Pulled Through Time

Veronique Holloway

Pulled Through Time

Time and Other Lies
Volume 1

Veronique Holloway

VH Books

Cover design by David Sorum
Cover image: Haviland Cove Beach, Glens Falls, NY

Pulled Through Time
Time and Other Lies Volume 1

Printed book ISBN: 979-8-9994779-2-7
ebook ISBN: 979-8-9994779-3-4

VHBooks.net

Dedication

For everyone who has ever wanted to escape from life.

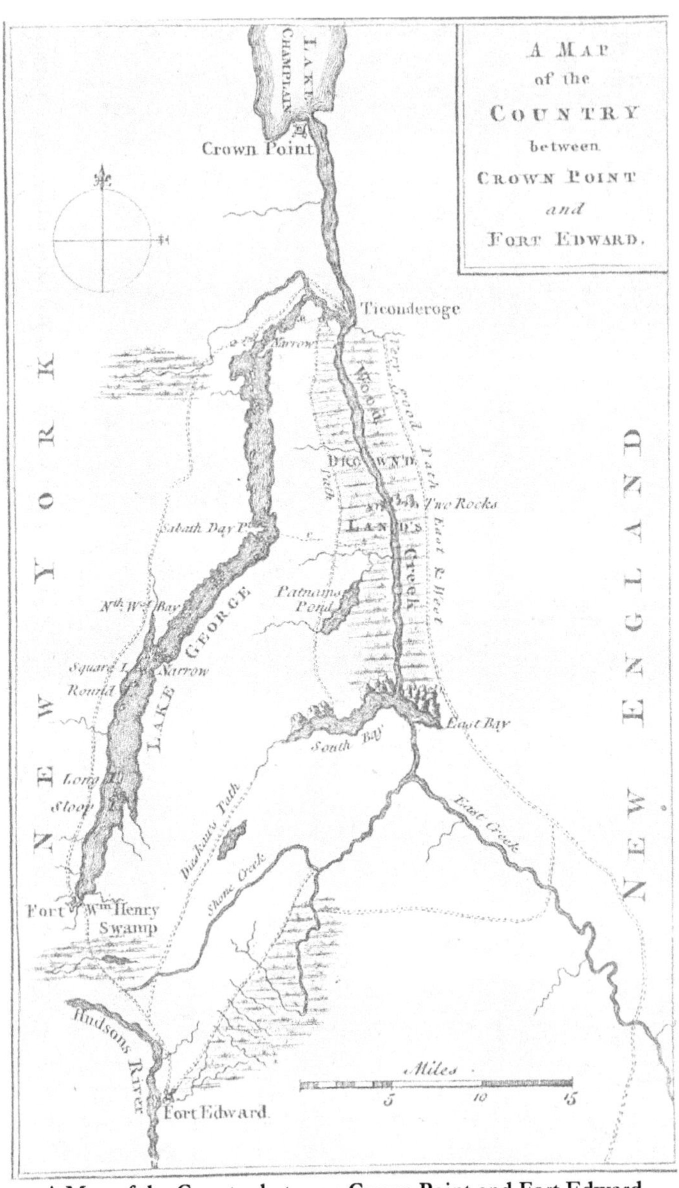

A Map of the Country between Crown Point and Fort Edward
From *Gentleman's Magazine*, London, 1759

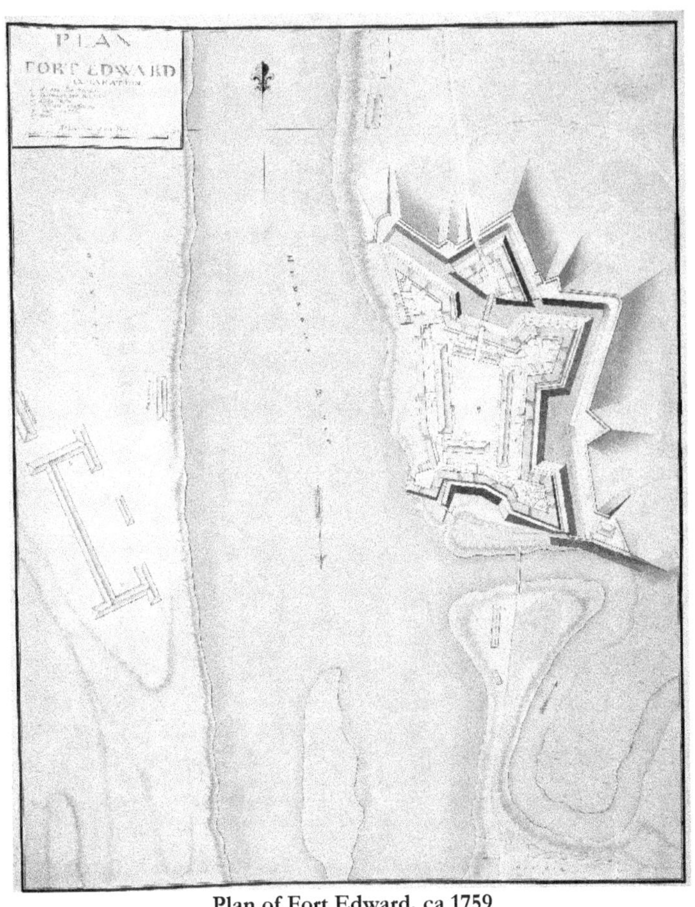

Plan of Fort Edward, ca 1759
Map reproduction courtesy of the Norman B. Leventhal Map &
Education Center at the Boston Public Library

July 28, 1758

Ellie would be dead within minutes. The arrow had pierced her heart, and she was quickly bleeding out. Even if she had access to modern medicine, there was likely nothing that could be done to save her. Yet, it was not her life that flashed before her eyes. Instead, it was her friend's words that swam through her head.

"Are you happy, Ellie?" Lisa had asked.

"I don't think I know how to be happy," she had replied flippantly in lieu of admitting how unhappy she had been.

She used to ask herself how she got here all the time. Ellie Sorenson had been happy once. With the world at her fingertips, how could she possibly have become so miserable? How did she become trapped in an impossible situation? Twice? The first time, she could retrace her decisions and the events surrounding her life and see how one thing led to the next and how all of those small decisions, coupled with the traffic accident had impacted everything. Maybe it was inevitable. Ellie blamed a lot of it on the accident. If she had only taken a different route. If the other driver had only been paying attention to the red light. Maybe, just maybe, she would have still been happily married. Maybe her mother would still be alive and her husband would not have been seriously injured. Maybe her father would not have blamed her for her mother's death. Maybe she never would have gone to New York for an escape. And maybe she would not be lying in another man's arms with an arrow in her chest, 263 years in the past.

This time, she could not figure out how she got there no matter what she did. She retraced the steps that had brought her there, but her mind simply could not make sense of them. Ellie understood the decisions she had made. What she could not understand was how she came to be caught up in the past. How had she, a twenty-first century, educated woman with a career, a husband, a mortgage, cars, and motorcycles travel through time and end up dying in a war in colonial America? She knew this was a fatal shot. Had she not seen enough death at the medical examiner's office to know this was fatal, her paramedic training would have told her there was nothing to be done. Even if she had been in her own time, this would have killed her. As the ambush continued around her, she gave up trying to understand how she had magically traveled through time and accepted this as her fate.

Chapter 1

August 2021

While standing on the observation deck of the Empire State Building, Ellie Sorenson watched her cousin dig around in her purse for a few minutes before asking, "Did you lose something?"

"I can't find my lip balm," Kristy Benson replied. "Wearing these face masks gives me chapped lips."

The Covid-19 pandemic was waning, but it was still spreading rapidly enough that face masks were required to be worn in public and social distancing was still in effect. As if wearing the masks and maintaining a six-foot distance from other people was not enough, they had the added bonus of having to present proof of vaccination anytime they went inside restaurants or other public buildings. While many businesses were still closed, there were enough that had reopened that they were able to explore as long as they adhered to the safety requirements put into place by the state of New York. Everyone hated all of it, but Ellie knew firsthand why the restrictions were still in effect.

"I always have extra." She looked in her own purse and passed her cousin a new tube.

Ellie went back to staring out over the vastness of the city. She never could fathom the sheer number of people who lived there. The city went on forever in every direction, broken only by the Hudson and East Rivers. In addition to the five boroughs around them, the clear sunny day allowed them to see New Jersey, Pennsylvania, Connecticut, Massachusetts, and Delaware, though she could not tell where one ended and the next began.

Kristy looked at the label and asked excitedly, "Is this one of yours?"

Pretending offense, Ellie replied, "Of course it is. It's the best."

Lisa McFie took the tube from Kristy and looked at the label. "Where do you get it?"

"I make my own," Ellie replied.

"Of course you do. How did you ever get into that?"

"Really, Lisa? You have to ask? You know how Ellie is."

"Right. The Ellie rabbit hole," Lisa replied sarcastically. In a mocking tone, she continued, "I want to make s'mores, but in order to do that, I need to make my own marshmallows, chocolate, and graham crackers from scratch. That means I'll spend weeks researching it all and experimenting until I get it just right. God forbid I just go to the store and buy everything already made like a normal person."

Lisa and Kristy snickered while Ellie tried to hold back the smile at her friend's teasing words. The woman was not wrong.

"Ha ha. I didn't hear you complaining when I made cheese you could actually eat despite your allergies."

"Mmmm. Cheese. It was so good, too."

"You're welcome. But I recently started making all kinds of products other than food. This particular rabbit hole all started with goats."

"Goats?" Lisa asked, not understanding. She handed the tube back to Kristy who pulled her face mask down in order to apply the balm.

"My neighbor got some goats, and she found herself with more goat's milk than she could use for the cheeses she makes and sells at farmer's markets. With all the excess milk, she convinced me to try making soap with her. Turns out she was no good at it, but I was. And I rather enjoyed it. After a while, I started expanding into lotions, then lip balm, and whatever else strikes my fancy. I even learned how to make activated charcoal, which I then add to my soaps. I make the products, and she sells them alongside her cheeses."

"God, you're such a hippy."

The women laughed at Lisa's description of Ellie. Kristy had become friends with her cousin as a teenager shortly before Lisa moved away. The three had been close for a short time in high school, but when Lisa moved to New York immediately after high school, her and Ellie lost touch for a while. She had always been closer with Kristy since they grew up together. Ellie had moved to Utah only a year before Lisa left, when Ellie's father retired from the navy. Kristy had seen Lisa a few times over the years since, but this was the first time the three of them had all been together for more than a brief lunch or dinner since high school. It seemed like ages ago for them all.

They were enjoying a much-needed girls' trip, reminiscing and feeling young again. Kristy had recently beaten breast cancer, and this was a celebratory trip to mark the occasion. They all lived in different states now, so Ellie and Kristy had agreed to come to New York to see Lisa. Ellie had spent a significant amount of time in the city during the covid lockdown the previous year but had never been upstate. Kristy had never been there either. They flew into Albany then drove up to Glens Falls, where Lisa lived. They were staying with her for two weeks and took the train to go sightseeing in the city for a couple of days. Wanting to see as much as they could, they split their time between the city and the areas upstate closer to Lisa.

After returning from the city, they decided to spend a few days in nature, exploring what else upstate New York had to offer. Lisa took them to some of the dozens of caves in Schoharie County west of Albany. Ellie and Kristy always tried to get outdoors for new adventures when they got together, and this was perfect. They traversed the area, spending half the day exploring. The caves were cold, dark, and eerie, and Ellie loved it. There were crevices hidden along walls that could not be seen until they were only a few feet away, narrow passageways and wide-open caverns, stalactites and stalagmites, waterfalls and pools of water. It was beautiful.

With the city and the underground world sufficiently covered, it was time to enjoy the sun. They decided to go up to Lake George to enjoy the lake for the day. As much as Ellie had loved the caves, she loved the water even more and was looking forward to that one.

While driving up to the lake, Kristy updated Lisa and Ellie on the latest family news. "My brother and his family just moved to Philadelphia. Ellie, you probably already heard from Johnny, but I don't think I told you, Lisa. Steve's teaching at the University of Pennsylvania."

"I hadn't heard," Ellie replied. "Steve talks more to Johnny than he does to me. And of course, Johnny doesn't talk to me. I guess that's what I get for marrying your brother's best friend."

"I'm sorry he ever introduced you," Kristy said.

"Well, at least we had a few good years. I just should've gotten out when I still could."

They continued to drive around the lake, looking for a place to get out and dip their feet in the water. In late August, the weather was still nice outside, but the water was starting to cool. Ellie and Kristy both hated the cold. Kristy had even moved away from Utah the first chance she got, going to Las Vegas where the winters were significantly milder.

Ellie was jealous that Kristy did not have to deal with the snow. If she could move, she would in a heartbeat. She never wanted to move to Utah in the first place, though she had not had a choice in where they moved when her father retired. Still in high school, she had not gotten a say in the decision. She always thought she would move away the first chance she got, but then life happened. Before she knew it, she had been there twenty-nine years with the exception of a brief stint in Las Vegas. Where had her life gone? She never imagined it would have ended up the way it had. Most of the time, she felt like she had wasted it all away. With no kids, a loveless marriage, and only her hobbies and work to sustain her, she felt empty; as though she had no purpose; nothing to drive her. She had put all her focus on her career when her personal life fell apart all those years ago, and now all she had to show for it was a career that, albeit successful, was not even particularly fulfilling anymore. Most days, she wished she could go back to high school when she first started getting to know Kristy and Lisa and start over again. She missed her youth when she had the world at her feet. She hated feeling old.

Trying to pull out of her self-pity, Ellie worked on being present in the moment. They were sitting on the warm sand at Lake George Beach by the edge of the water when her phone rang. She saw the caller ID and pressed ignore, but it only rang again. She knew if she did not answer it, he would keep calling. Sighing, she answered.

"No. We have olive oil," she said.

After a brief pause, she replied, "It'll work."

"It doesn't have to be vegetable oil. It–"

"No. I get that the recipe says vegetable oil but olive oil is healthier and cooks the same way. It'll work just fine."

Ellie let out a long-suffering sigh, shaking her head and rubbing her temple. "Ten minutes in the insta-pot with a natural release."

When Ellie hung up the phone, Kristy was rolling her eyes and shaking her head. "Is he capable of doing _anything_ on his own?" she asked after listening to one side of the conversation.

Ellie understood her cousin's frustration. It was a reflection of her own frustration at her husband, but some of Kristy's was also directed towards Ellie at her inability to leave the marriage.

"I mean, he's a grown-ass man. He's what? Fifty-seven years old now? He doesn't need you to tell him how to cook breakfast from two thousand miles away."

Ellie agreed completely. It was nothing they had not discussed before. She could not count how many times this discussion had come up between her and Kristy. Bracing herself for yet another lecture from her cousin, Lisa cut in, trying to get caught up.

"Johnny was so sweet in high school. What happened?" she asked.

"He was," Ellie agreed. "Everything was great for the first several years. But then we were hit by a car one day. T-boned at an intersection. I was driving and he was in the back seat behind my mom on the passenger side. It left him with a traumatic brain injury and a busted knee. The brain injury affected his personality, memory, and his demeanor. He has trouble with impulse control and he has massive mood swings where he's easily agitated or quick to depression. It's exhausting but I'm sure it's just as exhausting for him. It's frustrating that he can't do the things he used to do or remember things the same way. He can't hold down a job, and I think it affects how he feels about himself."

Kristy was quick to point out, "That doesn't mean you should have to put up with his outbursts. You do everything for him, and he just takes everything out on you."

"There's so much he can't do for himself. He doesn't realize he's being mean or hurtful." Ellie defended him like she always did.

Lisa's face showed concern as she immediately thought the worst. "How hurtful is he?"

"Oh, it's not like that. He doesn't get physical. He just yells a lot and says mean things."

Kristy was getting angry. "Do you hear yourself? You used to never tolerate that sort of behavior. You could never understand why women stayed in relationships like that."

"Honestly, why do you stay with him?" Lisa asked.

"I can't afford to leave him. With his health and how long we've been married combined with our respective earning potentials, I'd have to pay him half of my income in alimony. I barely make enough to survive on now. Splitting it in half would be catastrophic. I wouldn't even be able to afford rent." That was only part of the reason, but it was easier than admitting how strong of a hold the guilt had over her.

Lisa and Kristy exchanged a knowing look and shook their heads as they knew nothing they could say would make a difference.

"But are you happy, Ellie?" Lisa asked.

"Does it matter? I don't think I know how to be happy."

Ellie made excuses for him, though in truth, she felt trapped. It was not a simple situation that could easily be solved by her leaving. Kristy knew how she felt, but she was not comfortable sharing that with Lisa. They had only seen each other a handful of times in almost twenty years. Ellie always got defensive when she felt people were attacking Johnny. It was her fault after all.

The truth was the marriage had ended years ago. With virtually no communication and no physical contact between them in years, they were little more than roommates now. She had mourned the marriage and moved on yet could not actually leave. Ellie had looked into a divorce, but his disability did not pay out enough to support him. With the alimony hanging over her head, she felt trapped. It was not as though she lived an extravagant lifestyle. However, not being able to cover rent in even the most basic studio apartment if she cut her income down any further was quite a deterrent for leaving. She desperately wanted out but could not find a way to do it.

Ellie did not want to talk about it. Nor did she even want to think about it. She wanted to enjoy her girls' trip and pretend she was free while she had the chance. They had seen several signs as they came into the Lake George area for various attractions. When she saw the historical fort two blocks from the beach they were enjoying, she knew Kristy would want to see it. As a history buff, it was right up her alley. Ellie knew this would be a great diversion, so she suggested they go visit it. Kristy was all too eager to let the matter drop for now in favor of seeing a little history.

The women wandered around the fort on their own for a while before their scheduled tour started. There were several copies of books and DVDs of James Fenimore Cooper's *The Last of the Mohicans* available for purchase in the gift shop. They had found themselves at Fort William Henry, which was the fort under siege in the story.

Standing at the back of their small tour group, they were shown the different areas of the fort while the uniformed tour guide began by describing the Battle of Lake George in 1755 prior to the start of the French and Indian War and the fort being built.

He then explained how the fort had been built and used in the early days of the war.

"The garrison was built by the soldiers in forty-four days," he informed them.

He continued on with the story of the fort, building up to the siege by the French in 1757 featured in Cooper's book, when it was burned down. It had only been rebuilt in the 1950s. Their tour guide was rather knowledgeable about the history in question and Kristy was thoroughly entranced as he spoke of the siege. Lisa and Ellie laughed at her enthusiasm and exchanged a knowing look. Ellie enjoyed learning, regardless of the subject and was having fun, but Kristy was glued to his every word. It did not hurt that he was rather attractive. With his long blonde hair pulled back into a ponytail at the base of his neck, he looked the part of the eighteenth-century British soldier in the replica uniform he was wearing. As they moved along, he said, "The garrison evacuated the fort and began the march back to Fort Edward, south of here when they were attacked again."

Lisa's brows scrunched as she whispered, "I'm confused. I thought the fort was the garrison. How could it evacuate the fort and march?"

She and Kristy both turned to Ellie with expectant faces.

"Why are you asking me? I don't know."

Kristy replied, "You're the military brat. I thought you knew these terms."

"First, that was a really long time ago. Second, I don't think they still use that term. If they do, it's not one I ever remember hearing."

Lisa asked their tour guide, who turned his attention to them while he answered. "A garrison can refer to both a place and the people in it. It... it was often used interchangeably to describe the troops and anyplace they were quartered."

He initially looked at Lisa when he answered her question. As he continued, his eyes scanned her companions, landing on Ellie. He paused in his explanation, then continued to look at her while he explained it, his voice faltering briefly. They thanked him, and he continued his tour, occasionally sneaking looks at Ellie. Lisa and Kristy whispered teasingly to her throughout.

"Apparently, someone has a new friend," Lisa said.

Kristy joined in with, "This may as well be your own private tour. I don't think he knows the rest of us exist."

"It's the blonde hair," Lisa said. "I give it five minutes before he comes over here and hits on her." Ellie was the only blonde amongst them while Lisa had deep auburn hair and Kristy's was black. Rolling her eyes, Ellie shook her head while Kristy agreed with a knowing smirk.

After the tour ended, their guide ushered the entire group to the courtyard for the musket demonstration. With tunnel vision locked onto Ellie, he caught up with them at the back of the crowd and spoke to her.

"Have we met?"

"I don't think so." They all snickered at the obvious pickup line.

He accepted her answer with a nod and a look of uncertainty and said, "It must've not happened yet."

"Is that your way of asking for my name?" Ellie asked as they found seats in the courtyard. He continued standing behind them, watching her closely.

"I know your name, Ellie Wilde. It must've been fifty years ago now but I could never forget you." He looked her up and down as she turned in her seat. "I thought it was you but you look so different. I suppose that was inevitable."

Stepping in closer, he pulled her in for a hug. When he drew back, he searched her face but saw no recognition there. This must have been how she felt all those years ago.

He had not said the words as though they were a pickup line. He sounded sincere and that was not what Ellie was expecting from him, nor did she have any idea how he knew her name. There was an affection in his voice she did not understand. They had all thought he was fixated on her because of her looks, but this was something different. He genuinely seemed to think he knew her. Ellie was certain she had never met him before. She certainly did not understand the reference to it having been fifty years ago. She was old, but not that old. Not yet anyway. She still had another five years to go. And he looked to be barely out of high school, making the comment even more bizarre.

With the demonstration over, they went over to watch the cannon loading and firing demonstrations. Their tour guide continued to watch her while his companions performed the demonstrations. Despite the weirdness of it, Ellie enjoyed the attention. Even at her age, she still managed to catch attention from men wherever she went. It was the only thing that still made her feel young.

After the demonstrations, he asked Ellie out for a drink.

"Are you even old enough to drink?" she asked him.

"I'm older than I look," he replied.

Kristy encouraged her to go out with him and Lisa quickly got on board as well.

"But I'm married," she tried to argue. Having an open marriage, it was a weak excuse, but she was not looking for anything. Casual sex had long since lost its appeal and she saw no other reason to meet up with someone who lived on the opposite side of the country from her.

"Only on paper," Kristy said. "You don't have to do anything with him. Just go have a drink and enjoy a night out for a change. You deserve it."

"Please, Ellie," he begged. "I'm off duty in an hour."

Though Ellie had no idea who he was, he not only knew her name, but had known her maiden name. It had been nearly thirty years since she had gone by that. For a moment, she considered the possibility that they had known one another as children but he could not possibly be old enough to have known her that long ago. Curiosity won and Ellie agreed to see him for coffee rather than for alcoholic drinks. She was not convinced about his age, regardless of his insistence.

Chapter 2

August 2021

"I can't remember the last time I went out with someone. It's probably been almost thirty years," Lucas said enigmatically.

Ellie laughed. "So why me then?"

"Because I've been waiting for you. I haven't seen you in so long, and I've missed you terribly."

Ellie was confused. They had only been at the coffee shop long enough to get their drinks and find seats, but Lucas Anders was still as strange as he had been at the fort. "You seem to have the advantage here. I'm sorry, but I don't remember ever meeting you before."

"Because we haven't met yet. Well, I've met you, but you've only just met me."

Ellie wondered if he was trying to use pickup lines on her, but he chose weird lines to use to pick her up. Why he would pretend to know her was beyond her.

"You are such a freak," she said on a laugh.

At the troubled expression on Lucas's face, she quickly jumped in and added, "Oh, no. That's not a bad thing. I prefer the company of freaks. I say it as a compliment. Normal is overrated. It's—"

"A setting on the dryer," he finished before taking a drink of his coffee.

Ellie smiled. "Exactly. You've heard that one? I've been saying that for years."

"I know. That's where I learned it. It's been ages since I've heard it."

She squinted at him, knowing she should be alarmed at his statement yet feeling comfortable in his presence. She jokingly asked, "Are you a stalker then?"

Trying to be nonchalant when she asked the question, she took a sip of her tea and played it off as a casual question. Lucas did not appear troubled at all. He looked as though he was simply catching up with an old friend, which intrigued Ellie.

"Not at all. It's complicated."

Instead of explaining it, Lucas changed the subject then and started asking about her.

Ellie enjoyed his company but found him enigmatic. He seemed to be looking for an answer to some unasked question. Her tea turned cold while they talked. She found this man fascinating, though she was not sure why. As the conversation flowed, she completely forgot how young she had initially thought him to be. His manner of speech gave the impression of someone much older.

As they visited, Lucas found her to be lonely and in need of an out to an emotionally abusive relationship. Despite how long it had been since he had seen her, he remembered her as if it were yesterday. After she saved his life, how could he ever forget her? She looked different than he remembered but he could see the intelligence and cynicism, the reluctance to trust anyone, and the confidence. The last was buried deep down, but it was there. The woman that sat in front of him now was a shell of the woman he had once known. What he saw now was a desire to be seen; a longing for something more. He knew he would give her that, but he still did not know why.

She had been in love with Lucas once. He never felt quite the same, though he had loved her and had waited decades for her. She was not yet the person he had come to hold so dear, but she would be soon. He owed her everything. She brought him out of a dark time when he had wanted nothing more than to give up. He had not seen the point in continuing on any longer when she came along. Ellie Wilde had been bossy and persistent and would not give up on him. He knew this was the beginning of that relation-ship. This had to be when she had fallen in love with him. Would he finally feel the same? He may not know what was yet to come for himself, but he knew where her journey was headed. Some of it anyway. He had not let her tell him everything; only what he needed to know. Despite how important she was to him, he had never understood why he would do what he was about to do. He had waited fifty years to find out and was eager to do so.

They talked late into the night, walking along the Feeder Canal Heritage Trail beside the Hudson River in Glens Falls after leaving the coffee shop. Kristy and Lisa had driven back from the lake leaving Ellie at the coffee shop in Lake George. She had texted them and let them know she was fine, and Lucas would drive her back. This was very uncharacteristic for Ellie who was always more cautious around people she had only just met, but there was something about this man that she trusted. He seemed to know her somehow and he was always polite. They talked like old friends and Ellie felt like she could tell him anything.

When the conversation turned to her marriage, her instinct was to close herself off and not discuss it, but Lucas had a way of making Ellie feel comfortable. When he asked why she did not get divorced, she told him, "What's the point? It's not like I'm looking for a relationship with anyone else. And just because it's not great, doesn't mean it's bad. It could always be worse."

"But it could be so much better. Don't you want someone to love? Someone to love you?" he asked.

"I don't believe in love."

"How can *you* not believe in love?" This was quite a departure from the woman he knew. She was the one who had convinced him to love again.

"It doesn't last. People change. Jobs and homes change. People come and go. Everything in life is temporary."

"Why did you get married in the first place then?"

"I was young and naïve. I won't make that mistake again."

Lucas looked sad and was quiet for a minute. When he spoke again, he said, "I used to believe this, too. I was lonely for a very long time and did not think there was a point in opening up to anyone when they all inevitably left me. But then someone made me see there was more to life than spending it alone. Experiences mean nothing if there's no one to share them with. I have hope now that someone will come along and spend forever with me."

Lucas knew she was that someone, but he could not tell her yet. He was still trying to understand it all himself.

"I hope you find that. I'm not a forever kind of girl."

"Not yet. But you will be. When you find him."

Ellie wanted to argue but there was no point. Lucas was entitled to his opinion; it did not make it right. She knew better and would not be changing her mind about it.

When he dropped her off at Lisa's house, Lucas offered to take them to another site that he thought Kristy would love. Ellie had mentioned her cousin's love for history and Lucas wanted to see her again but did not want to monopolize her time in New York. He also knew he needed to plant the seeds of history in her brain for what was to come next. When the other women agreed, they made plans for the next day.

Lucas took them to a place called Rogers Island. It was a small island in the middle of the Hudson River that once housed part of another fort. The main fort was on the east side of the river while the island had housed troops stationed there during the French and Indian War. It was the birthplace of the US Army Rangers. The fort was no longer standing, having long since been torn down, but there was a visitor's center and museum on the island with various exhibits, more live demonstrations, and an eighteenth-century French and Indian War encampment with reenactors performing live drills.

Lucas talked with Ellie more but was also inclusive of the other women while they watched the reenactors and wove through the demonstrations. Ellie noticed him occasionally watching Lisa when she was not looking. She wondered if perhaps she had been too talkative during their time together the previous day and had bored him so much that he had already decided to move on to her friend. She could not blame him. Lisa was beautiful. She was short and built much like Ellie but had auburn hair that turned red in the sun. Often feisty, she was always smiling and laughing and had the most positive outlook on life. Her and Ellie were polar opposites, yet they still managed to be close friends.

Her cousin Kristy was the middle ground between Ellie's dark cynicism and Lisa's bright, bubbly optimism. Kristy was fun but fell somewhere between the darkness and the light. She was tall and gorgeous with long black hair and large breasts. The large breasts ran in the family, but Kristy recently had implants after her mastectomy and cancer treatments. They were opposites in height. Where Kristy was tall, Ellie came in at only five foot two. They were the same age, but Kristy had maintained her figure while Ellie had gained weight over the years. While they both still looked rather young, Ellie had always thought Kristy much prettier than herself.

Ellie found she was not jealous of Lucas's wandering attention at all. She liked him but did not see things going anywhere with him. He was attractive, but he was much better suited for Lisa or Kristy than for herself. Aside from the minor inconvenience of being married, Ellie was not into history quite as much as he was. Though, really, she thought Kristy would have been a better match for him. Kristy and Lisa were both divorced, but Kristy loved history. Of course, Lisa was the one who actually lived in the same place as him.

When they finished on the island, they all decided to grab a bite to eat. There were a few restaurants to choose from a few blocks away and Lucas took them to one that stood on the site of the original fort. Leaving the island, they turned south onto Broadway and pulled into the parking lot of The Anvil Inn Restaurant. The parking lot wrapped around the building, and they found a spot right up front between the building and the road. Kristy was the first to notice the historical marker on the property indicating that the location was the original site of Fort Edward and another marker indicating the location that once held the northeast bastion of the fort.

After eating, Kristy and Lisa stopped in the restroom while Ellie and Lucas wandered outside to wait for them. It was such a beautiful day, Ellie wanted to enjoy it as much as she could. They stood beside the car on the driver's side, talking while they waited. Lucas enjoyed hearing what Ellie had thought of the reenactors on the island and the various demonstrations they had seen. He encouraged her to talk about it as much as she wanted. Seeing Kristy and Lisa exit the building, Ellie turned to move around the back of the vehicle to climb in on the passenger side.

As she passed the rear of Lisa's car, Lucas shouted, "Watch out!"

She felt a hand on her back, but before any force could be applied, she was crushed between their car and another vehicle that had come out of nowhere. It was only belatedly that the sounds of the squealing tires and the crunch of metal impacting metal registered in her brain. Lisa and Kristy were both screaming and the world was filled with sound, yet none of it was identifiable.

The restaurant was on the outer edge of a curve in Broadway. The speed limit was thirty-five, but most drivers flew down the road much faster than that. The truck had been driving north on Broadway and came around the curve too fast, causing the driver to lose control. Instead of going around the curve, the truck continued straight, jumping the curb and sidewalk and continuing into the parking lot to hit Lisa's car. Had her car not been there, the truck likely would have continued on and plowed into the restaurant.

Pinned between the two vehicles, Ellie struggled to move, steam coming from the engine of the truck in front of her. She could feel nothing below the waist and could barely move her head which now rested on the hood of the truck. Somehow, Ellie still managed to see Lucas out of the corner of her eye. He had tried to save her from the approaching vehicle but was hit as well. Though he was not pinned like she was, he looked like he was in worse shape than her as the blood pooled beneath his head on the asphalt of the parking lot. Having been flipped up over the hood of the truck, he was now on the passenger side of the vehicles while Kristy and Lisa were running up to them on the opposite side.

When the truck suddenly reversed, Ellie fell to the ground, blood flowing from her everywhere. There was so much blood, she could not tell where any of it was coming from. Traffic stopped and a crowd started gathering. Lucas was moving, trying to crawl towards her. She was not sure how he was even moving with the amount of blood that had been pouring from him. Having autopsied enough traffic accident victims, she knew the blood flowing from them both was only part of the story. The extent of the internal injuries in this type of accident were likely fatal and she knew she would not last long after being pinned the way she had been. How ironic that she would die in a car accident after what had happened to her husband and mother.

Everything slowed down and Ellie could not make sense of anything. She was dying. Lucas was there beside her, holding her hand one moment then cradling her head the next. She could feel his hand on the back of her neck. He was on his hands and knees, low to the ground, with his weight on one arm, every movement seeming to take a Herculean effort. She saw him reach up to his own neck, then there was a small pinch on hers. Was that a knife in his hand? That did not make any sense. Lucas collapsed beside her as Kristy and Lisa made it to their sides and everything went black.

Chapter 3

August 2021

Ellie stared into the mirror at the fine lines around her eyes. Her age was starting to show in those lines along with the wrinkles in her hands and neck and in the gray hairs beginning to poke through the long blonde strands that fell to her lower back. She continued inspecting herself and let her eyes fall downward.

Her biggest tattoo started on the back of her left shoulder and flowed down her rib cage, skirting her left breast, wrapping around to the front of her body, and coming to an end on the left hip bone. She had a handful of others, but they were all small, micro tattoos. Ellie got the large one done when she was much younger and thinner. At the time, it had elongated her torso and gave her a sleek appearance, despite her curvaceous form.

Those around her had always described Ellie as voluptuous. Even though she did yoga every morning and tai chi every night along with her occasional outdoor adventures, she had put on weight over the years, and the tattoo no longer looked as sleek. She had always been curvy, but the curves used to be in all the right places, while the rest of her was slender. Now the slender was gone and she was just curvy. The hourglass figure she was once proud of had changed over the years. With the middle almost as large as the top and bottom, she felt more like a snowman with legs those days.

Having taken pride in her figure once, Ellie had even worked as a stripper for a time during college. She used to be much more adventurous and free-spirited but had become more conservative in her old age. Should she continue to keep all the extra body piercings? Was there a point when one became too old to sport them? Her eyes went to the multiple rings dangling from each earlobe and the three posts going through the helix and the two in the forward helix. Between both ears, she had ten piercings. That was only the ears. It did not include the one above her lip or the ones below the neck.

Ellie was not really that old, but she felt like she was. She missed being young and carefree. Now, she felt old and broken, trapped, and alone. Life had taken a toll on her.

The traffic accident had her questioning her mortality. She did not understand why she was alive, let alone how she did not have massive internal injuries. At the very least, she should be in a hospital somewhere with tubes sticking out of her and everything bandaged up. After three nights in the hospital, the doctors declared her fit to be discharged. She was still a little sore, but that was the bulk of it. No major injuries, all she had were bruises and abrasions marring her skin. Even the doctors were stymied. The paramedics had declared her deceased on scene, but then they found a faint heartbeat. The first two days in the hospital had been spent unconscious, but when she came to, she was more than ready to leave. The doctors were adamantly against discharging her, but when her scans all came up clean, they had no reason to keep her, even though they were reluctant to believe she could have healed that fully in such a short amount of time.

Perhaps she had only imagined the truck pinning her to Lisa's car? In her excited state, maybe her brain misinterpreted the details of what had really happened. Lucas had pushed her out of the way after all. Maybe she only thought she had been hit in the impact.

Then why could she still recall the feel of it?

Shaking off the thought, Ellie let her mind linger on Lucas. He was another mystery. She was not sure what it was about him that had impacted her so deeply in such a short time. She did not understand why his death was affecting her this much, seeing as how she did not even know him, and she was certainly no stranger to death given her career choices. As a paramedic, she had occasionally lost patients. The pressure of not making mistakes and dealing with the families of patients eventually got to be too much for her, so when a position came open with the medical examiner, she took it. Having spent her days assisting on autopsies for the previous eleven years, she had seen bodies in every possible condition. Perhaps it was her own brush with death this time that had affected her so deeply. She had believed she was going to die. How could she be standing there now?

There was one advantage to Kristy disliking Johnny as she did: she had not called him after Ellie's accident. She told Ellie that she was going to wait until she knew what to tell him, but then when she miraculously got better, Kristy decided to leave it up to her to tell him whatever she wanted to share. Ellie was grateful Kristy had not called him. Unable to deal with him hovering over her, he was the last person she wanted to see or talk to right then. She needed space and even the thought of spending the day with Lisa and Kristy had been too much for her, resulting in her sending them on their way to go enjoy the day without her. Their vacation would be over soon, and Ellie did not want them to miss out on any of the remaining time they had.

Ellie tried to rest like she promised the women she would, but the days in the hospital had given her more than plenty of rest. There were far too many unanswered questions and unresolved emotions flowing through her. Needing to process it all, she decided to go for a walk. After loosely braiding her hair on the side and putting on her workout attire, which for some reason was rather loose on her, she headed out the door. She had tried putting in her contact lenses, but her eyes were not cooperating. Since waking up in the hospital, her vision had been blurred. It seemed her eyes were the one thing that had been affected by the accident. She would likely have to get new glasses. Her vision had already been extremely poor, having worn corrective lenses her entire life, and she hoped she was not going blind altogether now. It was one more thing she would have to deal with. Squinting through her glasses, she made her way through the neighborhood.

With Lisa living only a block away from the Hudson River, it was inevitable that Ellie would end up there. Walking along the same trail she had walked with Lucas only days ago, she stopped to sit on the edge of the water for a while, contemplating life. A couple of kayakers made their way to the bank near her, and she suddenly wanted to be on the water. It had always been her happy place. Whenever she needed to recharge her batteries, Ellie found a body of water to help her do so. She would meditate, swim, or kayak in order to get what she needed to ground herself. She ran back to Lisa's house and found the kayak and cart on the side of the house. Rolling it down the street, she launched it into the river at Murray Street.

Ellie had grabbed a life vest which she put on before launching. Being adventurous, but not a risk-taker, she was always diligent about that sort of thing. Looking up at the sky, she would not be able to be out very long, but she did not need long. Anything would help. She would paddle as hard as she could and then turn back after thirty minutes or so. Ellie kicked off her shoes once she was inside the vessel and locked her phone with its attached wallet inside a dry bag and placed it safely within the hold. Once she was settled, she was off.

Paddling as hard as she could, like she planned, Ellie quickly lost track of time, though she knew she had not gone far. She kayaked often at home and knew how long she could go until she was fatigued. Going with the flow of the river to get back, her return trip would not take as long. While she was out, she kept an eye on the increasingly darkening sky. The clouds overhead looked angry, but they were not as angry as her. Why did people have to drive so recklessly? The driver had been drunk and took off after hitting them, but there had been enough people on scene that they got a license plate number and description of the driver. It had not taken long for the police to find him and arrest him. It was little consolation for Ellie.

She wondered about Lucas Anders. He had died to save her life yet she knew so little about him. Did he have a family somewhere? Where did he come from? Who would mourn him? In the small amount of time they had spent together, he spoke very little about himself. She had done most of the talking. When he did speak, it was always of the past. Not his past, but *the* past. They had spent most of their two days together talking about the French and Indian War.

It struck her that she had never thought about that period in history. Last week, if anyone had asked her when it had happened, she would not have been able to answer. It had always been some abstract period about which she knew nothing. Now, it was all she could see. She kept picturing Lucas in his British Army uniform, standing on the top of the fort near the cannon.

It was not until the thunder boomed overhead that Ellie noticed the storm coming nearer. It startled her out of her reverie, letting her know it was time to turn back. She was not particularly worried about getting wet but did not want to be out in the open on the water if the lightning started getting close. The paddle was a quality one with a carbon shaft which would be an excellent conductor. While Ellie was turning her kayak around, she realized how much the wind had picked up. The journey thus far may have been against the current, but the wind had been at her back. Now she was heading directly into it. Every time she thought she was making progress, she was kicked back several yards by the wind. Having come that direction, she knew there was nowhere nearby for her to put in. The bank along that stretch was nothing but dense forest. Her only options were to try going all the way back to where she started or turn back around and continue on a little farther. She recalled Lisa saying that she normally launched from Murray Street and went as far as the dam a few miles away before turning around. Sometimes, she would stop at a place halfway between her and the dam at Haviland Cove Park. Ellie knew she had to be close to the park and decided to push on. As she came around a bend, she could see the sandy stretch of beach on the north side of the river where people had likely spent the morning before this storm rolled in. There looked to be some sort of park there and she began paddling in that direction so she could get out of the water. There was even a small structure that was most likely a bathroom if she needed shelter. Once she was out of the water, she could either wait out the storm there or walk back to Lisa's house. As long as she was off the water, she would feel better.

The storm was directly overhead before she made it to the beach, and the rain was pouring down hard, the wind whipping her around like a rag doll, making the water feel as though she was on the ocean. White caps swelled in the river, splashing her relentlessly and making her effort that much harder. The closer she got to the cove, the further away it seemed to get. It did not help that her vision was worsening by the minute. Between her poor eyesight and the storm, she could not see the houses beyond the park or the parking lot beyond the beach. The park was heavily wooded, and it was difficult to make out anything other than the sandy beach and the trees beyond. As she finally got closer to the cove, a large log floated directly in front of her, being pushed around by the stormy waters. She did not see it until it was right in front of her, and she was unable to turn to avoid it. Combined with the churning water, it threw her balance off enough that the kayak flipped, dumping her in the rough water.

Surfacing, she sputtered, spitting water out of her mouth and wiping at her eyes. She immediately reached for the kayak, grateful she had put on her life vest. Ellie was so focused on getting back to shore safely and not losing the kayak in the process that she did not notice that her glasses had fallen off in the water. At least the paddle had been on a leash which kept her from losing it. She tried grabbing the kayak so it did not drift away with her phone and wallet inside. Finally making contact with it, she looped her foot into the handle. She was close enough now that she could swim the rest of the way. It would have been harder to right the kayak and climb back in than it would have been to drag it with her. As she started pulling the kayak to shore, she thought she saw Lucas on the shore waiting for her in an old British Army uniform. Looking again, she saw that no one was there.

The mind did strange things when it was grieving. It was not uncommon for people to imagine seeing their dead loved ones and she knew that was all this was. It was only her imagination conjuring up what she wanted to see.

To avoid thinking about all of the possible negative outcomes while she struggled to reach the shore, she let her mind wander back to him and everything he had shown her in the previous days. He had a passion for history, and it showed. She had enjoyed seeing the reenactors at the fort and the period encampment on the island and she allowed herself to imagine what it would have been like to actually have lived then. A sense of nostalgia for a way of life long since forgotten washed over her; a life with no modern trappings, no vehicles to destroy people's lives. This was the second time she had personally been involved in a serious car accident, which ultimately ended with fatal consequences. What would it be like to live without them? As her thoughts landed on Fort William Henry and the reenactment at Rogers Island, she could picture what it would have been like long before the Revolutionary War when the country was still under British rule.

As she stared at the shore only feet away, wondering about life in the eighteenth century, she finally felt the ground under her feet and stood up, grabbing the kayak with her hand. Fighting to make her way out of the water, she dragged the kayak along, with thoughts of life in colonial America swimming through her mind.

Pulling the kayak onto the sandy beach, she heard the boom of thunder. The lightning was only a fraction of a second behind it and suddenly, every nerve ending in her body was on fire. Her skin burned so hot she thought she would burst into flames any second. Everything spun as the world fell out from under her feet. She felt weightless; not falling but not floating. It was as though she had no corporeal body. Had she just died? The whole experience seemed to last a lifetime yet passed in the blink of an eye. And for the second time in a week, everything went black.

Chapter 4

Completely dry by the time she awoke, Ellie was not certain how long she laid on the shore unconscious. The storm had cleared, and it was bright and sunny out. The first thing she did was try to get her bearings in order to get back to Lisa's house. The kayak was gone. It must have drifted back out onto the river. Well, along with replacing her shoes, phone, driver's license, and credit card, it looked like she would also be replacing Lisa's kayak. Ellie kicked herself for not paying better attention to the weather. She knew better; she was anything but careless. Too busy reprimanding herself, she was not thinking straight. Forcing herself to calm down and focus, she started walking away from the river. Given how heavily populated the area was, she would not have to go far. Taking off her life vest, she started walking but all she could see were trees. That was when she realized that she could see with perfect clarity, despite not having her glasses or contacts. Ellie's vision had been poor her entire life, so she was not sure what was happening. Had she actually put her contacts in and only thought she was wearing her glasses? Maybe the accident was beginning to affect her memory. Had she gotten a concussion? It looked like she had another hospital visit coming up very soon.

Surprise registered when she did not reach a parking lot to the park on which she thought she had landed. She checked again to see that the river was at her back, which meant she was going north, where she thought she remembered seeing the parking lot. Instead, there was nothing but trees. The branches intertwined overhead, blending one tree into another. It was becoming clear to her that her memory had been affected more than she had thought. Confused, she looked around and decided to continue going north. Eventually, she would run into someone or something.

The sun beat down on the forest surrounding her. It was far thicker than she remembered it being. It was a hot day, but at least the trees gave her some shade from the direct sun. Being barefoot, it was taking much longer to get anywhere than she expected it to. At least that was what she told herself as to why she had not run into civilization yet. She stepped carefully at first, but it was no use. The underbrush was dense there. Every rock and sharp twig she stepped on bruised or cut her feet a little more. She was not going to be able to walk for a week when she finally made it back. If she ever made it back. What was taking so long? How could she have gotten this far out?

Holding up her baggy stretch pants the whole way, Ellie had been trudging through the thick forest for hours, dodging branches, and tripping over roots. She had scratches all over her arms, chest, and legs, and her stomach told her it had been a long time since she had eaten. It felt as though she had not eaten in days. Since she had no way of knowing how long she laid on the riverbank, she thought it was entirely possible. The scratches were not the only new marks on her. A reddish tree-like image now covered her upper right arm, from her shoulder to her elbow. She knew from her training that this Lichtenberg figure that developed was from the lightning. It heated up the capillaries under the skin and caused them to be visible as burn marks on the skin. Though she had studied the phenomena, she had only seen it once, during an autopsy on a man who was killed after being struck by lightning. She was lucky to be alive after being struck. She rather liked the pattern that developed and thought it too bad they usually disappeared after a few days. Maybe she could get a tattoo over the top of it before it disappeared. It would forever remind her of this trip with her cousin and every weird and tragic thing that had happened.

After what felt like an eternity, Ellie heard some screaming and shouting along with what sounded like gunshots or fireworks, though it was not yet dark. She thought it odd but decided it was likely a party of some sort going on. Reinvigorated, her pace picked up as she eagerly headed in the direction of the noises. They got louder and louder and as Ellie brushed back the branches, she took in a scene consisting of people in various uniforms and costumes reenacting a battle of some sort. They were spread across a dirt road, spilling over into the trees near a brook. A long line of wooden horse- and oxen-drawn wagons blocked the road in each direction as far as she could see. There had to be hundreds of people there.

Ellie immediately recognized the same red coat of the British Army that Lucas had worn at Fort William Henry. Various Native American garb and even everyday clothing common to the same period were also easy to recognize. Though, there was another uniform she did not recognize. After studying it for a moment, it reminded her of some of the uniforms she had seen while visiting the museums with her new friend. Was it French?

The reenactors were putting on quite a show. She wondered where the audience was and how they got so many of them there. From her vantage point, she could not see anywhere that was open enough to be visible. There was no one on the small dirt road watching and everything else around was trees. For that matter, where did they find so many Native Americans for this? The men dressed as Natives actually looked the part; they were not merely White men dressed in Native American clothing. And where were all the women in uniform? Most reenactments incorporated women amongst their numbers.

As she watched, Ellie could see that the uniforms of the men falling were torn and they were all bleeding from various wounds corresponding to the tears in the uniforms. She had spent enough time around reenactors to know they did not go to these lengths. Those uniforms were expensive, usually handmade, and they were not about to ruin them. They also did not use makeup and blood for their reenactments. Maybe it was a Hollywood production. She looked again for any lights, cameras, or other electronic equipment but found none. Again, there was no audience; no directors or producers yelling "cut."

While Ellie was becoming more and more confused as to what this could be, a man stumbled in front of her and fell. He was bleeding profusely, and her paramedic training kicked in, despite the years since she had practiced. Dropping her life vest, she turned the man over onto his back and saw that his leg had been cut almost completely off. Blood was pouring out from the thigh where his leg should have been attached to his body. While she tried to stop the bleeding, she watched him lose consciousness. Hovering helplessly as he took his last breath, she suddenly knew this was not a reenactment, nor a Hollywood production. Unsure what was happening, she knew this was somehow real.

Ellie started becoming concerned for her safety when she saw a young boy in the middle of the foray. He was not in a uniform, but in regular clothing of the same era. She thought him to be around sixteen years old and wanted to pull him from the danger before she left. With his bare hands, he was fighting a Native American who held what she assumed was a tomahawk when a man in a blue and white uniform noticed the boy. Several voices began calling for retreat but the Frenchman had his sword drawn and was running towards them. The boy and the Native American were only feet from her, but the boy had his back to the Frenchman. She watched for a moment, long enough to see that the Frenchman was not going for the Native American. The boy was now facing two opponents.

Before she could think, Ellie ran in and stood between the Frenchman and the boy, pushing the Frenchman out of the way. It bought the boy enough time to defeat the Native American but as she turned back to face the Frenchman, he shoved his sword through her stomach. She looked down in surprise at it sticking out of her belly.

The Frenchman removed his sword and spun to finish off the boy who had picked up a flintlock pistol from a fallen soldier nearby and shot the man.

Ellie fell to the ground and lay there, bleeding out. She tried to put pressure on her wound but was too weak to be effective. She watched the battle rage around her. The boy fought a few more men around him, then he came back. He was kneeling down beside her, holding her stomach and speaking to her, though she could not make out what he was saying. He cradled her in his arms, lifting her off the ground. She was slowly losing consciousness and the last thing she remembered was being lifted up. Was she on a horse? Ellie let the darkness take her yet again.

***

Ellie woke to chaos all around her. People were yelling. She could hear men's voices with the occasional female voice mixed in. One of the men was yelling at another to treat a girl. "You must take care to not let her expire," he yelled.

The other voice replied calmly, "She is already dead."

Ellie wondered who they were talking about as she slipped into darkness again.

Unsure how long she had been unconscious this time, she woke to someone pulling at her clothes. No. Not pulling, her tank top was being cut off of her.

She fluttered her eyes enough to see two women standing over her. One was cutting her shirt while a younger one watched, holding something in her hands. A hospital gown maybe?

The younger one was asking the other, "What kind of cloth is that? I never seen such a thing."

The other replied as she removed the fragments of Ellie's tank top. "I know not, only what kind of stays is those?"

"There 'tain't no laces nowhere. How did she ever get these on?" the younger one asked.

Ellie was so tired. She wanted to ask what was happening, but she did not have the strength and let herself drift off again.

The next thing to enter Ellie's muddled brain was the feel of being weighed down at her shoulders and feet, quickly followed by a searing hot pain shooting through her abdomen. Her eyes flew open, and she saw a woman at her feet and a boy at her head, each holding her down. Was that the boy from the battle? She could not think about that now. A dark-haired man with an equine nose and a dour expression was holding a searing hot metal rod to her stomach.

"What the fuck are you doing?" she screamed out while struggling to free herself.

Somehow managing to free her upper body, she shot up in the bed and punched the man in the face. He recoiled and dropped the burning rod next to her. Ellie snatched it up quickly and held it out, threatening anyone who came near her. A handsome young man in a white vest and pants ending at the knees hurriedly made his way across the room when she started screaming and was by her side now, trying to calm her down.

"Don't tell me to calm down. That man was just shoving a red-hot iron against my skin. Why the fuck should I calm down?"

The young man instructed the others to see to the other wounded and they all left. Ellie immediately felt less threatened but was still full of adrenaline and not yet ready to calm down.

"Do not fret. They've all gone. No one is here to hurt you, miss. We only mean to help."

"You sure as fuck have a funny way of showing it," she screamed. She had curled up on whatever makeshift bed on which she had been placed, with her feet underneath her, ready to pounce. The pain in her stomach told her she likely would not get very far, but she would figure that out later.

"I regret you were startled but you've a rather severe injury which needs to be closed. Mr. Anwar was only trying to do that."

The man was speaking in a calm, even tone while sitting perfectly still so as to not startle her any further. She recognized it for what it was yet still appreciated it. However, she still had a lot of rage fueling her.

"How? By removing all the flesh around it?"

"He was cauterizing the wound."

"Cauterizing? Are you kidding me?" she asked, incredulous.

The young man looked at her quizzically and tried to explain what cauterizing meant. She held her hands up, interrupting him. "It's all good. You don't have to mansplain cauterization to me. I'm not an idiot. What you can explain, though, is why the hell he was doing it in the first damn place."

"As I said, we must close the wound in your abdomen."

"Uh, have you ever heard of sutures? You could've just stitched it up," she said sarcastically.

"In the field, we cauterize wounds. It takes too long to stitch them."

"Well, you're not cauterizing me," she challenged. "Bring me a needle and thread and I'll stitch up my damn self."

The young man looked at her as though she were a specimen in a zoo. He somehow managed to look confused, appalled, and impressed all at the same time.

Ellie watched as he stood up and walked away, speaking with the woman who had been holding her feet. The woman left and came back a few minutes later and handed something to the man who then came back over to her. He again sat down on the chair next to her bed that had previously been occupied by the dour man and handed her a needle and thread. The look on his face was challenging her to do what she had threatened to do.

Well, if they were not going to do it, Ellie thought. It was not like she did not have plenty of practice sewing human flesh. She did it every day in the morgue. And she had plenty of piercings and tattoos to prove that not only was she not afraid of needles, but that she could handle the pain. She could do this. Thrusting her chin up in defiance, she took the needle and thread from him.

"You have any iodine to sterilize the thread? A little alcohol for the needle?" she asked.

"Sterilize?" he asked.

Ellie did not have the capacity to think about why he was asking this right now. Could he not break from whatever damn role he was playing for five minutes? This was her health with which they were dealing. Why she was not in a proper hospital was beyond her, though after her recent stay she was in no hurry to return. She stared at him, waiting for him to comply with her request. He stood again, walked across the room, and brought back a bottle.

Holding it out to her, he said, "I know not what iodine is, but I have alcohol."

Setting to work cutting the thread and inserting it through the eye of the needle, Ellie then sterilized both the needle and thread the best she could. When she was ready, she lifted the gown she was wearing, exposing her midriff. After cleaning her stomach with the alcohol, she then proceeded to shove the needle through her skin. She winced as the needle pierced her tender flesh but gritted her teeth and continued. The young man and the woman both watched on in amazement. Ellie was more than a little annoyed at the entire situation, even if she had no idea what that situation was. But instead of taking her to a proper hospital or trying to treat her there themselves, she was stitching up her own injury. As soon as she could get out of there, she would get to a real hospital and make sure she was seen by a doctor. The last thing she needed was an infection. And she could get her head examined for a brain injury while she was there.

Ellie finished stitching herself up, cutting the excess thread after tying it off. She handed everything back to the young man, and the woman held out a strip of cloth and helped her wrap it around her stomach. When it was securely in place, Ellie pulled the gown back down and laid back in the bed. The adrenaline had begun wearing off and all she wanted to do now was sleep. She certainly did not want to think about what just happened, how she got there, or where she even was for that matter. All she wanted was the dark oblivion of sleep. Turning her back to her audience, she pulled the covers up over her shoulder, trying to ignore everyone in the room. She heard them walk away and drifted off to sleep.

Chapter 5

With no idea where she was, Ellie tried to take in her surroundings when she woke up sometime later. It seemed to be some sort of primitive building made of wooden logs. She was laying on a bed made of straw inside a cloth bag spread over a wooden pallet. Reminding her of a bean bag chair without the extra give, it was surprisingly more comfortable than she would have expected. There was wooden flooring and no insulation or light fixtures. The only light seemed to come from windows or candles. A small amount came from the fireplace along one wall which had a desk nearby. A red British Army uniform coat hung from the back of the chair. The room was filled with a few dozen other straw and pallet beds, each with an injured man on it. It appeared as though she was the only female patient in the room. She looked around the small room, trying to find anything that would indicate this was all fake. If she could only catch a glimpse of something anachronistic, something from the twenty-first century, she would know she was being set up and that this was all some sort of reenactment after all. Of course, most reenactors typically still adhered to modern hygiene practices. Just looking around the room, she could tell this was not the case. The smell of rotting flesh filled her nostrils, as if to further prove it was not a reenactment. Combined with the memory of a sword being shoved through her stomach, it was all enough to make her want to vomit. The panic began settling in as she looked at the people around her.

"Tip us your daddles," a woman was saying while holding out her hands in front of a man lying on a pallet. He responded by holding out his hands to her.

Across the way, the man whom she had punched in the face was sitting beside another patient while a woman stood at the man's head. "Make the cull easy," he was admonishing her.

Ellie had understood the people who had spoken to her before, but now she wondered if that had all been a dream. Pushing the covers back, she tried to sit up enough to see her stomach. Dressed in a long white loose-fitting cotton dress and her stretch pants, her tank top and sports bra were gone. Pulling the dress up enough to see her abdomen, which was covered by a bandage, she remembered stitching herself up, thinking that had been part of the dream. Ellie also remembered a hot metal rod and burning flesh. Which was it?

About to rip off the wrapping around her middle, she saw a rather good-looking young man walking towards her. It was the same young man who had brought her the needle and thread. He had a thick head of honey-colored hair tied into a ponytail at the back of his neck with a black ribbon, much like Lucas had worn. His chest was broad and tapered down into a thin waist. Like everyone else around her, he was wearing clothing that was not from the twenty-first century. He was again in the white pants and vest with a white cotton shirt underneath, the sleeves rolled up, revealing sinewy arms. Stockings covered his muscular calves, and he had on black shoes. The only thing missing was the red coat of the British Army uniform. She wondered briefly if the one hanging on the chair at the desk belonged to this man.

When she tried to sit up further, he rushed forward to help her. Removing her hands from her bandage, he pulled the covers back up over her as far as they would go. As he did so, Ellie was fixed on the striking cobalt blue eyes that stared back at her.

"Good evening to you, miss. You must allow that to heal. We did not get a chance for introductions earlier. I'm Captain Thomas Burke, physician, at your service. How do you do?"

Too busy trying to figure out what was happening to her, Ellie could not answer. Was any of this real? The pain in her stomach told her it was. But how could it be? Had she received her own traumatic brain injury during the accident? What would happen to her if neither her nor Johnny could work? How would they support themselves?

Captain Burke was speaking again, asking her more questions. "Do you speak English? You didn't seem to have a problem with it earlier this morning."

She wished he would go away so she could slip out and find her way home. While she was trying to find an exit, he kept trying to converse with her. It looked as though he was not going anywhere. Maybe he could give her some of the answers she needed.

"*Parlez-vous français?*" he asked when she still had not said anything.

Her face was scrunched in confusion. "What? Why would I speak French? I am still in the US at least, am I not? I didn't somehow end up in Canada or something?"

"The US? I know not where that is. But no, you're not in Canada. You're in the colony of New York."

He confirmed what she already knew but was afraid to admit. "Colony? Is this real? Am I dreaming? Or did I get brain damage from the accident, and nothing has been real since? This is just a coma of some sort."

Ellie's eyes darted around the room as she asked her questions, desperately hoping to find something that would make sense.

"I assure you this is real. You're not in a coma, nor are you dreaming. I checked your head for injuries after you stitched up your stomach but found none. What's your name?"

"Ellie. Ellie Sorenson."

"Where are you from Miss Sorenson? And how did you end up in the middle of a raid?"

"I'm not sure." Ellie continued looking around, trying to make sense of this. How had she managed to travel back in time? And why this time? For that matter, what time was it exactly? Was she in the middle of the American Revolution? Judging by the number of British uniforms, she was not in a Patriot hospital.

"What year is it?" she decided to take a chance on getting some answers.

"1756."

"Shit."

The French and Indian War was at its beginning, with another seven years to go. It was only days ago she had been exploring the fort and talking about that war with Lucas. How had she ended up there? It had to be a dream; something that her subconscious had locked onto and made her believe was real.

The captain looked at her questioningly and continued trying to get some answers from her about where she came from, but she had none to give. How could she possibly explain that she had traveled through time, 265 years into the past? Was it magic that brought her there?

The world felt like it was spinning out of control. Ellie had never been one to believe in magic. Could she trust anything to be real? While Captain Burke asked his questions, a woman across the room called for him urgently when a man was carried in by other soldiers.

"Captain, it's Ensign Hunt."

One of the soldiers began explaining that the man had collapsed on the parade ground. "He's been proper sick for several days, he has. While we was drilling, he started a-sweating profusely and then he collapsed."

The soldiers placed the patient on a table and the doctor examined him. They removed his coat, and Captain Burke put his ear to the man's chest.

"His heartrate is fast. What was he sick with?"

"I know not. He been in the flux and a-retchin' for a few days now. He even been a-speaking and walkin' like he were drunk but I ain't seen him drink nothin'."

Ellie watched on in amazement. She kept waiting for the so-called physician to do something. There was no sense of urgency. Why was he not doing more for this man? They were not far from her, and she could tell from where she was that his breathing was shallow and rapid and he was sweating profusely while his skin was flushed. She suspected the man was dehydrated and suffering from heat stroke but he was fairly far gone. They would lose him if they did not do something quickly.

That was when she heard the doctor say, "I can no longer hear a heartbeat. I'm afraid he's expired."

Ellie watched the scene unfold in shock. As the captain began walking away from his patient, she was appalled. He had not done anything to try saving this man's life. Standing from her bed, she ran across the room to him. Once again, her paramedic training kicked right in. She stood next to the man and checked his wrist for a pulse while listening for a breath. His eyes were sunken in while his lips and fingernails were blue. When she found neither pulse nor breath, she climbed on top of the table, straddled the man, and started doing chest compressions. At her height, she was too short to get over the top of the man while he was on the table. Captain Burke and the woman assisting him were both horrified. They were by her side in an instant, trying to pull her from the young ensign.

"What has come over you? Remove yourself, madam," he demanded.

She was not budging. Brushing them off, she continued doing CPR on the patient while they yelled and pulled at her. She yelled right back at them. "Back off!"

The venom in her voice must have been enough to convince them to let her continue.

Captain Burke shook his head and said to the woman, "Let her enervate herself. When her own injury reopens and causes her enough pain, she shall stop."

As they turned to walk away, she called after him while continuing compressions, "What the hell kind of doctor are you? This man is in shock. He needs an IV and an ice bath."

"He's already ceased to be," the captain replied.

Ellie was not going to let him off that easily. She seethed at him, "Get your ass over here and treat your patient."

Before the doctor could respond, the patient drew a gasping breath. The captain immediately rushed over to stand next to Ellie and checked on the man while she sat back on her heels. He looked over at her in awe.

Climbing off the table, she stood beside the man and pressed on his fingertip until it turned white. Releasing it, she watched to see how long it took for the color to resume. The color was slow to respond, causing the corners of her mouth to pull down. Pinching the skin on the back of his hand, she could see it was also slow to return to normal. She then looked at the mucous membranes inside his mouth, seeing they were dry.

"He's dehydrated and suffering from heat stroke. He needs fluids and an ice bath. Do you have an IV?" The doctor looked confused, and she tried again, "Intravenous tubes to administer electrolytes?" When the doctor still appeared confused, she let out an exasperated sigh and said, "Never mind. He needs to cool down before his organs shut down. Help me remove his clothes and get something to cool him down with. Do you have an ice bath?"

Ellie was met with blank stares with no attempts to help her remove the man's clothing.

"It's the middle of summer, madam. There's no ice anywhere," the doctor informed her.

Having already removed the man's shoes and stockings, Ellie elevated his feet and was working on removing his vest while everyone around her stared in confusion and disgust.

"Get some water, preferably as cold as possible, some cloths, and some fans. We'll cool him the best we can that way."

The captain nodded to the young girl standing nearby and she ran out the door. He moved closer to Ellie now and helped her remove the man's clothing, leaving him in only his linen shirt. The girl came back carrying two buckets of water while the older woman had brought some cloths. Together, they set about soaking the cloths, dripping the water onto his bare skin, then placing them around the man while Ellie began fanning him.

"Put one under each arm, on his neck, under his back, and at his groin," Ellie directed, a fan in each hand. "Rinse the cloths again and reapply them every minute or so."

The young girl began fanning the man alongside Ellie while the captain and the older woman hurriedly changed out the cloths. As soon as they had changed out each one on his body, they started over with the first, repeating their actions. It took several minutes but eventually, the man's skin began to return to a normal color and he was slowly regaining consciousness, though his speech was still slurred and he seemed quite confused. When his heartrate and breathing returned to normal, Ellie decided to leave his care to the others.

"Get him some bone broth or some lemon water with salt. You have those?"

Captain Burke nodded at the older woman, and she set about acquiring the drinks.

"Don't let him drink it fast."

Ellie made her way back to her bed without another word, feeling everyone in the room watching her as she went. She knew the man still had a long road ahead of him and was not out of the woods yet, but without proper medical care, there was little else they could do for him. He likely would not make it but it would not be for lack of trying. She hoped they had sufficiently cooled him quickly enough and that the orally administered fluids would help, even if they were a long shot.

After tending the young ensign, the older woman approached Ellie. "I be Mrs. Gibbons. That were rather remarkable. Where did you learn that?"

Ellie shrugged, trying to downplay what she had done. There was no way she could explain her education and training. "Just something I picked up somewhere."

Mrs. Gibbons looked at her with disbelief but did not push further. She tried a different tactic instead. "Undoubtedly this somewhere 'as a name? Do you dwell nearby?"

Once again, Ellie did not have an answer. She was frustrated by her situation, but now the reality was starting to set in. The last several days had been beyond trying and she could not stop the tears from falling. It was the first time she had cried since the accident. Mrs. Gibbons was beside her in an instant. Wrapping her arms around Ellie, she drew her in for a motherly hug, holding her while Ellie cried.

When the tears slowed, Ellie lifted her head and looked away. "I'm sorry. I just realized I'm stuck here with no place to go, and I don't even know anyone. I have no idea how I got here or how to get home."

The tears again gained momentum as her situation really sank in. Ellie had never been much of a crier and was horrified at the display now in a room full of strangers, but the tears continued to fall. With her face buried in her hands this time, she did not see the captain approach. He had been checking on another patient nearby and heard the exchange. Captain Burke and Mrs. Gibbons exchanged a look. They seemed to have had an entire conversation without words, and he nodded his head, then turned to walk away to check on another patient. Before leaving, he placed his hand on Ellie's shoulder briefly.

When she looked up, he smiled down at her. "All will be well. We shall endeavor to find a solution."

Ellie did not know how they would figure out a solution to anything, but she was grateful for the kindness of these two individuals. Mrs. Gibbons gently urged her to lean back on the cot and get some more sleep. Night was setting in and she found she was more tired than she thought. She was happy to comply. But first, there was something far more pressing.

"Is there somewhere I can," she paused, trying to find the right term, "relieve myself?"

Mrs. Gibbons pointed to a chamber pot at the foot of the makeshift bed. Ellie had not thought about that aspect of being in the past. Assuming she was actually in the past; she still had her doubts. She eyed the pot and looked around the room.

"Oh. Okay. And what do I do with it when I finish?" she whispered.

Mrs. Gibbons informed her one of the nurses would come by to empty it later. Ellie had to remind herself that even hospitals in her time used bedpans. There was a small privacy screen at the end of her bed, and she used it now to keep herself out of view of the rest of the room, angling it so she had more coverage while she did her business before falling back into bed to sleep more, in the hopes that when she woke, this would all have been a dream.

Chapter 6

June 19, 1756

Captain Burke marveled at the strange woman who had found her way into his hospital. He had written her off as dead when she came in to them. By all accounts, she was brave enough to put herself between a French soldier and a young boy, had enough fortitude to stitch up her own flesh, and was somehow able to bring a dying man back to life while challenging anyone who tried to stop her. Yet, she was so vulnerable that she was in tears when asked about her home.

When he saw her strike Gideon and scream profanities at him, he initially took her for a common whore. Having arrived in the most immodest attire he had ever seen a woman wear in public, she had even walked around the hospital in only a shift and climbed atop a man with no shame; how could she be anything else? Yet that somehow did not fit. She acted like no whore he had ever met; certainly nothing like the ones in France.

The woman was strikingly beautiful. She had no armpit hair, though she was clearly a full-grown woman. Her skin was smooth and unblemished, with no scars from disease or callouses from a lifetime of hard work. Even her hands were delicate and smooth. What she did have on her skin were the strangest markings. The designs painted on her resembled those of the Indians yet were vastly different. Theirs were far more geometric in design while hers had more flourish. They were intricate, delicate, and had colors he had never seen on an Indian.

She also wore more jewelry than anyone he had ever seen. It was far too much for someone of the lower or middling sort. The rings that appeared to have been pierced through her ears and naval were unlike any he had ever seen. It was common practice amongst the Indians to bore holes through the ears and noses, but theirs did not look like this. This woman had several small holes all around her earlobes and the front of her ears while Indians typically only bore one large hole in each lobe. He could not figure out how the smaller pins above her lip and in the upper portion and front portion of her ears were staying attached.

In addition to the peculiar jewelry, the way she spoke had him constantly trying to understand what she was saying. She spoke English, yet it was no English he had ever heard. She used strange words and when she did use words he recognized, they were often strung together in a manner he had never before heard. He had been intrigued by her when she seemed to recover from near death as if by some divine intervention. But now, after her performance with Ensign Hunt, he wanted to know more.

When Ellie woke again, the sun was streaming through the small windows and the young boy she saw on the battlefield was sitting beside her cot. She was surprised to see him. He looked younger now than he had on the roadway. She guessed him to be maybe fourteen or fifteen. Despite him being seated, she could see that he was tall and gangly. His dark hair was to his shoulders and looked as though it had not seen a washing in some time.

He stammered out an introduction. "I know not if you remember me, but we met a couple days ago. Well, nearly," he said shyly. "I'm Isaac Huntington. You saved me from that Frenchman proper good. He woulda kill't me sure. I'm awful sorry he got you instead, but I made sure you had proper good care from the doctor. I brung you back here and told him what happened, I did, and he fixed you right up. I just knew you was going to get better."

The boy was talking fast, but he finally stopped long enough for Ellie to introduce herself. She told him her name but little more. What more could she tell him? He had not been wearing a uniform and was likely too young to have enlisted, but then, they accepted young boys in the military during this era, so she supposed it was possible. She knew very little of history, particularly this period. Most of what she knew was gleaned in the previous days spent with Lucas and exploring the fort and museums in the area. She decided he was probably with the militia.

Isaac was all too happy to do most of the talking. He brought Ellie some food and happily answered the questions she asked. He told her she was in a hospital at Fort Edward at the *Great Carrying Place.* Ellie remembered from the Visitor's Center on Rogers Island that was what the spot on the Hudson

River had been called in the eighteenth century. The historic marker outside the restaurant had even said *Great Carrying Place*. This was the last place she had been with Lucas before he died. She asked Isaac to clarify what he meant by Fort Edward. When she had visited there, it was the name of the city. It had been named after the fort that was built there during the French and Indian War and torn down sometime during the Revolutionary War. The fort had never been rebuilt. It certainly helped support the captain's claim that she was in 1756.

While she talked with the young boy, she watched the captain and Mrs. Gibbons tending their patients. The dour looking man she had punched in the face for trying to cauterize her wound was back. Setting some dirty medical instruments on a small table next to a nearby cot and tying on an apron, he motioned for a couple soldiers to come over and advised them to hold the patient down. As he grabbed a saw from the table, it looked like he was getting ready to amputate the man's leg below the knee. He moved toward the patient being held down on the cot, and she could see dried blood on the saw.

She called out to him, "Are you going to clean that blade before you use it on him?"

The man stopped what he was doing and looked at her with disdain. "Mind your business and don't interrupt me again."

He started moving towards the man again, and this time, she stood up out of bed to interrupt him.

"You need to clean that instrument." She looked over his tray full of tools and added, "All of these instruments, in fact. They're disgusting. They all need to be sterilized before you use them on anyone else."

"I shan't take orders from doxies, and I told you to not interrupt me again," he seethed.

Ellie could see the contempt in his cold dark eyes, and he raised his empty hand to strike her, but the young Isaac was suddenly there between her and the man. Captain Burke and Abigail Gibbons came over to see what the commotion was about, and the other man immediately started spewing hatred about her interfering with his work.

Captain Burke turned to Ellie and asked why she was interfering, and she told him. "Those instruments need to be cleaned and sterilized. They're covered with filth and blood, and god knows what else. If you don't want this man dying from infection, you need to use proper disinfecting techniques."

She pointed at the injured man in question who had been quietly watching the confrontation play out. His dark eyes were like saucers, the white standing out in his ebony face as he now pled with the captain to not let the other man kill him. Captain Burke looked at Ellie, who was not standing down. He huffed out a breath and relented, having already seen her stubborn streak. It was clear she would not be placated.

"And precisely what proper disinfecting techniques would you have us do?" he asked, folding his arms across his broad chest.

"For starters, you could wash them all with soap and hot water. Then, follow that up with some bleach or alcohol. Throw out anything rusty or dull. And stitch him with sterilized sutures instead of attempting to cauterize him."

She pointedly stared at the dour man as she said the last. Ellie knew there was only so much they could do there, but that would be a good place to begin.

Captain Burke looked between her and the other man, then back to Mrs. Gibbons. He was not convinced this would do anything to stave off infection, but she had already saved one patient's life. Infection seemed to take more patients than the initial injury ever did. What could it hurt to try it?

"How long will it take?" he asked her.

Judging by the state of the instruments, it would take some serious scrubbing before she could sterilize them. "An hour," she told him.

He turned to the other man. "Mr. Anwar, go check on Corporal Illsley. Come back in an hour."

Then he turned back to Ellie and said, "Mrs. Gibbons shall show you where you can find the soap, water, and alcohol. Though, we may not have any alcohol to spare for such a thing."

With that, he turned and walked away. It appeared she would be the one cleaning the instruments. She was fine with that as it not only gave her something to do but allowed her to make sure they were disinfected properly. He had not said anything about the bleach, and she thought that like the iodine, maybe he had no idea what it was. When were bleach and iodine discovered? She had not thought about that. It was going to be a constant struggle trying to figure out what was available and what was not. At least alcohol was almost universal to every time period and every culture. If they could not spare any right now, she would simply boil the cleaned instruments for twenty minutes. It was certainly better than what they were currently doing.

Isaac volunteered to assist. "Supposin' I could carry a bucket of water for you. I wouldn'a want you a-hurting yourself."

She chafed at his implication that she was weak or incapable of doing a simple task but welcomed the company.

Before they could set about their task, Mrs. Gibbons brought a stack of linens over. Ellie thought perhaps she was to do laundry after she finished with the instruments. She did not mind since she had no other way of paying back the medical care they provided for her nor anywhere else to go, but she wondered what it would entail there. It was not as though she could throw them into a washing machine. Mrs. Gibbons handed her the pile and told her, "You'll be changing into these afore you leave here."

Mrs. Gibbons must have seen the confusion on Ellie's face because she added, "'Twon't do to have you walking 'round in such a state, parading 'round afore all these men with practically nothing on. It's no wonder they're all in a hullabaloo. Neither the doctor nor the surgeon's mate has taken their eyes off you since you got yourself up out of bed. 'Tis bad enough in here; 'twould be most unfitting to go outside dressed in only a shift."

Ellie wanted to correct her. The doctors had only been watching her to ensure she did not interfere with their work. The man she had called the surgeon's mate, Mr. Anwar she believed he was called, was the dour one who tried to cauterize her. He glared incessantly at her as if he wished her to burst into flames.

"Here?" she asked, incredulous. Ellie looked around the open room full of people who were mostly men. The small privacy screen hiding one end of the bed she had been in did not provide much privacy. Mrs. Gibbons shook her head and walked away as if she could not be bothered with such a ridiculous question.

Ellie looked down at the long white linen dress she wore over her loose stretch pants. She had no idea what happened to her tank top and sports bra, but it did not matter. She could not wear them there and would need clothes. Gratefully accepting the pile she was given, she stared at the contents. Most of it was easy enough to understand, though she had no idea how she was going to lace up a corset by herself. Maybe she could get away with not wearing one. What she could not understand was why there were so many skirts. She supposed Mrs. Gibbons wanted to give her some options to choose from, though only one appeared to match the bodice she was given.

Looking through the pile of clothes, Ellie found a skirt she liked and pulled it on under the gown she was wearing. Most of the skirts were an off-white color which she imagined would be difficult to keep clean. She opted for one of the colored skirts, tying it at the waist, then she dug around again to find a corset. Turning her back to the room while trying to stay behind the privacy screen as much as possible, she pulled her arms from the sleeves of the gown, letting it fall loosely over her shoulders, keeping herself covered as much as possible while she changed. She pulled the corset under the gown, slipping her arms through and working the laces down the front before pulling the gown off over her head.

Mrs. Gibbons was close enough to watch her from around the screen, and must have seen Ellie's confusion. She let out an impatient huff and started assisting her in changing. Ellie had never been modest when it came to her body, though she had become more self-conscious as she aged and put on a few extra pounds. However, it seemed she had shed several pounds over the previous week or so and did not feel this way with Mrs. Gibbons. After taking off the shift she was wearing, the woman stopped her.

"What is you doing, child?" she asked.

Ellie said, "I thought I was getting dressed."

"Then why would you take off your shift?"

"Isn't this just something to sleep in?"

Mrs. Gibbons laughed. "Oh heavens, no. 'Tis your underdress. It's only the first layer."

Ellie wondered how many layers there were.

Mrs. Gibbons had her put the shift back on, then remove the skirt and corset she had already put on. She then handed Ellie the stockings first. Reaching under the shift, she removed her stretch pants, which had somehow become even more loose-fitting since her arrival there. When she was up walking around, she had to keep pulling them up. After removing her leggings and putting the stockings on, Mrs. Gibbons handed her a ribbon.

"Tie it 'round the leg beneath the knee," she informed Ellie at her questioning stare.

Sitting back on the bed, Ellie tied the stockings in place. Mrs. Gibbons handed her a pair of shoes next. Ellie bent to put them on but stopped to examine them first.

"Which foot is which?"

"What is your meaning?" Mrs. Gibbons asked, not understanding Ellie's confusion.

"Which shoe goes on which foot?"

Mrs. Gibbons's brow furrowed, her mouth pulling downward at the same time. "Put either one on whichever foot you wish."

Ellie followed her directions, putting each shoe on a foot, then switching them to the opposite feet when they felt uncomfortable. Switching did not help. Neither was made for a specific foot which made it feel awkward to wear them. Settling into the uncomfortable shoes, Ellie stood.

"What's next?"

"Your stays is next." Pulling the olive-green corset from the pile on the bed, Mrs. Gibbons wrapped it around Ellie. It laced up the front and back, but the front was unlaced. Mrs. Gibbons began threading the laces through the eyelets up the front then pulled it closed and tied it off. There was a gap in the front where the laces stretched across her torso and Mrs. Gibbons grabbed a V-shaped panel which she shoved down inside the laces. It was not as restrictive as she would have expected, but it was still limiting. Instead of bending over, she would have to squat if she had to reach anything on the floor. Grabbing the next item, she wrapped a cord around Ellie's waist and tied it in the front. Two large pouches hung from the cord on Ellie's hips. At her questioning stare, Mrs. Gibbons again explained. "These be pockets."

Ellie was happier than she probably should have been by this prospect. More often than not, women's clothing in her own time did not come with pockets. She loved not only that she would have them, but that they were so large. Each one was larger than the purse she normally carried back home.

Over the pockets, Mrs. Gibbons had Ellie step into a lightweight cotton pink skirt which was split on the sides and gathered onto ties at the waist. The tie on the back panel wrapped around the front and tied there while the other wrapped around to tie in the back, leaving gaps on the sides where she could access the pockets underneath. The skirt reminded her of Japanese hakama pants.

When Mrs. Gibbons pulled another skirt out, Ellie asked, "Just how many skirts do I need?"

Mrs. Gibbons corrected her. "These be not 'skirts;' they be petticoats. And 'twould be indecent to go without them all. You absolutely mustn't wear them out of doors on their own, either," she said sternly.

The last one was a heavier olive-green linen which matched the stays but wrapped around and tied the same as the first. Once it was tied, a light-weight piece of white fabric with small black squares that reminded Ellie of polka-dots was wrapped around her shoulders and tucked into the front of her stays.

"This is your neckerchief," Mrs. Gibbons explained before Ellie could ask. By now, she had gathered that the girl had no idea how to dress or what anything was and had decided it was best to explain it as she went. "'Twill keep you warm while providing modesty from the low cut of your other garments."

She then held out a tan jacket and Ellie put her arms inside the short sleeves. It was also a light-weight linen for which Ellie was grateful. With all these layers, she was worried she was going to quickly overheat. The sleeves ended right below the elbows and the bodice was fitted around her torso, flaring at the waist into skirting that ended a few inches below the waist. Mrs. Gibbons stretched the front across her chest and pinned it closed with straight pins tucked toward the stays. Next came a striped, brown apron nearly as long as the skirts and extended from hip to hip, tying in the back. When Mrs. Gibbons pulled the last piece from the bed and tried to put the cap on Ellie's head, Ellie jerked back. That was where she drew the line. She did not mind the dresses, but the bonnets were a little too *Little House on the Prairie* for her liking. Though, given the time she spent in Utah, it might have had something to do with the Mormon pioneers as well. Either way, it conjured up conservative, closed-minded old ladies in nightgowns and she could not bring herself to wear one.

"'Tis indecent to leave your hair uncovered lest in the privacy of your own home," Mrs. Gibbons informed her, scandalous at the idea. "You may as well be undressed altogether."

Ellie laughed at the horrified expression on the woman's face. "Yet I have on enough layers to remind me that I am anything but undressed."

The corners of Mrs. Gibbons's mouth pinched in a frown but she did not argue further. Between explanations of each item, Mrs. Gibbons chatted amiably all the while. She told Ellie the clothes had belonged to a nurse who was with them but had wandered off in search of herbs and was killed by Indians. Ellie made a mental note to not wander off by herself.

Ellie tried counting how many layers she was now wearing. There were three layers on top and three on bottom; four if she counted the apron. How did anyone get anything done? The clothes were simple, worn, and designed for working in, yet with the corset and all of the layers, Ellie could not help but feel like a princess. It was so rare that she ever wore dresses at all that this was very much outside of her norm. She suddenly felt like a young girl again playing dress-up in her mother's clothes. Though the shoes were a little big, thankfully they fit well enough that she would not trip over them. The skirts, on the other hand, were far too long. She would have to hold them off the ground when she walked, or she would be tripping over them.

Mrs. Gibbons gave a curt nod of her head. "That's better. We'd best be gettin' you what you need to get on with your cleaning. Mr. Anwar will be a-wanting his tools for surgery."

Ellie came out from behind the screen with the biggest smile on her face that she had experienced in a long time. She did not care that she was off to clean dirty medical instruments. She was a princess. When she glanced up, she saw that the captain was watching her. He looked briefly stunned, and she did a little twirl to show off her new clothes. Unable to hold back his own smile, he nodded his head once in approval. This only increased her own smile while Mrs. Gibbons rolled her eyes at Ellie's antics.

"Come along now," Mrs. Gibbons said while Ellie chased after her like a child, Isaac trailing along behind her.

Chapter 7

June 19, 1756

In the small room, it had been difficult to not overhear the women talking as Ellie was dressed. Captain Burke quickly realized that this strange woman had never before dressed in this manner. She had no idea what to call any of the articles nor how to properly layer them or fasten them. He immediately decided she had likely been taken from her family at a young age and raised by Indians. It was the only explanation, though it was odd that she spoke English so well without knowing anything about the dress of the English. Most of the non-commissioned personnel there were uneducated and their speech reflected it. She did not speak the way the lower sorts did. He would have to find out more about her origins.

Ellie was starting to relax a little. Still terrified she would not be able to find her way home and with no idea how long she would be there or how she was going to survive when they inevitably threw her out, for the time being, she had a purpose and now she looked as though she fit in, as much as that was possible with her piercings and tattoos. Most importantly, she knew she was safe with these people. Both Mrs. Gibbons and Captain Burke made her feel welcome and safe. She asked Mrs. Gibbons what her first name was.

"Abigail."

"Ooh. Can I call you Abby?" Ellie asked. She felt like she was acting like a teenager but could not help herself. Filled with an energy she had not felt in years, she somehow felt so young and alive there. Though it was hard to argue with men dying of battle wounds all around her, she still was not entirely convinced that any of this was real, so she decided she was going to enjoy whatever came. It was almost like having a temporary free pass from her life.

The woman glared at her and replied sternly, "You may call me Missus Gibbons."

Everyone was so formal there. It was going to take Ellie some time to get used to that. She understood military life and addressing people by rank, but everyone else was addressed by "Mister," "Missus," or "Miss."

Abigail Gibbons took Ellie to a large fireplace in another room surrounded by shelves with pots hanging down, Isaac following closely behind. She pointed to two buckets hanging from a wooden plank that Ellie could use to haul water, then showed her where she could find the other supplies she would need. Mrs. Gibbons left them to their task, and they set about getting the job done. Looking at the buckets, Ellie started removing them from the board, but Isaac immediately took it from her, placing the board on his shoulders while the buckets hung on either side.

"'Tis a yoke," he explained at her confusion before leading the way to the well outside. When they got back to the door of the hospital, he said, "Supposin' you shan't mind dubbing the gigger? 'Tis a difficult thing while the buckets are full."

"Dubbing the gigger?" she asked.

Isaac looked at her in confusion, then nodded to the door. Understanding dawned on Ellie and she opened it, gesturing for him to walk through first.

"I'll be thanking you, miss. I may not be able to get it meself at the moment, but I'm still enough of a gentleman to allow you to enter first."

Ellie instructed Isaac while they worked and idly chatted. He told her of his life on the farm in Massachusetts and how he was the eldest of seven. When they called up the militia, his father was proud that he wanted to join him. This had been his first battle, and it was not at all what he had expected.

When they finished, they carried the now almost sterile instruments back to the main hospital area where Ellie had Isaac lay out a clean cloth before setting them down. He had stayed as long as he could but had to get back to his company. Captain Burke came by to check on them, and she said, "We did what we could with what we had. They're better than they were. As long as he makes sure his hands are clean and the wound stays clean, the patient has a better chance of surviving."

The captain nodded his head and called Gideon over to proceed with his amputation, instructing him to thoroughly wash his hands first. The surgeon's mate was not particularly happy about that and grumbled while he left to wash his hands.

With Captain Burke already off to tend another patient, Ellie found herself with nothing to do. The man awaiting amputation looked terrified and Ellie sat with him, trying to alleviate any of the fear that she could. She certainly did not fault him for being afraid; she would have been, too. Ellie had been on the peer support team as a paramedic and helped implement a program at the medical examiner's office. She used her training now to be a support to this man who was about to lose his leg and could quite possibly die from the surgery.

"What happened?" she asked after they had chatted for a bit.

"I took a ball to the leg. Shattered everything below the knee proper good."

"I'm sorry? A ball?" Ellie asked.

"Musket ball," Thaddeus replied. "Me master shan't be 'appy to find me leg missin'. I know not what he'll do with me when I return to his home."

"Your master?" Ellie asked before she could stop herself. Taking him in, she noted for the first time that the man was likely enslaved. She never concerned herself with skin color at home and it had not occurred to her that his dark skin had implications she could not comprehend. "I'm sorry," she said quietly before he could respond.

Instead of dwelling on it, she began telling him how brave he was and tried to offer what comfort she could. Two men came over and held Thaddeus down while Gideon began the procedure. He wrapped the leg with a leather strap attached to a metal corkscrew which he then tightened down, cutting off the blood in the leg. One of the men pulled a small metal ball from his pocket and placed it inside Thaddeus's mouth.

"Bite down on this," he said as he inserted it.

"What is that you just gave him?" Ellie asked.

"'Tis a musket ball."

"Wait. Really? Did you just tell him to bite the bullet?" she asked with an amused grin. The men did not understand her amusement and she turned her attention back to Thaddeus. As Gideon grabbed the scalpel from the tray, Ellie had a sudden thought.

"Wait," she exclaimed while Gideon looked at her with more irritation than she thought was possible. "Musket balls are made from lead, aren't they?"

When the men nodded in confusion, she quickly went across the room to the fireplace and grabbed a small piece of wood and ran back. "Give me the ball. Bite on this instead."

Thaddeus spit the ball out and took the stick instead though everyone else was asking what difference it made.

"Lead is poisonous," she explained. "You should never, ever put it in your mouth."

The men laughed at her. Gideon shook his head. "Be you quite finished interrupting my work? I'm a busy man and I don't appreciate your nonsense and whimsical notions."

Sitting down next to Thaddeus, she raised her eyebrows in objection to his demeanor but told Gideon she was finished, then continued chatting with the man and held his hand as Gideon finally began.

Watching the amputation was something that would stay with Ellie for the rest of her life. It was so primitive. The poor man was awake the entire time while the surgeon's mate hacked away at his leg. The entire procedure took less than ten minutes and Ellie was grateful it was relatively quick, though it felt like it went on forever. When Thaddeus squeezed her hand, Ellie thought he might crush every bone in it, but she sat there and let him. She did everything in her power to not show any discomfort. If he could endure what was happening to him, she could endure this.

When the amputation was finally over and Thaddeus drifted off into a laudanum-induced slumber, Ellie once again found herself with nothing to do. She offered to again clean the tools Gideon had finished using and to her surprise, he let her take them. When she finished, Ellie looked around and started cleaning whatever else she could. When a man in a cot nearby asked for a drink, she went in search of some water. Upon her return, another patient was asking for some as well. She began tending to the patients' basic needs as best she could. Ellie did not want to interfere with the work Captain Burke and Mrs. Gibbons were doing but rather tried to supplement it and take on the jobs to which they could not attend. When she came across a man whose bandages were filthy and seeping with blood, she found the supply and changed them out, washing the wound before redressing it. After finishing, she went back to cleaning.

It was no wonder so many people in this era died of infections. The place was horrendous. She did not think even the poorest modern hospitals looked like this. Ellie wiped down every surface she could and swept what she was able to. When a patient needed something within her capabilities, she would see to it. Every time she interacted with a patient, she engaged them in conversation. Starting with asking their names, she would then ask where they were from or if they had families at home. She was surprised to hear how many of them had families there with them.

Ellie was aware of being watched the entire afternoon. Abigail Gibbons periodically watched her at first, but then she watched less and less as the day went on. The captain continued to watch her throughout. Every time she looked up from her work, she would see his eyes on her. It made her a little uncomfortable. He probably did not trust her and was keeping an eye on her after the trouble she had already caused since her arrival. She was careful to not overstep.

As the day came to a close, Ellie did not know what she thought would happen, but she had not made any progress in figuring out her situation. She debated going out on her own and taking her chances. She did not have a problem sleeping on the ground outside and was not entirely helpless. She could probably find food along the way, though that may prove the more difficult challenge. With no weapons to use for hunting, no tools for fishing, and not enough knowledge of flora to find edible plants that would not kill her, she did not relish her chances of survival. Then there was the small matter of two armies and a whole lot of Native Americans at war with each other. She had already stumbled onto one skirmish; she did not want to stumble onto another one.

***

As the sky darkened, Ellie realized she should have been trying to figure out how she was going to eat and where she was going to sleep. Instead, she had thrown herself into her work with barely a thought for herself. Ellie had not seen Abigail for a time but had been so busy she did not notice when the woman had even left. Eventually, she came back, another woman following her, and they each had some food that she asked Ellie to help her deliver to the invalid men. When they came back in from getting the last round of bowls, Ellie saw that all of the patients had been tended to. Mrs. Gibbons took the bowls she carried and set them down on a table away from the patients.

"Come, foul a plate with us," Abigail said.

At Ellie's confusion, Abigail indicated that one of the settings was for her. She sat eagerly and happily ate the concoction of beans and some sort of pork. As she made her way through the meal, she found there was bread at the bottom of the bowl. There was light chatter as they ate, with Gideon speaking to everyone but her. She was completely fine with that. He was entirely unpleasant.

As the conversation flowed, it inevitably led to questions about her. Where did she come from? How did she end up there? Did she travel by sea or by land to get there? Of course, she had no more answers to give now than when they first asked. They would not believe her if she told them. She thought it best to not tell them anything. This resulted in her saying, "I don't know" over and over again and appearing confused.

Of course, this led Gideon to accuse her of being a French spy, at which she laughed. She did not even know any French. He was wary of her, though. She would have to watch herself around him.

The captain came to her rescue with, "Of course she's not a spy Mr. Anwar. Were she one, she would have a much better pretense about from where she came and how she ended up here."

Ellie was grateful for his acceptance of her situation and defending her to his colleague. Giving him an appreciative smile, he winked at her, which, to her surprise, sent butterflies dancing through her stomach. If she was twenty years younger and single… She did not want to think about that right now and pushed the thought aside.

There were a few questions about herself that did not require explanations she did not have which Ellie attempted to answer. When they asked if she had been traveling with a father or husband, she was unsure what to say. The one thing she was trying the hardest not to think about was now being asked of her directly. She imagined Kristy had actually called Johnny this time and he was probably looking for her, but she could not tell them that. How would she explain that he would never find her or that he did not even exist at that moment? She suddenly wanted to cry again, and she never cried. Not that she missed her husband. She was glad to be free of him for however long she was there. But it was the reminder of everyone else back home that had her emotional, even if the emotion was an oddity. Ellie was the least emotional person she knew, often joking that she had no heart. However, in that moment, the exhaustion and overwhelming despair of her situation began to sink in.

What was Kristy going through right now? Had she reported her missing? Was there a search party combing the water for her? Was this what happened to all the people who went missing and were never found? Would she ever see her family again? How would her niblings feel about her disappearing?

Ellie had never been particularly close to most people in her family, but there were a select few. As teenagers, she had become close with her cousins, Kristy and Steven, even marrying Steven's best friend, resulting in them spending a lot of time together over the years. Her sister had passed as a child from diabetes, but she still had three brothers. She had never been particularly close with her brothers and had been estranged from them for years, but when they all started having their own children, she tried to make more of an effort to have relationships with them. It may have been difficult to reconcile with her brothers, but she loved her niblings dearly. In return, she was always the favorite aunt to them all.

Ellie's mother had passed away a decade ago from a drug overdose. Having become addicted to OxyContin after the traffic accident, she had ended up on fentanyl when the Oxy was not enough, which then killed her. Ellie's relationship with her dad was also estranged. They had never been close, but when her mother became addicted to opioids, Ellie was the only one who saw it as a problem, making the distance between her and her father that much greater. She tried getting her mother help, but everyone defended her, saying the drugs were necessary for the pain. Ellie had seen this far too many times in her line of work and knew better. It had caused a rift between her and her family when her mother first became addicted, which only intensified when she passed. They blamed Ellie for the accident since she had been driving. The other driver had run a red light and Ellie was the only one of the three in her car to escape with no serious or permanent injuries. If blaming her for the incident was not enough, after she died, her father accused Ellie of not doing enough to get her mother off the medications. She had done everything she could and was met with nothing but resistance. Eventually, she stopped talking to her father altogether and barely spoke to her brothers.

Her hesitation in answering questions about her marital status, combined with the melancholic expression on her face and the wedding ring on her finger led Mrs. Gibbons to her own conclusion. "He's expired, han't he? Oh, you poor lamb. To be an ace of spades so young," she tsked.

"Ace of spades?" Ellie asked.

"Widowed," Thomas filled in for her.

Ellie did not correct them. Technically, he was not alive right then, so she let them believe she was a widow.

While cleaning up the dishes, the captain stopped Ellie and asked how her stomach was doing. She had not even thought about it in hours. It felt like it had already completely healed, though she knew that was not possible. Then again, her injuries from being pinned between two cars had healed in two days and now she was in the middle of the eighteenth century. At that point, she was ready to believe anything was possible. She told him it was fine.

"You've had a rather busy day. You must be in a great deal of pain. Do you need some laudanum?"

"Laudanum? As in opium?" Ellie responded. That was the last thing she wanted. She never took drugs if she could avoid them, particularly anything addictive.

He nodded.

"No thank you," she said. "I'll deal with the pain." It was no longer particularly painful, but she did not want to share that with him. He would probably insist on seeing it if she did and she would not be able to explain if it had somehow healed itself as it felt like it had.

He studied her as if she were some sideshow curiosity. "You ought not need to suffer. The laudanum shall help."

"I'm sure it will," she huffed. "But it's highly addictive. I'll stay away from opioids, thank you." Even the thought of it left a bad taste in her mouth after what she had gone through with her mother.

"Do not fret. There's no cause to think a medication addictive. It's very commonly used to treat patients with all manner of ailments."

She gave him a tight-lipped smile and declined the offer again without further explanation. It was not worth arguing over.

"Come see me if you change your mind."

"I will. Thank you."

When they finished up for the night, Mrs. Gibbons asked Ellie to follow her. They went outside toward the encampment positioned around the fort. Walking east of the fort, in the opposite direction from the Hudson River, they walked through hundreds of tents set into neat rows. The tents surrounded the fort in an arc with a creek separating them from other structures to the south. They walked and walked as Abigail expertly weaved her way through the city of tents until she finally stopped at one about a mile from the hospital inside the walls of the fort.

"There be an empty bed in 'ere. You may stay 'ere for now. We shall start bright and early tomorrow morn, so get some respite. Get up with reveille and come directly to the 'ospital."

Ellie put her hand on Abigail's arm before she could leave. "Thank you, Mrs. Gibbons. I really appreciate everything you've done for me. Truly."

Mrs. Gibbons nodded her head and said, "You're welcome." Then she turned and walked away.

Chapter 8

June 20, 1756

Ellie slept more deeply than she thought possible, given her unknown surroundings and her current situation. She attributed it to the energy her body was expending to heal itself combined with the busy day she had the day before.

When she went inside the tent the night before, she found five other women already in there. Spotting the empty bed Mrs. Gibbons had mentioned, she went over to it. The women immediately started asking questions which Ellie again did her best to answer without actually telling them anything. Thankfully, their questions were mostly sated with the explanation she gave about saving Isaac's life and helping out in the hospital after being injured. She kept her story very basic in an attempt to not raise more questions, telling them she was likely only there for a couple of nights until she could find someplace to go. This seemed to help placate a Mrs. Charlotte Spencer, who was particularly put out by Ellie's presence there. When they were satisfied, they started turning in, one by one. Before they did, the one closest to her, a Miss Anne, told her she could use the trunk at the foot of the bed. It had all belonged to the previous nurse Mrs. Gibbons had mentioned who had been killed by Native Americans. The other women had salvaged what they could of her belongings and left the rest. There had been nothing of enough importance to send back to her family. The clothes had not fit any of the women in the tent and they were going to distribute them to some of the other women, but Abigail Gibbons had beaten them to it. The woman had only died shortly before Ellie's arrival.

Ellie had undressed down to her shift when she crawled into bed the previous night. Now, in the morning light, she wanted to inspect her wound and make sure infection was not setting in. Once she got the dressing off, she would clean it thoroughly and put on a new, clean dressing. Assuming she could find one.

The other women were up early with reveille, leaving Ellie alone in the tent. Mrs. Gibbons had told her to come directly after reveille, but she assumed she would allow her the few minutes it would take to tend to her injury. After removing her shift, she unwrapped the cloth that was wrapped around her middle. She was shocked to see the wound was already closed. How was that possible? She was really going to have to stop asking that question. The scar that was forming consisted of a clean, smooth line near the top, with a much larger, messy pattern towards the bottom where that oaf had burned her. Regardless of how it looked, at least it was healing well and was not infected. She would have to clean the area later when she could get some soap and water, but at least her mind was put at ease by seeing the condition of it.

Looking around the tent, she did a brief inventory of her surroundings. Aside from the six beds of straw on the ground, each covered with bedding, the only other items in the tent were the aforementioned chests at the foot of each bed. Ellie opened the one that now temporarily belonged to her and found a sewing kit with a small pair of scissors, needles, and threads. Those would come in handy to hem her numerous skirts. For now, she used the scissors to remove the stitches from her stomach that were no longer necessary. There was also another dress, petticoats, and a hairbrush inside, but nothing else.

It was a good thing she had never been high maintenance. Ellie had grown up camping and while she did not get out as much as she would have liked anymore, she still enjoyed the outdoors whenever she could. She was no stranger to cooking over a fire or using cast iron pots and pans. Her beauty regimen minimal, she did not wash her hair daily or wear very much makeup, when she wore it at all. Her hair was kept long, but simple, and often worn in a loose side braid that fell over her left shoulder. Living without a hair dryer or curling iron would be easy for her. Ellie would miss pedicures, and she would have to figure out how to wax herself or use a straight razor, but those were small things. It would certainly be an adjustment, but she would manage.

Ellie took a moment to look at herself closely before redressing. It was difficult to see much without a mirror, but even without one, she could see she had somehow lost a significant amount of weight in the last handful of days. Some weight loss was to be expected with everything she had undergone. She had barely eaten anything since the car accident. Her clothes had been feeling looser, but she guessed now that she was probably down fifteen or twenty pounds since the accident. A few pounds would not have concerned her, but how she had dropped that much in only a few short days was beyond her, as was everything else that had happened since. Had it only been a few days? The accident already felt like ages ago. Would she ever make it back to her own time again?

Putting her unanswerable questions aside, she prepared to begin her day, making a point to ask Mrs. Gibbons about personal hygiene. She would find some hot water and soap that she could use with a cloth for a sponge bath, but she was not sure how people washed their hair or brushed their teeth, if they even brushed their teeth, in this time. She was going to have a lot to learn there.

The day progressed much like the day before. Ellie spent her time cleaning and tending to the patients the best she was able while staying out of Gideon Anwar's way. By midmorning, Captain Burke approached her and asked her to walk with him.

They went outside, and he began showing her around some of the areas she was allowed to access. The fort appeared quite different than it had in the model and drawings she had seen at the visitor's center with Lucas. Though, looking around, she could see that quite a bit of construction was still underway. She knew the fort to have been roughly square in shape with large arrowhead shapes sticking out on each of the corners, the one in the southwest corner being smaller than the rest. These arrowheads were where the canons were positioned high enough to reach the enemy from afar or sound alarms to the other forts in the area. The hospital was in the north-west corner of the interior of the fort with a second building next to the one she had been in, though a larger structure was under construction to replace the two buildings. Along the north wall of this inner courtyard were the officer's quarters and a set of barracks were along the east wall. An L-shaped storehouse was in the south end of the courtyard and a 'necessary house' was to the west of the storehouse.

Once again, Ellie had needed an explanation. The captain looked rather uncomfortable explaining that this was the privy. The chamber pots were generally only used in the hospital or at night. The rest of the time, the men inside the fort used the necessary house. When someone was walking out as they passed by it, Ellie's curiosity had her peeking inside. It was essentially a long, wooden, communal porta-potty. Two benches were built-in along the length of the walls with holes cut in the top. The benches ran the entire length of the small building and allowed twenty men to do their business at once, all while facing each other. Ellie was suddenly not sure that the chamber pot was so bad.

Being in the encampment outside the fort, Ellie had been shown to another area designated for the women to do their business, though it was not introduced to her as a necessary house. It was not fully indoors, but was a pit dug into the ground with similar boards placed over the pit where they could sit to do their business. Before they moved on, Ellie noted the basket of corn cobs in the corner. There was a similar basket at the privy near her camp.

"Why are all of the corn cobs piled up here?" she asked, looking up at the captain.

Instead of answering right away, he blushed a deep red and simply stared at her, willing her to come up with the answer on her own so he would not have to speak of such things aloud to a lady. How could she possibly not know? Even Indians used corn cobs to clean themselves after doing their business.

When she did not understand right away, he coughed as he tried to sputter out an answer. This was far worse than explaining what a necessary house was. He fumbled over his words, but in doing so, she somehow managed to finally understand. The look of surprise on her face was not what he had expected.

"You've got to be kidding me," she exclaimed. It was his turn to be confused.

"I'm not certain I understand your meaning."

"Never mind." Ellie shook her head.

"You're welcome to pull leaves from the surrounding brush if you prefer."

"Those are my only options?" she queried.

"Unless you're aware of an alternative? It's not uncommon while traveling to use grass, moss, sticks, or handfuls of straw."

Thomas was again struck by the surprise and horror on her face. He desperately wanted to ask what other options were available, but that would be extremely inappropriate. He held his tongue instead.

Once again, Ellie was grateful that she was not high maintenance. The bathroom habits there were going to take a lot of getting used to.

As they continued the tour, Ellie was beginning to wish she had paid more attention to the terminology Lucas had used during the tour at Fort William Henry. She was proud of herself for remembering that the ramparts were the walls used to fortify the fort and the hollow cutouts underneath them housing the cannons were called casements.

Men passed them as they walked, all in uniforms of different kinds. There did not seem to be a standard, but rather many different styles and colors, though the red coat of the English was easiest to recognize.

Ellie had always prided herself on being open-minded and non-judgmental. She allowed people to show her who they were through their actions rather than by their appearances or social status. Growing up with a racist mother taught her how not to treat people. She gave everyone the same deference. Therefore, it surprised her to realize the level of unease she felt being surrounded by so many 'redcoats.' She knew they were not her enemy, nor were they even the enemy of the American people at that point in history, yet she could not shake the feeling that she was in enemy territory. Apparently, that concept was deeply ingrained into her.

As they walked, they came to an opening leading outside the fort and she looked out to the west. "That's the Hudson then? And Rogers Island?" Ellie pointed to the uninhabited island directly across from where they now stood.

"Roger's Island? I like the sound of that, I do."

The new voice was attached to a man who had come up behind them. Ellie and Captain Burke turned, and the men greeted each other with a slight bow. "Mrs. Ellie Sorenson, may I introduce to you Captain Robert Rogers?" Turning back to the other captain, he added, "Mrs. Sorenson has come to us from the convoy that was attacked near the Halfway Brook."

"How do you do, Mrs. Sorenson?" the other captain replied as he took her hand and kissed the back of it. "You shall be heartily glad to hear that my men and I shall be seeking out and engaging the party which attacked your convoy. They shan't be bothering anyone anytime soon."

Ellie was not quite sure what to say to that, nor to the fact that she was standing in front of the man who created the US Army Rangers. Navy or not, as a military brat, she was all too familiar with the Rangers. There was a healthy rivalry between the Rangers and the Navy SEALs, both of which were elite forces, each believing themselves superior to the other. It was strange to think of this young man in front of her now as the person who started that unit. She settled on a simple, "Thank you."

The man smiled, then said, "And yes, that is Hudson's River, but what's this about Roger's Island?"

Captain Burke changed the subject before Ellie could answer. "I was showing Mrs. Sorenson around. She may be staying on with us as a nurse. She's already been so good as to assist on her fellow patients since her arrival."

"Is that so? Well, I wish you the best, and hope to not have need of your services," he said with a teasing smile. Captain Rogers excused himself, and Ellie watched him as he left, still slightly in awe.

As they continued their tour, it suddenly occurred to Ellie that she could very well be standing in the exact spot where her and Lucas had been hit by that truck. The landscape was obviously significantly different, but she thought it possible. They had made their way along the east wall and were now standing south of the north bastion. For a moment, she felt as though she could not breathe.

Captain Burke noticed Ellie suddenly pale and asked if she was alright. He worried that she had not allowed herself enough rest after such a significant injury, though she had seemed to be doing well. She assured him she was fine, but he could see that something had left her distraught. He wanted to know everything about this peculiar woman. Try as he might, she simply was not sharing any information about herself. He found himself becoming perturbed.

"How did you come to be at the site of the raid, Mrs. Sorenson?"

"I really don't know. I was lost and stumbled on it. I heard the noise but had no idea what was going on, so I went in closer to see. I watched for a few minutes and that's when I saw the man coming at Isaac with his sword."

"And you thought to put yourself in the way instead?"

"I was trying to push him out of the way. He's just a kid and he was facing the opposite direction and didn't see it coming. I didn't expect to take his place."

Thomas looked closely at her. How could she describe Isaac Huntington as "a kid" when she was likely not much older than him?

"How did you become lost?"

"I was on the water and my k–" Realizing she could not say kayak, she thought to find another way to explain it and decided to keep it simple. "I capsized. I swam to shore but didn't recognize where I was, so I started trying to make my way into," she paused again, "civilization. I was surrounded by trees and was trying to find a town or a village or something."

"You were on the water by yourself?"

Ellie nodded.

"Where was your escort?"

"I didn't have one."

"Why not?"

"Because I'm a grown-ass woman fully capable of doing shit on my own."

Ellie knew she was getting defensive, tired of being asked questions to which she did not have answers. She took a deep breath, let it out slowly, and tried again.

"My friend had just passed, and I needed time to myself to process what I was feeling."

She could not explain much, but she wanted to be as honest as she could in her answers.

"Do you make a habit of going on the water by yourself, Mrs. Sorenson?"

Ellie nodded again. "If I don't have anyone to go with me, yes. And you can call me Ellie, you know."

It chafed her that everyone there was calling her Mrs. Sorenson. She had gone by that name far longer than she had ever gone by her maiden name, but it still felt wrong. It was a constant reminder that she was anchored to Johnny and felt like a weight around her neck.

"Were you unconcerned with the Indian warriors or the French Army in the vicinity, *Mrs. Sorenson?*" He deliberately emphasized her name when he said it that time. He was trying to rile her up.

Ellie sighed. "I didn't know I needed to be."

"From where did you begin your journey on the water?"

She wanted to say, *"In 2021,"* but did not think that would be very helpful. As this was yet another thing Ellie could not explain, she remained quiet.

He tried again. "Did you carry yourself off from someone?"

"No."

"Where do you dwell?"

Ellie continued her silence. She knew it only raised suspicions, but the truth would raise questions as to her sanity. Or worse yet, her 'supernatural abilities.' She thought they were probably no longer burning women at the stake during this time but was not certain and did not know if they still punished women for witchcraft in any other way. It was not something she wanted to find out. As for her mental state, she knew enough to know that any suspicion about her being insane could get her locked up and that people in the past had bizarre notions of what constituted insanity. She was afraid to say anything that might make her situation worse. She tried to give the captain enough to get him to believe her but not enough to question her sanity.

Ellie could feel her eyes beginning to burn and knew the tears were not far behind. They seemed to remain annoyingly close to the surface since her arrival in the past. She desperately wanted to tell him everything. She wanted to confide in someone and have them tell her she was not crazy. She wanted help in figuring out what had happened to her and how to get home. But that would not happen there, so she did the only thing of which she could think and continued her silence. When she stayed quiet this time, he stopped walking and turned to face her.

"Mrs. Sorenson, I understand there's something from which you may be hiding or don't wish to speak, but I've a responsibility here. I need to know if I can trust you if I'm going to petition the colonel to allow you to stay. I lost a nurse of late and could use the help. There are a number of other women here who would be happy to take on the endeavor, but you seem to know your way around the patients, and I think you should be an asset in the hospital. But I must know where your loyalties lay or if there's a husband or father or owner out there looking for you. You are clearly unfamiliar with our clothing or medicine, and you have those marks on your stomach and heels and the rings through your ears and navel. You speak English, though I don't recognize the accent or your manner of speech. You are not an Englishwoman, are you?"

She wanted to say that she came from there; that she was more American than he was, but she did not say it. Her ancestors had come from England eight or nine generations before her, so she clung to that.

"Yes, I am," Ellie protested. "My family is English, anyways."

"Have a care what you say. I'll not be fobbed off so."

Looking up at him in confusion, she admitted, "I have no idea what you just said."

He studied her face for a moment, before explaining, "I was warning you to not lie to me. I'll not be deceived by false pretenses. I'd have the truth."

While she nodded, he continued, "Does someone hold papers over you?"

At her confused expression once again, he clarified, "Are the marks and rings a sign of ownership? Are you indentured to someone?"

"Gods, no," she exclaimed, trying to rein in her offense. "No one owns me."

"Were you held captive by Indians? Did you live amongst them? I've seen similar marks on them, though nothing quite as detailed and colorful as what you have."

When she paused to figure out how to best explain them, he took it for something else and said, "I need to trust you, but I also need you to trust me with whatever you tell me."

Ellie wanted to believe him. Desperately wanting to trust him, she had always had a hard time trusting people she did not know. She considered her response carefully.

"Look Captain, I wish I could give you the answers you're looking for. I can tell you no one owns me. I'm not beholden to anyone at all for any reason. I am my own person. I've never been held captive, nor have I ever lived amongst the Native Americans."

"Native Americans?"

"Indians." Ellie was surprised he was unfamiliar with the designation.

"Who put the marks on you?"

"These ones," she held out her arm and showed her Lichtenberg figures, "are from getting struck by lightning."

He looked as though he wanted to interrupt again, but she pressed on.

"The rest of them, I did myself. Well, I didn't actually do the tattoos because I'm not an artist, but they were entirely my decision. The belly button, too. They aren't marks of ownership or association with any particular person or tribe. They're just artwork. I find them aesthetically pleasing. And where I come from, they're rather common. It's no different than any other adornment like a necklace, except that it's permanent."

He did not look satisfied with the explanation and pushed again, "And where is it you're from that this is so commonplace?"

"Far away from here," she said wearily.

Thomas let out a frustrated sigh. Ellie understood the sentiment. It felt as though they were going around in circles.

"Your accent is not French or Spanish." When she did not respond, he tried again. "You don't appear to be Spanish or Portuguese. Are you Dutch?"

Her continued silence caused him to try a different angle. He wanted to believe what she told him, but how could he when she was not forthcoming about herself and from where she came? "You did not appear from nothing. From whence did you come before yesterday?"

Ellie played with her necklace while staring out across the grounds of the fort. There was nothing more she could say to this man without him declaring her insane or worse, a witch, and locking her up.

Thomas sighed, running a hand across his clean-shaven jaw. He had never met a woman so obstinate. He was trying to help her, but she would not give him anything on which to go. He watched as she played with the pendant hanging from a cord around her neck. Was it a tell that she was not being honest with him or was it simply a nervous tic?

"That's a peculiar cross," he observed. "I've not seen one quite like that."

"That's because it's not a cross," she replied.

He looked at her skeptically.

"It's an ankh," she explained. "It's also called the Key of Life. It's Egyptian. It predates the cross by a few thousand years and represents eternal life."

Ellie knew she was rambling. She was hiding behind useless trivia to cover for her nervousness.

Thomas perked up at the small amount of progress. "Are you Egyptian then?"

"No," Ellie shook her head. "I just like the ankh."

What would she do when this officer told her to leave there? Where would she go? How would she survive in this world with no money or work? Could she even get work? Other than as a maid anyway. Just how limited were opportunities for women in this era? And how was she going to get home? Her fate was in this man's hands. She needed to give him something, even if she could not tell him the truth.

"I can't tell you where I'm from, Captain. I don't know how I ended up here. I never thought it possible that I could ever be here."

"You know where you are then? How is it you've heard of this place, yet refuse to tell me from whence you came?"

"All I can tell you is that I'm not from the colonies." Ellie sighed her own frustration now while Thomas continued to look at her expectantly. He was waiting for more and she had no more to give him. She wanted to get off this merry-go-round but did not know how.

"It's complicated," she said in exasperation. "Too complicated for me to even understand. And if I can't understand it, how the hell am I supposed to explain it to you? If I knew how the hell I got here, I could find my way home, damn it. I sure as hell wouldn't be stuck here with no money or resources or a way to survive. I can't wrap my goddamn brain around what's happened to me, and believe me, it's far more frustrating to me than it will ever be to you." She was almost yelling now, and her eyes were stinging with the unshed tears. A few soldiers nearby turned their heads at her raised voice.

He finally accepted this explanation. She wished she had thought of it yesterday. He had been quiet while she let out her frustration. Ellie turned her back to him for a moment to gather herself before turning back to him. When she did, he had one eyebrow raised and a smirk on his lips.

"And is it common where you're from for ladies to use such language?"

Ellie laughed. "As a matter of fact, it is. Though, I typically use much worse language which is not quite as common. I've been holding back out of politeness."

"Yes, I heard some of it yesterday."

They both laughed at this. It was a good release, and his laughter was like a balm to her frayed nerves. Maybe he was not as stuffy as she had initially thought.

As they walked back to the hospital, he asked, "Did you say the designs on your abdomen and heels were called tattoos?"

At his hesitant tone, she asked, "You've never heard of tattoos before?"

He laughed at this. "Oh, I most certainly have. A tattoo is the sound of the evening drum that calls soldiers to their quarters."

"That's weird. I wonder if that's why they're called that. Maybe it has something to do with the tapping. Tattoos—my kind of tattoos—have traditionally been done by tapping the ink into the skin with sharpened sticks or bones."

"You allowed someone to drive ink into your skin with sharp sticks?" he asked in horror.

"Multiple times," she replied with a smirk, not correcting him that hers were done with needles rather than sticks.

"That sounds horribly painful." His face was a mixture of shock and disgust.

"It is."

"And you did this willingly?"

It was her turn to laugh. "It only hurts for a little while. The pain is temporary, but the artwork will last a lifetime."

Captain Burke shook his head in non-understanding while Ellie laughed. She was not surprised by his reaction. There were plenty of people in her own time who had the same reaction.

Before going back into the hospital, the captain asked if she would be interested in staying on as a nurse. "It would primarily entail cleaning, making beds, mixing medicines, emptying chamber pots, and holding patients while myself or Mr. Anwar operate."

"Just like that? You don't need to see my qualifications or hear a list of my training and experience?"

His eyebrows raised at this. "Would you tell me if I asked?"

Okay, she walked right into that one.

"I don't suppose I can," Ellie said wistfully.

"I thought not. Most of the nurses here have never done this before. They've no training. They only have a desire to help and a loved one serving with the army, be it Regulars, provincials, or militia. They follow the army as it moves, so we are always in need of people to help care for the sick and wounded and make hospital supplies. I suspect you've more training than even my surgeon's mate. Though, I shan't say that to him. Mr. Anwar believes women shan't be here at all."

Thomas would not admit that she had training he himself did not have either. Though she did not know much of the basic ailments they saw, she had additional skills that he felt would be useful. If he was being honest, he wanted to learn what she knew and enhance his own medical training. She could be taught whatever she did not already know.

Ellie accepted his offer. Aside from having nowhere else to go, she decided if nothing else, it would buy her time to figure out how to get home or how to adjust and survive there on her own.

That evening, Captain Burke once again asked Ellie to follow him. This time, they were going to see the colonel. The captain had petitioned for her to be allowed to stay, but the colonel wanted to meet her before making a decision. Thomas watched her fidgeting with her clothes and necklace as they got closer to the colonel's quarters.

At somewhere around thirty years old, Ellie thought Colonel Nathan Whiting was young to be in command of an entire fort. With his brown hair in curls at the temples, he looked every part the eighteenth-century gentlemen. He looked tired, but Ellie imagined it must be exhausting to be in his position, in charge of a military fort in the middle of a war.

Ellie sat across from the colonel while he sat behind his desk. Captain Burke stood behind her and a servant stood in a corner of the room waiting to be called upon if needed. She immediately felt as though she had been called into the principal's office for doing something wrong and did her best to not fidget. The colonel quickly put her at ease, offering her tea and making small talk. He asked after her comfort since her arrival at the fort. She assured him that everyone had been friendly and helpful, deciding to leave out anything about Gideon Anwar.

"I've been informed as to the disagreeable circumstances under which you've come to be here," he said. "That was a remarkable thing you did for young Mr. Huntington."

Ellie did not say anything. What could she say?

"And then for Ensign Hunt as well," he added.

She nodded. "I was just trying to help, sir."

"Well, young lady, from what I hear, you saved the lives of two of the men under my command. If I allow you to stay, am I to presume you shall continue to do what you may to help?"

"Absolutely, sir," Ellie replied. She found it odd that he was calling her young lady when she was obviously older than him.

"My priority is to the men of this army. If you are to stay, you must be industrious and moral. We shan't allow women of bad character. If you are found to be immoral or of drunken character, or if at any time, you refuse to work for the men, be warned, that you shall not be permitted to remain."

The colonel was no nonsense. He was strict and stern in his lecture, filling Ellie with no doubt that he meant what he said. This was no empty threat. He continued, "Now, we shall not simply turn you adrift on the world as such an act would disgrace the corps. Under normal circumstances, if it came to that, we would normally write to any friends or family you may have who may be able to take you in. I understand this may not be possible in your situation?"

Ellie looked away and shook her head. She hated admitting this vulnerability to anyone but forced herself to say, "No, sir."

"Well, under those circumstances, means shall be taken to have you received into some poor house, or some other situation where you may earn your bread."

Ellie made a note to ensure that did not happen. What she knew of poor houses made her resolved to stay out of one. Homeless shelters in her time were rough enough; she could only imagine how awful they would be there.

The colonel nodded his head, seemingly satisfied. Ellie thought it much easier than she had expected.

"If there's anything of which you have need, Captain Burke shall see to it. Good day, madam."

The captain stepped forward to escort her out of the room. Ellie had apparently been dismissed. She stood and walked out, thanking him for his time while dipping her head with an attempt at a slight curtsy in deference to his position and generosity before walking out. Having done the same when she was introduced, Thomas had been impressed by the way she presented herself to the colonel. She had addressed him as 'sir' or 'colonel' when speaking to him and was polite and courteous the entire time, without fidgeting as she had before the meeting. She behaved as a lady should, which had surprised him immensely. It was completely opposite from the way she behaved around Gideon. She clearly had some breeding that contradicted a lifetime spent with Indians, though how she had come by it, he was not certain.

He found himself more and more intrigued by this woman.

As they rounded the corner, Thomas was called back. He waved her on and went back in to talk with the colonel.

"I expect you to heed her behavior," he told Captain Burke. "We've no need for any spies or trollops in the camp. If she causes any mischief, she will be dismissed."

"Yes sir," said the captain.

He paused before leaving. The colonel gestured for him to speak, yet Captain Burke was hesitant. "I wondered, sir, if she might be allowed a bounty for agreeing to stay on."

The colonel scoffed. "A bounty? Come now Captain, those are for men who sign on with the regiment. We cannot possibly give one to a woman."

"I understand, sir. I thought since she arrived with nothing, she would be in need; something to help her get by until she can be paid."

"She has been given quarters and half-rations. That will have to suffice until she can be paid. Good day to you."

Captain Burke dipped his head in a slight bow and left. He was disappointed, but it was what he had expected. He would have to look into his own purse to help the girl out.

Chapter 9

June 1756

"**M**rs. Sorenson stays to herself most of the time," Private Javon Simms reported to Captain Burke. "I hardly catched her interacting with others, and then, only minimally."

Thomas did not look up from his writing. He had assigned his servant the task of keeping an eye on Ellie Sorenson when not in the hospital in order to make sure she was settling in and not breaking the camp rules. He did not believe her to be a spy, yet he was not yet ready to trust her. Something was not right about her, and he intended to find out what it was.

"What does she do in her solitude?"

Javon wrung his hands together and gave a partial answer. "She spends much of her time by the creek."

"What does she do by the creek? Is she meeting anyone?"

"No," the boy said evasively.

Thomas finally looked up from his desk. "Then how is it she is engaged?"

Javon looked uncomfortable. He stuttered, "Sh– she washes."

"She spends her time washing her clothes. That's all? Anything else?"

Javon looked upward, avoiding eye contact with the captain. "Not only her clothes, sir."

Thomas sat back in his chair. With a reproving tone, he asked, "You watch her bathe?"

"I– I didn't. I mean. I don't." The private collected himself the best he could. "No, sir. The first time, when I saw her begin to undress, I turned away. I only listened to see if anyone else came along."

"The first time?" Captain Burke's eyebrows were raised at the wording the private chose to use.

"Every time, sir."

"It's only been a few days. How many times has this occurred?"

"Nightly, sir."

Thomas fought to conceal his surprise. He knew no one who washed that frequently. A daily splash of water about the face, neck, and arms was sufficient. This woman was more peculiar than anyone he had ever met. He shook off the thought of her bathing and continued with Private Simms.

"Is that all you've observed?"

With a shift of the eyes, he answered, "No, sir."

Thomas waited for the boy to elaborate. Shifting from one foot to the other, he said, "Before she washes, she... she dons breeches... and, and performs a series of... of movements."

Private Simms had turned even redder with this last report.

Thomas was even more confused now. The redness in the private's face belied something that said his discomfort was not only in seeing Mrs. Sorenson in breeches alone. There was more to this that the private was too embarrassed to report. The captain pushed further.

"What sort of movements?"

"As a dance, but not. Very slow, very... obscene movements."

Thomas was not sure whether to laugh or be annoyed that the suspicions of her being a camp trollop seemed to have been proven correct. When Javon could not elaborate further on how her movements were obscene, he moved forward with his questions.

"For whom is she performing this dance?"

"No one, sir." He was quick to report. "She's always alone when she does it."

"Has she engaged in any other inappropriate behavior? Interacted with any of the men?"

"No, sir."

"Have you anything else to report?"

"No, sir."

Thomas nodded and dismissed the private. He would have to investigate Mrs. Sorenson's actions himself and determine if she needed to be expelled from the camp. He was greatly disappointed as he had not thought her to be a strumpet. He had always thought himself a good judge of character, but this may turn out to prove him wrong.

Ellie spent the next few days acclimating to her new surroundings and taking in as much as she could. The encampment surrounded the fort on the three sides of land with additional encampments on the island to the west. Parade grounds made up an open area between the encampments and the walls of the fort and a large garden on the island allowed the soldiers to grow their own food while a smaller one was designated for the officers. There was a smaller stream south of the fort, cutting the garrison in two. Additional structures were being built, and Ellie knew some of them would be ovens to bake bricks that would be sent to other locations around the area. There was a designated spot in the stream for the washerwomen to do laundry and she could easily slip in to do hers beside them. She went upstream a little way to find a secluded spot to bathe every chance she got. Whenever she could not make it to the stream, she would use a bucket of water and a cloth to give herself a sponge bath.

Personal hygiene products were among the first things Ellie had asked about. She had asked both Anne and Mrs. Gibbons but neither had heard of deodorant or conditioner. Mrs. Gibbons informed her she could get soap from the sutler, who was a local shopkeeper that set up a table in the fort for the soldiers and other people there. Ellie had no money yet and decided to wait to visit him. Though she did not relish the idea, she could go a week without soap if she had to as she had done so many times over the years while camping. She ventured to say she would still be cleaner than many of the other people in the fort.

Whenever she was outside the hospital, she watched the soldiers drilling. There were thousands of them at the fort at any given time, though the specific companies and regiments were constantly changing. Her father's last duty station before retiring was on a marine corps base on the North Carolina coast. Ellie had been a teenager then, but she loved spending time on base, watching the marines drill. It was like a well-choreographed dance. She found it amazing that they could all be in complete unison the entire time. Watching these soldiers now took her back (*or was it forward?*) to that time. There was something beautifully terrifying about watching a group of well-trained soldiers practicing their drills. The sight in this time had an added bonus of drums and fifes being played while the soldiers learned how to march and operate their muskets.

Each regiment consisted of over five hundred men and was broken down into companies. There were ten companies per regiment with approximately fifty men per company, though they were rarely fully staffed. Each regiment also had drummers, fifers, non-commissioned officers, and staff that included a quartermaster to assign equipment and lodging, an adjutant to act as personal aide to the commanders, a surgeon, who may or may not be a commissioned officer, and a surgeon's mate. Regiments were commanded by colonels, though the colonel of a regiment could also be a general or commander-in-chief of the entire army. In these instances, command of the regiment fell to a lieutenant colonel. The colonel, lieutenant colonel, and major made up the field officers while sergeants and corporals made up the non-commissioned officers. Each company was commanded by a captain with two lieutenants assisting. Ellie had never learned all of the ranks in the military as a child, but she knew most of them. Of course, the insignia were all completely different there and she had no idea what rank anyone was by simply looking at them, but it helped her to understand the structure better, knowing the layout of the regiments and companies.

The women who followed the army were incredible. Ellie had every respect for them. Also referred to as 'necessary women,' they spent their days doing laundry, mending uniforms, or being nurses to the men. It was long, hard work that never ended. Twice a week, each soldier would drop off a shirt, 'necessaries' or underclothes, and a false frill, which Ellie learned was the collar worn by the men. One set of clothes would be cleaned and dropped off by the washerwomen every Wednesday when they would pick up the next round of clothing and drop them off on Saturday afternoon. They would then receive their pay on Saturday nights from the pay-sergeant of the company. Sundays they were free to catch up on their own chores or visit with their family. They would receive four pence for the entire week or two pence for each set of clothing. The women would then use that pay to purchase more soap for more laundry. It was a never-ending, thankless task which was physically demanding and barely covered the costs of their supplies.

These women were typically wives of the soldiers and were primarily from the lower classes. The army did not want the women in camp, thinking them a distraction, but permitted a select few to take care of such tasks that would otherwise pull the men away from their duties. Most of the time, only three or four women were allowed per company, or approximately thirty to forty women per five hundred men. With so few positions available, they were highly coveted, and wives were placed on a roster to await being allowed to join a regiment. Were it not for the skills she had demonstrated after waking in the hospital,

Ellie likely would not have been allowed to stay. On top of the meager pay they received, the women were also provided rations half the size of what the men received.

Most of the women who were there were too poor to stay at home. They often had children along with them as well. It was a hard life, and Ellie was in awe at the fortitude they displayed. The women of the camp were as much family to each other as their husbands and children were. This was something Ellie understood all too well as that had not changed over the centuries. It had been that way when she was a child as well. She could not help but be reminded of her mother following her father around during his service. Being a military wife had been hard on Ellie's mother, but it was easy in comparison to what these women endured.

Ellie's days were filled with making supplies, caring for the basic needs of the wounded like fetching food and water and doing whatever else was needed. The doctor and surgeon's mate spent their days treating various fevers, dysentery, bloody flux, scurvy, venereal diseases, and other disorders. The days after a battle, such as these last few, were spent dressing wounds, boring and binding fractured skulls, and amputating appendages.

Ellie asked questions every chance she got. On her first day in the hospital, Abigail Gibbons was initially patient, but it quickly waned. She pawned her off on another young nurse, Miss Patti Woodford, whose youth and inexperience left her unhelpful in answering any of Ellie's questions. Instead, Ellie found herself explaining medical concepts to Patti. When Patti showed Ellie the doctor's supplies which included jalap, bark, opium, mercury, cream of tartar,

Epsom salts, calomel, camphor, and nitrile, Ellie was filled with even more questions about what each was used for and why they were administering poisons. Of course, she had known this was common practice, but having book knowledge was completely different from seeing it in practice. At her multitude of questions, Patti was becoming more and more uneasy. Captain Burke came over and relieved her of Ellie's company and endless questions.

"I believe your curiosity to be insatiable," he scolded gently. "It may be too much for Mrs. Gibbons and Miss Woodford."

"Sorry. I just want to understand how things work here."

"I would venture to say that's a rather admirable quality, not something for which to apologize."

Ellie's mouth lifted into a half smile and the captain took on her education. Unlike with the women, Ellie was no longer simply asking questions. With the captain, it became a two-sided discussion in which they both learned from the other. The captain asked nearly as many questions as Ellie did. She answered what she could, but found it was not nearly as much as he answered. After that, Ellie spent most of her spare time close to the captain, learning what she could.

Captain Burke enjoyed the endless curiosity Mrs. Sorenson seemed to have. Initially he simply meant to relieve the women from having to answer her multitude of questions, but he quickly found himself engaged in exchanging information with her, learning as much from her as he taught her. Her questions were insightful, and they challenged him. This only served to draw him into her more than he already was. She was a truly fascinating woman.

One of the many things Ellie learned was that nursing duties included shaving men as needed.

"Captain Van Etten is in need of a shave," Thomas informed her. "His aide has gone to fetch his kit but shan't be able to do it himself with his hand mangled as it was in the raid." Captain Burke looked to the leg he was applying balm to and did not continue any further instruction.

"I'm sorry. Are you asking me to shave the man?" Ellie was concerned by the request. She had only ever used safety razors, and it had been years since she had used one on anyone else. In the early days of her marriage, she would sometimes shave Johnny, but that seemed ages ago.

Without looking up, he asked, "Is that a problem?"

"I've never used a straight razor before. I'm more likely to slice the man's skin clean off than just the hair."

The captain looked up at that. "You are not to slice the man's skin off," he said sternly. "Private Johnson shall instruct you when he returns. He may assist you with his good hand."

When Captain Van Etten's aide returned with the shaving kit, Ellie had to tell him she had never used that type of razor before. He looked at her with doubt as she requested instructions from him. When the aide looked to his captain, the man nodded his assent. Private Johnson showed her how to sharpen the blade prior to use, then moved on to the proper way to hold the blade and the appropriate angle and pressure to use on the skin. He showed her how to prep the face and lather, then began explaining where to start, that she needed to move with the grain, and keep the skin taut. She wanted to tell him she knew the last parts but let him explain anyway. It was easier than arguing.

Private Johnson was reluctant to hand over the blade to her, though she could not blame him. She was a little nervous, and this was not a small thing. The blade was rather sharp, and she would be holding it against someone's neck. When he finally relinquished it, she opened it up again, and instead of going to work on the captain right away, she placed it against her own forearm and began shaving the light hairs there. She figured it was as good a place as any to practice. Captain Burke was walking by and stopped to watch her for a moment. When she caught his eye, he nodded once and moved on.

When she was as confident as she thought she would ever be, Ellie proceeded to resharpen the edge, then lathered the captain's face and neck and began.

Working as slowly as she could, Ellie concentrated on the task in front of her, blocking out all sound and movement around her as much as she could, using her task as a form of meditation. The captain dutifully held as still as he could, without speaking or attempting anything else that would cause his face to move. The private hovered over her shoulder the entire time, injecting additional advice and instruction, reminding her of this or that. It was all she could do to block him out along with everything else going on around her. By the time she finished, she was quite proud of herself.

Thomas sought out Ellie that evening and found her in a corner at the edge of camp in a pair of breeches and a man's shirt with her calves and feet bare, in some sort of strange pose, much as Private Simms had described. She was facing away from him with her arms outstretched, one forward and one to the rear. Her legs were spread wide with one ahead of the other. The forward leg was bent at the knee while the back leg was straight. She held still for a few moments, then tilted her body, reaching her forward arm up to the sky while dropping the rear arm toward her back leg. Then she leaned forward, bringing the forward arm down to the ground and the rear arm up to the sky while she straightened both knees. Her rear arm came forward then to join the other, and she stepped her forward leg back. She was now on her hands and toes with her rear in the air.

Thomas suddenly felt as though he had been watching her in an intimate moment, though the fact she was well hidden away from others certainly alleviated his concerns about her being a trollop. Clearing his throat, he quickly turned his back and stammered out an apology. When he heard her laughing, he spun around to face her. She was standing now with her hands on her hips, her face flush from the exertion. Could she have been more beautiful? She had an exotic quality to her that he could not place. It did not change the fact that she was laughing at him.

"What are you apologizing for? Geez, you'd think you just caught me in the throes of passion or something."

Having come to standing after he cleared his throat, she was teasing him and enjoying his discomfort, his face turning a nice shade of pink.

He studied her for a moment. "Are you always so brazen, Mrs. Sorenson?"

"This is anything but brazen, Captain Burke. If you want brazen, I can show you brazen." She was deliberately being as sultry as she could now while still maintaining a physical distance. Holding eye contact with him, she lowered her lashes and her voice while tilting her head coyly. She slowly licked her lips while he stared openly. Teasing him was all too easy.

He shook his head as if to clear out the thoughts running through it and stammered again, his face a bright red now. Ellie was enjoying this a little too much. He was so proper; it was fun to see him ruffled. As much fun as it was for her, she could see it was not so for him and decided to cut him a little slack.

"Okay. I'll stop. Did you need me for something?"

"Yes. I– Why are you dressed in such a manner? Where did you get those clothes?"

Ellie looked down at herself. "I got them from Isaac. I needed something I could do yoga in, and a dress wasn't quite cutting it."

"Yoga?" he questioned. His brain felt like it had left him, and he grabbed onto the only part of the sentence he could.

"It's a form of exercise. It's very meditative. Helps keep me healthy and my mind focused."

The poor man still looked uncertain, so she asked, "You do know 'meditative?'"

"Yes, I know meditative," he barked.

Ellie held up her hands in surrender. "Just checking. We seem to have had plenty of other language barriers."

He mumbled something and started to turn away to leave. Ellie reached forward, grabbing his arm. "Captain, wait. What did you need?"

Thomas stopped, having completely forgotten that he had come looking for her to begin with. It was difficult to not openly stare at her dressed as she was. It took him a moment to collect himself, and then he held out his filled hand to her. Not expecting anything, she was immediately confused but held out her own hand to receive whatever he carried. He placed a few coins in her open palm.

"It's a bounty for you staying on with us," he said shyly. He was uncomfortable lying to her, but she seemed like the kind of woman who would not ask for help. Though, he had still referred to it as a bounty, he was careful not to imply that the colonel approved it. She would not know any better.

Ellie was surprised. The captain seemed almost embarrassed to be there, handing her money. She knew she would be paid but did not expect this, thinking she was only receiving rations and billeting until payday, whenever that was. This would certainly help; she could buy soap now. She thanked him and asked him to explain what a bounty was, knowing the word but not the context in which he was using it now.

"It's extra pay to entice men to join a regiment."

"A sign-on bonus," she said in understanding. He nodded in agreement.

She looked at the coins in her hand. Thomas mistook the confused expression on her face. "I fear it's not much, but it shall help you get by until you receive your pay from the pay sergeant on Saturday. Of course, that won't be much either, but nurses are the highest paid of all of the camp followers."

How did Ellie explain this?

"It's not that. I just," she paused. "How much is it?" She blushed at her ignorance of something so mundane.

Thomas was visibly surprised by her question. When he told her the total, she stared blankly back at him. He then tried telling her it was a week's worth of pay at six pence a day, but she still looked confused.

"I'm sorry," she said sheepishly. "I don't know anything about your money here."

Thomas explained to her that they used pounds, shillings, pence, or sterling. Each colony also printed their own money but they did not use those local currencies which were less valuable than sterling. He picked up different coins from her outstretched palm. "This one is a shilling, and this one, a pence." Pulling another coin from his pocket, he held it out, saying, "This is a pound."

"And how much is a shilling, a pound, and a pence?"

"Well, there are twelve pence to a shilling and twenty shillings to a pound."

She was following along up until that point. Counting out the coins in her hand, it was equivalent to three shillings. When he started breaking it down further into thruppence, tuppence, pennies, halfpennies (which he pronounced "haypennies"), sixpence, and florin, she was lost.

"Yeah, it's gonna take me a while to learn all that."

Her head hurt trying to wrap her brain around everything he was trying to teach her. She pocketed the coins for further inspection later.

As she moved back to resume her yoga, he warned, "Mrs. Sorenson, you mustn't go too far away from camp. Indians are always lurking in these woods and will not hesitate to take you captive or kill you."

"I'll stay close. Thanks, Captain Burke."

He bid her goodnight and left, though he did not go far. Thomas had tasked Private Simms with watching her, but he was also worried for her. She was so innocent regarding life there; he did not think she took his warning seriously. Finding someplace nearby where she would not detect him, he watched over her until she finished her 'yoga.' In truth, it was not only the Indians that worried him. If other soldiers saw her, she would be in danger from their lustful desires. If his own lustful desires were any indication, she would be in trouble quickly. He did not want to see any harm befall her and decided to take over this part of the task he had given to Javon.

Now that she had a little cash, Ellie decided to pay a visit to the sutler. When she had a break in her duties inside the hospital, she managed to purchase some soap, a toothbrush, and tooth powder. That was all she managed but she decided it would go far. People there did not wash their hair as they did in her time. Typically, they used flour, wood ash, or other powders to soak up the oils and brushed out any debris, then dressed it up with pomades, covering it with some sort of cap. Ellie was glad she had taken up soap-making with her neighbor and decided to make some of her own products the first chance she got.

Back in the hospital, Captain Burke asked her how often she did her yoga.

"Daily if I can," she replied. "Either yoga or tai chi."

"What is tai chi?"

"It's a different discipline, but it's similar to yoga. It also uses controlled movements to help maintain the body and the mind."

"These movements help keep you healthy?"

"I know it doesn't look like much, but they're both really good for your muscles. They also help you breathe and relax, which are good for the mind."

As she left the hospital that night, Ellie saw a couple of Native Americans doing trades with some of the soldiers in the yard. Her feet had been killing her every night after standing in those awkward shoes all day. Not only were they designed to be worn on either foot, they also had a low heel and no cushioning. How did women wear these? The men's did not appear much better. She would rather work in the six-inch platform heels she used to wear while dancing. At least they were made to fit the foot and had cushioning.

Ellie had a little of the money the captain had given her left, but she wanted to save as much of that as she could, not knowing how long she would be able to stay there at the fort. Knowing the bartering system was alive and well-used in this time, she thought of the jewelry she always wore. There were two necklaces, one with an ankh pendant and the other, given to her by her nieces, was an obelisk-shaped amethyst. She also wore several stone bracelets, a few rings, and a hemp anklet. She was not willing to trade all of them, but she would not miss some of them. She went to see what wares they had.

One of the Natives spoke enough English to understand what she was after. He did not have any with him that day but said he would come back the next with a pair of moccasins that would fit her. It would cost her the blue sodalite bracelet she had made several years ago. It was her second-favorite, after the amethyst one, but if she could get some shoes that she could stand in all day, it would be worth it. Assuming they would be significantly more comfortable than what she was wearing every day, she wondered briefly if she could trade for some of the clothes they wore as well. She almost asked but then decided that might be pushing it. It would cause her to stand out even more than she already did and not in a good way. Dependent on keeping her position there in order to eat, be sheltered, and basically stay alive, she did not want to be perceived as a 'woman of bad character' or do anything to jeopardize that.

After starting to walk away from the Native American traders, she turned back and asked them if they had any hygiene products. After several questions and explanations, they informed her they could bring some back for her with the moccasins. They smelled and looked far cleaner than most of the Anglo-European men and women there, so she looked forward to seeing what they had.

That night, Thomas grabbed a book and took it to the spot he found the night before. He got comfortable and settled in to keep an eye on Ellie while she did her exercises. He tried not to watch her, fighting to keep his eyes on his book, while only looking up occasionally to make sure she was safe. He found he had to reread the same passages multiple times before he remembered what he had read.

Chapter 10

June 24, 1756

After nearly a week, Ellie was starting to feel slightly more settled. The excess casualties from the raid she had been caught up in were either gone or in the other hospital building for recovery, so they were slightly less busy. Their primary customers now were the soldiers within the fort with various ailments.

There were several books lying about the captain's desk. When she looked through some of the titles, she saw most of them were medical books. She carefully started flipping through one titled *Observations on the Diseases of the Army*, written by Sir John Pringle, stopping on the table of contents and reading through it. Next, she looked at a book titled *The Method of Treating Gunshot Wounds*, by John Ranby. Excited to see such books, she thought they may give her a better understanding of the diseases of the period and treatments available to them.

Ellie began to wonder what valuable information she would be able to find in these books. While the knowledge was dated, so were the available tools at her disposal. Amongst other things, she had been trying to figure out how to make simple hot and cold compresses without having electricity. Perhaps something in these books would help her with such concepts. When Captain Burke walked by, she asked if she could borrow them.

"Do you read?" he asked.

She wanted to be offended but then remembered illiteracy was common there.

"As often as I can."

"Would you not be more interested in poetry, Mrs. Sorenson? Or perhaps the bible? I have both of those amongst my library as well."

Ellie turned up her nose. "No thanks. I've read the bible. Not interested. The poetry, maybe when I finish these. I'd rather learn something, though, and these will help me do that far better than the poetry will."

Thomas laughed at her honesty. He felt the same about the bible but rarely ever said so aloud. He again brightened at her curiosity, considering himself a life-long scholar and always thirsting for knowledge. How could he refuse her access to his library?

"By all means, then. I've more over here," he pointed to a shelf, "and in my quarters. If there's anything in particular in which you're interested, I may have it."

The smile that lit up her entire face was reward enough for him, but she thanked him anyway. He shook himself of the inappropriate thought that popped into his mind and went on his way.

While watching Ellie that night, Thomas heard the footsteps approaching only when they were close upon him. He started at the intrusion but relaxed when he saw that it was Isaac Huntington. He should have known; the young boy had taken to following her around as often as he could. Thomas could see the infatuation and did not begrudge him in the least. She was rather bewitching.

When the boy saw him, he called out a greeting which Thomas returned reluctantly, knowing his presence would no longer be hidden to Ellie.

At hearing the voices, Ellie looked around. She saw Isaac talking with the captain and cheerily greeted them while waving, causing Isaac to smile as he approached her. Thomas slowly stood from his seat under a tree and came over as well.

"You look like a proper boy in those clothes, Miss Ellie," Isaac laughed.

She shrugged and said, "I needed something I could easily move around in. They work well."

Ellie directed her attention to Thomas, who was looking her up and down. He disagreed with Isaac's assessment. The clothes showed every curve of her body and made her appear all too womanly. His eyes lingered on her bare feet for a moment longer than was proper. She had the smallest feet he had ever seen on a woman, but they were decorated unlike any he had ever seen. The nails on all of her toes were somehow colored purple and she wore rings on two of her toes and a bracelet around one ankle. He had never thought a woman's feet could be beautiful, yet hers were.

The wealthy women in Europe had begun coloring their nails during his time there, though they looked nothing like hers. The colors he had seen were typically soft pink or red, and they were not as glossy as hers were. The stains they used were not generally available to women of the lower sorts. Those women might be seen wearing light colors on their nails, but even that was not common. How had she stained hers such a vivid purple? Was it another indicator of her social standing and from where she came?

"What are you guys doing here?" she asked, pulling him from his thoughts.

Isaac spoke first. "I came to see if'n you fared well in the breeches and if'n you be needin' anything else."

"I'm good. Thank you, Isaac."

He shrugged but made no move to leave. Ellie looked to Thomas. "And your excuse, Captain?"

Thomas looked sheepish but tried to avoid telling her the real reason he was there. Holding up his book, he said, "I was endeavoring to read. I noticed when I was here last what an agreeable spot this was to remove myself from the rest of the camp."

Ellie did not believe him for a second but decided not to call him out in front of Isaac. A mischievous thought crossed her mind. If they were so interested in what she was doing, she would put them to work.

"Well, since you're both here, you may as well join me."

Both men started stammering, trying to make excuses to leave, but Ellie was not having it. "Nope. Come on. Shoes off."

She walked far enough away to give them each some space and show them she was about to resume her practice. To her surprise, they both complied, removing their shoes. When Thomas also removed his waistcoat, Isaac followed suit. Now they were both only in their shirts and breeches.

With only his shirt on, Ellie could tell Thomas was well defined under his clothes and wondered how he managed to build muscle mass and stay fit while being a doctor. It was not as though he was going to a gym every morning. She tried not to stare and instead focused on the movements ahead of her.

Beginning by having them stand in mountain pose, she eased them in slowly. They stood tall with both feet planted, hands down at their sides, while she had them controlling their breath and learning to move with it. After an hour of increasingly difficult poses, the men were both more than ready to be finished. She had them end the session in corpse pose, allowing them to finally come to a rest, lying on their backs.

When she released them from the session, Isaac was eager to go, but Captain Burke continued to lie there on the ground. Ellie had sat up when they finished and was sitting cross-legged, laughing at the captain for just lying there. When he did not move, she crawled over to him to check on him. She teasingly poked his arm and asked if he was still alive.

"That was more challenging than it appeared," he said. "My legs are convulsing more than they do after a day of marching."

Ellie laughed at his acknowledgment of her claim. She kneeled and reached out her hand to help him up. He looked over at it, then up at her, and he was suddenly afraid if he took it, he might pull her down on top of him instead and ravish her. He slowly made his way to standing without her assistance. Not trying to slight her, he also wanted to show her that she had not bested him. It earned him one of her radiant smiles for his efforts.

———————————

June 25, 1756

"I do believe every muscle in my body is in distress," Captain Burke announced the next morning.

Ellie laughed. "Does that mean you won't be joining me again tonight?"

With a sigh, he reluctantly agreed to come. Now that he had been found out, he would not be able to hide his presence. If he wanted to ensure her safety, he would have to join her.

Laughing at his reluctance, she said, "Don't feel like you have to say yes. You really don't have to."

The captain asked, "Would you prefer it were I not there?"

Ellie thought he sounded a little hurt.

"Not at all. I enjoyed having you there. I just don't want you to feel obligated to be there. If it's not something you want to do, then don't come."

"I shall be there."

Abigail Gibbons and Patti Woodford had heard them speaking and immediately jumped to the wrong conclusion. Mrs. Gibbons admonished them not only for engaging in inappropriate activities, but for then speaking about it aloud within the company of others.

Ellie laughed while the captain looked scandalized. He tried to deny her accusations, but she was not having it. Ellie jumped in to explain. "We were doing an exercise to keep the mind and body healthy.

You're both welcome to join us. I will warn you that you'll want to lose your stays before you come by, but you're more than welcome to. It's not only healthy, but it's a lot of fun."

To Ellie's surprise, Captain Burke told them, "Do not heed her words. It's not fun at all. She is rather disagreeable, and the exercises hurt."

Ellie was horrified at his assessment until she saw the smile on his face. He was teasing her as she had so often done to him. They both started laughing and Mrs. Gibbons shook her head and walked away. Patti stayed though and asked questions about it.

Patti was a shy young girl of about nineteen. Tall with big brown eyes and mousy brown hair, Ellie often wondered who she was there with. The other camp followers were there with their husbands or fathers. Ellie was a rare exception to this. Though she thought Patti young to be married, she reminded herself she had been married at seventeen. As much as Ellie enjoyed the private time alone with the captain, she thought it would be good for the girl to get out and join them for these sessions. It might even build up her confidence a little.

"Truly, I'd not be an interruption, Mrs. Sorenson?"

"Of course not. Why ever would you think that?"

Instead of answering, Patti looked over at Thomas. Ellie followed her stare and said, "The captain wouldn't mind."

"I think he'd not be agreeable to me taking away his time with you," she said shyly.

Ellie scoffed. "I'm way too old for him. Even if I wasn't, he doesn't think of me that way."

"I seen the way he looks at you, miss. He undoubtedly thinks of you that way," Patti insisted.

"I think you're mistaking his pity for something more."

"There's no pity in his eyes when he looks at you. I may be inexperienced, but even I can see it."

Ellie was not sure she believed what Patti was trying to tell her. She certainly was not looking to get romantically involved with anyone in this time. Not only was she not in the right frame of mind for it, but she still hoped to find a way home. Even if she was looking for something, Thomas was far too young for her. Though she had no idea how old the captain was, she assumed he was somewhere in his mid- to late twenties. She had never put much stock in age differences, with her own husband being twelve years older than her. But this was different, was it not? Ellie tried to put her finger on why the age difference bothered her this time. Was it because he was younger than her? She had always been attracted to older men, but this time, she was the older one. Did that matter? Or was there a difference between twelve years and twenty?

Was it a generational difference? If she had been in her own time, would she ever consider dating someone his age? Or would growing up in different eras make them too different? In that case, there was no one there that Ellie would ever be able to date, even if she wanted to. Growing up in different centuries, she would have vastly different life experiences from everyone there, so they could never have that commonality. The situation put her in mind of all the fantasy books she used to read. She wondered if authors of stories about vampires or other immortals ever considered this conundrum. If a person lived to be five hundred years old in a world where immortality was not the norm, how would that person ever date? Would being with anyone else always make the immortal feel like a pedophile?

Not that Thomas made her feel like a pedophile. He was more mature than men she knew in her own time who were older than him. He was responsible, intelligent, and led others well. She often forgot how young he was. Until she looked at him. If anything, he made her feel young, which she loved.

Perhaps it was the stages of life in which they both found themselves. His was only beginning, and hers? Well, Ellie was approaching menopause and old age. What could she possibly offer him? It was flattering to think that Thomas might be interested, and she was not immune to his looks and his charm. She would certainly enjoy any attention he wanted to direct her way, but she found it highly unlikely that it amounted to anything.

Brushing away the thoughts, Ellie went to the shelf where they kept dressings and pulled out a few pieces of cloth then found a sewing kit. She thought she had finally figured out how to make hot and cold compresses and decided this would be the perfect opportunity to test it. Between patients, she began cutting and sewing up various sizes of square or rectangular pouches of fabric, leaving one end partially open. Going down towards the river, Ellie began filling each of the pouches with the course black sand found along the riverbank, then sat by the water, closing them up. As soon as the first one was done, she placed it on the edge of the river, allowing the cool water to flow over it. By the time she had finished sewing the rest of them, it was nice and cool. Squeezing the excess water from it, she went back into the hospital and handed it to Thomas who was sitting at his desk.

"What is this?" he asked, flipping the cold, wet pillow of sand over in his hands.

"For your sore muscles. It's a cold compress. I made a bunch of them so we can use them on the patients, but I thought you could try it out."

Thomas looked at the sandbag, then back at Ellie doubtfully. "What shall I do with it?"

"Where does it hurt?" she asked, taking the cold compress back from him.

"Everywhere."

Ellie chuckled, recalling how she used to always feel when she was starting out with yoga. "How's your neck?"

Thomas stretched his neck then nodded. "It's rather unpleasant."

Walking around to stand behind him, Ellie lifted his low ponytail and placed the compress on the back of his neck, holding it in place for a moment. Thomas stiffened at her touch. Her hands in his hair sent goosebumps across his skin before she had even placed the cold pillow on him.

"That's quite cold," he said with a start as soon as it touched his skin. He was grateful it covered up the goosebumps.

"That's the idea," Ellie laughed. "Hold it here for twenty minutes. If it gets too cold, place a dry cloth between your skin and the compress. We don't want to burn you."

Ellie let go of the compress and came back around to stand in front of Thomas while he held the compress in place.

"And this is supposed to do what, exactly?"

"Cold helps with inflammation and fresh injuries. It's really good for sprains and strains. Heat increases blood flow and helps with chronic injuries. I wish I had a way of heating these, but at least we can cool them off in the river."

"What's inside?"

"Sand."

"It's nothing more than sand inside cloth?"

"That's it."

"You may consider putting it beside a fire. It should heat quite well."

Ellie nodded. "That's perfect. The sand should hold the heat nicely. Probably even better than the cold." It was hard not to picture walking on a beach in the summertime. How many times had she burned her feet doing that?

"How did you think of such a thing?" he asked.

"I've been trying to figure out how to make them since I arrived. They'd be quite useful here in the hospital, but I wasn't sure how to hold the temperatures other than maybe rocks, but they're not particularly flexible. I noticed the sand along the river the other day while I was washing and how warm it was under my feet, and it made me think about how well sand holds temperatures."

"Yes, but how did you know of the healing qualities of the temperatures?"

Ellie gave him a pointed look. "Really?"

"My apologies. For a moment I forgot your secretive life prior to your arrival with us," he teased. "Well, if it works, we shall use them on the patients."

Ellie smiled proudly and nodded before turning to leave for her other duties.

Ellie finally had some spare time to do a little reading. It was always busy there, and she had not yet been able to do so. Grabbing a book at random from the captain's desk, she sat down to read. It appeared to be a handwritten account of injuries and illnesses, and she wondered if it was the captain's account of the things he had encountered. It was difficult to read. The spelling was inconsistent at best. Some words were incorrectly spelled the same throughout, while others were incorrectly spelled in a different way each time. The word 'they' was spelled 'thay' and the words 'there' or 'their' were both spelled 'thare.' Those were the easy words. Some, she had to use the context to figure out. What gave her the most difficulty, however, was the lack of punctuation. With no periods, it was difficult to tell where one sentence ended and another began. She could not even rely on capitalization as random words were capitalized while those which should have been, often were not.

Ellie gave up on that one and grabbed another book. This one did happen to be the captain's journal. It was obvious by the dates that this one was his, which meant the last one was not. Her first thought was to put it down, so she did not invade his privacy. However, the passages appeared to be very simple accounts of each day, listing the weather, where they ate or slept, and slightly more detailed accounts on days where they encountered anything of significance. There was very little personal information in there at all, instead primarily being accounts of what illnesses and injuries they had faced, much like the previous one. This one had much better grammar, spelling, and punctuation, but was still difficult. She struggled to understand what she was even reading.

As she read, her brow furrowed in confusion and concentration, Gideon walked up and asked in a snarky tone, "Is you enfeebled of the mind?"

He snatched the book from her hands.

"That be the captain's personal journal. I hardly think he would be content with you a-reading it," he scoffed, then added, "Only I suppose 'tis harmless. If the look on your face were any indication, you can't even read."

He sneered at her while flipping through the pages himself.

She snatched the book back from him and started reading one of the passages aloud. When she finished, she gave him a look that said, "I told you so."

"There, 'tis as I said," he replied. "You struggled to even get through that little bit, you did."

"It's not the words; it's the font and the way they're written. This is like reading another language."

"Only it's not another language. What you read aloud was English. Perchance you only read French?"

"Oh my gods. This again? I'm not a damn spy. I read English just fine. This is just unlike any English I've ever read."

It was difficult to not see and hear everything going on around them in a space so small and though he had not meant to, Thomas had been listening to the exchange. It had been equally as difficult to not watch Ellie as she absentmindedly twirled the end of her braid around her finger while she read. Unlike when she played with her necklace whenever she was nervous, it was something she frequently did when concentrating on anything. The woman was always fidgeting in some manner, seemingly unable to sit still and he found it endearing.

Thomas took pride in his handwriting and level of literacy, being more so than most. Even Gideon could not read or write more than those words they frequently used in the surgery. But Thomas was an educated man. Her words now stung his pride, and he approached them both, gently taking the journal from Ellie's hands.

"We shall leave this one be. Help yourself to any of the others," he said and walked away.

Ellie could see that she had upset him. Was it something she said? Had he not meant for her to read that one? She immediately played the conversation back in her head to try and remember if any of it was belittling or mean and went after him.

"Captain, wait."

Ellie caught up to him outside as he headed toward the officer's barracks.

Thomas had not understood why Ellie's words had stung as much as they had. Coming from anyone else, he did not think they would have bothered him. He did not wish to let her see how much she affected him, so he had chosen to leave in order to compose himself. Yet there she was. He stopped and waited for her to speak.

"I'm sorry. I shouldn't have read your journal. I should have put it down as soon as I realized what it was."

When he did not respond, she continued almost shyly, "I thought it might help me understand what was happening here. Everything in this place is so different than where I come from. I was trying to get a better understanding of where I've landed."

The captain nodded and took the opportunity to ask, "And where is it exactly from whence you come?"

Ellie smiled at his attempt to get the information out of her again. "Nice try," she said.

"You said you struggled with the font, and it was unlike any English you've ever read. Was my writing so bad as to be unreadable? And how is the English different?" Not concerned with the content of the book, he was more concerned with his handwriting. Always looking for ways to better himself, he thought perhaps he could learn how to improve.

"Oh, no. You have beautiful handwriting. I wish mine was half as nice as that. No, it's the use of letters and words here. I feel like I'm reading with a stutter. I noticed it in some of the other books, too. The letter 's' looks like an 'f' and the letter 'u' is often replaced with a 'v.' The word 'ye' is used in place of 'the'. It's just like the struggles I'm having to understand some of the speech. The vernacular here is vastly different from what I'm used to. There are so many words I don't recognize at all. And there's a lot I do recognize, but don't recognize the way they're used."

It was the simplest explanation she could give without telling him about where she came from. Thomas beamed at her praise and accepted her explanation.

"Did my words help you achieve a better understanding of this place then?"

"Some," she nodded. "It helps me learn the syntax used here. It also gives me an idea of the recent history and what's happened so far during the conflict. I know the war has only just begun and there's still seven more years to go until it'll be over, but this helps give me a foundation and sort of catches me up to where we are now."

Thomas's head perked up. "War? We are not yet at war. Though we likely soon will be. You believe this will continue seven more years? That is rather precise."

Oops! Ellie was struggling to remember to police her words before she spoke. At least he used the word 'believe.' She could use that.

"I meant to say *several*, not seven," she covered. "Do you see an end in sight anytime soon?"

Thomas sighed, "I suppose not."

He handed her the journal and turned them both back toward the surgery, instinctively putting his hand on her lower back as they began walking. As soon as he realized what he had done, he quickly removed his hand, dropping it to his side. Ellie missed the warmth of it immediately.

***

"Good evening, Captain," Ellie said as she saw him approach for their nightly exercise session. Tonight, she thought she would mix it up and do some tai chi, thinking it might help the captain to be able to use different muscles. Patti had said she would come but she could not make it that night. Ellie was glad to have the captain to herself for one more night.

"You may call me Thomas when we are not in the presence of others," he told her.

This brought a smile to her lips, "Does that mean you'll finally call me Ellie?"

He nodded in affirmation.

"Good. I hate all that formal crap."

Thomas's laughter warmed her. "So I've noticed."

"How are your muscles tonight?" Ellie asked while guiding him through a warm-up before they began.

"They seem to be much mended. Thank you. Your cold compress seemed to help."

Ellie beamed at being able to help.

"I'm glad to hear it."

"Of course, Mr. Anwar has already informed me he does not plan on using them."

"He is such an ass! If it works, why wouldn't he use them?"

Thomas raised a brow at her. "He won't use them merely because you created them. That's reason enough for him."

"I don't know what his problem with me is, but I don't care. If it helps the patient, why not use it?"

"I am of the same sentiment. However, Mr. Anwar is traditional. He still bleeds his patients and does not always look to new treatments. Nor does he believe women have anything to contribute to medicine. Combine that with the fact that you were particularly hostile upon meeting him while he was trying to treat your injury and it is not difficult to see where his animosity with you lay."

Ellie tried to look sufficiently chastised, but Thomas saw right through it.

"Come now, you are not even a little remorseful for having been so."

"I'm really not," she admitted. "And the more I get to know him, the more I'm glad I punched him."

"He may be a sneaksby but he's a good surgeon's mate. He's needed here."

"Sneaksby?"

"A cur. Someone who's mean-spirited," Thomas explained.

Ellie nodded. She certainly could not argue with that.

Chapter 11

June 26, 1756

Despite having enormous respect for the women in camp, it was not mutual. Ellie often found herself being the topic of gossip and rumors. She was no stranger to this as her easy nature tended to draw out the nastiness in other women who were typically jealous of either her looks or her ability to not care what others thought of her. It was very freeing to not have to constantly worry about how others would judge her actions and that meant she did not consider herself in competition with other women. Unfortunately, other women never felt the same way. She had always gotten along with men better than she ever had with women and women found this threatening. Given the extent of how different she was there, she fully expected this. Though she had hoped it would not be the case, it was.

It did not help matters that Ellie took the spot of someone in her tent who had been hoping to move up to nurse from washerwoman. Nursing was far less physically demanding and paid slightly more, though still not enough to survive on. Charlotte Spencer wanted the extra pay for what she perceived was less work. Anne Houseman defended Ellie, but she, Patti, and Mrs. Gibbons were the only women who treated her nicely. Outside of the hospital and her yoga/tai chi sessions, Ellie stayed to herself as much as she could, knowing she was drawing attention from others in the camp by doing so, but it was not as much as she otherwise would have by interacting with people. She stood out like a sore thumb and knew from experience that was not always a good thing. When she was younger, she had loved dying her hair bright colors like purple or blue and had loved her time as a dancer, but when people had seen her hair or found out about her dancing, she was inevitably treated differently. People would look down on her or be rude to her simply because she chose to do something outside the norm. It would be no different there with the exception that the consequences would likely be much more severe than ostracism or rudeness. Though she could handle the talk and the glares, her very survival now depended upon how well she could fit in.

It was not only that Ellie 'stole' what Charlotte felt was her position. With no history, she was suspect. Everyone thought she was a whore. Spending her time with both Thomas and Isaac did not help that perception, but she was not about to stop being friends with them simply because they were the opposite sex. Of course, suspicion transferred to Thomas given their friendship, and he was labeled as her paramour.

"No one knows from where she came," he heard Mrs. Olsen tell another woman. He thought her companion was called Mrs. Spencer.

The other woman replied, "I wager she lived with the savages, I do. She immerses her whole self in the river and cleans her teeth and clothing every day. She also even put soap and water to her hair twice this week already. And she won't drink anything but water, at that, only if'n 'tis been boiled first."

The women giggled at the idea. Thomas did not condone gossip in his hospital but tried to let the women be. When their voices lowered, he knew the conversation had taken a turn. When he heard the suspicions of Ellie whoring in order to purchase a new pair of moccasins, he quickly put an end to it, instructing them to return to their duties.

Ellie's new moccasins were made of a soft leather with intricate beadwork covering the tops. She had only been looking for something basic, but these were beautiful. They fit like booties that enclosed her entire foot, with a flap around the top that could be worn up over her ankles or folded over around her feet. The Native American who brought them for her said they had been coated in beeswax to help keep out moisture. She loved them and they worked perfectly. They fit her feet and were comfortable enough to stand in all day. Modern shoes, they were not, but they were like wearing slippers which suited her fine.

Mrs. Olsen scoffed at her when she walked in wearing them. Ellie had no interest in what the woman thought of her, so she ignored her. When the woman started vocalizing her distaste, Ellie stopped and held out her foot for a better look.

"Aren't they beautiful? And they are so comfortable. I may have to get three more pairs."

Ellie turned and walked away with a smirk on her face. Some things never changed. Women had always been catty and bullied other women about their fashion sense or any other thing they could. Never having paid those women any attention, she was not about to start now. Her words may not have done anything at all, but at least the woman would know she had not embarrassed Ellie like she had planned. Maybe next time she would not bother.

Thomas had watched the exchange between the women. Mrs. Olsen had always been disagreeable. She had been replaced in almost every job she took on. She was only in the hospital now because no one else wanted to work with her. For some reason, Gideon seemed to tolerate her and Thomas did not want to see her children turned out of camp. If she continued behaving this way, he may have to send her to the laundry. He wanted to defend Ellie to the woman, but she did not need his assistance. She held her own nicely. Catching her eye as she walked away from the nasty woman, he smiled and winked at her. She paused and her smile now lit up her eyes.

Before Ellie could settle into making up the recently vacated beds, Captain Burke asked her to join him.

"Where are we going?" she asked as they left the hospital with a leather satchel full of instruments.

"We've a patient to attend," was his only reply.

They walked across the field to the stables. As they entered, Ellie immediately looked around for someone with some sort of injury that would bring them out there. This felt more like her days as a paramedic, responding to an injury in the field rather than sitting around in a hospital waiting for people to come to them. She did not see anything amiss, but then a man approached.

"This be her," he said, pointing them to a large brown horse with a white nose inside a stall. "She gots herself a runny nose, flux, and she's swelled up under her jaw."

Thomas immediately set to examining the horse, curious what Ellie would have to say about this, if she had advanced knowledge that could help him there, too. He liked talking out the problem in front of him on occasion, finding that it helped him reach a conclusion more quickly, particularly when a patient could not speak. "Runny nose, flux, swelling under the jaw." He felt along the horse's jaw for the swelling and found it right away.

"Have you noticed any change in her breathing? Any coughing or fevers?"

When the attendant answered in the affirmative, Thomas turned to Ellie who had been surprisingly quiet the entire time. He was alarmed to see her seemingly frozen in place outside the stall looking visibly confused.

"This is the patient?" she asked.

"Yes."

"It's a horse." As if he did not know.

"Horses get sick, too," Thomas replied slowly as if talking to a child.

"But don't you have a vet for that?" she asked, still confused.

"A vet?" Thomas's brow furrowed as if her confusion was spilling over onto him. He did not understand what had gotten into her and she was not clearly articulating herself to help him understand.

"Veterinarian."

"Veterinarian? Do you mean *veterinarius*? Beasts of burden? I thought you did not know Latin?"

"I don't. But no. I mean veterinarian. As in, an animal doctor." Ellie knew she was not particularly coherent at the moment, but she could not understand why they were there. Worse, she did not have words that Thomas would understand to clear up her confusion. The attendant was scowling at her and Thomas looked at her as though he was not sure what to make of her.

"I'm the physician here. We do not have separate doctors for animals. There's a farrier," he said, pointing at the attendant, "who tends to them, but he's not a doctor. It is up to us to determine whether the horse has a cold, strangles, or glanders."

Ellie continued to stare at him blankly. She understood a cold and she understood the word strangles but somehow thought it did not mean the same thing as what she was thinking. The last word, glanders, was a new one altogether. "Strangles or glanders?" she asked.

Thomas stared at her quizzically, trying to maintain his patience as he explained what the illnesses were. "Both illnesses are highly contagious. We must determine what is afflicting our patient and treat her accordingly. Are you able to assist me with this or shall I send you to retrieve Mr. Anwar?"

The last thing Ellie wanted was to be sent away. It may have been a horse, but she wanted to learn. "What do I do?"

Thomas gestured for her to come inside the stall with him. As she did, the horse coughed, then shook her head and stepped backward. Ellie's blue eyes became large, and she backed up with a start, jumping away as quickly as she could. Thomas was confused by her behavior until something finally occurred to him.

"You're not afraid of horses, are you Mrs. Sorenson?"

He could not imagine this woman being afraid of anything after what he had witnessed of her thus far, but her behavior now would seem to indicate otherwise.

"Not afraid," she said defensively while keeping a close eye on the beast. "Just trying to be safe. I've never been this close to one before. It's bigger than I imagined. I don't want to get stepped on or kicked or something."

Thomas stopped his examination. "You've never been this close to a horse?"

If what she said was true, it disproved his theory that she had been born of good English stock, but then spent years with the Indians, resulting in her often-conflicting mannerisms. Though, her claim did not make sense for someone who had come from a family of the lower sorts either. Horses were everywhere. Even had her family never owned one, it was near impossible to avoid them. Many Indian villages did not have horses, but had she spent her life entirely amongst them, she would not have the education she did. He could not fathom how she came to have an advanced education without having spent any time near horses.

While Thomas tried to puzzle out the conundrum that was Ellie Sorenson, the farrier brought his attention back to the horse. "Do you think it to be glanders? Might'nt it only be a cold?"

"It might, though I'm worried about the flux and the fever."

To Ellie's astonishment, Thomas coaxed open the horse's mouth, checking under her tongue. When he found no swelling, he decided it was not likely strangles.

"It's good that you caught it early," he praised the farrier. "If it is glanders, we might yet contain it still before it spreads."

"How do you treat it?" Ellie asked.

The men exchanged a glance. "There is no treatment," Thomas informed her.

"So, it'll just run its course and the horse will recover on her own?" Judging by the men's reactions, Ellie could tell this was not the case but did not want to jump to conclusions and think the worst.

Thomas gave Ellie a sympathetic look. "I fear not, Mrs. Sorenson. If it is glanders, the horse will die within weeks."

"What will you do then?"

"If it's glanders, we must put the animal down."

Ellie gasped but understood. It was not unusual even in her own time to euthanize sick or injured animals that could not be treated.

"The difficulty lies in that it might only be a cold. We do not wish to kill her for a cold, but if it is not, she may spread the illness to all of the other horses. Then we might lose the entire stable."

"So, you'll quarantine her then, until you know?"

Thomas looked to the farrier once again. "Do you have a place sufficient to quarantine her away from all of the other horses?"

"Supposin' I could keep her in her stall," he replied with a nod.

"No," Ellie said, shaking her head before Thomas could jump in. "If it's that contagious, she needs to actually be quarantined, not just separated.

She needs to be kept in a place where she's not sharing the same air or provisions with the other horses."

The farrier looked at Thomas, questioning the instructions. Thomas nodded at the man, instructing him to do as Ellie suggested.

"Continue watching over her. Look for white discharge from the nose followed by brown discharge and a fever. If these develop, do inform me. We may take measures then. Hopefully, it's only a cold and she shall soon be mended."

Despite being indoors, Ellie smelled the rain before she heard it. It was not surprising really, considering the fort was a simple structure made of wood with no real insulation. It could barely be called 'indoors.' Closing her eyes, she inhaled deeply, enjoying the scent. Captain Burke and Patti Woodford watched on and the captain asked if something was amiss.

"Do you smell that?"

He sniffed the air and replied, "The only thing I smell is rain."

"What you're smelling is called petrichor. It's the smell emitted by the ground as the rain penetrates the earth. It's one of the best smells in the world," she explained, almost dreamily.

The captain watched her as she took in this simple joy. He could see the pleasure on her face and immediately wondered what it would be like to be the reason for that look of pleasure. He shook off the inappropriate thought when Patti spoke.

"I always did fancy that smell. I knew not that it had a name."

They could hear the rain coming down in a heavy pour and Ellie moved toward the door to watch it come down. "I love the rain," she said to no one in particular. She really wanted to go out and dance around under the downpour but only had two sets of clothing. If she got this one wet, it would take a long time to dry with all the layers she had on. She had to be more aware of her use of clothing there than she did at home. As it was, she washed her shifts nightly and decided to wash the overclothes once each weekly or more often only as needed.

The thought of home had her watching the sky for any lightning that might be nearby. It occurred to her that might be her way home. She had enjoyed Thomas's company and learning as much as she had, but she had a life to get back to and needed to get home. As soon as the thought entered her mind, she immediately questioned it. Did she need to get home, though? Was that what she wanted or was she simply going along with what was expected of her, yet again.

Her time dancing and dying her hair bright colors had been her little acts of rebellion when she was younger. She had repeatedly been accused of being a free spirit throughout her life and she tried to live up to that, but when it came down to duty and responsibility, she had always done what was expected of her, knowing she would this time, too. Though she loved the adventure she had been having, she did not belong there. She needed to get back to her career, her nieces and nephew, and her cousin who was probably going crazy trying to find her. The thought of Kristy and her niblings had her searching the sky even harder.

Thomas watched Ellie in the doorway enjoying the rain. He was sore from the yoga and tai chi sessions and had wanted to skip but did not want her out practicing on her own. Thomas had recommended she only continue with the tai chi moving forward as the movements were less scandalous. He was thankful she did not argue with him over it but instead agreed to alter her practice. It did not escape him that the rain would prevent her from doing it that night, leaving him grateful when it started coming down. He would not have been any help if she found herself in trouble, though he would miss her company that night.

When there was no lightning in sight, Ellie reluctantly closed the door and came back in.

"You seem to have an aptitude for grammar and spelling. Do you write as well?" Thomas asked her.

Ellie ignored the reference to her appraisal of his journal. When she nodded her head, Thomas continued, "Perhaps you would act as a scrivener to us?"

Ellie's brow bunched in confusion. "What's a scrivener?"

Gideon Anwar mockingly replied, "How might she be a scrivener when she don't even know what one is?"

"How can you be a surgeon when you don't even know how to pull your own head from your ass?" Ellie retorted. She had not meant to let him get under her skin, but he was so good at it.

Patti covered a laugh with a hand over her mouth while Gideon stood and moved closer to Ellie, raising his hand as if to strike her. Ellie stood even taller, raising her chin up in defiance at him. She may not be able to do much damage in return, but she would be damned if she cowered before him or let it go unanswered. However, she would not throw the first punch and waited for the blow to land. Before it did, Thomas's hand shot up to intercept Gideon's arm.

"Have a care, Gideon. If anyone is to dole out punishments, it shall be myself as the ranking officer in this hospital. Now, I believe Mr. Harris is in need of some attention."

The use of his first name by Thomas was a deliberate slight. It was a reminder that Thomas was his superior and would not hesitate to pull rank on him if need be. Gideon left but not before giving Ellie a glare that told her this was not over.

Thomas turned to Ellie. "You really ought not provoke him."

She was appalled. How was this her fault? Okay, maybe she did go a little too far with her comment, but she did not say anything that was not true.

"I couldn't help myself. The man is an ass. He constantly belittles me and does anything he can to make my life miserable." Ellie realized she was whining but could not seem to help herself. She stopped and took a deep breath before continuing. "I'm sorry, Captain Burke. I can't promise it won't happen again, but I will try harder."

"I do hope so, Mrs. Sorenson. It would be disconcerting to see you lose your position here or be punished in another manner. If he had a mind to take it to the major, you could lose your rations, be removed, or worse."

Ellie did not want to think about what the 'worse' option was. She had seen both soldiers and female camp followers being whipped for disobeying orders and did not want to face that herself. Sufficiently chastised, she said, "I'll behave myself."

Thomas gave a short nod of his head and got back to the matter at hand.

"Now, a scrivener is a clerk or a scribe. Do you know what either of those are?"

Not meaning the question to be condescending, he was simply trying to ascertain if either of the words were within her vocabulary since they had encountered so many that she did not know or words that she recognized but held a different meaning to her.

"I know both of those," Ellie said while nodding her head, taking his question as it was meant. "What do you need written?"

"Some of the men here wish to write home but are unable to do so. The fort's scrivener is rather busy and often does not have time enough to perform this task for the men in the hospital. Is this something you might be able to do?"

Ellie immediately agreed but then thought about what it would entail. She had never used a quill and ink, though her favorite writing instrument was a fountain pen. Hopefully, they were not so different that she would have any problems using one. Her biggest hesitation though, was her handwriting. She used to practice calligraphy as a teenager but that had been decades ago. Her everyday handwriting was rather atrocious and difficult to read. The handwriting from this time was much more standardized, even if the content was not.

"Do you have a pen and paper that I can practice with first? I've never used a quill pen."

This woman never ceased to surprise Thomas. "Do you use chalk instead? Perhaps graphite?"

"I've used both," she almost added, 'among others,' but caught herself in time.

Thomas took her over to his desk where he pulled out the journal she had read. Flipping to an empty page, he pointed to the quill and ink on the desktop and showed her how to use them. After writing a few words, he grabbed another item off his desk which consisted of a wooden handle in the middle of a thick rectangle base with an arc-shaped block underneath. The rounded portion was covered with a linen cloth. Thomas pressed one side of the linen arc on the paper where he had written and slowly rolled it across the page without lifting. As he demonstrated the technique, he said, "Have a care to use the blotter frequently to prevent the ink from smudging."

Ellie recognized it as an ink blotter but had never seen one used. She had not known it was covered with cloth and had always wondered how the wood absorbed the ink quickly enough to be effective. Nothing else he showed her was new to her, but she let him explain in case there was something she did not already know. Taking the offered quill and journal, she began to write her name. Thankfully, it was easier than she had expected. It was not unlike her fountain pen with the exception that the ink flow was inconsistent and she constantly had to keep dipping the quill in the ink. She repeated writing her name for a few lines and quickly got a feel for it. Thomas stood behind her with a hand on the back of her chair while she practiced. He leaned in so close that she could smell his earthy scent. While many of the inhabitants of the fort did little in the way of bathing, he was clearly not one of them. She tried to ignore it and focused on the page in front of her.

Nodding at her skill, he told her, "I'll show you how to care for the quill and cut a new nib later. Just practice for now."

Ellie was excited to learn this new technique, having always considered herself a nerd and loving all things pen and paper. Though she never spent much money on her jewelry, she could easily justify spending a couple hundred dollars on a pen. She had always wanted a Mont Blanc but could never afford one. They were a little out of her price range. Ellie began writing out the alphabet in the hand she used to use for calligraphy. After writing it out, she followed it with the sentence she learned when learning to type: 'The quick brown fox jumps over the lazy dog.' After writing this out three times, she felt she was ready. She excitedly asked who wanted a letter written. Thomas laughed at her eagerness and pointed her to one of the patients.

Carrying paper, quill, ink, and blotter inside a small portable writing desk, Ellie went to the soldier. She set everything up and waited for the soldier to start dictating. Thomas hovered nearby, pretending to tend to a patient in the next bed over. Ellie was not fooled by his actions. As soon as the letter was finished, he held out a hand for the page and she handed it over to him. She waited while he read it, knowing he was checking to make sure it actually said what the soldier wanted it to say.

"Satisfied?" she asked smugly.

Thomas nodded as he fought the grin that was trying to spread across his lips.

"I've not seen a hand like this before," he observed.

"I know. My handwriting is a little sloppy. Hopefully, it's readable."

"It's perfectly readable. In fact, your spelling and grammar are both perfect, which is not something I've seen often outside of printed books," he said while staring down at the page in his hand. Without looking up, he asked, "Where did you study?"

"School." It was all she could say.

At that, he looked up from the page to study her face instead. Once again, he knew there was more to her story, but she was clearly unwilling to tell it. He decided to let it go for now with a single nod of his head. Perhaps she would tell him in time. He handed the page back to her.

"Have Mr. Simms show you how to send it off."

While Ellie was occupied with writing letters, Thomas sought out Gideon and scolded him for his behavior. "I understand you do not approve of women in the hospital, but they are here to help. Unless you wish to assume their responsibilities as well as yours, you shall not continue to provoke Mrs. Sorenson. I will have peace in my hospital."

Gideon reluctantly agreed and Thomas hoped the man would stick to his word. He knew Ellie would continue to defend herself and he did not want to see her catch the attention of the colonel. He had made himself clear about what would happen if she were causing trouble within the camp.

Chapter 12

June 1756

Ellie watched Thomas often. With his usual stance of feet planted wide, broad shoulders back, he exuded confidence and authority. It was difficult to tell how old he was. Though he looked young, he was quite mature and led the hospital, overseeing the entire operation, such as it was. He commanded the operation as well as someone twice his age. There was no cockiness or arrogance, yet he was sure of himself and carried himself with an air of confidence, never hesitating in his diagnoses. When a soldier came in that afternoon after having difficulty maintaining his balance, Ellie was surprised to see his confidence falter and hesitation set in.

The man had been reluctant to come in, but when he nearly fell off one of the ramparts, he was ordered to see the doctor. Thomas examined him and was hesitant to diagnose him. He stood, telling the soldier to stay there on the table and he would return. Gideon Anwar followed Captain Burke, asking why he did not tell the soldier what ailed him.

"It's a clear case of epilepsy, it is. Lemuel Barnes has evil spirits and must be banished from here before they inhabit anyone else," Gideon argued.

Thomas responded, "I'm not yet convinced. Mr. Barnes needs further examination."

He was not sure what further examination he could do but did not want to be the one to destroy this man's life. He would if he had no alternatives, but he would exhaust all of his resources before he did. His instincts told him something else was amiss with the man. To his surprise, Thomas found himself seeking out Ellie for her opinion. He did not tell her anything about the man or his history, but instead, asked her to examine him.

Abigail Gibbons watched on with Gideon, who was aghast. For once, she was in agreement with him. Why would the captain be asking Ellie's advice? This soldier had clearly been invaded by evil spirits and they needed to remove him as quickly as they could. He needed an exorcism, not a doctor. They watched on in disbelief as Ellie went to examine the man. Captain Burke stood beside her but did not say a word.

Ellie asked the soldier his name and what brought him in. Lemuel was again reluctant to say anything. He looked around the room and twisted his hands nervously. When he finally spoke, he said so quietly that Ellie had to strain to hear him, "I has the evil spirits, I do."

"I beg your pardon," Ellie said. That was an expression she never thought she would use. Her mother used to say it all the time and she had always hated it.

The man repeated himself and Ellie realized they were not going to get anywhere. She needed clarification. "Why do you think that?"

"I fall down a lot. A spirit takes possession of me body and I lose control of meself."

Ellie was confused but thought maybe he was describing seizures. Turning to Thomas, she asked, "Do you know of seizures?"

He nodded his head sadly while looking defeated. Ellie did not understand why that was such a bad thing. Thomas was ready to take control back when Lemuel spoke again.

"It never used to 'appen. It came on sudden-like after a smite to me costard during construction of the fort."

"I'm sorry, what?" Ellie asked, thoroughly confused by the expression. Looking back and forth between him and Thomas, it was the captain who explained, "He received a blow to the head while building the fort."

This triggered something in Ellie, though she had still been having enough misunderstandings that she wanted more information. She asked the man to describe these episodes.

"What happens to you physically, Mr. Barnes?" she asked.

"Everythin' spins and I lose me balance, I do. Sometimes I fall," he said sheepishly.

"Is it like being drunk or spinning around in circles?" she asked.

"'Tis, yes."

"Does it happen when you turn your head or change positions from laying down or standing up?"

"It does."

"Okay, I want to do a test on you. Is that okay?"

He looked at the captain, and asked, "What do that mean?"

The captain's lips turned upright at the corners at being a translator for both him and Ellie. "She means 'is it alright?' Mrs. Sorenson was asking your permission to perform a test."

Surprised at this exchange, she only now realized that she had never heard anyone there use the word 'okay,' immediately leading her to wonder when it came into usage. She would have to watch her use of that one when she was around other people. At least Thomas had figured out what she meant.

Lemuel reluctantly nodded his approval for her to proceed. Ellie could tell he was afraid of whatever test she had planned, but she thought he was more afraid of being filled with these 'evil spirits.' Trying to put him at ease, she talked him through what she had planned. Instructing Thomas to stand beside her and assist, she explained to him what to look for. Tilting the soldier's head to the correct angle, she assisted him in lying down slowly while instructing him to keep his eyes open. Watching his eyes, she saw the telltale signs of nystagmus. As his eyes began jumping all over the place, side to side and up and down, his arms shot out for something to hold onto.

"I'm going to cast up me accounts," Lemuel warned, slightly panicked.

It only took Ellie a second to understand the strange expression this time. She knew that feeling all too well and almost wanted to vomit in sympathy with the poor soul. Mrs. Gibbons was right there with a chamber pot for him, though he ended up not needing it.

Convinced that the man had the same type of vertigo she herself had suffered from for years, she performed the Epley maneuver on him. She did a series of head tilts until she was satisfied she had fixed the problem. Afterward, she helped him sit up again and he sat still for a minute, regaining his equilibrium. She gave him instructions on limiting his movements over the next few days and told him to return if he experienced it again. The soldier was clearly hesitant to believe she had done anything to rid him of the evil spirits, but said the spinning was gone.

Ellie was smiling widely, feeling like she had helped. Everyone else was clearly as hesitant as the soldier to believe she had done anything.

"That was remarkable," Thomas praised. "I admit, I was skeptical, though I had hoped there was another, more rational explanation than what previous medical knowledge would have us believe it to be."

Ellie's lips quirked up. "You mean a better explanation than demonic possession?"

Fighting a roll of the eyes, Thomas replied, "Yes."

"Are you saying you don't believe in demonic possession like everyone else around here?"

Thomas expelled a heavy breath. "I believe in reason and science, physics and mathematics. I believe what can be proved."

Ellie frowned. "So, you're saying you wouldn't believe in, say, being able to transplant a heart or kidney from one patient to another?"

"Only if you wish to kill both patients," he was quick to reply.

"What about humans being able to soar through the air in machines that can fly?"

Thomas laughed and shook his head. "No."

"Having foreknowledge of the future?"

"No."

"Being able to travel through time?"

Thomas continued shaking his head, but more in disbelief now. "From where do you derive such fanciful notions?"

Shrugging, she avoided giving him an answer. "If someone came in here claiming those to be true, what would you do?"

"If any of those could be proven, I would be inclined to believe them. But none can be. If a patient persisted, I would have to treat him for madness."

Ellie had been testing the waters, wanting to share her story with him but still reluctant to do so. Now she was even more so. If she ever told him, he would think she was insane. She would certainly lose his friendship along with any trust that she had managed to build up with him. Knowing he still did not fully trust her, she knew now that she would lose the little ground she had gained if she ever told him.

Gideon interrupted their conversation, curious as to what she had done. "Are we to believe you actually did anything to cure that man? He's catched evil spirits and only a priest can remove them. He shall be back if he does not do something accursed first or convey them along to others."

Ellie rolled her eyes, turning her back to them to return to her work, deciding to let Thomas handle this one. Before she could go, he stopped her with a hand on her arm.

"Mrs. Sorenson, how did you know Mr. Barnes did not have evil spirits?"

"He has a condition called Benign Paroxysmal Positional Vertigo, or BPPV."

When she was met with a bunch of blank faces, she explained, "The ear has several canals inside it.

There are calcium crystals inside each canal. Sometimes, particularly after a head injury, the crystals come loose from the canal. It throws off the equilibrium and causes dizziness, making the entire world feel like it's spinning."

"How have you come to know of this?" Thomas asked.

"Gee, I don't know. I don't want to be burned at the stake or imprisoned for being a witch," she responded sarcastically.

Thomas smirked, dropping his hand from her arm. "We no longer engage in such behaviors. You shall undoubtedly be happy to learn it's illegal to accuse someone of witchcraft."

Ellie's head jerked back in surprise. "Illegal? Really?"

Thomas nodded. "Since the Witchcraft Act of 1735. Though it generally stopped being a practice around the turn of the century; shortly after more than two hundred people were accused in Massachusetts. It took Parliament a while to become enlightened on the matter."

She looked at him skeptically. "Of course. They had to wait until *after* the Salem Witch Trials that killed twenty people."

It was his turn to be surprised. "You've a familiarity with it?"

"Oh yeah. I'm familiar with it." Ellie had visited Salem with her cousins. She had been equally appalled and fascinated by the stories of what the women had gone through and it had made her angry. "Why is that so surprising?"

"Most outside of Massachusetts are unfamiliar with it."

"How is it you know of it then?" she challenged. "Are you from Massachusetts?"

The corners of his lips turned up at her disbelief. "No. My dear friend is a lawyer. I oft helped him study. How is it you come to have knowledge of it?"

"Stop fishing," she said teasingly with a smirk.

Thomas looked around the hospital. "Fishing? We're not near the river at the moment."

Ellie could not help the laughter that bubbled forth at his confusion. "You're fishing for information."

"I'm trying to clarify," he corrected. "You said you were not from the colonies, yet the only people I know who have heard of the witch trials that occurred in Massachusetts are those who lived in the surrounding areas or have studied law. Have you studied law, Mrs. Sorenson?"

"I haven't. But I have studied the Salem Witch Trials. A little, anyways."

"You never cease to surprise me."

Ellie smiled widely at the compliment. Thomas was momentarily blinded by her smile, then remembered the waiting Gideon. "We seem to have meandered away from our original discourse. How did you diagnose and treat Mr. Barnes?"

Sighing, Ellie resigned herself to share a little bit of herself with these people. "Unfortunately, I know from personal experience. I've suffered from BPPV since I was a teenager. It's awful. I'd rather have pain than nausea any day. The Epley maneuver helps immensely, though. The crystals need to be realigned and placed back into the correct position within the ear canal."

Ellie had learned about different types of vertigo after her husband's head injury, but this type was one she had learned about decades ago. The Epley could potentially be a permanent fix to the problem, but sometimes it came back. With her years dancing, then her yoga, it occasionally came back for her if she did too many inversions or other movements that caused the crystals to come out of alignment. She could not do headstands at all without them bringing the BPPV back.

Thomas told Lemuel Barnes he wanted to see him back in a week and released him. Ellie taught him and a reluctant Gideon everything she knew about Benign Paroxysmal Positional Vertigo including how to diagnose and treat it.

Afterward, Thomas asked, "From where does your knowledge of medicine come?"

She decided to once again stick to the truth as close as she could, while keeping it vague. "I went to school."

Gideon scoffed and asked, "What school let in a woman?"

Turning to him, she said simply, "The one I went to."

He snorted and walked away.

Ellie could not keep from saying, "Jackass."

Thomas chuckled at her curse, and she turned her attention to him. "Where did you learn medicine?"

"I also went to school. Though I've been studying it as long as I can remember. My neighbor was a physician, and I knew it was what I wished to do, so I studied under him as much as I was able. In my youth, I did small chores then worked my way up to bloodletting and eventually performing surgeries. My father sent me to school abroad in the hopes I would lose interest in medicine and learn a more respectable trade." Thomas smirked at the memory. "He was not much pleased to find I simply furthered my knowledge in the pursuit of my own interest."

Ellie smiled conspiratorially with him, knowing all about pursuing interests against a parent's wishes. Perhaps if she had gone into the military like her brothers had, her father would have been proud of her. At least her short stint as a paramedic was a brief reprieve from his disappointment.

"I've had plenty of jobs my parents didn't approve of. They were ecstatic when I learned medicine." Ellie tried to carefully police her words.

That she had shared that much about her parents and having had other jobs was a small victory for him. Thomas desperately wanted to seize on it and ask more, but he knew she would not be forthcoming. Instead he shared more of himself, hoping to put her at ease enough to continue sharing more of herself. "I like to think it will be different with my own children when they come along."

It was easy to imagine this man with children. A natural leader in the hospital, disciplined but fair, he would probably dote on daughters while being stern and demanding discipline from sons.

"However, you're quite adept at the medical arts," he continued, pulling her from her thoughts. "We're lucky to have you here with us."

"I'm glad to hear it. I haven't practiced in a long time."

"Why ever not?"

"It got to be too stressful. People we tried to help would yell at us, fight with us about receiving treatment, or outright assault us. Then I had five small children in one month all die on me. There was nothing I could do to save them. As the last one slipped away, her mother was screaming at me to do something. I did everything I could, but it wasn't enough. All I could do was look at the poor girl's mother while her heart broke into pieces."

Fixing her stare across the room, she recounted the memory that still haunted her. She shook herself. "After that, I focused solely on the dead and autopsies."

"Autopsies?"

"Right. You don't do those here." She had forgotten autopsies were not widely conducted until much later. "It's the examination of the dead to determine cause of death."

"I know what they are. I believe they do them in Italy. I'm surprised to hear that you come from a place that is conducting them. There are few places which do." That seemed to rule out her dwelling with the Indians who would never engage in such a practice.

Knowing he was fishing again, trying to get her to give him something more about where she came from, Ellie was not giving anything up that easily.

"This place from where you come sounds rather unconventional. They seem to allow women to engage in many activities within the realm of men."

Ellie fought to keep her tongue. He did not mean anything offensive. It was merely a reflection of this time. Losing her temper would not help get her point across and it was not an argument. He was not advocating for women to stay 'in their place.' He was simply asking about where she came from. Guarding her thoughts so she would not say anything circumspect, she replied, "They're afforded many liberties they're not afforded here."

Thomas smirked at how expertly she avoided his underlying question. She was quite intelligent indeed. This only drew him into her further.

"I should be most grateful to learn any other techniques you know that are not common practice here," he said.

Ellie cocked her head in question. "Short of CPR or the Heimlich, I wouldn't know what else I could teach you. I don't know what I know that you don't."

"Why don't we start with those?" he suggested. "We physicians often spend more of our time searching for medicines than doing any actual healing. I'd be most agreeable to learning anything you're able to share with me."

Happy to share her knowledge with him, she knew most of that knowledge was useless there since the cures were unavailable. She admired that he was so inquisitive and was always open to learning something new. This was so rare in most adults, regardless of what century it was. It was refreshing, and she loved it while simultaneously finding it exhausting as it required her to always be on guard.

Ellie taught Thomas what she knew of sterilization, CPR, the Heimlich maneuver, and any other modern medical interventions she could, and he taught her about doing medicine in the eighteenth century with the help of Mrs. Gibbons. Gideon wanted nothing to do with any of it as he did not believe Ellie could teach him anything.

Trying to find people to practice maneuvers on while not being accused of impropriety was exhausting. In the end, she demonstrated each technique on Miss Woodford while he practiced on male soldiers. Even that raised eyebrows as the movements were considered indecent. Ellie shook her head at the accusations.

"You won't be saying that when it saves your life," she always countered.

Chapter 13

June 29, 1756

"The men with more severe injuries shall be a-taken to the 'ospital in Albany in two days' time. 'Tis a nurse they'll be wanting to accompany them and see to their needs."

Ellie had been at the fort for nearly two weeks when Abigail Gibbons approached her first thing in the morning. The hospital had been filling up and many of the men that were there had been there since the raid in which she saved Isaac from the Frenchman. She had learned that immediately prior to her arrival, there had been reports of a large party of enemy soldiers that had been working in the area near the fort, creating a new road. They had gotten a little too close to the fort for anyone's liking, and a detachment of four hundred men were sent to reinforce the garrison at the fort. The men were sent with a convoy of one hundred wagons. When they reached a place called Halfway Brook on Thursday, June 17, the convoy was attacked. A large number of British soldiers were killed and scalped, the oxen were slaughtered, and the wagons were plundered. The victory had gone to the French that day. Ellie and Isaac had both been lucky to get out with their lives. If she had not taken a thrust of the sword for him, he might very well be dead.

The retreat had been sounded shortly after her arrival and he had not hesitated to scoop her up onto the horse he claimed from the Frenchman he killed and race back to Fort Edward. Captain Burke had initially refused to treat her, saying that she had been too far gone for him to do anything. He had to treat the soldiers first, which she did not like for selfish reasons but almost understood. She was in a military hospital and that was why he was there after all. It was only when he had seen to his other patients and she had refused to die that he tried treating her. After doing all he could for her, he sent Gideon Anwar to cauterize her wound.

A few days later, Captain Robert Rogers and Captain Israel Putnam took the Rangers to the Narrows at Lake Champlain and attacked the same party that had attacked the convoy. This time, the victory belonged to the British. Ellie remembered from her visits to the museum with Lucas that this was the first time the British had encountered this type of warfare and what was learned during this war helped the Patriots win their freedom from the British in the American Revolution a few years later. Both wars were more a series of raids and skirmishes instead of exclusively being the open warfare in which the British had always engaged.

Absorbed in her work, Ellie responded, "That's good. It's just what they need. Hopefully, they'll get the care there that we can't give them here. Are you going with them then?"

"I care not to go on these travels. My children need me 'ere, they do. Miss Woodford went last time but I thought you might be agreeable to the journey this time. You'll be like to provide more assistance to them, you will."

Though surprised, Ellie accepted the offer. Mrs. Gibbons had three children there with her, having followed her husband and son from Boston. They were both attached to the militia, and she came along to help. Her son was only sixteen, but that was old enough to join the militia in that time. Ellie could only imagine the anguish Mrs. Gibbons must have felt all the time. Her three younger children were fourteen, twelve, and eight. Given that this war was only just getting underway, it was entirely likely the fourteen-year-old would soon follow in his father's and brother's footsteps. The younger two were girls, so she would not have to worry about them as much. Though once this war ended, another would not be far behind it.

"'Tis not an easy journey." Mrs. Gibbons brought her back to the present. "There is no bateaux available, thus you shall be long on the road. If'n the roads is clear, it ought to take you maybe two days each way. If this rain continues, it might could take longer."

Looking forward to it, she wanted to see something other than the fort. There was a small part of her that was still in denial about her situation. Maybe she was merely in a bubble there of people reenacting this time period. Perfectly. With no anachronisms. And really killing each other. Okay, so it was a long shot. But she still needed to see the outside world for herself. She was eager for the journey ahead of her.

"The fire is gone out yesternight," Gideon came to inform them. "Make haste that it gets started again."

He stopped only long enough to order them about, then left as quickly. Mrs. Gibbons turned to Ellie. "Supposin' you could see to it if'n you please, Mrs. Sorenson."

Before Ellie could say anything, Mrs. Gibbons left to begin her duties for the day. Ellie had noticed that the fire seemed to always be going, even though it was summer. It was not only used to keep warm but to heat water and cook as well. There were several fireplaces around the fort and while all of them were not always kept lit in the warmer weather, many of them were.

Making her way to the fireplace inside the small hospital, Ellie looked around the mantle and the shelves surrounding it for matches of some sort but did not see any. Suspecting that much, she had hoped she was wrong. She stacked wood and kindling, trying to at least prep it until she could figure out what to do. Once she finished, she stared at it trying to figure out what to do next.

Thomas saw Ellie standing by the cold fireplace looking confused. "Is there something with which you need assistance, Miss Ellie?"

Looking up at the captain, Ellie was not certain she wanted to admit her ignorance. She hesitated before saying, "The fire went out last night."

With his attention on the stone hearth, he nodded. "So it would seem. I see you've gathered wood. Are you planning on setting it ablaze?"

Wringing her hands, Ellie looked back at him with pleading eyes. "I'm not sure how," she admitted quietly.

"There's flint and steel just here," he said, turning to the shelf she had searched for matches.

It had not occurred to her to look for flint and steel, though never having used them, she probably would not have recognized them as such had she been looking. Thomas picked them up and handed them to her but she simply stared at them, not having any idea what to do with the objects. She was familiar with the theory of using flint and steel to start a fire but had never done it or seen it done.

Again, she looked up at him with confusion on her face, her eyes imploring, trying not to vocalize her lack of knowledge. He managed to understand the look she gave him and took back the flint and steel from her.

"How do you know not how to start a fire?" he asked, gently. It was not an admonishment nor was he passing judgment. He was genuinely surprised.

Unable to tell him about matches and lighters, Ellie simply shrugged. Of all the people to come to assist her, she was both grateful and mortified that it was the captain. She felt like an idiot for not knowing, but she had already exposed the depth of her ignorance to him, so this should come as no surprise. Regardless, he did not treat her any differently for her lack of knowledge. He was always patient with her and this was no exception.

Kneeling down, Thomas urged her to do the same as he arranged new tinder beside the wood she had carefully piled up. He used much smaller pieces and included a few small scraps of linen that he had grabbed along with the flint and steel. Holding the flint and cloth in his left hand and the steel in his right, he demonstrated the technique to Ellie before handing the tools back to her. It took her several tries while he guided her and corrected her positioning a few times, but she kept at it. Seeing her frustration, he began to take the tools back from her, but she yanked her arms back stubbornly.

"I'll get it," she declared, "even if it takes me all damn day."

Biting back a smile at her obstinacy, he sat back on his heels and left her to it. He corrected her a couple more times, but eventually, there was a spark and the linen caught. In her excitement, it went out before she could place it inside the nest of tinder he had created, but she was encouraged and eagerly tried again.

This time, when the linen caught, he quickly guided her to place it inside the tinder while blowing on it gently to ignite it. Smoke poured out from the nest and she continued to blow on it until a small flame rose up. Her eyes sparkled at her triumph and her face split into a broad smile. He helped her arrange the wood so the fire would grow before finally helping her stand up.

"Next time," he informed her as he pointed, "you might take the shovel and bucket beside the hearth here and go to any of the other fires in camp to retrieve an ember that's already burning. It's much easier and quicker."

Her hands immediately flew to her hips as she cocked her head. "You let me go through all that when all I had to do was go steal an ember from someone else?"

"I know how curious you are and thought you might wish to learn the technique," he shrugged.

The smile returned to her face, warming him more than the fire now roaring beside him. "Thank you."

Bowing his head slightly, Thomas headed away, returning to his duties before he decided to see what else he could teach her. The smile on her face made his stomach flip and he would gladly teach her more if she continued to look at him like that.

"Where are you from?" Ellie asked the soldier for whom she was drafting a letter home.

"Gloucester, miss."

"Massachusetts?" she asked.

"Yes, miss. Is that your home as well?"

Captain Burke stood at the table nearby, mixing medicines and Ellie was very aware that he was watching her, awaiting her response.

"Me? No. It's way too cold for me there," she teased, skirting the answer.

"Only, you know Gloucester is in Massachusetts, miss. 'Tis not very large; you must be from near there," the patient insisted.

Ellie shook her head. "No. I've just heard of it."

She had actually driven through there and stopped for lunch on her way to see Lexington and Concord years before. Ellie had always loved the Boston area and had even considered moving there after college, but she preferred much warmer climates.

"What do you do in Gloucester?" she asked.

Before he could answer, the man next to him spoke up, "The only thing these Massachusetts boys be knowin' how to do: he's a fisherman."

The boy smiled at the ribbing. "'Tis not the only thing. I saved your bloody hide from that savage, I did. We know how to fight, too." He turned back toward Ellie and blushed, realizing what he had just said. "Beggin' your pardon, miss. Forgive me language. I meant not to be vulgar in front of a lady."

Ellie's mouth turned up in a smirk, and she caught Captain Burke's eye. "It's alright. I've heard worse."

The captain was smirking now himself.

"So, I take it you're not from Massachusetts?" she asked the other man.

"No, miss. I come from Pennsylvania."

"Philadelphia or somewhere else?"

"Lancaster, miss," he said proudly.

"Oh. So further west," she replied.

Captain Burke looked at her with curiosity, pausing in what he was mixing. "You've a familiarity with Pennsylvania as well as Massachusetts?" Thomas asked from the table across the small room.

"Some," she replied vaguely. She knew he was going to use this opportunity to ply her with questions about her past. Thankfully, the soldiers held his questions at bay by asking their own.

"Where else might you be familiar with?" another one of the men asked. "Do you know of Hartford?"

Ellie thought for a moment. "That's in Connecticut, right?"

The men all let out a small cheer. Ellie was a little confused by their surprise and how impressed they were by something as simple as recognizing the names of these cities. Apparently, this was all they needed to begin quizzing her on her knowledge of geography.

"That's three for three," one of the men said. "I'm supposin' you'll be knowin' the names of all the colonies?"

Ellie's brows scrunched in thought for a moment, and she set down the quill she had still been clutching. Unsure how much of a challenge this would be, she raised her head in thought and started naming them in order from the south since she was more familiar with that region. Seeing them in her mind as if on a map helped her keep them all straight and not miss or repeat any.

"Florida and Louisiana aren't British colonies, so I guess I'll start with Georgia. Past that, we have South Carolina, North Carolina, Virginia, Maryland, Rhode Island, Delaware, Pennsylvania, New York, New Jersey, Massachusetts, Connecticut, and," she paused for a moment, thinking. Ticking them off on her fingers as she went, she knew she only had one more to go but was not certain which one of the remaining two possibilities was correct. "And... shit. Just one more. It's either New Hampshire or Vermont."

She looked back to the men, who all wore expressions of both awe and surprise. They looked to each other, as if trying to verify her answers.

"Is that right? I always get my New England states mixed up."

None of the men answered, so Thomas spoke up while resuming the stirring in his bowl. "You named all thirteen on the continent. There are many more elsewhere. New Hampshire is the final one here. But where is Vermont? And why did you call them states?"

"Vermont? Really? Is that not a place yet?" she asked, pointedly ignoring the other question. Ellie looked around her, and none of the men seemed to recognize the name. Apparently, it did not exist yet. She had been certain that it was one of the original thirteen, and if not, that it was at least established by that time. Oops. Oh well, it did not seem as though any of the men knew better.

The captain on the other hand was shaking his head. "*Ver mont* is French for 'green mountains.' There's a region not far from here that goes by that moniker, but it's not a colony, only a part of New York. Is that from where you derive?"

Ellie brushed off his question. "I must have heard it somewhere." She turned back to the men. "So, I may have had an extra one, but I named all thirteen. Do I still pass the test?"

They looked to each other, and when they all agreed that she had, they issued another challenge. "Only, can you name the capitals of them all?"

There was laughter and cheering as the men urged her on, more of them listening closely now.

Ellie's eyes widened at the new challenge. "That one is a little harder. Let's see." She began naming them all, working in the same order she had before. She was not as certain about the capitals. Not only had she never memorized capitals before, but she knew some of them may not have remained the capital over time.

"Georgia would be Atlanta; then there's Charleston, no, wait, Columbia; then Raleigh; and Richmond. No. That's not right. She remembered visiting the governor's mansion in Colonial Williamsburg as a kid and changed her answer. "The capital of Virginia would be Williamsburg." It must have changed over the years because it was Richmond in her time. She continued working her way north, slowing down as she made her way further up the coast. "Damn it. I can't remember Delaware or New Hampshire."

The men laughed as one said, "You could make somethin' up, and we wouldn't know no better."

Ellie feigned being appalled as she swatted him lightly on the leg.

"You're testing me on things you don't even know the answers to?" she asked, pretending to be aghast.

"We need not know the answers. 'Tis fun only to watch you try to answer 'em."

She pursed her lips and put her hands on her hips, pretending to be put out by them. "I see how it is. Well, I'm glad I can keep you amused."

The men laughed, and she smiled back in response, shaking her head. She picked the quill back up and finished the letter she was writing for one of the men. After cleaning up her supplies, she took them back to the desk to put everything away. Thomas had finished his medicines and was now logging his daily notes in his medical journal.

"You've an aptitude for geography. Where did you learn so many diverse subjects?" he asked.

Ellie shrugged, avoiding his gaze, "Just picked it up over the years."

She could not tell him that she had been to most of the places she had named or that colonial history was taught to every kid in grade school. Instead of giving him a chance to further quiz her, she asked, "Is it really so surprising that I could know these things?"

Thomas cocked his head to the side, studying her momentarily before answering. "Do you truly not know?"

Staring back at him, she answered, "Know what?"

"Most men do not know geography well. Women typically know even less. Only those who own land have a reason to know it, and many who fall into that category only know what's immediately around them. You not only knew all of the colonies and most of the capitals, but you named them in order from south to north, suggesting a visual familiarity with where they are located or how they relate to one another. Though, the capital of Georgia is Augusta. I've not heard of Atlanta. Have you studied maps?"

Ellie avoided answering his question with one of her own. "If most people here don't know it, then how do you know it so well?"

"I've studied. I had to learn it from a young age. My father demanded a broad education for his sons."

"I see."

Thomas did not know what to make of this woman. She clearly had some extensive education to be able to recite what she had about the colonies, which she could only have obtained if she was a woman of means. Though, even that did not guarantee an education for women. At least, not to the degree she seemed to have. Yet, she did not behave or speak as a genteel woman, and her appearance did not match that either. No woman of means he had ever met would allow herself to be painted in the manner of the Indians or have holes bored into her naval or her ears to the degree she had. Then, there was her use of the word 'states' when referring to the colonies of New England and her declarations of a place called Vermont. Despite knowing his geography well, he had only heard of such a place as a small area not far from where they were. He was not certain what that meant. She continued to be an enigma to him and wanted to know more. Hoping one day she might answer, he continued to ask questions whenever he could, even when he knew she would not answer.

Chapter 14

June 30, 1756

Thomas set down a stack of supplies on a table already filled with other items. They had been packing for two days and were getting ready to load the wagons.

He turned to Ellie standing nearby and said, "These are ready to be loaded."

"Okay. Where do they go?"

"All of our supplies shall go into the last cart at the very back of the train."

Grabbing an armful of items, Ellie took them outside, looking at the train of wooden transport vehicles waiting to take them on their way. There was a welcome break from the rain as they loaded their supplies. She walked to the back and set down her load on the bed of the very last one, then went back inside and grabbed another load, continuing until she had almost taken everything outside. On her way back in to grab another load, she heard Thomas call her from the back of the line after having passed her as he also brought out a load. As she started walking towards him, he asked, "Where is everything?"

Ellie was taken aback. "What do you mean 'Where is everything?' I put them all in the last cart like you said."

Thomas pointed to the one next to him which was the second from the last one. "Then why is it empty?"

"You said the last one. That's not the last one." Ellie pointed to the one behind them and said, "That's the last one."

Exasperated, Thomas said, "That's the last wagon. I said to put them in the last cart."

Ellie looked between the two vehicles. "Seriously? There's a difference?"

Thomas sighed and ran his hands down his face. In as calm a tone as he could muster, he said, "Yes, there's a difference. A wagon," he said pointing to the one behind them, "has four wheels and can stand upright on its own. A cart," he placed his hand on the one beside him, "only has two wheels and cannot stand on its own. One has two of what we call axles, and the other has only one." He again gestured to each as he described the number of axles they each had.

Ellie was a little offended that he was talking to her like a child, yet having no idea there was a difference between the terms, she was glad he took the time to explain them.

"Okay. So, do the ones that have seats for people to sit in have different names depending on whether they're open or enclosed?" she asked.

Thomas's frustration quickly left him as he realized she had not known the difference between the various transport vehicles they used. He should have known better. She was highly competent and did not make a habit of being difficult with anyone other than Gideon. Losing the condescending tone, he explained to her that there was no difference; both of those were simply called carriages, though there were many different types of carriages.

"Oh," she said as understanding came to her, "a carriage is like a car, a wagon would be a truck, and a cart would be more like a trailer."

She had not meant to say it aloud. It was merely a way of clarifying the differences in her own mind, but Thomas scrunched his brows at the unfamiliar terminology and asked, "Is that what you call them where you're from then?"

"No. Well, maybe. I mean, I suppose they might still be in use in some parts of the world, so they probably have the same names. But we use different kinds of transportation altogether. A car, truck, or trailer would be the most similar vehicles."

She debated using the phrase 'horseless carriage' to explain further, but did not want to add too much, and this explanation seemed to satisfy Thomas.

He showed her around the wagon and cart at the back of the train, pointing out different parts while calling each by its proper name. He was patient while she learned the terminology and asked endless questions yet again.

As they walked back towards the cart, one of the retainers pulled out a strange-looking saddle and put it on a stand she had seen others use to temporarily hold their saddles. This was not like the other saddles she had seen there. It was rather lopsided with the skirting coming down lower on one side than the other. On the shorter side, there was a rail attached to one of the two horns at what she assumed was the front, and continued down the length of the saddle, and instead of stirrups, there was a single bar on one side. It was opposite the side with the rail.

Ellie stopped walking and asked, "What is that?"

Thomas looked where she was pointing and answered with considerable confusion, "Do you refer to the saddle?"

She looked at it questioningly. "I assumed it was some sort of saddle, but what the hell kind of saddle is it? How would you sit on that?"

He took a moment to look at her before answering. "It's for the colonel's wife. Have you never seen a woman's saddle?"

Ellie again blushed at her lack of knowledge. She must seem rather naïve, but Thomas was not mocking her. He was genuinely surprised.

"No." She was not uneducated and knew most women rode side-saddle throughout various historical periods, yet she had never seen a saddle built for that. How did a woman control the horse on that thing? What if they encountered an enemy and had to run? How would she stay on a running horse?

"How have you never seen one before?" Thomas asked in surprise before remembering their time in the stable with the sick horse. "I suppose if you've never seen a horse, you'd have no reason to have seen a lady's saddle."

Ellie shrugged, not wanting to further embarrass herself or heighten his suspicion of her even more than it already was. It would be too easy for him to once again start asking questions that she could not answer.

Thomas took her silence for embarrassment over being found out as having come from a family of a lower means. Though, this did not seem to fit her either. Despite her initial attire and mysterious appearance, he had never thought her inferior or having been poor. He found himself constantly tallying up her words and behaviors, trying to determine her origins, as he was doing now.

People of lesser quality were not educated as she was, nor as well groomed. The amount of jewelry she wore would imply that she came from a certain level of wealth. He knew of no low born or middling class persons who wore as many necklaces and rings as she did. The woman had ten pieces of jewelry in her ears alone.

Most women who pierced holes into their ears only had one per ear. These women were from the gentry and the earrings they wore were often either a simple teardrop pearl hanging below a gemstone or something more elaborate and gaudy. They attached to a hook that hung from the hole in the lobe, often falling almost to the shoulder. Thomas had never seen a woman with more than one hole pierced through her ears, nor had he seen the simple hoops or tiny pins such as those she wore in her upper ears.

Though, Thomas also could not picture her spending her days idly in needlework while being waited on for her every need either. Ellie was the type of woman who was capable, independent, and used to doing things for herself. Yet, she did not have the hands of someone who had spent a lifetime doing physical labor and she was unfamiliar with how to do so many basic things. She was not lacking intelligence or fortitude. There was something else. Something that was missing. She was a bizarre combination of what he would expect in a gentlewoman and a woman of lesser quality. He wondered what kind of place could possibly have produced such a combination of characteristics in a woman.

The questioning ended when Mrs. Gibbons came back with her arms full. Thomas did not want to embarrass her in front of Abigail, for which Ellie was grateful. Though, Ellie had already done that enough all by herself. The clothing had been bad enough, but Abigail had been rather confused when Ellie had asked her about personal hygiene. Thankfully, they used toothbrushes much like what she was used to. The biggest difference being that they used powder instead of a paste. There had been far more things for Abigail and Thomas to explain to Ellie than a grown woman should need explained.

They each grabbed some of Mrs. Gibbons's load as it was all about to topple over, and they headed back to their cart. While loading it up, Isaac sidled up to them.

"Great news, Miss Ellie," he began.

Mrs. Gibbons sternly corrected him, "*Mrs. Sorenson*, if'n you please, Mr. Huntington."

Ellie tried to suppress a smile while Isaac looked contrite. "Mrs. Sorenson. I found out of late that I be joinin' you in Albany." Ellie told him she was delighted they would have his company along the way. He looked suspiciously at Thomas before saying, "I wished to tell you, only I shan't stay. I must be packin' my things. I shall see you on the morrow."

The look did not go unnoticed by anyone except Ellie. After he left, Mrs. Gibbons said to Ellie, "That one fancies you, he do."

"Isaac? He couldn't possibly. I'm far too old for him."

"You're not so old," said Thomas.

"I'm older than I look." People had always thought Ellie was younger than she appeared. By the time she reached her forties, most still thought she was in her early thirties. She did not mind at all.

"That does not accord with his interest. You're still young enough to remarry and have a family, you are," said Mrs. Gibbons, undeterred. "Isaac comes from good stock and stands to inherit a large farm. He'd be a proper good 'usband, he would."

Incredulous at the suggestion, Ellie could not help sneaking a glance at Thomas to see his reaction. His face darkened slightly, but he kept his opinion to himself.

"Mrs. Gibbons, I'm old enough to be that boy's mother. I've been married plenty long enough already. I'm in no hurry to do it again anytime soon. And I certainly won't do it simply to be a broodmare to someone who stands to inherit some property. I'm perfectly happy to remain single, thank you."

Thomas snickered, but Abigail looked confused. "Surely you be not as old as that? Why, if'n I weren't twice his age and already wed, I'd consider 'im meself. I may yet try and arrange a match for me own daughter, though I fear she is still some years away from marrying age."

"But twice his age is too young for you?" Ellie had always thought the woman to be older than herself, but she was having a difficult time determining people's ages there. Everyone looked so much older than they were.

"Certainly." She looked appalled at the notion.

"Well, I'm more than twice his age."

"Mrs. Sorenson, dishonesty is unbecoming of a lady, even if'n 'tis in jest," she scolded.

"I wish I was only jesting, but unfortunately, I am not," Ellie said with a sigh.

Mrs. Gibbons shook her head, not believing it, but Ellie let it drop. She knew she would not be able to convince the woman, and it was not worth trying.

While Mrs. Gibbons went back for another load, Ellie and Thomas stayed behind to move everything from the wagon to the cart.

"You shan't tease Mrs. Gibbons," he admonished gently.

"About what?"

"Telling her you're not jesting about being older than she. If she's twice his age, that makes her around two or four and thirty years old."

"I wasn't teasing, Thomas. I know how to do math. What I said was the complete truth. I passed thirty-four a long time ago." She wondered, not for the first time, how old he was.

Seeing the doubt on his face, she pointed to the crown of her head. "See the gray hairs?"

He leaned in close enough that she could smell his earthy scent with hints of leather and wood smoke. There were no colognes or scented soaps on him. What she smelled was all him, and it was entirely pleasant. Ellie shook off the thought. She did not need to be having thoughts about him like that.

"I see not a single gray hair," he said.

Squinting her eyes at him, she tried to tell if he was teasing her again or if there really were none. Ellie had not seen a mirror since her arrival there. She assumed some of the officers may have one but none of the camp women did that she had seen. Given everything else she had experienced, it would not surprise her if the few gray hairs she knew had set in had all disappeared as well. She inspected her hands and the lines on them seemed to have disappeared.

They did not look nearly as old as she had seen them looking over the last several years.

"You can't possibly be more than two or three and twenty," he said, confused. "And I would venture to believe even that unlikely."

She laughed, not about to tell him she was twice that. Instead, she said, "Well, I certainly appreciate the compliment. But, as I said, I'm much older than I look."

"Yet you don't know the difference between a wagon and a cart, nor have you ever been near a horse? You certainly are an enigma."

She smiled at what she considered a compliment and said, "Thank you."

He laughed despite himself and shook his head.

Chapter 15

July 1, 1756

They departed early the next morning. As they were getting ready to leave, Isaac came over to where Ellie was standing.

"'Twould be my honor to offer me horse for the journey." he said. Having earned it in battle, it was part of the 'spoils of war' that the soldiers in that time were entitled to as part of their pay. Ellie was surprised by the generous offer but declined.

"You'll be certain? 'Tis a long journey, it is."

Ellie briefly looked at Thomas, who had been standing beside her, then asked, "And what will you do without your horse?"

"I'll march, I will," he said simply.

"Thank you, no. I'll be fine walking," she said, smiling at him and his kind gesture.

Isaac shrugged and headed towards his horse. Having remained quiet throughout the exchange, Thomas spoke up now. "It truly is a long journey. You may wish to reconsider his offer."

Ellie laughed. "And just what am I going to do on a horse I don't know how to ride? The first rabbit he sees, I'll be bucked off. Either that or when everyone else turns left, I'll probably end up going right. Nope. I'm good. I'm not afraid of a little walking. How far is it anyway?"

The corners of Thomas's mouth lifted in humor. "Fifty miles."

"And how many days do they expect it to take?" she asked, confident in her ability to cover the mileage with no problems.

"Three days or thereabouts. It may be done in two, but this rain will slow us down."

That made Ellie feel significantly better. She was not afraid of walking fifty miles. In fact, she relished it, greatly looking forward to the journey. Her concern had only been for the pace, having been afraid she would not be able to keep up. But she had always loved hiking and it was not uncommon for her to do fifteen- or twenty-mile hikes a couple times a year. Fifty miles over three days was completely doable. She wondered how much longer it would continue to rain. With the exception of a few breaks here and there, it had not stopped for about five days. As much as she loved the rain, it was the one part of the journey to which she was not looking forward.

The narrow dirt road followed the Hudson River and was surrounded by thick forest on both sides. The river peeked through in some spots while the trees completely obscured it in others. This was essentially the same path the train followed from New York City north in her own time. She had taken that train with Kristy and Lisa past Albany and down to the city then back again at the beginning of their vacation. It was difficult for Ellie to reconcile the two paths as being the same place. She never thought she could imagine a New York that looked like this.

Ellie enjoyed the journey to Albany. They left bright and early on Thursday at five in the morning, going steady all day and making it to Saratoga by nightfall. The pace was not grueling but walking through the mud started to be cumbersome after the first few miles. She tread carefully at first but quickly gave up. By the end of the night, the mud had caked onto the bottom few inches of her skirts, making her wish she had some pants. She was glad she had at least traded for the moccasins. There was no way she could have done this in the other shoes.

Their party consisted of twenty wagons and carts and a company of fifty soldiers including the company captain; a subaltern, which she had learned was the same as a second lieutenant; two sergeants; and eight militiamen. The officers on horseback took the lead, followed by the provincial soldiers who marched two abreast. The wagons and carts came next, followed by the colonel's wife and about a dozen servants and retainers to do the cleaning, laundry, and cooking. The militia brought up the rear to guard their backs with those on horses at the very rear.

The twenty wounded men were placed inside two covered wagons that reminded Ellie of the pioneers. She learned it was called a Conestoga wagon. The cover would keep the rain off of them and keep them as comfortable as possible during the journey. Ellie followed directly behind the colonel's wife, so she was closer to the injured men if she was needed.

Though she expected the sexism, she was still annoyed to learn she was considered part of the bag-
gage. However, it was some small consolation that
the colonel's wife was even considered as such. She
had joined them to make her way back to Albany.
Mrs. Whiting had only been visiting the fort but now
she was headed someplace safer. Ellie was excited to
see how she rode in that odd side-saddle. It looked
horribly uncomfortable, and Ellie still could not see
how the woman could control her horse on it. As far
as Ellie could tell, it did not matter at the pace they
were going. She supposed it would not have been
proper for a lady to ride any faster than that anyway.

Mrs. Whiting was the only woman on horseback
while all of the other women were expected to walk.
There were only four of them and occasionally, one
of them or the other retainers would try to climb
onto one of the wagons to avoid walking but was always caught and reprimanded. Thomas had been alternating between riding in one of the wagons with
the injured men and occasionally marching alongside
his charges. Going where he was needed, he would
only call her forward if she was needed as well. He
had offered her a place in one of the wagons with the
wounded men in order to keep an eye on them, but
she declined, not wanting to take up the space, nor
be seen as being given special treatment. There was
already talk about her and the captain and she did not
need to add any more fuel to that fire. When he said
that she was not directly needed inside the wagon,
she decided to walk.

In addition to stops to pull carts or wagons out
of the mud or doing other repairs, they stopped every
five miles or so for rest breaks and Thomas and Isaac
always came to check on her. Each of them repeated

their offers of the horse or the wagon and she thanked them but declined. Ellie found the journey to be more meditative than her yoga and tai chi. With her walking in the middle of the train between her two friends, she did not get to pass the time talking with them and did not really converse much with the others near her in the convoy. Instead, she used the time to consider her situation for the millionth time.

With no idea if she would ever make it home, she wanted to be able to survive for however long she would be stuck there. She had already made every effort to learn everything she could and vowed to continue doing so, not wanting to be with the army any longer than necessary. Knowing women there were second-class citizens, subservient to men regardless of where they were, she also knew military life. Regardless of the century, some things never changed, and the male-dominated culture was always worse in military units than in the civilian world. She may stand half a chance if she could break away from the military. Not to mention, Fort Edward would only be there for a few more years. She could not remember when it was torn down, but she thought it was sometime during the Revolution. That was another thing to consider. Twenty years could go by in a flash, and she needed to figure out what she was going to do if she was still there that long. There was a lot for her to figure out. If she was stuck there, she wanted to be able to stand on her own.

Figuring out her living situation and how to survive in that world was only part of what occupied Ellie's mind. She also found herself thinking back over the last several years of her life. As far as Ellie was concerned, she was not married there; therefore, she was single. Living as an unmarried woman these last two weeks had been amazing. Despite the highly restrictive overreach of being attached to the military, Ellie found the freedom of not being married intoxicating. She used to love being on the marine corps base as a teenage girl. Flirting with all of the marines and getting attention from them was like an addiction. The adults around her all thought she was going to end up as a teenage mother, but she never did more than flirt. She knew she could not behave that way there, nor did she feel a need to. Instead, she found herself doing the opposite, and staying to herself, avoiding attention. With her luck, she would somehow be married off without her consent to some knuckle-dragger who thought she was his slave. No, she would keep her head down as long as she was there. But she would also use the time to figure out who she was.

Ellie had lived so long for other people, she needed to figure out what she wanted. Was she still the free-spirited stripper with pink hair who did whatever she wanted? Was she the academic nerd who had obtained five college degrees? Was she the morbid, conservative morgue technician who followed all of the rules? Was she a medic, whose purpose in life was to help others? Or was she something else entirely? Would she leave Johnny if she ever returned home? Did she want a divorce? Did she ever want to be married again, whether it was there or in her own time? Ellie knew she could confidently say the answer to the last question was a resounding 'No,' but she decided to take the time to figure out the rest, even if it took her months to figure out.

While she knew definitively that she no longer wanted to be married, she had never been able to find a way to go through with it. Even in the worst moments, her guilt kicked in, reminding her that Johnny was the way he was because of her. How could she walk away and simply move on while he suffered, unable to provide for himself?

Most of the road was enclosed on both sides with trees. Ellie loved being in nature this thick. Living in Utah, she missed the forests that closed a city in like this. Utah had a few trees here and there, but it was a desert. The trees were mostly in the mountains, and they were nowhere near this dense. Of course, even the cities in which she grew up in the south did not have forests like this. Perhaps two hundred years before she lived there they did, but in her time, the forests did not compare to these. Often closing her eyes on the journey to take in the quiet and the fresh air, she held onto one of the carts for guidance and walked with her eyes closed as far as she could go. The sounds of the convoy varied as people were often more talkative sometimes than they were at other times. There were also the sounds of the horses and the wagon train adding to it. But it was still nothing compared to the constant electronic and vehicular sounds that barraged her in her own time.

The second day of their journey started much later. It had been surprising how quickly the camp had been set up the night before. These men were an efficient machine. With only four women on the journey, Ellie shared a tent with all of them. The colonel's wife was the only woman who did not have to stay with everyone else, though even she had a lady's maid with whom she shared with.

Though setting up was quick, it took longer to tear down and get back on the road again. The rain was coming down in a heavy downpour, and they tried to wait out the worst of it. Ellie kept her eyes on the storm, but there was still no lightning any-where near them. They finally got back onto the road and made it to the halfway point by sunset.

As they walked that day, the other women and retainers often engaged her in conversation. Ellie was not rude and always joined in as long as was polite, though she tried keeping them talking so she did not have to, asking them questions about themselves so they felt compelled to continue talking. They stopped in Stillwater for the night and set out early again the next morning.

On the third day of their journey, Thomas had a patient with which he needed help. Ellie had helped care for the men every time they took a rest stop, helping them walk if they were able to stand, making sure they had food and drink, changing dressings as needed, and making them as comfortable as possible. When they departed camp that morning, Thomas asked her to walk with him to keep an eye on one of the men who was not doing as well. Worried that they would need to do her CPR on the man and not yet confident he would be able to do it correctly, he wanted her there with him if it was necessary.

After spending less time together on the journey than he had become accustomed to, Thomas wanted to hear her voice but Ellie was quiet while they walked. It did not even matter what they spoke about, he just wanted to hear her.

"Pray tell, Miss Ellie. How is it we conclude every night covered in mud to our knees, yet you start every morning with clean skirts?"

Ellie looked down at her feet. "I wash every night in the river."

She said it as if it was no big deal, but no one else was doing that. Even the colonel's wife had mud on her skirts that had not been washed since they left.

"Every night? And they dry by the morning?"

"Not even remotely," she laughed. "But I figure I'm going to be wet anyways from the rain, so what difference does it make?"

"Why clean them nightly then if you know they will only get muddy again in the morning?"

"Because I can't stand being dirty. There's no point in bathing myself every night just to put dirty clothes back on."

Thomas was not expecting that answer. He tried not to think about her bathing herself and instead asked something that had been bothering him, though he was hesitant to ask. "Every night? Do you not believe excessive bathing to be opening yourself up to infection and illness?"

"Quite the opposite. Cleanliness keeps infection and illness away."

Seeing the doubt on Thomas's handsome face, she went on to explain germ theory to him, enjoying having these discussions. He was like a sponge, soaking up everything she had to teach him. He asked questions to better understand the concepts she told him about and even shared his own experiences and viewpoints on things. The time flew by.

As they walked, Thomas kept an eye on his patient, who was not doing well, checking the man's pulse regularly. When his eyes rolled back in his head and he became quite pale, Thomas looked closely but could not see his chest rise and fall. He jumped up on the wagon and checked the man's pulse once again. When he found none, he called the convoy to a halt. He held out a hand to quickly help Ellie up and she guided him through the chest compressions, telling him where to hold his hands and how fast to go. After she counted thirty chest compressions, she had him stop and administer two breaths while she checked his clammy skin for a pulse. She took the next round of compressions, but Thomas again administered the breaths. Propriety was not his only concern this time, though he would use that as an excuse had he needed one. He simply did not want to see her lips over another man's mouth for any reason. When he took over the next round of compressions, the man finally gasped a breath and opened his eyes. Thomas looked over at Ellie and saw that her smile was as big as his felt. He got so tired of losing patients. It felt amazing to save someone's life for a change.

When they looked up, they saw they had drawn quite an audience. Everyone was looking on in amazement. The company captain asked if they needed any assistance. When they replied in the negative, he ordered the convoy to continue.

Isaac was by the side of the wagon telling Ellie how impressive that was. She shrugged and said, "Thanks."

Ellie jumped off the wagon as it started rolling forward. A confused Thomas told her she had earned a ride for a while. Smiling up at him, she said, "I've walked this far. I'm not going to miss out on the last few miles."

Once again, he was in awe of her mettle and humility.

After the next rest, Thomas again walked beside Ellie, keeping her near the wagon in case she was needed. His patient was sleeping and there was nothing more Thomas could do for him at that moment but he still used the man as an excuse to keep her close. She was quiet again. When the rain started lightly drizzling once more, she turned her beautiful face up towards it, placing her hand on the side of the wagon and closing her eyes. It was impossible to keep his eyes off of her. When she was about to step in a puddle, he took her other hand and placed it on his arm, guiding her away from the puddle. She opened her eyes and looked at him in surprise but when she realized what he was doing, she simply smiled at him and closed her eyes again, enjoying the feel of the rain on her face. It was a simple pleasure, but the joy on her face filled his heart.

The journey was slow, the road little more than a dirt path cut out from the trees. It was not even graded and was incredibly uneven, making it all too easy to twist an ankle. With rain or snow, the road became even more difficult and potentially treacherous to pass. Wagons and carts got stuck, which not only left ruts behind but took time to dig out. Once the wagon or cart was dug out, it often needed a wheel or axle replaced after breaking in the process. What would only take an hour in her time took them three days to accomplish.

They finally made it to Albany by nightfall, stopping at the hospital first to unload their wounded men. Part of their party left to find quarters for them all, while another part escorted the colonel's wife to her residence in the city. Ellie helped unload the injured men and escort them into the hospital. It was a two-story building shaped like an 'H' with a large, covered veranda supported by columns in front. It contained forty wards which could hold up to five hundred patients along with storage rooms and rooms for surgeons and other officers. Ellie was impressed by the size of it, though it was small by comparison to buildings at home. She was well-traveled and had seen plenty of buildings from the Revolutionary Era in Boston, Philadelphia, and Virginia, but they were all small compared to this. Those buildings were all statehouses or churches, not a hospital. The governor's mansion in Williamsburg was also large, but it was elaborate. This was purely functional. She wanted to explore it, going room by room to get a feel for how they lived and worked in this time. How was a hospital run in this era?

"Have you never seen a building such as this before, Mrs. Sorenson?" Thomas asked while watching her take in every detail.

Ellie had no idea how to answer that. Instead, she responded, "It's beautiful."

By the time they got everything unloaded, it was late. It had been a long day and Ellie was tired. Looking forward to sleeping that night, she wondered where they would set up camp for the next few days.

They headed back out on the road again and to Ellie's surprise, they ended their journey at a farmhouse. Most of the men went towards the barn and the field where the tents were already set up. The officers went towards the house. Ellie started heading towards the tents when Thomas called out to her. Catching up to her, he took her by the arm, escorting her to the house, leaving her rather confused.

"I've made arrangements for you to stay inside with the officers. It shall be cleaner and perhaps your skirts will be dry in the morning."

Ellie wanted to cry at the thoughtful gesture. It was so simple, but it was the sweetest thing anyone had done for her in a long time. She gladly accepted the room offered to her. To her shock, she even got the room to herself and did not have to share with anyone. The introvert in her had been slowly dying since she had been there. This space to herself was more than she ever could have hoped for. It was heaven.

July 4, 1756

The next day was Sunday, July 4. Ellie was not sure how to feel about that. At that point in history, it was just another day. While she had never been particularly patriotic, being there on the eve of the nation's birth felt strange. She was suddenly homesick, though she did not miss her husband, her job, or the overpopulated cities. Nor did she miss the constant barrage of electronics and technology. However, Ellie did miss certain modern conveniences like music on demand, a washing machine and dryer, a shower with hot running water, and indoor plumbing in general, and she missed some of her family. But she could not quite put her finger on exactly what else it was she missed. Perhaps it was simply a general feeling of knowing what to expect, the comfort of understanding her place in the world, the security of having a successful career and a home. Everything there was something new. She was constantly guessing as to whether she was doing things correctly or what was going to happen next.

She had to police her words and continuously ask for explanations. It was all exhausting.

Given that it was Sunday, they had been granted a day of rest. Ellie had nowhere she needed to be and nothing she needed to do. Between the introspection over the last three days, and the reminder that she was very far from home today, she was grateful for the rest.

She wanted solitude.

She wanted to explore the city.

She wanted to stay curled up in the bed and ignore everyone and everything.

The latter won for the first few hours of the day, but she could only hide out for so long. Thomas came to check on her when she had not come down for breakfast, wanting to make sure she was not sick. Ellie thanked him, reassured him that she was fine, and sent him on his way. Next, Isaac came up looking for her. She did the same to him. She tried crawling back into bed but quickly began to feel restless. It was almost midday and she had not slept this late in two weeks, usually being up at the crack of dawn every day when reveille was called at the fort.

Taking her time dressing, she examined herself in the mirror that hung on the wall in the bedroom, much like she had after the accident with Lucas. It was the first one she had seen since her arrival in the past. The sight of her reflection shocked her. Though she knew she had lost a lot of weight, seeing how much she had lost was more surprising than she would have expected. It was not so much that she looked sick. Quite the contrary, she looked healthier than she had in years, all of the excess weight having melted off of her, leaving her as thin as when she had been dancing. Her weight was not the only shock.

When Thomas had said he had not seen any gray hairs, he had not been kidding. She could not find any herself. It was not only her hair either. The fine lines and wrinkles were all gone and she looked at least twenty years younger than she actually was. It immediately reminded her of Lucas telling her that he was older than he looked when she had met him. She had always looked younger than her years as well, but never by this much. The appearance of her age seemed to have reversed itself and she somehow looked and felt healthier than she ever had.

Shaking off the strangeness of her appearance, she finally dressed and slowly made her way down the stairs. Isaac and Thomas had heard her stir and were both at the bottom of the stairs waiting for her. They each wanted to escort her wherever she wanted to go. They were so sweet; how could she refuse them?

Ellie let the men escort her around the city together. She was in awe of Albany. It was shocking to see the size of it. The men took her awe as being due to never having seen a city this large, but it was anything but by her standards. She had heard someone at the hospital tell them that Albany was normally a sprawling city of seventy-five acres with about 335 households, but there was currently estimated to be an additional four thousand soldiers, Natives, and refugees there. As they walked the 'city' streets, Ellie noted the muddy roads with pigs and cows everywhere. She had seen rural towns larger than this.

It had been as shocking to see very little else along the way. In her time, New York was one enormous city melded into the next all the way along the Hudson River. However, they had passed very little in the three days it took to get there. She really was not in Kansas anymore. The thought made her want to cry. No one there would even get that reference, which made her feel even more alone. Ellie closed her eyes, fighting back the tears. They had been roaming the city for hours and Isaac had stopped to talk with one of the other soldiers they had run into. Thomas asked her something, but she did not hear him. She was desperately trying to not lose control.

Thomas repeated himself. "Have you been to Albany before?"

Ellie took a deep breath before answering. "No."

It was not true. She had flown into Albany and driven up to Lisa's house from there, but she could not say that. Ellie consoled herself with the fact that she had never been to *this* Albany, so it was not entirely a lie.

Thomas could see the unease on her face and the tears she was fighting to hold back. Was she lying to him about having been there before? She seemed to take in everything they passed as if she were seeing it for the first time, yet how could this place have this kind of effect on her if she had not been there before? Was this where she came from? Was she running away from someone there? Maybe he was wrong. Maybe her mood was for another reason.

"Does something ail you, my dear?" he asked gently.

"Only everything," she whispered, turning her head away as a tear slipped out and rolled down her cheek. She really was there, stuck in the past.

"What was that?" he asked. He knew she was avoiding looking at him and it irked him.

Ellie shook herself and replied, "Nothing. Doesn't matter."

Her eyes brimmed with the tears she was trying to hold back, and he reached over and put his hand on her shoulder, stopping their stroll. He turned her and placed both hands on her shoulders, so she had to face him. To his great annoyance, she still avoided his gaze, looking everywhere but at him.

"Miss Ellie, I hope you know that you may speak freely with me."

Ellie closed her eyes. If she lost control now, she would never regain it. Taking a deep breath before opening them again, she looked up at Thomas, her gray-blue eyes moist. He was a full foot taller than her, so she had to arch her head a little to see him while he was that close.

"I know, Thomas. Thank you. I'm fine, really."

She knew he did not believe her for a minute, but she did not care, briefly patting his hand on her shoulder for reassurance. Before he could push further Isaac had rejoined them, informing them he would be on guard duty that night at the farmhouse, so he was going to head back. Not wanting to be alone with Thomas, she suggested they all go back. She was afraid if she was alone with him, she might just share her secret with him. He was far too kind to her to resist opening up to him much longer, though she feared the consequences of doing so. He had already made it clear he would not believe such a concept as time travel. They listened to Isaac talk the whole way back, leaving Ellie grateful she did not have to say much.

Initially glad to have been going back to the farmhouse, once there, she found herself restless once again and did not want to be in the same room as Thomas. Due to 'propriety,' there was always someone else in the room with them. This helped keep Ellie from telling him where she came from, but there was a tension there that she could not shake. Excusing herself, she went to her room where she paced across the floor, her reflection in the mirror mocking her as if to reinforce her new situation.

She wanted to cry.

She wanted to scream.

She wanted to hit something.

When she no longer trusted herself to not start throwing things, she decided to go for a walk. Ellie knew she would not be allowed to go on her own, so she quietly snuck out. The last thing she needed right then was company. She needed some space.

Wandering aimlessly through the streets, Ellie wondered if she would ever get home. She tried to clear her head of everything that was on her mind and focus solely on breathing. It was dark before she started feeling a modicum of control again and began returning to the farmhouse. The control was tenuous, but it was better than it had been all day.

As Ellie walked, she heard someone behind her. She had never been paranoid before but had always tried to be aware of her surroundings and take necessary precautions to stay safe. Having walked the streets of New York City and Philadelphia alone in her own time, she had never had any issues. But, she had also seen enough throughout her career to know what could happen to a woman on her own and picked up her pace a little to determine if the footsteps she heard would follow suit. When they did, she walked a little faster and tried to look for a tavern or someplace that she could either lose them or hide out until they passed.

Unfortunately, she was surrounded by houses and not in a part of town that had anything open to the public. For a moment, she considered approaching one and knocking on the door but then decided against it. That could potentially have worse consequences. She would keep that as a last resort if she needed it.

The streets were so much darker there than anywhere she had ever lived before. The moon was almost full, which helped, but only a little. It sounded like the footsteps were getting closer. She tried to make out how many there were and counted at least two sets but could not tell where they were. Ellie looked over her shoulder when she turned a corner but could not see anything. Her nerves were starting to get the better of her now. Trying to rationalize the sounds, she told herself it was only a couple people heading home. But then, why were they keeping pace with her?

As quickly as they began, the footsteps stopped, and Ellie breathed a little easier; until two men came out from behind a building, stepping in front of her, blocking her path.

Trying to sound as calm and confident as she could muster, she said, "Good evening, gentlemen," while simultaneously trying to go around them, on her way. She tried to make it clear she was not interested in whatever they had to offer. One of them grabbed her arm, preventing her from leaving. Ellie tried not to show the panic she felt inside, refusing to be a victim. She looked at his hand on her arm then lifted her chin and said with as much confidence and authority as she could muster, "I'm due back at my quarters with the army. I appreciate your offer of an escort, but I'm fine. I really must be going."

The man sneered at her but before he could do anything else, she heard another voice behind her say sweetly, "There you are, darling. I told you not to go on without me."

Ellie turned to see Thomas walking up, glaring at the man with his hand on her arm. It was enough for the man to release her, though her would-be attackers internally debated whether they could take this newcomer. Thomas was not in uniform but stood tall with his hand on the sword he still wore at his side, waiting for them to do something. They must have decided she was not worth the risk and started leaving.

Grabbing her arm where the other man had released it, Thomas started walking forward angrily with her in tow. He had not said a word to her but looked ahead while dragging her along. Ellie was not about to be manhandled by him after having just faced off two real threats. Shaking off his hand, she stopped in her tracks. He immediately stopped with her and turned on her.

"What, pray, are you doing walking around the city alone at night?" he spat.

"I'm sorry. I didn't realize I needed an armed guard," she said sarcastically.

Thomas snarled, "Well you do. It's not safe for a lady to be out after dark on her own."

Ellie scoffed. She was not some fragile flower. While she had not known exactly what she would have done had Thomas not interfered with the plans of those two men, she knew she would have handled it. She would have fought them if she had to. It may not have ended well for her, but she would not have let them off easily.

Walking past him, she continued on her own towards the farmhouse. Thomas followed closely behind. She was grateful to him for getting rid of those men, but she was pissed that he needed to do it to begin with. Already feeling trapped and helpless about being there, now she was upset that Thomas was treating her as though she was helpless to look out for herself.

Ellie was used to doing things on her own. She had moved out of her parents' house when she was seventeen and had been on her own since. In the early years, she had her husband to help her out. Since his brain injury, that had changed. Over the previous several years, she had gotten very little help from him. When they traveled together, he would throw temper tantrums if he did not get his way. He was completely inflexible and could not handle the slightest change in schedule. And he spent the entire time generally hating the existence of every other human around him. Subsequently, she had long since stopped traveling with him.

Ellie had become extremely independent over the last two decades and she resented having to rely on others now. She depended on them for money, food, and shelter, which was bad enough, but now she could not even walk down a street on her own. This fueled her anger, and she lashed out at Thomas.

"What are you even doing here anyway?" As soon as she asked the question, it occurred to her that he was never far away. "In fact, why is it you're always there?"

He became indignant, and answered, "It's a good thing I was."

Ellie narrowed her eyes at him. It did not escape her that he did not answer the question. "Are you spying on me?"

Instead of answering, Thomas looked guilty. She turned on him now, jabbing a finger into his substantial chest. "You are, aren't you? How dare you? Have you been spying on me this whole time? Is that why you join me for tai chi? Have you just been pretending to be my friend this whole time?"

The emotions Ellie thought she had under control were now a raging hurricane tearing through her.

"Miss Ellie, that is not the case." Thomas felt guilty knowing that it had started out that way, with him spying on her, but it had quickly turned into something else. Now he found he craved her company. Anytime she was not around, she consumed his thoughts and he could not wait to be in her presence again. He could not tell her this, though. "You showed up as if from nowhere with no family, no home, and nothing to indicate who you are. I've a responsibility to ensure you are not a spy or something otherwise detrimental to the army."

"A spy?!" Ellie was incredulous. "I thought we already had this conversation. You actually think I'm a spy? How the hell would I be a spy? I don't know a single person on this goddamn earth other than you and the people at the fort. Who exactly am I supposed to be spying for?" She shoved at him, but he was so solid that he barely budged.

"I don't believe you to be a spy." He tried taking her hands in his, but she pulled away. "Yet I also have a responsibility to ensure your safety and that your," he paused, looking uncomfortable, "behavior is appropriate while you're attached to the army. I spoke for you to the colonel; therefore, the responsibility falls to me."

It was not the whole truth, though he did fear for her safety and felt a need to protect her. But it was more than that. What he could not say was that he could not get enough of her. He craved her voice, her thoughts and opinions, her touch. In no time at all, she had somehow managed to affect him in a way no one ever had. He was not sure what it was, but until he figured it out, he wanted her near him, and he wanted her safe.

"You are unbelievable!" she screamed at him. "I can see to my own safety and as for my 'behavior,' don't you worry about that." Ellie narrowed her eyes and said calmly, "My plan is to bed every soldier at the fort and I'm making my way around the camp, but I'll eventually get to you."

Ellie said the words ever so sweetly, while dripping with sarcasm, yet they still stung. Thomas was not sure why the thought of her in bed with anyone else rankled, particularly when he knew it to not be true, but it did. As much as her anger at him did. He suspected there was something else bothering her, but she would not say what it was. He wished she would trust him and share her burdens with him. Perhaps he could help.

Before he could respond to her scathing remarks, Ellie picked up her pace as she had only moments before. Thomas easily kept up with her. She continued walking increasingly faster until she was outright running, holding her skirts in both hands, lifting them almost to her knees. The exertion felt good. She had been tired all day from the journey but her encounter with the men followed by the argument with Thomas left her with some excess adrenaline she needed to burn off. Not surprisingly, Thomas kept up with her the entire time. By the time they reached the farmhouse, Isaac, who was standing guard, stood tall, on alert.

He stopped them, asking, "What's happened? Is all well?"

Their urgency had him looking behind them to see who or what was pursuing them. For some reason, this struck Ellie as funny, and she burst out into laughter. The men looked at her as though she had lost her mind, which she was beginning to think was a distinct possibility. Her usually nonexistent emotions were now all over the place. She was brimming with so many that it was almost overwhelming. If she did not laugh, she would start crying and would not be able to stop. Apparently, her laughter was contagious because Thomas suddenly began laughing with her. Isaac was visibly confused as he watched them laugh uncontrollably.

When Ellie slowly regained her composure, she told Isaac, "Sorry. No. Everything's fine."

Thomas sobered up as well and he and Isaac both looked at her questioningly. "I just needed to burn off some energy," she said.

Ellie turned to walk back to the house, bidding the confused men behind her a good night. She left Thomas where he was, knowing she was headed for a good breakdown soon, but for now, she needed to control her emotions. It would not do to have a meltdown in front of everyone there.

Chapter 17

July 7, 1756

They spent the next two days in Albany, loading supplies and getting ready to travel back to the fort. Thomas was weary and kept his distance from Ellie, though he remained close enough to keep an eye on her. He did not know what was really bothering her, nor how to fix it. He had tried apologizing the morning after they argued, but she was not receptive to it. After that, he thought it best to give her some time, though he did not like seeing her like that. It pained him that she was angry with him. Worse, he hated that he had hurt her and hoped that she would eventually come around.

They left Albany on Wednesday. The rain had continued, and the journey back was even slower than the journey out. The roads were horrendous. They constantly had to stop and dig the wagons out of the mud. Every step felt like twenty-pound weights had been strapped to Ellie's ankles as her feet stuck in the thick, wet mud. The return trip was nowhere near as enjoyable as the trip out had been.

The rain was heavier than it had been as well, but still no lightning. On the trip out, they mostly encountered light drizzles with bouts of sunshine to break it up. This time, it was a relatively steady downpour. Ellie's numerous skirts were additional weights, threatening to pull her down. Part of her wanted to be swallowed up by the mud and the puddles once and for all. She did not even try to wash her clothes every night this time. After spending her days completely soaked and muddy, it seemed pointless. She settled for washing herself and rinsing off the excess mud from her clothes when she could.

Her only condolence was that the weather matched her mood. Despite the added difficulties, Ellie wanted it to continue pouring down on her, not wanting to feel like this on a beautiful sunny day. Preferring to wallow in her misery, the rain complemented her mood perfectly. She avoided Thomas as much as she could, but in such a small party, it was difficult to do so. Isaac continued to sidle up to her every chance he got but she was never good company. The way she was acting towards him made her feel guilty, but she could not make herself do anything differently. She would apologize to him later.

They arrived in Stillwater at sunset on Saturday and would stay there near the small Fort Lyman and rest Sunday. They always took Sunday as a day of rest whenever possible. It was nice, but she missed the three-day weekends she had gotten used to in Utah.

Though Ellie wanted to stay inside the tent all day and keep dry, with three other women in there with her, there was no peace. Her social battery had long since been depleted and she could not deal with the other women. The rain had finally eased up to a light drizzle and she wandered out. Ellie had seen the copious amounts of pine gum resin on the trees surrounding them on the journey out and had wanted to collect some to make a salve. It was one more of the natural remedies she used to make at home in her own time. She always kept some on hand and knew it would be far better than what they currently used in the hospital, which was typically nothing at all.

Ellie had waited for the return trip to collect the pine gum so she would not have to transport it both ways. After looking for a container she could collect it in, she went in search of what she could salvage. There was a large amount on the trees near the fort, but she was constantly being warned to not wander off. *With Thomas watching my every move, he would probably stop me before I could even make it to the tree line*, she thought bitterly.

"The ruffmans are full of savages, they are, miss. You ought not wander off by yourself," Isaac called to her as she got to the edge of camp with her bucket.

"I'm not going far, Isaac. I'm only gathering pine gum from the trees around us."

"Supposin' I could attend you then," he replied, reaching for the bucket.

While holding the bucket underneath her against the tree as she scraped the residue, Isaac hesitantly asked, "Miss, did Captain Burke wrong you in Albany?"

Ellie was confused. He could be referring to anything. She continued scraping resin into the bucket and innocently asked, "Wrong me?"

Isaac put the bucket down and faced her. "Only, did he hurt you or... or violate your honor?"

Stopping what she was doing, she asked, "Why on earth would you think that, Isaac?"

"I seen the way you be together. I watched you the whole of the way to Albany. Only since we left there, you barely said any words to him a'tall. I know 'tain't none of my business, but if he did wrong by you, I would defend your honor, I would."

Ellie put her hand on his arm. "You're so sweet, Isaac. Thank you. I assure you nothing like that happened. I just have a lot on my mind, and the captain..." How did she explain it? "Well, I just need some space from the captain right now."

Isaac nodded before working up the courage to say the next words. He looked at his feet and said, "I know he would be a proper good match for you, only I would make a good husband, too. Me family has more than three hundred acres of land, and we bring in corn, wheat, squash, and beans and aside from cattle, we've chickens, Cornish hens, and turkey. I would be kind to you, Miss Ellie. I would hold affection for you, always, I would."

"Oh, Isaac." Ellie's heart softened, knowing the kid had a crush on her. It had taken her a while to see it, but once Mrs. Gibbons had pointed it out, it became obvious. She had assumed it would run its course. Apparently, this was the course. She needed to nip it in the bud before it got any worse.

"I do appreciate your offer, and I'm very fond of you, but I can't marry anyone right now. You still have plenty of time to find someone better suited to you; maybe someone who hasn't already been married and broken."

She hated rejecting the poor kid, but it was better than leading him on.

"I pay deference to your opinion, miss" he said, nodding dejectedly.

"But Isaac, I would very much like it if we could still be friends." He looked doubtful for a moment, and she added, "I'm afraid I don't have very many of those at the moment, and I would be very sad to think that I've lost your friendship."

Isaac perked up at that, feeling like he was still important to her. Accepting her offer, they continued their foraging, filling the bucket in no time at all. Without much human interference with nature, there was an excessive amount of pine gum available. Ellie took the bucket back to their cart and found a spot for it while Isaac went back towards the center of camp.

When she turned to go back to her tent, she heard the screams. One of the women was dropping to her knees after having the top of her head removed. The Native American who took her scalp cried out in triumph and held it up like a trophy while the rest of his party came out of the trees to wreak havoc on the camp. The scene before her was complete chaos. People were running everywhere. Soldiers were shooting their muskets and drawing their swords while the Natives stabbed, shot arrows, and fired guns. They scalped when they could and whooped and hollered all the while.

Ellie frantically searched for Thomas and Isaac but could not find either of them. Against her better judgment, she ran into the fray, trying to find them. She immediately started questioning why she did not stay at the cart and hide underneath it. But she could not bear the thought of anything happening to Thomas after the way she had left things. When a soldier fell at her feet with half of his head gone, she bent and picked up his sword. She had no idea how to use it properly, but she would figure it out. She knew which end went into the other person and decided in that moment that was all she needed to know. Ellie continued searching desperately until she saw Isaac in a fight with a Native American. Isaac was fierce and killed the man quickly and effectively before moving onto the next one.

Another Native American was trying to take one of the women and Ellie ran towards them. The man saw her approach with the sword in her hand and laughed at her. He actually laughed at her. That was all it took to fuel the rage that had been burning within her for days and she thrust the sword at him. Forgetting the other woman, he sidestepped her attempts a few times with another laugh, as though it were a game. Each time, his laughter burned through her. After a few minutes of playing with her, he lunged at her, easily removing the sword from her hands and grabbing her. He was behind her now, holding her against his body with his arm around her neck, slowly choking her while grabbing her hair. She knew she was about to be scalped. He had dropped the sword and instead held a large knife in his hand, placing it against her forehead.

Thomas watched from across the glen as Ellie was held against the chest of a savage, a knife to her forehead and he knew what was coming next. He could not bear to watch yet could not look away. Screaming her name did nothing as it would not carry over the noise of the battle. He fought to make his way to her before it was too late.

As the blood from the initial cut trickled down toward Ellie's eyes, she got a surge of adrenaline and stomped her heel down hard onto the center of the Native's foot while lowering her arm with her fisted hand, aiming for his groin. It was enough to get him to release her, and she grabbed the knife, wrestling it away from him. She had grabbed it by the blade as he had a firm hold on the handle. It sliced deep into her hand, but she did not care, barely even feeling the pain through the adrenaline. When she finally got control of the knife, she did not hesitate. Swinging her arm upwards, she shoved the knife into his solar plexus as hard as she could. When she made contact, she buried the knife deep, shoving it in as far as it would go. As he fell to his knees, she pulled the knife out and thrust it back in again and again, falling along with him. Ellie continued stabbing him, releasing all of her pent-up frustrations and anger until she felt someone grab her hands. Her head immediately jerked up to see this new threat, ready to attack. When she saw it was Thomas, she dropped the knife and leaned into him as he wrapped his arms around her.

The relief that flowed through Thomas that Ellie was unharmed knocked him to his knees. He pulled her to him and held her for a moment, whispering words of comfort. He was not certain if the words were meant to soothe her or him, but they flowed forth anyways. Wrapping himself around her, he protected her from the raiding party who were now beginning to flee. When he gathered his senses, he stood, pulling her up with him, lifting her into his arms. Breathing her in as if she was the very air he needed to survive, he could smell her citrus and honey scent over the smell of the blood and carnage around them. He carried her away from the chaos as the last of the raiding party ran off into the woods. Thomas took Ellie to the cart holding all of their new medical supplies from Albany. As they reached the cart, she climbed out of his arms before he could set her down. She looked down and he was immediately hurt that she still could not look at him.

Ellie took a moment to compose herself before turning back to Thomas. Looking up at him with her eyes red and brimming with tears, she softly said, "Thank you."

It was not much, but it was all she could muster. She was grateful he had tried to get to her and that he now tried to make her feel safe, but she had just killed someone. Ellie was not the helpless woman he thought her to be and she did not want to encourage him in thinking that she was. Biting back the tears that were threatening to spill, she looked at her hand. It would need wrapping along with her head and she wanted to do so before tending to the numerous injured that would be waiting for them both. If she did not take care of herself, she could not take care of anyone else. Ellie started reaching for the dressings and other medical supplies but Thomas stopped her, pulling out a cloth himself and wiping at her hand, removing the blood. When he cleared off enough of the blood to see her skin underneath, there was barely a scratch. She knew she grabbed the knife hard enough that it sliced her open, but her hand only looked as though she got into a fight with a cat. The wound was only surface deep. While she examined her hand, Thomas took the cloth to her forehead.

When he wiped away the blood, he said, "He must have not cut you. I saw the blood and thought him to have done so, which gave me such a fright. It must have only been blood that was already on his knife."

Ellie's hand flew up to her forehead, where she felt nothing but smooth skin and sticky blood. She nodded numbly. This was like all of the other injuries she had received since being in New York with her cousin. "We better go help the injured."

They grabbed some supplies and made their way back to their party and started working through the injured and dead. It took hours to see to everyone. Thankfully, those who survived the attack had only relatively minor injuries. No one needed an amputation or major surgery.

The party stayed there overnight as the soldiers at the fort were now on higher alert after running out to assist and chase off the Natives. If they were willing to attack them that close to a fort, they would attack anywhere. Though they were still safer staying near the extra soldiers. They posted extra guards regardless but no one in camp slept. They were all eager to be on their way in the morning and left as soon as it was light out. It took another two days to reach Fort Edward. It had been a somber two days. By Tuesday evening, they were all more than ready to be there. Ellie helped unload everything for the hospital and headed back to her tent with few words to anyone.

July 14, 1756

Thomas watched Ellie for two days after they returned from Albany, walking around as though she was barely there. She was a ghost. His heart broke for her. Talking to her did little good as she barely responded. It was not only him, either. She conversed with people only as much as she needed and usually let them do all the talking. She rarely laughed and did not even fight back when Gideon said something that he knew upset her. Thomas missed the spirited Ellie he had come to know. What had happened in Albany to result in this? Surely it was not merely their argument or the attack from the Indian war party. She had been upset even before then. He hoped she would come back to them soon.

It was not only Thomas who noticed the change. Everyone else in the hospital commented on it as well. Abigail Gibbons asked what had happened on the journey. When Ellie told her nothing, she asked Captain Burke. He told her of the raid, but nothing else. Everyone at the fort already knew of the raid but the rest was not his story to tell, even if he knew what it was.

Ellie's tent mates even asked after her. No one seemed to get through to her. If Ellie was being honest, she could not get through to herself. Reflecting back on everything that had happened recently, she realized it had been less than a month since she left Utah. In that time, she had possibly died or came close to it three times, been in two battles, and killed a person. She had seen more than her share of death over the course of her career and had even watched people die before. But none had died by her hand. None had been trying to kill her. She was not sure what to do with that. This never would have happened in her own time. She suddenly had the urge to get home now more than ever.

While the other nurses discussed who would replace the woman that had been killed in Stillwater, Gideon said something snarky about women not belonging there. Ellie did not even have the energy to argue with him.

Mrs. Gibbons tried to cheer her up. "The sutler shall be able to get the tallow you be looking for in order to make your pine gum salve. It shan't be cheap, only supposin' you could split the cost over a few weeks 'twere it necessary."

Nodding noncommittally, she responded, "I still have most of last week's pay and the bounty from the colonel for staying on here."

When Gideon heard her, he began laughing. "The colonel ought never have approved a bounty for you, you bottle-headed bunter. Women do not receive bounties from the army. Those be for the men."

Ellie was momentarily confused by what he said as well as his obvious insult. The insult would have to wait. She had more pressing things on her mind.

"Where did it come from?" she demanded.

Without saying a word, Gideon Anwar looked over at Thomas who was across the room attending a patient. Ellie was immediately pissed. She had been squirreling away as much money as she could in the hopes to be able to leave at some point. With no way to lock anything up and not trusting other people in the camp, she had been carrying all of her money in her pockets. Finding a corner, she pulled it all out and counted out a week's worth of pay, leaving her with almost nothing but that did not matter now.

Storming over to Thomas who was now at his desk, Ellie slammed the coins down on the desktop and yelled at him, "I don't want your pity or your charity!"

It was Thomas's turn to be confused, but when he saw the smug, self-satisfied look on Gideon's face, he knew this was his doing. He watched Ellie walk out of the hospital and considered chasing after her but decided against it. The entire staff was watching the scene unfold as were the patients, and he tried instead to retain his composure. He put the coins in his pocket and resumed his work, deciding to deal with Gideon later.

July 17, 1756

Saturday afternoon, Ellie was going through the motions in the hospital when she heard the thunder pick up again. She had gotten used to listening for it, but this time she could tell it was close and continued listening for a while as it got louder and louder. Other people inside the hospital had now begun to take notice as well. People outside were bustling about, trying to take cover. Isaac came in to check on Ellie, saying that the storm was almost directly overhead.

When Ellie asked him how bad it was, he said, "They spotted lightning from the ramparts a-moving near to the fort and everyone is ordered indoors."

Ellie's eyes got big as the thought rolled through her head. She was out the door before she even knew what she was doing. Isaac called after her, but she ignored him. She was running, trying to find the most open patch of ground that would not be under surveillance from the soldiers around the garrison. If she had to go outside the fort, she would. With any luck, she would not be there long. Wishing she had a lightning rod of some sort or at least a kite and a key, Ellie looked to the sky, trying to see where the lightning was striking. When she made it down the road a little way, she looked up to the sky and stretched out her arms. She yelled and screamed at the sky, "Here I am! Come on! Take me home!"

The thunder boomed and the lightning rolled across the sky, lighting up the entire area, but it never reached the ground. While she waited for the next round, someone grabbed her from behind, wrapping her up small and lifting her off her feet, carrying her back towards the fort. Struggling to get away, she thrashed around and kicked her feet. When one made contact with a shin, she heard a man yell out, "Damn it, Ellie, hold still."

Thomas Burke. Of course. She should have known. He set her down when they reached the casement inside the fort, sheltered from the storm. Ellie immediately turned to face him and kicked him in the other shin on purpose. He hopped on one foot while she turned around to go back outside. Regaining his footing, he caught her quickly and held her to him tightly, her back to his chest, her arms locked at her sides. She struggled to get away, screaming at him to let her go.

"Do you endeavor to get yourself killed?" he yelled.

"I'm already dead," she responded.

Ellie could hear the thunder moving off into the distance as she was held captive, unable to reach it. She collapsed then, becoming dead weight in his arms, pulling him down with her. There was no way she could hold the tears back this time. On her knees, she curled in on herself and bawled with her face in her hands. Feeling Thomas moving behind her, he pulled her into his arms like a small child and held her while sitting on the soaking wet ground. He wiped at the rivulets of water falling onto her face from her drenched hair, letting her cry while he held her and kissed the top of her head.

As her tears slowly abated, Thomas whispered soothing words to her. She was mumbling now, and try as he might, he could not make out her words. He lifted her chin to look into her face and she quickly looked away. There was no anger there. What he saw instead was despair, heartache, and shame. He did not understand any of it.

"Speak to me, darling, please," he begged.

She shook her head, and said, "I'm never going home."

"How could a thunderstorm help you get home?"

Ellie continued shaking her head. Thomas could see her starting to close off again and kept pushing. "Miss Ellie why were you standing in the storm? Was it your aim to attract the lightning to you?"

"It doesn't matter."

When she tried standing up to leave, he knew he was losing her again. Pulling her back down, he placed his hands on either side of her wet face, forcing her to look at him. He hated seeing her in such despair and wanted nothing more than to see her blue eyes light up again.

"It matters a good deal, Miss Ellie. Why do you wish to be struck by lightning? What vexes you so? Do you know what shall happen if it hits you?"

Barking out a bitter laugh, Ellie broke free from his hands. "I have absolutely no idea, but I have a sneaking suspicion. It doesn't matter anyway. I'm never going home. I'm stuck here forever. Destined to be half a person. Some subservient, obedient woman who has no rights, no autonomy, nothing. My family is gone. My home is gone. My career is gone. My rights. Gone. Everything. Gone. My entire fucking life. Gone."

Feeling sorry for herself, Ellie was ranting now. The words did not matter. Nothing would change, but she needed to vent. She had been locking everything up since she got there, and her dam had finally broken. The words poured out of her as the rain poured from the sky. Thomas sat patiently with her and let her get everything out. He did not run from her emotions like she would have expected a man from this time to do. He merely listened, asking questions when she paused, though she still had no answers. Her emotions swung like a pendulum from despair to anger and back to despair again. When she finally felt like she got everything out, she was exhausted. Ellie took a deep breath and slowly exhaled. As the breath left her, she looked up at him and had the sudden realization that she had taken this man on her emotional rollercoaster and unloaded on him after making him drag her sorry ass out of the pouring rain. She was mortified.

Thomas saw the moment she released everything and suddenly became embarrassed at having shared so much with him. She need not have been. He was still as much in the dark as he ever was with no idea where she came from or what her life had been up until she arrived there. All he knew was that she had lost everything, felt trapped there, and somehow thought a lightning storm would take her home again. When she began apologizing for 'dumping all this on him,' he stopped her.

"You need not apologize, my dear. I told you I'm here if you wished to talk. It is clear you needed to do so. I regret being unable to do more. But Miss Ellie, you really shan't make a habit of running forth into a lightning storm. I know not what you thought to happen, but lightning is made up of something called electricity and it's quite dangerous."

When Ellie looked at him blankly, he continued, "A man in Philadelphia, a scientist, only recently discovered that lightning is made up of this electric fire and it is rather powerful. Powerful enough to kill."

Unsure of what else to say to Ellie, Thomas thought to fall back on something educational as so much of their relationship had been built upon the exchange of knowledge.

Ellie could not help the laughter that erupted from her lips. "Electric fire? You did not just try to mansplain Benjamin Franklin, lightning, and *electricity* to me."

Thomas was thoroughly confused both by her laughter and her words. She had heard of Mr. Franklin? Ellie stood while trying to bring her laughter under control. When she stretched out her hand to help Thomas up, he grudgingly accepted it, if only to prolong contact with her.

The laughter having brought in fresh tears, Ellie wiped at her eyes. She slapped Thomas on the chest and said, "Thanks. I needed that laugh."

Turning to leave a thoroughly confused Thomas, Ellie turned back around while she sobered up. Hesitantly placing her hand back on his chest, tenderly this time, she focused her gaze at his collar, unable to meet his eyes.

"Thank you for being here," she said softly.

He put his hand over hers, then used the other to tilt her chin up until he could look down into her beautiful eyes. "I am your obedient servant, Miss Ellie, and it was my most sincere pleasure."

A small thrill rolled through her and her heart immediately started racing. Ellie left before she did something stupid, like throwing herself at him. As she walked back to her tent, she told herself he was only a friend, despite his latest actions and despite the way he looked at her. There was no way there could ever be anything more. He really was from Mars and herself from Venus. There were simply too many differences between them, even if he was interested, which he most certainly was not. Isaac Huntington, sure. Not Thomas Burke. Nope. He was only being a gentleman, who perhaps felt some sense of responsibility for her.

July 29, 1756

"Women ought to be at home, not with the army, you bunter."

Having started feeling more and more like herself again, and slowly beginning to accept her situation, Ellie's disposition improved over the next few days, but of course it would not last; not with Gideon Anwar around. It was only a matter of time before they started arguing again.

She had little patience with him anymore. "If I could teleport my happy ass home, I would in a heartbeat!" she yelled at him and stormed off.

Thomas heard the shouting and watched the display before finishing up the returns on which he was working. Hating all of the record-keeping and numbers he had to turn in regularly, he would have preferred nothing more than to work exclusively on his patients and learn more about medicine. As soon as he finished his paperwork, he went in search of Ellie. Finding her down by the river, he sat down next to her. They sat in silence for a few minutes until he finally nudged her with his shoulder.

"You have a happy ass?" he asked teasingly.

He meant to cheer her up, but it was not working. "It's just an expression."

"I thought as much. But tell me, what was that other thing you said? Tell a port?"

She almost smiled at his mispronunciation, but instead, she corrected him. "Teleport. It's a make-believe thing that doesn't exist. It transports something from one place to another instantly. Then again, maybe it does exist. Maybe that's how I got here to begin with."

Ellie thought back to the lightning again, knowing it had to have had something to do with how she ended up there, though it did not make any sense. People were struck by lightning all the time and never traveled through time. As far as she knew anyway. Maybe it was magic. At least her Lichtenberg figures had stayed on her arm. She had come to like them even more than she had initially. They would always be with her, a physical reminder of the event that changed her life.

"What's a bunter?" she asked, changing the subject. Thomas cocked his head in question and she explained. "Gideon called me that before. I get that it's an insult of some sort, but what does it mean?"

Reluctant to tell her, Thomas sighed. "It's a person who's part beggar, part prostitute. I shall speak with Gideon and ensure he does not use such language in front of you again."

To his surprise, instead of getting upset, Ellie laughed. "Wow. Okay. That's… that's something. I guess from his point of view, that's probably an apt description for me. I mean, with no money, home, or family, I'm essentially a beggar and I imagine he probably thinks all women are prostitutes."

"You are undoubtedly anything but," Thomas said firmly. "Neither a beggar nor a prostitute, I'll not have him saying such things of you."

Placing a hand on his knee, Ellie gave him a small smile. "It's alright, Thomas. It doesn't matter what he thinks."

Thomas searched her eyes for a moment before she turned away, looking back to the water, taking her hand with her. He immediately missed the warmth of it. They again sat in companionable silence for a while.

Thinking about her situation constantly since Albany, Ellie decided if she was going to be stuck there, she may as well make the most of it. She took this opportunity to ask him, "Will you teach me to ride a horse?"

"It would be my most sincere pleasure."

"Sweet." She immediately laughed at his puzzled expression, then decided to push her luck, "What about a gun? Would you teach me how to use one?"

Thomas was not as quick to agree this time. "You wish to learn to shoot a firearm?

"I know how to shoot a 'firearm,'" she said with air quotes, which were obviously only for her benefit. "What I want to know is how a musket works."

"You know how to shoot a firearm but know not how a musket works?" he repeated, not understanding her.

"Exactly. I've shot plenty of guns before. Just nothing like these ones you have. These are entirely different from what I'm used to. I have no idea how to load them. And I'm guessing shooting them is completely different without rifling in the barrel, but I'm sure that'll just take practice."

"You are quite a mystery, madam."

July 29, 1756

Ellie had finally accepted the fact that she may be there for the long term and tried to make the best of it, learning everything she could about life and medicine in the eighteenth century. While being as frugal as she could with her money, she purchased the tallow she needed for the salve and soap, along with baking soda for deodorant and dry shampoo, and hemp oil for lotions and conditioner. It took some doing to figure out what oils were available, and that baking soda was only referred to as sodium bicarbonate, but she eventually got what she needed. It did not even cost her as much as she had expected as she was able to barter for part of it with one of her remaining bracelets. She was also getting better at learning the economic side of life there.

At that time, soap was typically made using tallow and wood ash, but it was harsh, making it one more reason people did not apply soap to their skin to bathe. The washer women often had red, irritated hands from the harsh soaps they used all day. Thanks to her experimentations in her own time and a desire to learn how to do things from scratch, Ellie had already been familiar with making soap using wood ash in lieu of store-bought lye which was unavailable in colonial times. It had taken a lot of practice to get it right and she had thrown away many batches before perfecting her technique, but eventually she was able to make soap using traditional methods that was not harsh on the skin and was not too soft to hold its form. This was the most useful knowledge she had come to the past with and had never been more grateful for her hobbies and desire to not take shortcuts.

Ellie spent her Sundays doing laundry and making her various soaps and salves. This also gave her more commodities to trade for other items she might need. When she was not working on her chores, she was with Thomas, learning what she could about riding a horse and loading a musket. Unable to shoot one since there were restrictions about firing guns anywhere near the fort, she settled for learning how to load it. Since she carried a handgun on her regularly at home and practiced with it often, she was not as concerned about practicing with this one but would make do with learning to operate it. She did not have her own musket to carry anyway. It was simply a precaution in case she found herself in another situation like the one at Stillwater where she might be able to pick up a musket from someone who fell and use it.

Thomas taught Ellie to ride using his own horse, Boreas. He went slow with her until she was comfortable, then gradually picked up speed. There was not a lot of room to run around the encampment, but they did short bursts and went out on the roadway whenever they could, which was not often. Bands of French and Native American raiders still roamed the area, killing soldiers or taking them prisoner as close as half a mile from the fort. Though they were limited to where they could ride, Ellie found she rather enjoyed riding a horse. However, it made her miss her motorcycle.

Along with riding the horse, Thomas taught Ellie how to care for one. She had noticed that he was often at the stables, mucking the stall or feeding and brushing Boreas down whenever possible. He was a beautiful chestnut quarter horse with black socks fading above the knees and black mane and tail. Thomas's pride in Boreas was obvious. There were other people assigned to the tasks, but he did them himself as often as he could. If he was not at the stables or in the hospital, he was often seen chopping wood or teaching swordplay to Private Simms. He was always doing something. Ellie realized that was how he managed to keep his physique. When she asked him about it, he simply said he preferred to stay busy.

Ellie also enjoyed the simplicity of life there. In reality, it was anything but simple, though it was how she thought of it all. It was long, hard days filled with manual labor and no weekends. Labor laws were still nonexistent. There were no five-day work weeks or eight-hour workdays; no holidays, weekends, or overtime. They often worked when necessary, sometimes getting days off only sporadically. They did try to take off Sundays whenever possible though, since most were rather religious. But under the circumstances, it did not always happen.

Yet, with no electronics or internet or social media, people actually conversed with one another.

Everyone seemed to know everyone and there was a sense of community, even if there was still a lot of infighting. She hated the class system, slavery, and all of the restrictions and proprieties she was expected to follow as a woman, but she tended to ignore most of those. Never having been one to concern herself with what others thought of her, she was certainly not about to start now. Ellie was friendly enough to everyone around her and treated them all equally, regardless of rank, social status, or skin color. Well, that was not entirely true. She still struggled with Gideon Anwar and had a difficult time with the people she encountered who owned slaves. Ellie tried to avoid spending any time around those individuals if she could help it.

Her fair and equal treatment of people did not go unnoticed. After prioritizing several soldiers according to the severity of their injuries rather than rank or skin color, Thomas decided to have a word with Ellie. The officers had complained about not being treated first and it was his responsibility to run the hospital accordingly. He approached Ellie by the fire while she was heating a pot of water which held a tin bowl filled with what looked like tree bark and plant debris in a yellowish-brown liquid. As he leaned in for a closer look, the pine scent filled his nose.

"Is that pine pitch?"

"It is. I'm just rendering it down to clean it."

"Are you making turpentine?"

Ellie looked at Thomas with a question. "Turpentine? I didn't know you could make that from pine gum."

Thomas nodded, but asked, "How else would it be made?"

Ellie wanted to say, *With a bunch of chemicals,* but she held her tongue and shrugged instead as she set up an earthenware crock with a thin piece of linen over the top. Letting the fabric hang loosely inside the crock with the edges flowing out over the lip and down the sides, she gathered the fabric inside a cord and tied it around the neck of the crock, securing the fabric in place as best she could.

"If not turpentine, what are you making? Are you looking to make something watertight or perhaps grease some axels?"

He was trying to make her smile with the last suggestion, and it worked. Ellie's mouth turned up in a grin as she told him, "I'm making a salve."

"With pine pitch?" Thomas asked in surprise.

"You've never used it for that? It's a great antimicrobial and antiseptic. Works fabulously on burns, too."

"Anti-what?"

Ellie heaved a sigh, trying to figure out how to best explain it. "You remember what I told you of germ theory?" Thomas nodded and she continued, "Antimicrobial and antiseptic substances help kill those microorganisms. They help treat and prevent infectious diseases."

"Pine pitch can do that?" he asked skeptically.

Ellie nodded. "You should see what I can do with a beehive. Combining everything inside the hive makes for some of the best salve ever." At his unconvinced expression, she added, "Just believe me when I say it's got really good healing properties."

Thomas did not hesitate. "I do believe you. I'm merely surprised. However, I shall look forward to using it."

Looking up from stirring her resin, Ellie saw the faith and trust in his eyes. Her chest warmed and she could not help the smile that spread across her lips.

Thomas hated that the conversation he was about to have with her was going to remove that beautiful smile from her lips, but it needed to be done. He started to inform her that she needed to treat officers before treating anyone else, but then he stopped as he considered her.

"You regard everyone the same, do you not?" he asked, already knowing the answer. He had noticed it but had not considered it before now.

"Why wouldn't I?" she asked as if there was no alternative.

"What I mean is that you seem unbothered by a man's rank or station. You treat slaves and servants the same as officers and pay no heed to whether someone is your better or is inferior to you."

She shrugged. "Better? Inferior? No. I believe in equality. I try to live by the Golden Rule: Do unto others as you'd have done to you. If I wouldn't like being treated a certain way, I would never treat anyone else that way."

"Equality? The Golden Rule? Are you Quaker? New Light Presbyterian?"

Thomas latched onto this as it could potentially give him a clue as to where she came from. The Quakers had settled in Pennsylvania and the New Light Presbyterians were a new sect of Presbyterianism that had recently split during the Great Awakening of the previous decades. The sect had started in New Jersey and slowly spread across New England and into the middling and southern colonies, though it was still predominantly in New Jersey. He had only heard of it from one of the officers from the New

Jersey Regiment. The other captain had thought them absurd, explaining to Thomas that the foundation of their religion was that all souls were equal in the eyes of God regardless of rank or position.

With the pine gum fully liquid after more than an hour of slowly melting, it was time to strain it. Grabbing a pair of tongs, she pulled the tin out of the water-filled pot and set it down briefly on the table next to the crock in order to dry off the excess water from the pot so that it would not drip inside the pine gum while she poured it out. After drying it off, she slowly poured the hot liquid into the linen draped over the crock. Thomas carefully grabbed the sides of the crock, holding it steady and keeping the excess linen in place for her while she worked.

"I don't do religion," she said in answer to his question.

"No, I don't imagine you do," he replied. "Though those are both rather Quaker ways of thinking." He thought about the interactions he had observed. "I'd nearly venture to say slaves and servants fare slightly better from you than do officers. Surely, you don't think them to be equals or even greater quality to yourself?"

Continuing her pouring, Ellie went slow so as to not overfill the linen or slosh the hot liquid over the sides. Once it was fully strained, she would add the sheep tallow she had obtained in order to make it more spreadable and keep it from going back to a solid.

"I don't know much about Quakerism but we're all human. I'm not going to treat anyone differently simply based on skin color or their lot in life. No one is better than me and I'm no better than anyone else.

Okay, except maybe Anwar. I'm pretty certain I'm better than him," she joked.

Thomas chuckled. "You don't believe even rank has any bearing on a person's standing?"

Ellie considered this. "I used to," she replied slowly. "I used to respect a person's rank even if I couldn't respect the person, but that was a different situation. I find it much more difficult to respect it here in this army where rank is purchased, not earned. It's not given based on merit, but rather how much money a person has. And money has no bearing on a person's character or their merit. I'm not interested in how much money a person has, only what kind of person they are."

Thomas looked thoughtful, as though he was considering her words before responding. Ellie thought he was trying to choose them carefully so as not to offend her.

"I know that's like blasphemy around here," she added. "You probably think I'm ridiculous." Ellie looked up to see him watching her face instead of what she was doing.

"Not at all." Thomas shook his head, once again forgetting about his primary purpose in having this chat with her. She was always surprising him, giving him a great deal to consider, often making him see things in a new light. "I think it makes you rather remarkable."

By the end of July, word had finally reached the fort that war had officially been declared in England on the eighteenth of May. Ellie had not been sure when it had officially started when she arrived and had thought it long since underway. Surprised by how long it took for word to reach them, she knew it had a long way to come and would be slow but did not realize it would take over two months.

Isaac continued coming around as often as he could, remaining friendly with Ellie, but his eye had turned to the young Miss Woodford as Ellie had intended. Patti was a much more suitable match for him than she could ever be. Aside from the massive age difference, he was very much a man of his time. He was a farmer with no education and had no aspirations of learning about anything other than what affected his life directly. He did not understand intellectual pursuits and never would have understood Ellie's ideals and beliefs. Patti was much more suited for life on a farm.

Everyone who saw her and Thomas together over these last few weeks came to the same conclusion: the entire fort assumed they were having an affair. Thomas struggled with many of Ellie's beliefs but was always open to listening to what she had to say. Even if he did not agree with them, he enjoyed hearing her different perspectives. She challenged him and everything he believed, and he enjoyed the challenge. He had learned so much from her that she even had him bathing daily. He had always considered himself to have had good hygienic habits, but he now began adding soap to his daily washing, being far more thorough than he ever had before. Her germ theory had Thomas wanting to implement several changes within the hospital as well. Unfortunately, they were all met with resistance and when he tried to push for them, his relationship with Ellie was called into question. Knowing what everyone at the fort was saying about them, he tried to be proper and maintain a distance, but Ellie drew him in to her. He simply could not stay away. And propriety was something she understood but preferred not to practice. Her informalities only drew him to her more.

Of course, the rumors about her and Thomas were only that. While Ellie did not care about how they impacted her, she worried about his reputation. Though, she knew as the woman, it was her reputation that would take the hit, which was fine with her. She ignored them and let Thomas deal with them in whatever way he saw fit for himself.

While part of Ellie certainly would have enjoyed it if the rumors were true, she was not ready to be in a relationship of any kind. Twenty-seven years was a long time to have been married. Even if the previous fifteen had been more like having a roommate, there was still a lot to process and get over. Ellie had mourned her marriage years ago, but she needed to learn to be on her own now. Getting married at seventeen meant she had gone straight from her parents' house to being married. She had never lived completely on her own or been responsible solely for herself. While she was not technically living on her own now, she was not in a relationship, and she needed to sit with that for a while and get used to it before she jumped into another one. And as much as she liked Thomas, he was so young.

She had learned that he was only twenty-six and though she often forgot about the age difference, every so often it would pop up. He was not sure what he wanted out of life any more than she did, though he insisted he was not looking for a wife and that the army preferred their men to remain unmarried. But then he would make comments about how great it would be to have children. She could tell he longed for a family but maybe was not quite ready for one yet. It did not matter. Children were not something she could give him. Even if she was open to a relationship, there was another small matter of not knowing how long she would even be there. While she had reconciled herself to being there for the long term, she had no idea if that would actually be the case. For all she knew, she could leave tomorrow, and that would not be fair to Thomas. Part of her half-expected to suddenly leave anytime and every day she wondered if today would be the day.

Chapter 20

August 25, 1756

Living through the covid pandemic and even working in the New York City morgue at the height of death running rampant through the city did not prepare Ellie for the sickness that spread through the fort that August. Summer was winding down, though it was still warm, and people started getting sick.

Troops were constantly coming and going from the fort. It was usually a stop along the way to another location. The Rangers and a handful of other regiments were the only steady faces Ellie saw. Most of the ones she saw were strangers. Combined with the hygiene practices of the day, it was no wonder illness spread like wildfire. Another surgeon arrived in mid-July alongside several hundred more troops. Each regiment brought surgeons and surgeon's mates with them when they passed through, and the extra help was always appreciated, though it was typically short-lived. As much as Ellie hated the idea of having to deal with another version of Gideon

Anwar, she was even more grateful for the extra help this time as the hospital quickly filled up. Surgeon Thomas Williams was nowhere near as crotchety as Gideon, but also nowhere near as open-minded as Captain Burke.

Construction continued on the fort, and they had finally moved into the new hospital building which was built over the existing one. The new one now sat in a building which ran along the length of the wall parallel to the Hudson River. The building was two stories and housed barracks on one end and the hospital on the other end, which would hold one hundred men. It would not be enough.

When the first man came with a fever in July, Ellie had not been as concerned as everyone else had been. She knew that there were a lot of fatal diseases in this period which started with a fever, but it was still hard to be concerned over a fever, which was not typically fatal in her time. The next man with a fever to come in was examined by Ellie as the other surgeons and surgeon's mates were all busy. He mentioned he had been having soreness in his mouth and Ellie had him open it to examine him. When he opened his mouth, she could see the red spots on his tongue, some of them beginning to break open. Ellie had never seen anything like that before so she waited for the doctors to finish their other duties and isolated the man as best she could. There was another right behind him. This one had the sores inside the mouth, but they had begun spreading to the rest of his face as well. She put the men together away from other patients and had the captain examine them as soon as he came back. His concern was immediate as he pulled her away from the patients.

"Miss Ellie, have you touched either of these men?"

"Yes," she replied, not understanding why he was frantic. He was immediately crestfallen but recovered quickly.

"These men have smallpox," he said.

"Okay," Ellie said slowly. She needed a minute to process this.

Thomas misread her and assumed she had never heard of the disease. He began explaining how deadly it was and she did not interrupt him. Though she had heard of it, she knew very little about it. The bulk of what she knew about smallpox was that it had killed off massive numbers of Native Americans once European settlers arrived on the continent. The disease had not been in North America prior to that and had come over with the European settlers. It had been transferred to Native Americans when they came in contact with the settlers and on occasion through infected blankets and other items. It had been eradicated sometime shortly before she was born, and they did not even vaccinate for it anymore in her time.

They quickly set about quarantining the men and asking about who they had been in contact with over the last few days. They tried to isolate those men as well, but it was too late. The disease had already begun to spread through the camp. It was not only at the fort, either. By the end of July, smallpox had spread throughout the entire army across New York. There were reports from the other garrisons across the colony in the same situation. They estimated that in an army of approximately six thousand, there were as many as fifteen hundred infected. Connecticut was sending another eight hundred troops for reinforcements. With it being so prevalent, it even spread into the civilian population.

Thomas had been concerned that Ellie would develop small pox and she was concerned for him. When he first explained the disease to her, she went back to the hospital supplies and pulled out some of the cloth they used for bandages. She began cutting and sewing masks for the hospital staff. If covid had taught her anything, it was how to properly make masks. Ellie tried to pass them out to anyone who wanted one, but they all laughed at her. Thomas accepted one gladly as did Patti and Mrs. Gibbons, but that was it. Everyone else declined them. Together, they tried to ensure everyone was properly washing their hands and not touching their faces, but again, to no avail.

The sick kept coming. They opened up a small-pox hospital tent near Ellie's part of the encampment and it was full in no time. Throughout the first three weeks of August, the transmission rate remained steady. They did not see an increase in the numbers of infected, nor did they see a decrease, averaging two deaths a day. However, by the following week, the death rate jumped to five or six a day.

Soldiers were being taken from other duties to help bury the dead. Ellie was again put in mind of her time in New York City. She had been part of a federal response team that deployed on mass fatality incidents to help manage the deceased. When covid overran the city and the dead started piling up, they activated her team and she spent six weeks in a temporary morgue in Brooklyn, taking in dead bodies alongside the National Guard. The rest of the world was in lockdown, but Ellie had flown across the country to assist in a dire situation. They were taking in about a hundred bodies a day, but it did not compare to this. In Brooklyn, the bodies came in already enclosed inside body bags. They were empty shells of people whom Ellie had never met. She did not know any of them and it was just a job. This was why Ellie had preferred working with the dead; it was much easier to separate herself from her emotions. She had a strong empathic link with other people, so she typically did what she could to avoid the emotions of others.

Many of the men and women coming in now were people she knew and lived beside. The disease did not only affect the men; it passed to the women and children in the camp as well. One in three infected died from the disease. Ellie would sit with the infected person much like she had for Thaddeus when his leg had been amputated. She offered what care she could provide and when the patients were beyond her care, she sat with them while they passed, offering them any small comfort in their last moments she was able to offer. Though she had not been trained as a counselor, her training in peer support was more than what was available in this era; psychiatry was not even a field of study yet. She used what training she did have to get her through and help those around her. Ellie put her discomfort of other people's emotions aside and tried closing her own emotions off as much she could in order to be there for those people who needed her. When one of the children became infected, she stayed with the girl and held her hand. When the girl passed, Ellie cried.

Thomas hated seeing Ellie distraught over the smallpox deaths. When the child passed, he thought Ellie would leave them as she said she had left medicine once before after the deaths of several children.

He held her when she cried for the child, but there was little else he could do for her.

Ellie felt that she finally understood what the doctors and nurses around the world felt during covid. There were so many people dying and there was nothing she could do to help. Smallpox would eventually be eradicated, and medicines developed to fight it, but that did her no good there. Ellie did not take days off. She was in the hospital every day alongside Thomas and the others. They did what they could for these people to ease their suffering, but there was little to be done. There was a hopelessness that she could not shake. It would continue for months.

In mid-August, the provincial army was sent home, the Regulars were ordered into winter quarters, and the Rangers were ordered to return to Fort Edward. Abigail Gibbons, Isaac Huntington, and Patti Woodford had all left with the militia, and none were planning on returning for the following year's campaign season. For a time, Ellie was not certain what would happen to her with the fort going into winter quarters. Mrs. Gibbons and Isaac had both offered to take her with them to their homes, but it was not what she wanted. She was not yet ready to leave the fort. Thomas petitioned for her to stay on, but with the rumors, it was thought he only wanted her to stay as his mistress. When Surgeon Williams supported her staying, saying she had been invaluable thus far in dealing with the outbreak and her further help would be necessary, Major Sparks, who had recently taken over command of the fort did not hesitate to allow her to stay. Ellie was not sure what she would have done had she been ordered out, and was more than happy to stay, even with the outbreak.

"Isn't there a vaccine for smallpox?" Ellie asked after another man died from the disease. She remembered something about George Washington ordering all his troops to get it during the Revolution. Maybe it had not yet been developed.

"Vaccine?" Thomas asked.

When Thomas did not understand her, she remembered they did not call them vaccines yet. Ellie had to think about it and corrected herself. "Inoculation."

Thomas nodded in understanding. "There is. I spoke with Major Sparks about it only last week. I fear he does not wish us to inoculate anyone."

Ellie was aghast. If they had it, why would they not use it? How many lives would it save? She thought back to covid when the vaccines first came out and how many people had declined them, and she understood. No. Not understood, but she could relate. She argued against the decision anyway.

"If it stops the illness and saves lives, why not do it?"

Thomas sighed. He was tired. He had argued the same thing for inoculating the men. "The men would become sick and be bedridden for weeks. We are ill-prepared to handle the extra strain it would cause, leaving us in the most disagreeable circumstances."

Ellie thought it a weak excuse.

By early September, many of the men who remained began to desert. Sick men tried to leave and orders were issued forbidding them to do so. Surgeon Williams eventually adopted the mask as well, believing the illness to be due to bad air. He argued that if the sick were allowed to go to good air, they would surely survive. Ellie knew he was on the right path, but for the wrong reasons. However, when he said that the sickness was because the people were sinful and it would abate if people repented and reformed, she lost faith that he could be educated on the matter. She also wondered if he was referring to the rumors about her and Thomas. The thought that their alleged behavior could somehow bring on a plague that killed hundreds of people across the state made her laugh. It was the only spot of humor she had seen in weeks, so she held onto it.

Thomas began lacking energy and attributed it to the long hours, filled with hopelessness. He was glad when a majority of their hospital staff went home, as it would be less people to become ill, but he was not looking forward to having less help. He had fought to keep Ellie there, though he was not certain it was the best thing for her. Part of him wanted to send her far away so she did not catch this awful disease and part of him did not want to see her go. He had come to rely on her opinion as much as he enjoyed her company. If anything happened to her, he would never forgive himself, but she wanted to stay so he had petitioned for her to do so. He was rather surprised when Surgeon Williams argued in her favor as well. But the weeks had been hard and there was no end in sight. Thomas wanted nothing more than to rest.

Ellie could spot the early signs of the illness by now. Noticing Thomas rubbing his head more frequently to ward off headaches while moving more slowly and sitting more frequently as if he did not have the ability to keep going had her concerned. Initially, she thought it was the weight of the disease spreading through the fort as it had weighed on her, but this was different. When he started having chills and began vomiting, she knew he had contracted it.

Knowing the rate of death, she immediately became more frightened. Ellie ordered him to bed immediately. Thomas tried to argue with her over it, but she was having none of it. She told him he could either convalesce in his quarters or in the hospital; it was his choice, but he would be going to bed if she had to take him there herself.

Surgeon Williams backed Ellie's assessment of Thomas's health and he and Javon Simms helped him to his quarters. As an officer, he had a private room so he could isolate himself in there without risking spreading the disease further. Thomas tried to forbid Ellie from coming near him, but the stubborn woman would not listen, insisting on checking on him regularly and seeing to his needs. The fever lasted several days, even after the sores began to form. When they did, Thomas tried again to keep Ellie away. He was not a vain man, but he did not want her to see him like that. His face and body were covered in the pus-filled blisters so characteristic of the illness. There were times when he thought he was going to die and times when he wished he would. It was a horrendous disease. Ellie continued to attend him in between all of her other duties in the hospital. Having already had smallpox as a child, his servant assisted in caring for Thomas, but Ellie still insisted on tending to him herself, resulting in her and Javon alternating duties. She sent him to help in the hospital when she was with Thomas where he could help multiple people. Assisting Thomas not only helped reassure Ellie that he was still breathing, but it gave her a much-needed respite from the hospital. She sat by his bedside, holding his hand, wiping his brow with a wet cloth, and reading to him. Thomas constantly worried she would be next to fall ill. Ellie

wished she had gloves and a full Tyvek suit but settled for continuing to wear her mask. It was not
much, but it was better than nothing.

It had been awkward to hold Thomas's hand. Or
anyone else's for that matter. When Thaddeus had
grabbed her hand all those months ago, it had felt
incredibly awkward. Holding hands was not something Ellie did with people. She was not a very physically affectionate person, preferring to only have
physical contact with those closest to her. Even then,
she rarely ever held hands. She could kiss or have
casual sex with others but would not hold their
hands. It was far too intimate to her.

While kissing and sex could both be purely physical with no meaning behind them, holding someone's hand always had meaning. There was an underlying emotional connection with holding hands, even
with a stranger. The only exception she could think
of was to take someone's hand in order to physically
guide them somewhere. But that was not the same as
holding someone's hand on any other occasion.
Since she never guided anyone anywhere, she never
held anyone's hand. The first time one of her boyfriends had tried to hold hers after she began having
sexual relationships outside of her marriage, it had
felt awkward and uncomfortable despite having already been having sex. In that moment, she pulled
her hand away and decided that was where she drew
the line. If someone tried taking her hand, she always
pulled it back. She tried to be discreet or not allow
the opportunity to begin with, to not make it a big
deal, but she always avoided it.

There, in the hospital, she decided that while
holding the hands of the patients communicated an
emotional connection, that connection was one of

comfort, rather than any deeper feelings of intimacy. It still felt awkward to her and she disliked it, but her patients needed that connection in order to heal. She allowed herself this one exception to her rule. Still, it felt different with Thomas, even if she was only doing it because he was sick. She tried to limit the frequency and length of time over which she allowed it to happen.

Ellie had begun removing her rings and bracelets every morning when she arrived in the hospital and put them in her pocket. She normally never took her jewelry off, but without any nitrile or latex gloves, she wanted to minimize the chances of transferring anything from patient to patient. Her jewelry had far too many crevices to hold onto germs and bacteria.

One night, while walking back to her tent after seeing Thomas, she pulled her jewelry out of her pocket and began putting it all back on again. Ellie started mindlessly putting her rings on, looking at each one only enough to determine which finger each went onto. When she looked down at her wedding ring, she hesitated. She held it between two fingers, considering it. She had mourned her marriage years ago when she first realized it was over. As far as she was concerned, she had only still been married on paper. It was no marriage, though. That aside, he was not alive in this time. As long as she continued wearing the ring, she would never be able to move forward. And she desperately wanted to try to move forward, even if it was only temporary. She still had no idea how long she would be there but wanted to use the opportunity to try moving on. Perhaps if she ever found her way home, it would help her find a way free of her marriage if she was already living as a single woman. Sliding the ring back into her pocket, she had no intention of putting it back on ever again.

In mid-September, there was a new threat of an attack on the fort as Marquis de Montcalm's army moved to Crown Point and Ticonderoga. There was concern that Fort Edward would be next. General Loudon had already sent most of the British troops home and now had to amass new ones. He had another three hundred coming to help reinforce the fort. They arrived at the fort, along with additional Native Americans and Generals Abercrombie, Johnson, and Loudon by October 20.

Walking to the well to fill a couple buckets of water, Ellie saw Major Sparks approach. She would have thought he was too busy with all of the generals there and the latest threat to be wandering around. Apparently he needed a distraction from it all.

"Good day to you, Mrs. Sorenson. How do you fare this morning?"

"Good morning, Major. I'm well. And you? You've managed to stay away from the pox thus far. Are you still well?"

The major motioned to his aide who took the full buckets of water from Ellie. She began to protest, but Major Sparks insisted. The aide waited for instructions, then left to take the water back to the hospital, leaving Ellie with the major.

"I am well. Thank you for asking. How does our doctor?"

Ellie let out a deep breath in an attempt to steady herself. Thomas's health showed no signs of improvement, and she felt utterly helpless. She did not share that with the major, wanting to give him a positive report instead. "It's early yet, but I'm confident he'll recover."

Major Sparks nodded. "I am heartily glad to hear this. He could not be in better hands."

"Thank you, sir."

"Thank *you*, madam. Your conduct hitherto has given universal satisfaction. The men speak quite fondly of you."

Ellie's eyes widened in surprise. She thought of Gideon, but the major was obviously not referring to him. "They do?"

"Indeed. You've earned a reputation for being fair, competent, well-versed in medical matters, and having a caring bedside manner. Which is why I would ask you to stay on as matron of the hospital for the next campaign season. You shall receive an increase in pay, and I'll send my man to help you move into one of the closer tents that have been insulated for winter. With the provincials and militia gone for the winter, we shall be consolidating the retainers and taking down any of the remaining excess tents."

"Thank you, sir."

Ellie was surprised by the offer but was also ecstatic. Despite the rumors about her and Thomas, people still gave her credit for her work. It filled her with pride when she desperately needed it after feeling helpless for far too long thanks to this illness taking its toll on them all.

Thomas was still ill with smallpox. It had been over a month, and he was finally beginning to feel slightly better, but only just. As much as he had not wanted Ellie checking on him, he was glad she did. Not only would he have missed her company but seeing her daily helped assure him she was not sick.

The threat from the French passed and they all left by early November, unofficially ending the campaign season. General Loudon pulled the remaining troops from Fort Edward on November 25, officially ending the campaign for 1756. Unfortunately, it did not end the small pox outbreak. Even as the number of troops diminished, the hospitals remained full. The population had shrunk, but people were still sick and dying.

Captain Burke returned to the hospital in November. He was still weak and was limited in how much he could do, but he was out of bed and moving. It was a start. Thomas had worried about coming out of it with disfiguring scars or losing his sight, but he was one of the lucky few. He had minor scarring on his hand, and a small mark here and there, but that was it. Happy to be alive, but more so that he had fared so well, he continued to hope that Ellie would not contract it. Grateful that she had not listened to him and visited him despite him having asked her not to, she had kept his spirits up. It was under her care that he was able to recover at all. She had been crucial in tending the number of sick and more than one had been grateful for her attentions.

Chapter 21

Winter 1756

The winter of 1756 was unlike any winter Ellie had ever experienced. Not only was it the coldest with more snow than she had ever seen, but she spent it living in a tent. With so many troops having been dismissed for the winter, there were far less retainers now as well. Ellie had been moved into her new tent which was closer to the hospital. Her last one had been a mile away, but now she was maybe half that distance. When the cold and snow set in, she appreciated being closer to it, even if only a little. The tents which remained around the fort were covered over with small branches lashed tightly together to help insulate against the cold, though the iciness still permeated them. In some spots, the tents were replaced by huts built in the same fashion. It provided slightly more insulation, but they were reserved for soldiers, not retainers like her.

Having spent a good chunk of her life camping, Ellie knew the canvas she was in now held the heat better than the nylon tents of her time, so she was grateful for that, but it did little to keep out the chill, even after they insulated it. Ellie trudged through the snow to get to the fort and inside the hospital every day. Once she was there, she avoided leaving whenever she could. With the epidemic, it was not difficult to do. She stayed in the hospital for long hours, tending the ill men. It was not uncommon for her to fall asleep at the bedside of one of the men she was tending. She would allow herself whatever time she could get before waking and moving onto the next patient.

It quickly became too cold to wash in the stream and it was not long before the water froze over completely. Both it and the Hudson River had frozen which had surprised Ellie. She never knew that the Hudson actually froze in the winter. It was not only the top layer, either. It was solid enough for the men and horses to walk across to the island. Ice had to be broken down and melted in order to use it.

Her own standard of hygiene became difficult to maintain, though she was more grateful than ever for whatever strange changes had occurred in her body on this journey that prevented any of her body hair from having grown back in. Having waxed prior to her trip with her cousin, she was still as smooth as the day she left the salon, much to her surprise. It was one less thing she had to deal with now in the freezing temperatures. Long gone were the soaks in the river. She took to sponge baths much like everyone else of the era, though she still continued to use soap, unlike them. It was always a cold endeavor, but better than the alternative. Most people there used a rag soaked in warm water scented with herbs to wash their face, neck, and hands. Soap was rarely applied to the body in the manner in which she used it.

To her surprise, Ellie learned quickly that there was a difference between bathing and washing as it applied to the human body. One could wash without bathing and still be just as clean. The body did not need to be fully immersed in water to become clean. The daily sponge baths most relied upon were nearly sufficient. Combined with the shifts worn under the clothes, it was enough. The shifts being linen, they attracted dirt and moisture while also having a slightly exfoliating effect. Changing them out frequently helped remove any sweat that was released, preventing odors from building up. The man-made fabrics so prevalent in the future had the opposite effect, promoting moisture while not being absorbent, resulting in odors. Seeing people changing their underclothes frequently throughout the day had surprised her at first, but she quickly began to understand. Now that she had more than two shifts, Ellie had begun to do the same. She still missed standing under a hot spray of water and soaking her whole body in a shower, but at least she did not feel filthy all the time as she would have expected.

Of course, not everyone changed out their underclothes regularly, some even going several days between changes. This had more to do with economic limitations than anything else. White collars were a sign of prosperity, indicating the owner had the means to change frequently, preventing the collars from becoming dirty and stained.

With so many of the inhabitants of the fort being of the lower classes, they did not all have the means to change out their clothing as often, leaving their sweat to soak into their garments and remain there. The closed quarters smelled all the time and despite the cold, Ellie tried to keep a window open in the hospital whenever possible. Gideon usually came behind her and closed it back up again.

Washing her hair became a weekly task, leaving it as long as she could between washes before she could not stand it any longer. She always washed it in the morning before rushing into the hospital to do work that she knew would require her to stand in front of the fire. The first thing she did on these days was wash and sterilize all of the instruments. Then she would find any medicines that needed to be prepared by being cooked or heated. She never had any difficulty finding enough tasks to keep her in front of the fire until her hair was dry enough to put back into a braid.

In addition to changing her bathing habits, Ellie had to reduce her frequency of clothes washing. She still managed to wash her shifts regularly, but it was a struggle to clean her outer clothes once a week. It helped that with the massive number of smallpox deaths, she had been able to increase her scant wardrobe. Not only did she now have a few more stockings, shifts, stays, and petticoats, but she had a wool coat as well. Thomas had tried to give her one of his, but it drowned her. There were plenty of men smaller than him at the fort who had perished from the disease and she had been able to find one that fit her that was not contaminated with smallpox.

The smallpox outbreak slowed but did not fully go away. Captain Rogers was among those who contracted it in March and was sick for over a month. Like she had with her other patients, Ellie did what she could to make him as comfortable as possible, but it was very little. Though she did not know much of this period, she knew enough to know that Robert Rogers wrote a book on military tactics called *Ranging*

Rules. She had seen copies of the book for sale at the Rogers Island Visitors Center when she had visited it with Lucas, Kristy, and Lisa. He had not yet written the book, which told her he would survive the small-pox. She sat by his bedside whenever she could, fetching him a drink, wiping sweat from his brow, or simply holding his hand.

"You have no idea how important you'll be to the future. Just hang on and get better," she told him when he was fighting the worst of it. He did not re-spond, and she was not certain he even understood or remembered what she had said. It did not matter. It was merely an attempt to keep him fighting and boost his morale.

Ellie did not contract smallpox, though it contin-ued to run its course throughout the army. Many of the other hospital staff contracted it and she contrib-uted her immunity to her new magical death super-powers which was how she thought of her new abil-ities to heal. With Mrs. Gibbons, Patti, and Isaac gone and Thomas in quarantine, Ellie had begun ex-perimenting when she was alone. She would burn or cut herself to see if the different types of injuries all healed and how long they would each take to heal. Of course, smaller injuries healed more quickly, but everything always healed. She could still feel pain, but it only lasted as long as it took for the injury to heal. Ellie was afraid to do more than anything superficial. The pain aside, she worried she would do something from which she would not be able to recover. She had cheated death a number of times already but did not know how many more times she would be able to do so. She questioned how close to death she had come in any of those incidents. The paramedics had declared her dead after the truck pinned her behind

Lisa's car, yet what about when the lightning struck her or when she had been stabbed by a sword? Her training and experience told her she had died both of those times as well yet the fact that she was still alive had her questioning it.

It occurred to Ellie to test her abilities against smallpox leading her to inoculate herself. If she got the disease and healed instantly, she would know her regenerative abilities worked on illness as well. If she did not heal instantly, she would be sick for a couple of weeks, but it would be a much milder form of the disease; then she would be immune to it. She thought it worth the risk. Late one night when everyone else was away from the hospital, Ellie sat next to a man who was rather ill with the disease and lifted her skirts to her thigh. She had a knife which she used to make a small cut in her leg. As soon as it was open, she worked quickly to remove some pus from one of the sick man's pustules and transferred it into her leg. Her wound healed within minutes, and she waited.

It did not take long before Ellie began to notice the tell-tale signs of the disease. She developed a fever the next day and fought a headache throughout the day, but by the end of the day, it had all disappeared. She was back to feeling completely well. Ellie knew it could have been her own natural immune system shortening the amount of time she was sick but thought it more likely that it was her new regenerative abilities. Regardless of why it was the case, at least she had some comfort in knowing she did not have to worry about contracting the illness.

With more questions than answers, Ellie did not think she would get them anytime soon. She was still at a loss to explain everything that had happened to her. With a lack of anything better, she decided, half-jokingly, that she had died and jumped to an alternative universe either during the traffic accident or the lightning strike. She had dropped a good thirty or forty pounds within the first three weeks of that time with no ill effects. Once she got down to what looked like a healthy weight as far as she could see, she no longer dropped any additional weight. Her eye sight was perfect for the first time in her life, she felt healthier than she ever had, and she had somehow reversed aging. Instead of appearing to be the forty-five she now was, everyone thought her to be barely twenty. The few strands of gray hair that had previously been present had since disappeared without hair dye and the fine lines and wrinkles around her hands and face had somehow smoothed themselves out. Ellie had been on birth control before arriving in the past in order to regulate her cycles and prevent painful cramping and had received her three-month shot prior to her trip to New York. She had expected it to wear off, allowing her menstrual cycle to begin again, but so far it had not arrived. It could take up to a year after getting off the shot to return, so she was not concerned, but she wondered if her new status would affect that as well. If her cycle returned, it would be one more aspect of hygiene in this world she would have to learn.

On top of the continuing smallpox patients, the hospital staff also had to continue to treat all of the patients coming in with all of the other ailments they typically saw. Ellie even had to deliver a baby. She had delivered one as a paramedic in her time, and another one the previous summer with the help of Abigail Gibbons, but this was different. Abigail was not there to help now, nor did she have modern medicine and an ambulance, a partner, and an obstetrician a phone call away. The baby came and Captain Burke assisted her the best he could, but he had almost no experience in this side of medicine. This was the realm of women, he informed her. Unfortunately, none of the other nurses present had ever assisted in delivering a baby either. Ellie's nerves wreaked havoc on her, but she was well trained and knew she could do it. Thankfully, there were no complications, and Ellie was able to deliver the baby with ease. She was nearly as joyed as the mother when the delivery was over.

To the great annoyance of Gideon and the officers, who were used to always being treated before lower-ranking men, Ellie continued to triage patients when they came in. She always told them that if she did not treat people according to the level of severity of their injuries, they would have no troops to command. Many understood it and did not mind after she unruffled their feathers, though nearly as many would not hear of it. Gideon continued to treat officers first, but Ellie had decided long ago to stay out of his way as much as possible. The less she had to interact with him, the better. Many of the men would seek her out over the other doctors or surgeon's mates. Of course, this only drove Gideon's hatred of her even more. The people around her either loved her or hated her. There was little in between. It was a good thing she cared little about it.

———

There was an attack on Fort William Henry around St Patrick's Day. The fort sent signals to them at Fort Edward, which they answered back on the morning of the nineteenth. Ellie immediately thought back to the siege in which the other fort was lost, and the surrendered party that was massacred, but could not remember when that happened, save for the fact that it was sometime in 1757. She had not thought about that incident the entire time she had been there, but now, hearing about the attack, it was all she could think about. By all accounts, the siege and the attack on the retreating party had been a true massacre. The Indians attached to the French slaughtered not only soldiers, but women and children as well. She constantly asked for updates while her stomach knotted itself. She even tried urging Captain Burke to insist on sending reinforcements, though there was little he could do. Her anxiety over the matter did not go unnoticed, but she was reassured that they had it under control.

General William Johnson, along with twelve hundred militia and a band of Indians arrived at Fort Edward on the twenty-fourth. Word came the following day that the French had retreated after finding the fort better prepared than they had expected. General Johnson and the militia returned to Fort Johnson and life at Fort Edward resumed, giving Ellie's anxiety a temporary reprieve.

Things were quiet around the fort during April and May, which suited Ellie. She knew this was only a temporary lull but was happy to have it. Shortly after the attack on Fort William Henry, a man came into the hospital who was as tall as Captain Burke, with curly dark brown hair and deep brown eyes. Ellie was struck by his looks but immediately thought his health to be too good to be seeking out a hospital. She went to see what he needed, but before she could reach him, he had approached Thomas from behind and jostled his arm while Thomas was refilling the

ink in his quill to write in his journal. The inkpot toppled, sending ink across the desk and the man guffawed while Thomas jumped to his feet, cursing. Ellie ran over to help clean up the mess. Thomas
turned to give the impertinent man a thrashing but
as soon as his eyes rested on the man, his face broke
out in a smile, and he embraced the man instead.

When they finished their greetings, the man informed Thomas he had some letters for him from
home and dug through a satchel to hand some papers
to him. Captain Burke turned to Ellie to introduce
them.

"This is my dear friend, Captain Robert Jensen
with whom I grew up," he said with a smile. Captain
Jensen took her hand and pressed it to his lips in
greeting. Ellie controlled her instinct to curtsy at the
gesture. He maintained eye contact with her the entire time but as he straightened, he gave Thomas a
knowing look. Ellie was not certain what the look
conveyed, but something had certainly passed between them.

"Where did you grow up?" Ellie asked. She had
always been so focused on not revealing anything
about herself, she did not feel it was fair to ask about
his upbringing. She took advantage of this opportunity now.

"Williamsburg. Virginia."

Ellie smiled at the commonality between them.
She started to say that she had lived about forty- five
miles away in Norfolk as a kid and had frequented
Williamsburg often but caught herself before she
could say it. It would have raised far too many questions that she could not answer.

Captain Jensen informed them, "I know not how
long we shall be here, but there is word that we shall

be moving on to Fort William Henry before long." He turned to Ellie and explained, "That's where I spent last year's campaign." He had alternated between scouting for two days at a time, building the fort and its defenses, or building boats, wharves, and warehouses. "Likely, I shall be spending this year there as well."

Her concern immediately piqued, Ellie debated whether or not she should say anything. How could she possibly warn them? Would they even believe her? She could see how much this man meant to Thomas and would hate for anything to happen to him.

Thomas immediately noticed her face fall and her body stiffen. Something about this had her on edge. Making her excuses, she left while barely looking at them. He watched Ellie for a time as she moved about the hospital almost in a trance. Her demeanor put him in mind of her strange behavior after they returned from Albany. He did not wish to see her return to that.

While he watched her, he heard Robert say, "She's beautiful."

Thomas turned back to look at his friend who had been watching him. He looked at Ellie now, as Thomas had, which immediately made Thomas want to draw his friend's attention away from her. Robert had always had a way with women. They flocked to him and fell for his charms more often than not. Would Ellie fall for them as well? Thomas would have to keep them apart from each other. He told himself it was because he did not want to see her hurt. Before Thomas could redirect Robert's attention, his surgeon's mate approached Ellie and he knew it could only end in trouble.

Thomas watched as Ellie headed over to the supplies to begin making poultices. Gideon Anwar interrupted, saying, "Go reapply the salve on Lieutenant Campbell's leg."

With a sigh, Ellie set down the bottles in her hands and said, "You know, you could actually try asking nicely just once. It won't kill you. Promise."

Sneering, Gideon replied, "And you could endeavor to shut your potato trap and give your rag a holiday. Do as you be commanded by those superior to yourself."

Ellie's hackles raised along with her eyebrows, even if she was not entirely certain of his words; though, she could certainly guess the meaning well enough. "And just who exactly would my betters be in this scenario? Because I can assure you, I'm pretty damn certain it's not you."

Gideon was incensed and told her through gritted teeth, "All men be your betters, you impertinent doxie. You may be able to fool the captain that you not be a trickster only I see you for the shifting cove you be."

Ellie laughed at him. "It would be cute that you thought so if it wasn't so pathetic."

Prepared to leave it at that, Ellie started to go see to Lieutenant Campbell's wound, but Gideon was not finished.

"You will learn your place. I'll not be spoken to in that manner by a laced mutton such as yourself."

"As amusing as your attempts at insulting me are, you're wasting your energy. In order for them to be effective, it would require me caring what you thought of me. Nice try, though. I have no idea what a laced mutton is but it sounds really creative."

Gideon snarled.

Despite knowing it was pointless to argue with the man, Ellie was at a loss as to why he continued to treat her the way he did. Initially, she thought he would come around after a while. She had even apologized for punching him when she had first arrived, but if anything, it seemed his attitude towards her had worsened. Some people were just plain miserable and liked to take it out on everyone around them.

Before he could inject anything more, she added, "I have been wracking my brain trying to figure out what your problem with me is. Since day one, you have been nothing but nasty to me. You must have a truly tiny penis to feel such a need to constantly berate me and try to control me. I'm sorry I punched you, but it was a natural reaction to the situation. You really need to get over it."

Grabbing the dressings and salve from the shelf, Ellie walked away from Gideon as he continued spewing his hatred.

Robert turned to Thomas, adding to his previous assessment of Ellie, "And spirited."

Thomas raised his eyebrows at his friend. "Indeed."

"She must be wed to a colonel," Robert guessed. She was young enough that she could have been the daughter of a high-ranking officer, but Thomas had introduced her as 'Missus' and her demeanor certainly indicated a lack of innocence.

"No," Thomas replied. "She belongs to no one here. Nor will she say anything about from whence she came."

Robert was surprised by this information. "How did she come to be with the army then?"

Thomas told him her story, then added his own suspicions about her origins.

"She has some breeding, though she also behaves much as the red man. I oft wonder if she was born a woman of consequence then taken captive by the savages. Though she claims not to have ever lived amongst them, nor to know any other languages. Our Mrs. Sorenson is a mystery, indeed."

Thomas glanced at the letters from home after Robert departed and saw one addressed to 'My Dearest Captain.' He did not recognize the handwriting and glanced to the bottom of the page, where he saw the name of his sister's best friend. He frowned and immediately put the letter away to read later in private.

Thomas then turned and called out to Gideon, preparing himself for yet another lecture to the man about his interactions with Mrs. Sorenson. He would do the same with her later.

Chapter 22

May 1757

When Thomas found Ellie that evening for their tai chi session they had only just resumed after taking the winter off, he asked her if she felt alright. Of course, she claimed everything was perfectly in order as she was wont to do. Thomas was not fooled by this. The fact that she began playing with her necklace anytime the subject came up told him a lot. Something had her uneasy.

"You paled when Captain Jensen mentioned Fort William Henry. Does the recent assault still give you unease?" he asked.

Again considering what to tell him, she asked, "If he asked to be reassigned somewhere else, would they grant his request?"

Instead of answering her question, Thomas tried to reassure her that his friend would be fine, insisting that Robert would be in no more danger there than he would be anywhere else. Ellie knew this was not true. She tried again to convince him to keep his friend away from the other fort, but without telling him anything more concrete, she was not able to convince him of anything.

Ellie would get her chance to try convincing Robert herself. It did not take long before Captain Jensen began joining them for tai chi. Once he had heard about their odd nightly activities, he was immediately interested. Ellie was happy to invite him, though it surprised her to find the invite had bothered Thomas. She would have thought he would be happy to be able to spend this time with his friend. What she did not know was that Thomas did not want to share their time together with anyone, let alone the man whom he knew had charmed countless women.

Captain Jensen enjoyed the tai chi sessions, but it took him no time to confirm the suspicion he had upon first meeting Ellie. He confronted Thomas after a week of spending every night with him and Ellie.

"You love her," he accused.

Thomas immediately denied it. Still not certain he could trust her while she continuously hid her past, he did not want to feel the way he did about her. He certainly was not prepared to admit those feelings to anyone.

"She's rather gifted in her medical knowledge. I respect her and hold her in high regard."

Robert did not believe him even a little. He never would have thought Thomas could ever consider a woman to be so knowledgeable in medicine. That alone was rather telling. He was happy for his friend. He knew his parents were trying to arrange a marriage with a young girl in Williamsburg, but the girl was too young and not what Thomas needed. Ellie Sorenson challenged him and brought out the best in him. She was not some vapid young girl whose entire world was fashion and society. Despite how young she looked, Robert could tell Ellie was worldly and had an intelligence that spoke of experience. She could easily handle herself amongst the hardened soldiers by which she was currently surrounded as well as the officer's wives who now called her to join them at tea periodically. She would make an excellent wife for Thomas.

Robert decided if Thomas would not admit it to himself, he would help him see it. He began flirting with Ellie and turned up the charm he had used on so many other women. It pissed Thomas off, as he had intended. Ellie enjoyed the attention and Robert began to look forward to seeing the smile on her face, knowing he was the one to put it there. Though he did not want to poach the woman his friend was in love with, he could certainly see the attraction. Ellie was special, indeed. They became instant friends, which he had never done with a woman before. The three of them spent much of their down time together, laughing and enjoying what they could of this time.

As she got to know him better over the next couple weeks, Ellie appealed to Captain Jensen to stay at Fort Edward, telling him Thomas needed a friend there, which they both knew was not true. He was well-liked and they both knew it.

"What vexes you, Ell?" he asked.

Ellie appreciated Robert's informality with her. He had addressed her as Mrs. Sorenson in the beginning, but when she corrected him after the first time, he had always called her 'Ellie.' In turn, she called him by his given name, often shortening it to 'Rob' or 'Robbie' when she was teasing him. As they became closer, he started shortening her name as she had his, calling her only 'Ell.'

"I worry for you," she said simply.

Robert knew there was more to the story than this. Thomas had told him of her mysterious appearance and how she would not speak of her past. He saw the concerned look on her face anytime mention of the other fort came up.

"Thomas may be content to accept that as an answer, but I shan't. Tell me of what causes your disquiet. What do you believe to be happening at Fort William Henry?"

Ellie hesitated and thought about how to tell him what she needed to say to make him stay. He seemed to be as open-minded as Thomas, and this directly affected him more so than it would Thomas. She needed to make him understand.

"The French are going to attack it. A lot of British will die."

The vague prediction had Robert bursting into laughter. They were at war; it was a reality of their current circumstances. When he saw the seriousness on her face, he realized she was not jesting, and his laughter dried up quickly.

"Miss Ellie, the French are like to attack any place, any time. They may attack here and none of us would be any safer than the men at Fort William Henry. That is a fact of war. As soldiers, we shan't let that stop us from doing our duty."

"No. This will be different, Rob. Please, the siege will be long, and the British will surrender. When the fort falls to the French, the Native Americans will slaughter them while they retreat. It'll be a massacre."

The look of pleading on her face had Robert instantly believing her. Or at least, he believed that she believed this. He backed away from her slightly, concerned over what she was telling him, and decided to test how much she knew about this impending attack before he turned her over as a spy.

"When do you believe this siege and massacre shall occur?" he asked.

"I don't know. I only remember that it happened sometime this year. When the French attacked earlier this year, I thought that was it, but it wasn't. It's still coming. Please, Robert. Promise me you'll try to stay away."

"If the fort comes under siege, then it will be my duty to be part of the reinforcements if I'm not already there. I'll be involved regardless."

"No. That's not what happened. General Webb won't send reinforcements. Munro will be on his own. He'll surrender to Montcalm, but the Frenchman won't be able to keep the Natives under control. Montcalm promised them all the spoils of war they wanted but when he negotiates the surrender of the fort, he promises Munro they can keep everything. The Natives get pissed by the betrayal and attack the British as they leave. They massacred at least 185 men, women, and children and hundreds more were taken prisoner to Canada and held for ransom. Montcalm will burn the fort down before he leaves." Ellie had learned the names of the generals from her time there at Fort Edward but remembered Munro's from the movie. However, she could not remember his rank. She had tried talking of the event in the future tense, but it was hard to remember, leaving her to switch back and forth between future and past tense.

"I assume by Natives, you refer to the Indians?" When Ellie nodded, he added, "And do you also refer to Lieutenant Colonel George Munro?"

She nodded again.

"I know Munro. He is in no position to surrender anything to General Montcalm," he replied. "He's not in command of the fort."

Ellie said without thinking, "Not yet. But he will be. He'll be in command of it when they attack."

The way she had made it sound as though it had already happened was not lost on Robert. The additional information was the type which could not be planned. No army would plan to kill 'at least 185 people.' But it was the last that really caught his attention. Even a spy would not have knowledge of who would come to be in command of a fort in the future until it was about to happen. There had been no word that Munro was taking over anytime soon. Robert was immediately alarmed by her knowledge.

"How do you come by such information, Miss Ellie?" he asked quietly.

When Ellie turned away, not answering his question, he grabbed her arm gently and turned her to face him. Seeing the suspicion and concern in his eyes, she turned her chin up and said, "I'm not a spy,"

"I did not say you were," he replied. Ellie tried to turn away again, and this time Robert stopped her with his words. "Do you commune with Lucifer?" he whispered.

Ellie's brow furrowed and she pulled her arm from his grasp. Defiantly, she said, "I do no such thing."

Robert searched her face, then nodded, choosing to believe her. He tried a different tactic. "Ell, do you have visions?"

Ellie's shoulders fell. Of course she did not have visions, but she could not exactly say she was a time traveler, either. She did not know what to tell him and was suddenly afraid of what he would think of her; of what he would tell Thomas if she said she did have visions. If she said she did, would they think her insane and lock her up? Thomas had all but told her that was exactly what he would do. The alternative would have her as a spy, in which case she would also be locked up, but possibly tortured for information. It was one thing to not care what other people thought of her, but this was different. What they thought of her now could decide her fate. Her future and her freedom were in their hands.

Ellie could not stop the tears that sprang to her eyes. She pleaded with Robert, "Please, can you just take my word for this? Just this once? I'm not insane, I'm not a spy, and I don't commune with the devil. Please, just promise me that you'll stay away if you can."

Robert's instinct told him she was being truthful. She had been genuinely afraid for him, but now she was afraid *of* him. Unable to stand the look in her eyes, he sighed and drew her to him; something he never would have done with another woman, but there was something about this woman that made the gesture feel natural. With his arms around her, he promised, "Do not fret, my dear. I shall do my duty, but I will have a care. I'll not trust anyone if I find myself at Fort William Henry and I should be quite well."

Captain Jensen did not leave for the other fort any time soon but instead spent his time at Fort Edward going out on periodic scouting parties or work parties to clear nearby roads or staying in camp seeing to his company, performing picket duty, or taking his turn presiding over court martials. Ellie was happy to see him stay at the fort and hoped it lasted.

It was easy to see how close Thomas and Robert had been as kids. They reminded Ellie of her own brothers. There was a friendly rivalry between them, but there was genuine affection as well. They ribbed each other every chance they got, and Ellie enjoyed the familial feel to it in the middle of this war in which she found herself. With Robert's presence, Ellie found many opportunities to get to know Thomas better. It was easier to ask personal questions when they were not alone together. Somehow, it seemed less intimate and one-sided while she was still unwilling to share any of her own past.

"Why are neither of you married?" she asked one day.

Thomas looked away shyly while Robert answered, "The army discourages marriage. Thomas and I shall likely be lifelong bachelors." He slapped his friend on the back while Thomas nodded once in agreement. The lack of enthusiasm in his nod was not convincing Ellie that he believed what Robert said.

"Discourages but not bans?" she asked.

"No, it is not banned. We merely need petition our commanding officer for permission," Thomas replied.

"Okay, then I ask again, why are neither of you married?"

Thomas sighed as he answered, "I am unable to speak for Robert, but the opportunity has not yet presented itself for me. When I came of age, I went to Edinburgh to become a physician. I spent several years there but I was engrossed in my studies. When I returned, the war was beginning in earnest and I signed on with my regiment."

"Engrossed in your studies? Yes, as I recall, you did study anatomy rather extensively in France," said Robert teasingly.

Ellie loved seeing this side of the two men. The more time she spent with them together, the more she was privy to the insults and jesting that occurred between them as if they were brothers; a familiarity that came from having grown up together. They were not brothers, but they may as well have been. Longing for her cousins, she quickly put it out of her mind and enjoyed being included in the camaraderie.

Thomas gave him a warning look which did not go unnoticed by Ellie. To his horror, Ellie picked up on the innuendo immediately. He should not have been surprised; she was extremely intelligent. And where she was naïve in some subjects, she was anything but in others. Unless she misunderstood. The look on her face seemed to indicate that her opinion of him had gone up somehow. Though, there was a sparkle in her eye that made Thomas think she knew exactly what Robert had meant. Her next words removed any doubt.

"Did your anatomy tutor have a name?" Ellie teased. "Or was it tutors?" She deliberately placed an emphasis on the 'S' at the end of the word and winked at Robert conspiratorially.

This new development was intriguing, indeed. Perhaps Thomas was not as proper as he pretended to be. She began asking questions, but Thomas turned red and refused to answer anything on the grounds that he was a gentleman, and that topic would be inappropriate to discuss in mixed company. This only served to amuse and intrigue Ellie even more.

Robert was greatly amused by her teasing of Thomas. Having always been alone in that endeavor, he now found a kindred spirit in Ellie and instantly liked her all the more.

Captain Jensen sought out Ellie in the hospital weeks later and informed her that Lieutenant Colonel Munro had assumed command of Fort William Henry. Ellie paled and her eyes became big. The look of fear and panic that showed on her face immediately alarmed Thomas, but he was just as concerned about the look that passed between her and Robert. Ellie did not say anything but turned away to resume her care of the patient she was tending.

Thomas turned on his friend. "Why does it matter who commands Fort William Henry? Is Lieutenant Colonel Munro known to her?"

Robert tried to downplay the importance of the information and instead asked him, "Why not pursue her, Thomas?"

"Do not change the subject, Robert. How does this matter to Ellie? If you've knowledge of her, you must tell me. I've been endeavoring to learn of her past nearly a year, to no avail."

Thomas did not know it, but Robert was not changing the subject. Not entirely. If he did not act on his attraction to Ellie soon, he would miss his opportunity. His parents would see him married whether he chose his bride or not. As much as Robert hated hiding anything from his friend, this was not his to tell. He knew it had taken a lot of trust from Ellie to tell him what she had and that it was likely something she had not told even Thomas. He would not betray her trust.

"She would make a good wife," Robert told him.

"She has secrets. I'm not entirely certain I may trust her," he said with a sigh.

Robert put his hand on Thomas's shoulder and looked him in the eyes when he said, "You may trust her, my friend."

Thomas knew he would not get any more information out of Robert on the matter, but he also knew he could trust his word. Robert would tell him if there was something amiss. It left him with a feeling of hope he had not felt in a long time, even though he was still reluctant to formally court Ellie.

Chapter 23

May 1757

Captain Robert Jensen could not always join the tai chi sessions. With his duties often pulling him away to leave the fort and do night patrols in the surrounding woods, Thomas and Ellie found themselves able to visit together without him. Robert was glad to be able to distance himself from her a little while also giving Thomas the opportunity to spend time with her alone. Thomas seemed to be warming up to Ellie more now that he believed he could trust her. Though Robert could still see some hesitation, he hoped it would pass with time.

As the weather warmed, Ellie and Thomas visited later into the night. It was a welcome change after the long, cold winter. On a warm night in late May when it was only the two of them, they sat on the grass, talking and enjoying the warm breeze. The small, glowing lights of the fireflies sparkled through the air around them, giving the clearing a magical ambience, despite their surroundings. Ellie laid back in the grass in order to see them floating around above her. Stretching out her hand above her as if to grab the magic, her eyes were drawn further away, into the night sky. There were more stars than Ellie had ever seen before. She had camped in the middle of nowhere before and lived in some relatively rural areas for her time, but there was always still enough light pollution to obscure most of the stars. There, she felt as though she could see forever.

"There are so many stars. And they're so bright. I always knew they were there, but I've never been able to see them. Not like this. I've never seen them this clearly. Most nights, I find myself looking up into the sky whenever I'm outside. It's absolutely mesmerizing."

Thomas laid down beside her, looking into the sky as well. He pointed out a few constellations while Ellie asked questions. It was not long before his eyes were no longer on the stars, but on her.

"The stars shine but dimly next to the light in your eyes," he whispered. Ellie looked at him briefly and smiled shyly, unable to say anything.

While Ellie stared up at the stars and absently played with the end of her braid, Thomas could not take his eyes off her. Who was this woman? She was such a mystery to him. She had come to them knowing nothing of life there; nothing of horses, saddles, or other equipment used with them, nor the care and feeding of them; nothing of carriages or carts, scriveners or sutlers, or even money or clothing. Abigail Gibbons had even had to explain to her the use of a chamber pot when she first arrived, never mind what he had needed to explain to her about the subject. Yet she knew grammar and spelling; she could both read and write. Her writing skill surpassed even his own, though her penmanship left a little to be desired. And what she knew of medicine was simultaneously far more advanced than what he knew himself and severely lacking in some of the most basic knowledge. How was that even possible?

It was clear that Ellie had been educated, yet she knew nothing of basic life. Had she been locked away her entire life, never to see the outside of whatever dwelling in which she was raised? At times, her knowledge seemed as though it all came from books, but then she did something with a patient which told him she had seen the outside world as well. She had experienced life. Perhaps more so than him. She claimed to be older than him by a great deal. Could that be true? Sitting up to lean on his elbow, he voiced his thoughts aloud before he could think better of it.

"How can you be real, Ellie Sorenson? You've such knowledge, seeming at times to have learning beyond the rest of us, yet you do not understand basic things which every small child knows. You marvel at the simplest of things."

Turning her head to look at him, Ellie smiled enigmatically but did not answer. Instead, she shrugged and looked back up at the stars.

"I'm just me," was all she finally said.

What else could she say? With no way to explain herself, she remained quiet instead.

Thomas reached out and took her chin in his hand, tilting her face to meet his. He kissed her gently, then searched her face as if he could find the answers to the mystery that was Ellie. When he was satisfied that the answers were not there, he laid back down and pulled her into his arms. She happily curled further into him, and he held her close while they sat contentedly in the quiet stillness, staring at the sky. Thomas had never felt so conflicted. He cared for this woman far more than what was prudent, yet he knew so little about her and he still did not know if he could trust her. It would be smart to keep his distance, though he did not think that would be possible. She stole all thought and common sense from him.

⎯⎯⎯⎯⎯⎯⎯

When one of the seamstresses came in beat to hell, Ellie had to give her a sponge bath before she could even treat her. The woman looked as though she had been drug behind a cart for several miles. It was impossible to tell what was bruising and what was dirt. As she went along, Ellie found most of it was bruising. The woman had a broken arm and rib, and the entire right side of her abdomen was one giant bruise. She also had cuts and bruises all over her arms and legs. When Ellie asked the woman what happened, Gideon Anwar gave her a look that said, "Mind your own business."

Ellie ignored him. She could not thoroughly treat the woman if she did not know what happened.

Mrs. Thompson looked away and quietly said, "I denied me 'usband access to me bed when 'e were in the gun. He do not control his gross, brutal, lustful nature when 'e be that foxed. I tried to get 'im to leave me be, only he insisted on 'aving conjugal relations and held me by force 'til he accomplished his purpose. I ought not have refused 'im. He only took what were rightfully 'is."

Ellie was horrified. Not only at the acts this woman had suffered, but at the attitude that it was somehow alright. Was Mrs. Thompson trying to take the blame onto herself because her husband was drunk? Being foxed or in the gun was no excuse. If he could not control himself when he drank, he should not drink. Though Ellie was proud of herself for having been able to understand Mrs. Thompson, she was incensed on her behalf.

When she finished helping the woman and got her to sleep, Ellie went in search of Captain Burke. She tried to be discreet, but in such a small space, people were bound to overhear.

"I need to discuss a patient with you."

He looked up from his work and asked, "Is there a problem?"

"Yes," she said, exasperated.

When he made no move to stand or leave his desk, her eyes got big in incredulity and she tapped her foot, motioning with her head. "I'd prefer to discuss it in private. Patient confidentiality and all."

"Confidentiality?" he asked.

Letting out a deep breath, she said, "Never mind. Can we please just go have a conversation in private?"

Thomas finally stood from his desk and followed her outside where they found somewhere quiet along the river.

"What's this about, then?" he asked.

"Mrs. Thompson. She came in covered with cuts and bruises and I'm certain both her arm and ribs are broken. Or at least one rib." Ellie took a deep breath before adding, "And I'm pretty sure her husband raped her."

Thomas was quick to inform her, "A wife may not be raped by her husband."

"Bullshit!" Ellie exclaimed angrily before she could stop herself.

Thomas drew back and said, "You disagree."

"Yeah," Ellie said on an annoyed laugh. "Yeah. Abso-fucking-lutely I disagree."

"Regretfully, whether or not you agree, she belongs to him."

"Excuse me?" she gasped. "She's not a piece of property. Marriage does not give him the right to touch her without her permission." Despite knowing the law in this time meant that the woman was, in fact, her husband's property to do with what he will, she would never accept it. Hearing Thomas declare that the woman was her husband's property only added to her outrage.

Thomas folded his arms across his broad chest. "Does it not?"

"No! There's this thing called bodily autonomy," she said sarcastically. "It means that any physical contact with me without my permission is a violation." It was easier to make her point talking about it in the first person.

Thomas could not keep his eyes from roaming Ellie's body at her words. Noticing, a small chill went through her. She had to shake it off to stay focused.

"I fear she does belong to him according to the law. If it's not a violation of the law, pray tell me, what is it a violation of exactly?"

"My unalienable rights as a human being!" she shouted. "Not to mention my trust. Your laws are wrong."

She knew she should keep it about the woman, but she could not help her phrasing. Part of her thought it might get through to Thomas better if he thought of the situation as being more personal. Would it make a difference to him to think of her as the victim, rather than some random woman? She hoped so. The thought that he might blindly accept the law and feel that way was more than she could bear to think at the moment.

Thomas raised one brow. "Duly noted."

Ellie was even more frustrated now than she was before. She knew he was toying with her, allowing her to vent but not taking her seriously. Knowing women were property there did not make it any easier to accept.

"So, are you going to do anything?"

Thomas unfolded his arms and let out a deep breath before answering slowly. "I'm not certain what you believe I may do. I'm afraid he was within his rights in this matter."

Ellie let out a small, throaty growl while turning to look out at the water.

Thomas sighed. "I shall examine the woman's injuries. If they're excessive, we may be able to have him punished."

It was not much, but Ellie would take what she could get.

"Thank you," she said.

Chapter 24

June 1757

With the rivers being used for washing clothes and dumping waste, Ellie had been collecting her drinking water from upstream then boiling it before drinking it, but now that she had more time and resources, she decided to try making activated charcoal. It would come in handy, not only for filtering her water, but also for making deodorant and soap for herself and medicines in the hospital. It could help draw out ingested poisons and toxins received topically. She had made it before, and though it was messy and time consuming, it was not particularly difficult.

Ellie gathered the hardwood and lemon juice she would need to make it along with the pot to heat the wood, a mortar and pestle to crush the charcoal, and a container to put it into once it was complete. After chopping the wood into smaller chunks, she placed them in the pot over a fire near her tent. She went about doing her laundry and other chores while it cooked most of the day. Everyone who passed thought she was mad for cooking wood, but she was used to the confused stares that always followed her by now.

The next morning, Ellie took the materials into the hospital to work on it between her other responsibilities. Part of her duties included making medicines and salves, and this fell under that category. It was messy and loud so she worked in a separate room upstairs that she had to herself. Working in batches, she removed some of the blackened, cold wood from the pot and placed it on a cloth, wrapping it up as tightly as she could. Using a borrowed hammer, she began smashing the coals into smaller bits. Once she had smashed it into tiny pieces, she worked in batches, scooping some of it into the mortar and using the pestle to ground it into a fine powder. Ellie filtered out the larger pieces still remaining as much as she could and repeated the process until it was all a fine powder that went into another ceramic bowl. Once all of the charcoal was in the bowl, she added lemon juice.

While she worked, Ellie remembered cleaning the house when she was young. Her parents were often gone when she came home from school, so she would put on one of her favorite movies while she cleaned the house before they arrived home. She had always loved the sound of David Bowie's voice and used to let *Labyrinth* play in the background while she worked. If it was not *Labyrinth*, it was *The Princess Bride*. She had seen both so many times, she could recite each in their entirety. Smiling at the memory, she started humming *Magic Dance*. Her head began bopping, and her foot was tapping. With an affinity for remembering recipes and music lyrics, she could hear the music playing in her head and began singing.

In a room by herself, she let herself sing aloud. Soon, she was dancing along as well. It felt good to let go and dance as if she did not have a care in the world. She had always loved dancing and singing. Shaking her hips, she tried to remember when she first saw the movie. It must have come out in 1985, or was it 1986? Why could she not remember? *19-? 19-? 1985.* The thought brought to mind the song by Bowling for Soup and she started into it when she reached the end of that one.

Thomas came looking for Ellie to see if they would be doing tai chi that night. With the schedules they kept, it was always a question. The singing he heard as he came around the corner into the small room where she worked surprised him. Smiling at the sound, he stood nearby, keeping his distance, intending to listen for a few minutes, but the sound was like nothing he had ever heard before, the words having no meaning. He went further into the room as she was shaking her hips and belting out strange lyrics to this unusual song. He recognized very few of the words she sang and the few he did recognize were strung together in such a way as to have no meaning. What was a Prozac, an essuvee, or high school? What did the numbers 19 and 85 have to do with anything?

The movement of her hips was downright obscene. His jaw dropped, and all he could do was stare. After trying so hard to maintain a distance from her, to keep things between them proper, seeing her like this stirred something inside of him.

When she was done mixing, Ellie accidentally dropped the wooden spoon that she pulled from the bowl and squatted to pick it up while shaking her hips the whole way down. All that was left now was to cover the bowl and let it sit for twenty-four hours before rinsing it with her previously boiled and crudely filtered water, then allowing it to thoroughly dry. As she stood, she turned her head to see Thomas watching her. Momentarily startled by his presence, the look on his face told her he was enjoying the show, even if he was shocked by it. Deciding to embrace the moment, she continued singing the song by Bowling for Soup.

Ellie continued to dance while she sang *1985*. Despite being fully clothed in multiple layers, she was taken back to her days as a stripper, feeling freer than she had in a long time. She missed music and dancing. Grabbing Thomas by the hands, she started dancing with him. Or rather, she was dancing against him while he stood there watching her. Twirling herself around, he stood still, unsure what to do, standing there as stoically as he could while she danced around him.

The woman before him was the most beautiful and amazing woman he had ever met. Though he had allowed himself to kiss her once, he had been trying to maintain a little distance from her, as impossible as that seemed. It would be highly improper to give into his urges and he respected her far too much to treat her as anything less than a lady. Whether she was born one or not, he had no doubts that she was one. Though, he wished he knew from where she came. He wanted to trust her and believe she told him the truth, yet how could he when she continued to hide her past from him? If he knew, he would not hesitate to court her. But he did not know. Until he did, he needed to protect his heart from her, though that was becoming more and more difficult. She was breaking him down.

Coming to the last round of the chorus after singing one more stanza, she decided to end the song there, stopping her dance as well. Placing her hands on Thomas's shoulders, she smiled up at him, and on an impulse, she stretched up on her tiptoes and kissed him briefly on the lips. He had not kissed her again since their night under the stars, but she thought about it often. This was nothing more than a quick peck, but as she lowered her heels and started to pull away, his hands shot to her waist, and he held her in place. He looked into her face, searching for something. Her breath was coming heavy, both from the exertion of the dancing and from the effects of his gaze on her. Thomas pulled her in closer and lowered his face to hers. Closing her eyes, she felt his lips on hers, his hands sliding around her waist and up her back to draw her in even closer. Leaning into the kiss, she took everything he had to offer. He smelled earthy, like leather and wood, and she lost herself in his scent and his touch.

Ellie loved kissing Thomas. He gave her his full attention and had a way of making her feel like they were the only people in the world. He was good at it, too. It made her think he would be good at everything else in bed as well. As incredible as a physical relationship with Thomas would be, she was in no hurry to pursue one.

Casual sex was not exactly a norm in this time period, even if it was something she was looking for. It had been some time since she had been interested in casual sex. In fact, it had been so long, she could not even remember the last time she had been with a man. For Thomas, she would happily make an exception about what she was looking for, but it would still only be casual sex and Ellie did not want to mislead Thomas or make him think she was interested in more than she was capable of giving him. She valued his friendship too much for that. Instead, she decided it was best if she maintained boundaries between them.

Despite her decision, when Thomas pulled away, Ellie pulled him back to her, not yet ready to let this moment go. Boundaries could come after this moment ended. She wanted to continue feeling the passion coursing through her, to be desired for however long it might last, even if it was only a few minutes. Despite their age difference, or perhaps because of it, Ellie always felt sexy and wanted when this young man looked at her the way he did.

The kiss lingered, and when it ended this time, he did not release her immediately. Thomas held her a while longer. One hand still on her waist, the other reached up and brushed away a stray lock of blonde hair that had fallen out of the braid in which it had been. His fingers traced down the side of her face, making her feel as though he was dragging it through a field of butterflies inside her stomach, causing them to flutter wildly behind his trailing finger.

As a gentleman, Thomas knew he should not be thinking the thoughts that were going through his head. Ellie deserved more than to be ogled and ravished. But she was so breathtaking, he wanted nothing more than to consume her.

"Darling, you are utterly resplendent," he said, his voice a hoarse whisper.

"Resplendent, huh?" Ellie had always been uncomfortable accepting compliments and tried to downplay this one, but he was not having it.

"Yes. Your smile is the sun. It fills me with warmth and lights up my entire world."

Blushing under his compliment, her stomach did cartwheels and her heart fluttered in her chest. How long had it been since she had experienced this sort of reaction to a man?

"You must teach me this dance," he said when she found herself incapable of words.

Ellie smiled. "I can't teach it; you have to feel the music and move your body to the beat," she said while swaying against him.

His voice husky, he asked, "Do you hear music, Miss Ellie?"

The desire in his voice nearly brought her to her knees. "Don't you, Thomas?" she asked in a whisper.

Ellie did not dare speak any louder for fear the shakiness in her voice would give her away. Not trying to be seductive, she had not meant for her dancing to have had such an effect on him. It had simply felt good to let go and let the music take her over, even if it was only inside her mind that she could hear it.

"I always hear music when you are near me, for my heart always sings."

Thomas placed his strong hand on the side of her neck and kissed her again. This time, when he ended the kiss, his thumb slid along her cheek and jawline in a gentle caress. "Alas, I must withdraw myself from your company and return to the patients. Thank you for the dance."

Giving her a smile, he released her and left, forgetting the reason he had sought her out.

Chapter 25

July 23, 1757

As the drums beat for the changing of the guard on the morning of July 23, there came the sound of gunshots and the whooping of Native Americans in the forest near the fort. A work party of about eighty men had gone out early that morning to retrieve wood with a small detachment of troops as a covering party. As the ruckus reached the fort, everyone immediately jumped into action. Provincial troops ran into the woods like a mob, the picket advanced, and General Lyman led yet another party into the fray. Even Captain Putnam and some of the other Rangers came from the island to join in the defense. The fight lasted about an hour before the enemy retreated, after which, the injured started rolling into the hospital. Among them was Captain Jensen.

Ellie, Captain Burke, and Gideon made haste in tending to the wounded while the other nurses and regimental doctors assisted. There were not many injured, but it was enough to keep them busy throughout the afternoon. Robert had received a large laceration to his forearm which would need to be stitched, but it could wait until after the more severe injuries were treated. Ellie wrapped a bandage around his arm and told him to apply pressure and keep it elevated until they could get to him.

When Ellie finally made her way back to Robert, she began by cleaning his wound while he recalled what happened. The work party had gone out that morning and was at a thick swamp approximately a mile from the fort when they were attacked by about five hundred French Regulars and Indians. He thought them to be Ottawa based on the arrows they were using. Captain Jensen's company had been assigned to the detachment covering the work party.

"I'm glad to see you're alright," Ellie informed him.

"I'm well enough. Thank you for mending my arm."

"Make sure to keep it clean until it's healed. Come back and see me if you need help with it."

"Come with me," Thomas said, pulling her hands from the sewing implements she was cleaning after stitching Robert up. With a hand to her lower back, he guided her over to his desk and pulled out the chair. "You've not eaten all day. Have a seat." Atop the desk, a plate of food was waiting for her.

Ellie sat and looked up at him in wonder. The wounded continued to come in and they had all been working frantically to keep up all day. She tried to protest, saying she had too much to do, and she could work while she ate, but he was having none of it.

"You must care for yourself if you wish to care for others."

How often had she heard that over the years? It was something she had even said herself on a regular basis, but she felt fine. Trying to remember the last time she ate, Ellie was surprised to realize he was right; she had not eaten that day. She had meant to, but it had been a busy day, and she had gotten caught up in her work, not noticing how much time had passed.

"Thank you," she said simply while taking a bite. The army food was basic and bland, but it warmed her insides that Thomas had noticed her eating habits and was trying to take care of her. It was such a simple thing, but also the most thoughtful gesture anyone had made toward her in as long as she could remember.

The final numbers did not come through until late that evening, but they determined there had been no prisoners taken by the French. One sergeant, one corporal, and ten other men had been killed and scalped and several others were wounded. Two of the wounded died the following night, despite their best efforts.

Despite being exhausted after running around caring for the wounded, Ellie made sure to get up bright and early the next morning for the day's punishments. Corporal punishment was used often for a multitude of offenses including stealing, raising a false alarm, or even deserting, though the latter was more commonly punished with the death penalty. Normally the spectacle was something to avoid, but she was looking forward to it that day. Captain Burke had followed through on his word regarding Mrs. Thompson. Her injuries were considered excessive and upon questioning her husband, it was discovered that he had used a large branch with which to beat her. Apparently, if he had used something smaller, he would have been within his rights to punish her in that manner. However, since he used such a large object, it was considered excessive. Ellie had been pissed to know that no one cared that he raped his wife, but at least the man would be punished for what he had done to her. Finding a spot in the front row, she watched him receive his five hundred lashes from the cat of nine tails. The soldier enforcing the punishment did not hold back and the man's back was bleeding in no time. Ellie counted every single stroke.

Chapter 26

August 3, 1757

The reprieve after the attack on the work party was short-lived. It was not long before the French made another attempt, and it was the event Ellie had been waiting for and dreading.

Wednesday morning was sunny and warm. It was early August and the summer heat had not yet begun to dissipate. The sound of distant cannons going off at five in the morning woke Ellie. Initially, there were two or three shots within a minute of each other. When she dressed and made her way out of the tent, she could see the entire fort was in a frenzy. In the hospital, Thomas informed her that Fort William Henry was under siege. Ellie collapsed into a chair knowing what was to come and that there was nothing she could do to stop it.

As the morning went on, the cannon fire increased with sometimes as many as fifteen or more shots within two minutes. It continued throughout the afternoon until it finally ceased at six that evening. By nightfall, the entire camp had heard word of the French deserter who had been brought in by the Rangers. He had informed them that the French had come down the lake in three hundred boats, carrying with them numerous artillery, four thousand men, forty-five hundred Indians, four thousand Canadians, and thirty-five hundred Regulars. The French had placed thirty-six cannons and five mortars half a league away to the west of the fort. It was assumed the man exaggerated the numbers, but with only fifteen hundred men at Fort Edward, it was decided they were in no position to assist, and reinforcements were immediately called in from elsewhere.

The cannons ceased overnight, then picked up again slightly in the morning, increasing until noon. The Rangers were the only men who had been able to get close to the beleaguered fort to exchange correspondence. The message that was brought back informed them that nearly twelve hundred French had landed. With requests for reinforcements sent, General Webb declined to assist until the militia arrived. Ellie was glad to hear the cannons stop in the afternoon even if it was not to be the end of it.

The captains were both kept busy in meetings and councils. Despite knowing the outcome, Ellie begged them to urge the general to reconsider and send reinforcements. They had already been doing so. She was frantic and Thomas was at a loss to console her. Most of the men at Fort William Henry had passed through Fort Edward to get there and she had met several of them. She did not know them well, but many of them were only boys as Isaac had been the previous year.

By Friday, the cannon fire was less regular and spread out over greater intervals and the men at Fort Edward were all eager to assist their brothers.

Instead, they were preparing to evacuate their own fort. The general had issued orders to keep ready to march at a minute's warning. They would not be sending assistance from Fort Edward.

While the hospital staff were packing for evacuation, Robert came to speak with Thomas, who was occupied with a patient. He found Ellie instead.

"Will the French attack Fort Edward?" he asked her.

Knowing why he was asking her, Ellie paused what she was doing. In lieu of saying anything, she shook her head while locking eyes with him as Thomas walked over. Before Robert could ask her more, Thomas said, "You two appear rather grave, what is it you're discussing? Are you ready to depart?"

"Miss Ellie does not believe we shall have need to evacuate," Robert replied.

It was not entirely true. Ellie did not know if Fort Edward had ever been evacuated. She only knew that it had never been attacked during the war.

Thomas smiled patiently as though she was a child talking about Santa Clause. He took her hand in his and said, "It would seem Miss Ellie prefers to see the positive in our disagreeable circumstance and does not wish to admit the possibility. She believes in the might of His Majesty's Army, rightly so."

It took everything in Ellie to not snap at him or punch him in the face. She yanked her hand from his and said, "I'm more aware of the possibilities than you know. The British Army is not everything. They're certainly not some undefeatable, all-powerful force."

The look on Thomas's face changed to concern as his blue eyes darkened. As Ellie looked over at

Robert, she saw the same expression on his face. Robert chose his next words carefully.

"What, pray, does that mean? Do you believe the French shall prevail in this war?"

"Not at all. I just meant that the British won't always be the dominant force in this country."

"Then, you do believe the French shall prevail?" Thomas asked.

"No. The British will drive the French out. I'm just saying that there will come a time when they will also be defeated and chased out of North America. Well, everything south of Canada anyways."

Thomas and Robert were both looking at her expectantly now. Damn it. Would she ever learn? She really needed to think before she spoke. Her hand shot up to her necklace, seeking the solace of the familiar as she twisted and twirled her ankh, tracing the shape of it.

"Of what do you speak, Ellie?" Thomas asked, echoing Robert's words from months before.

Needing to deescalate this and find an escape, she changed tactics and decided to play the dumb blonde that had worked so well for her when she was a dancer. Smiling as disarmingly as she could, she shook off any seriousness, and said, "Oh, I don't know. I guess you're right. How could anyone possibly defeat the British? I guess I'm just stressed and nervous and I'm not thinking straight."

Putting on her best subservient smile, she looked at Thomas as though he knew everything in the world, and she was merely a lowly woman who could not possibly know any better. It nearly killed her to do so, but if it kept her safe, she would play the role of the submissive woman who did not understand the world and things best left to the men. For now.

Thomas's eyes traveled to Ellie's hand playing nervously with her necklace. Reaching out to steady her, he took it in his own, bringing it to his lips as he smiled at her. "I know you're concerned, but do not fret. All shall be quite well."

Robert watched Thomas walk away to see to his patients but had not been fooled in the least by Ellie's performance. He turned his deep brown eyes on her, giving her a look that said he knew better.

"What else do you see?"

Her hand back at her necklace, Ellie tried to dismiss Robert's question, but he was not so easy to dismiss as Thomas. She wondered briefly why she was not chasing after him instead of Thomas. Then she reminded herself that she was not chasing after anyone. They were both her friends, but if Thomas wanted to pursue her, she certainly would not object to a little more, but only so much more. At least as long as it stayed casual. Being free, even if only temporarily, she had no desire to ever get married again. Robert was waiting for an answer, and Ellie asked him to assist her in packing some of the medical supplies while she considered how much to tell him.

"The British will win this war. It will end in 1763 with the Treaty of Paris. Fort Edward will not be attacked the entire time. I don't know much more than that."

"With the exception of what shall become of Fort William Henry?" he reminded her.

Nodding in agreement, she said, "With the exception of that."

"If we are to win this war, then when shall we be removed from North America? Will the French return and defeat us in another war?"

Ellie's brow furrowed. "Kind of. It's a complicated answer."

"Simplify it," he demanded.

Ellie stopped packing and sat on a chair nearby, staring out of the window. Was this wise? She had already told him more than she should have, but maybe it was a good thing. If she could have corroboration that what she said was true, maybe it would help her in the future. Maybe he could help her convince Thomas if she ever told him. However, Robert already believed in her 'ability' to see the future; would this really help anything? Ellie decided to take a chance. The Revolutionary War was still almost twenty years away. Who knew if she would even still be there for it? Given that he had already kept her secret this long, Ellie decided to trust him. Hopefully, he would continue to do so.

"This war will cost the British more than they can afford. They'll try to tax the hell out of the colonists to pay for it, but the colonists will not sit back and allow it. They'll revolt, and the knowledge gained by fighting this war will allow them to win against the British, with the help of the French."

"The colonists ally themselves with the French after all this?"

Robert was incredulous at the absurdity of it but all Ellie could do was nod.

He noticed that Ellie spoke of these events with absolute conviction, as she had when she had told him of the current situation happening with Fort William Henry.

"You speak as though it's a certainty, as if it has already commenced."

"In my mind, it has."

"When shall this occur? If this war is the catalyst, how long until the colonists revolt?"

"Twenty years, roughly. Though, that's just the official war. Technically, the revolt happens almost immediately after this one ends. But it builds up to a war that begins in 1775."

Robert turned away, taking a deep breath and running his hand through his dark hair. He was not certain what to do with this information. Though it was no longer legal to accuse someone of witchcraft, it was still illegal to conjure spirits, foretell the future, and cast spells. Should he turn her in for her predictions? Did he even believe her? How could he not? She had been correct about the siege and about Munro. Robert decided he would wait and see if the rest of her predictions surrounding Munro's surrender and the ensuing massacre came true before he fully believed her. What he would do then, he did not know.

August 6, 1757

The cannons woke Ellie again early on Saturday morning. This was normally her day off now, but given the situation, there was no rest for anyone. Once back in the hospital again, she would be making sure they were all ready to leave at any minute. She wondered where they would go if they did have to evacuate. Albany, most likely. Though, she did not believe it would come to that. If the survivors had made their way to Fort Edward after the massacre, it would imply that it was still occupied, meaning they would not evacuate.

The first of the reinforcements began to arrive at Fort Edward throughout the day. General William Johnson arrived around nine that morning with Native Americans and militia and Lord Howe arrived nearly twelve hours later from Boston. Most of the militia came from various parts of New York, totaling around fifteen hundred men.

Every day they eagerly awaited word from the other fort. Ellie knew the siege lasted close to a week but could not remember specific details. There was still no decision made as to whether or not they would be evacuating Fort Edward. Everyone was on edge and people had pent up energy needing to be released. Sitting around waiting was getting to everyone. Ellie busied herself with emptying the hospital beds as much as she could, sending patients who were able to leave back to their quarters, and prepping the supplies to treat the men and women she knew would be coming.

On Monday, distress signals were flung up at Fort William Henry and by Tuesday, they heard little to no cannon fire after six in the morning. That evening, a Frenchman fighting with the English arrived at Fort Edward with news of Munro's surrender. The man reported that the French flag was hoisted at Fort William Henry that morning at eight and when he saw it, he jumped over the breastwork and made his escape.

On August 10, troops from the surrendered garrison came running into Fort Edward, extremely confused at the Native American's behavior. The troops reported that the Indians murdered everyone they could lay their hands on, tearing clothes off their backs, and ripping children from their mother's arms. Women were reportedly disemboweled, and children's heads were bashed against the rocks and trees. There was even a report of an Indian rushing into the fort ahead of the French upon Munro leaving and coming out carrying the head of one of the wounded left behind in the hospital. This all occurred while the French sat back and watched.

The men at Fort Edward were enraged by this. The French were helpless to prevent the attack by the Indians, but once it began, they sent a detachment of Regulars to protect the prisoners making their way to Fort Edward. Major Prevost was sent with five hundred men to meet the prisoners and take custody of them from the French. Despite this, several hundred Englishmen were taken as prisoners by the Natives, and many fled into the woods on their own. There were dozens of deserters on both sides, men upset by the course of events and how it was handled.

The following day, a large plume of smoke was seen across the countryside by those at Fort Edward. As the French deserters arrived, they reported that Montcalm had burned Fort William Henry and the Indians were departing, unhappy. Instead of searching for survivors or burying the dead, General Webb held Fort Edward ready for flight for several days, concerned with a further advance by the French.

The failure to support Munro and search for wounded left the men incensed. The only assistance that was provided consisted of firing the cannons at Fort Edward periodically to guide men into the garrison. Ellie, Thomas, and Gideon were all kept busy in the hospital as the injured poured in. They filled the beds in no time. Soon, they were spilling out everywhere, waiting to be seen. Women throughout the camp were pressed into service in the hospital. Each regimental physician, surgeon, and surgeon's mate was working around the clock.

Many of the survivors of the attack on Fort William Henry had sustained severe injuries. They did what they could for them, but many of them did not survive. With the assistance of Private Javon Simms, Ellie was spreading pine gum salve on a wound of one of the injured. Javon helped the patient move while Ellie applied the sticky salve after thoroughly cleaning the wounded area. They both heard Thomas swear under his breath and looked up to see him throwing a blood-soaked cloth down angrily on the floor. Ellie looked at the patient he was standing beside and could tell even from two beds over that the soldier had died. Thomas turned and stormed out of the room without a word to anyone. Javon turned to follow Thomas, but Ellie placed a hand on his arm and shook her head.

"He needs some time. If he needed anything, he would've asked."

Javon scoffed and pulled his arm away. He was there to serve Captain Burke and felt it was his duty to follow him. Turning to look at the door as if to follow him anyway, he then thought better of it. Ellie finished wrapping the wound she was treating, then moved over to the bedside Thomas had vacated, bringing Javon with her in an attempt to keep him busy so he could not go after Thomas. Together, they began the cleanup and preparation of the body for burial. She wanted to go after Thomas as much as Javon had, and it was all she could do to refrain herself from doing so, knowing he needed time to process the death that surrounded them.

Once she finished with everything she could do in the hospital, she considered seeking Thomas out to make sure he was okay but figured he had probably gone to his rooms to be alone, and it was not exactly someplace she could follow. With a sigh, she left, heading out to the river to release her own emotions before calling it a night. Catching up with Thomas would have to wait until the morning.

When Ellie arrived at the spot near the river where she usually went to meditate, she was surprised to find Thomas sitting by the edge of the water. With darkness setting in, it was difficult to see, but she knew instantly that it was him, leaving her glad she would not have to wait until morning to see him. He sat in the grass, throwing rocks into the water and did not look up when she approached. Sinking onto the ground next to him without a word, she removed her moccasins. They sat in companionable silence for a time, watching the water flow swiftly along. Ellie curled her bare feet underneath her and picked at the grass under her hands. It would not be long before it would be brown as the temperatures dropped.

"How do you do it?" he asked. "You've been beside me all this time and seen the hopelessness of it all, yet it seems to not bother you."

"Oh, that's easy," she teased, trying to lighten his mood. "I'm a cold, heartless bitch with no emotions."

Holding a rock still in his hand, Thomas turned and glared at her accusingly. "I know that to be a falsehood. I've seen how you tend the people in your care."

Shrugging, Ellie tried to downplay his words. They fell quiet again for a moment before he threw another rock into the water with more force than was necessary to propel it the short distance. It sank into the river with a loud splash.

"I find myself quite discontented to regularly be deprived of my efforts for which I've so labored and fatigued. I know not how many more men I may stomach losing."

Putting her hand on his leg, Ellie rubbed his thigh just above the knee. She wanted to hold him and comfort him but was reluctant to initiate any moves toward more physical contact than that. Happy to let him do so if he so chose, she convinced herself that if she refrained, she could still maintain a distance between them. Having been in his shoes, she knew there was little she could say to ease the pain and frustration he felt. Instead of speaking, she opted to listen.

"This is why you removed yourself from medicine is it not?"

Ellie nodded. "I lost five children in a month. I couldn't face the parents anymore."

"You were a midwife?"

Going back to picking at the grass around her, she shook her head but did not elaborate.

"I know you do not wish to tell me about yourself, but I am in need of a distraction. Pray, tell me something. Anything. Otherwise, I fear I may walk away from it all myself."

Sighing, she leaned forward, resting her elbows on her knees. "I wasn't a midwife, but I did deliver a few babies. I also saw a lot of kids, though most of my patients were adults. In retrospect, I don't think it was just the kids I lost that drove me away from medicine. It certainly was difficult enough by itself, but it also happened at the same time my mom began having difficulties. I tried everything I could to help her, but ultimately, nothing worked. Part of me thought that if I couldn't save her from something so stupidly simple, I wasn't qualified to help anyone else."

Thomas looked at her for the first time. "What happened to her?"

Choosing her words carefully, Ellie gave him a little bit of herself. "She became addicted to medication that killed her. It was supposed to be for pain management, and I couldn't do anything to get her to stop taking it."

Understanding dawned on him. This was why she did not want the laudanum he had offered her when she had first arrived. He studied her face for a moment before offering his condolences.

Ellie looked down from the intensity of his stare. There was still enough light surrounding them that she could see him clearly while sitting this close. When she looked up again, his gaze was still locked on her, unwavering.

"Thank you for telling me."

Knowing he was not only referring to the story, but the fact that it was something personal about herself, she nodded mutely.

Thomas reached out and put his big hand on her jaw, caressing her cheek with his thumb. Closing her eyes, she leaned into his touch. It was only a moment before she felt his lips on hers, so softly at first, she was not certain it was really happening. But then her lips were parting, welcoming his tongue. Despite having decided to maintain a distance, she could not keep herself from relishing his touch. His free hand went to her lower back, pulling her in closer to him. She could feel his need as his kiss grew more intense, more urgent. Her hands were on his neck, in his hair, and she welcomed everything he gave her, wondering if they could find a more secluded spot when he finally pulled back. Resting his forehead on hers, she watched him as he tried to regain control of himself. She was disappointed to see it return.

Sighing as he sat up straight, his voice husky, he said, "My apologies, Miss Ellie. You deserve not to be pawed at in such a manner. Please forgive me."

"I wasn't exactly complaining," she said with a smile, trying to lighten his seriousness.

"I'd not take advantage of you, darling," he said while looking away.

Ellie put her hand back on his knee again. "Thomas, you could never take advantage of me." She ducked her head to try getting into his line of sight. When he turned away again, she cupped his chin with her fingers, making him look at her.

"I'm here for you. Whatever you need, I'm right here. Okay?"

Nodding, he placed his hand over hers as she moved it to his jaw. Letting him hold her hand in place for a moment, she pulled it away as quickly as she could without making it awkward. As much as she wanted to let him hold her hand, she could not bring herself to close that gap. More than ever now, she needed to maintain some sort of distance from him and holding hands was where she drew the line. She had a lot of practice over the years with keeping things casual and the easiest way for her to keep that line drawn was to not hold hands and not share long, deep gazes into each other's eyes. Kissing was fine, but friendship was all she was capable of giving him.

August 1757

Men trickled into the garrison for days after the massacre. While filling buckets of water, Ellie looked up to see a man with white-blonde hair walking away from her.

"Lucas?" she called out, but there was no response.

She tried running after him but quickly lost track of him in the throngs of soldiers. It had certainly looked like him, but that could not be possible; could it? Going back to her buckets of water, she shook it off, thinking it was merely a reminder that she had not thought about him in a while. Her own guilt and grief were still mocking her, making her see things that were not real.

Three days after the massacre, there were still reports of the woods being full of French and Indians, though word also came that Montcalm had disembarked. Men were still deserting in large numbers with one company reporting thirty of the forty men in the company having deserted from Fort Edward. Four days after the massacre, a letter arrived from Montcalm expressing his remorse that the articles of capitulation granting safe passage of Munro's men were not carried out in full. A flag of truce was raised at the now burned fort to warn the guard to come and receive the remaining prisoners. The imprisoned Englishmen were then escorted to Fort Edward where they arrived on the afternoon of August 15. On the sixteenth, several of them left for Albany, escorting the wounded and sick to the hospital there. The last of the French were seen heading up the lake.

Soldiers continued to desert as more men continued to trickle in over the next several days. The Rangers took over the night patrol, much to Ellie's relief. At least she would not worry about Robert every night, having seen little of him over the previous days. Between the wounded keeping her busy and his duties keeping him busy, there was no time for socializing. Thomas saw him periodically in officer's meetings and he then kept her informed as to Robert's well-being. That was enough for her.

By early September, deserters were being condemned to death. On the fifth, the order was carried out at eight in the morning. This was nothing unusual, as the practice had been in place for the previous year. However, this time, the order was to be carried out by men from the deserters' own companies, who would execute them by firing squad. Other crimes were punishable by either five hundred or one thousand lashes from the cat of nine tails. Every attempt was made to restore order in the garrison after the events of the previous month. Ellie continued to do her job in the hospital, seeing to the sick and injured while keeping to herself as much as she could.

When Robert and Ellie both had a day off and Thomas was stuck working, Robert asked her to spend the day with him. They walked around the camp, talking about everything and nothing, recapping the previous few weeks. When they got to the quiet spot by the Hudson River where they spent their down time, Robert asked Ellie to tell him everything she knew about the next war that the colonists would fight against the Crown. It felt good to confide in someone and to be able to talk about such things, so she told him what she could. Ellie had barely paid attention in history class, so she could not go into much detail, but she surprised herself with how much she did know, telling him of the Boston Massacre and the Boston Tea Party, the start and end dates of the Revolutionary War, the Constitution, the Declaration of Independence, and everything else she could remember. Exact dates always eluded her, but she knew the years for most of those events. Robert's interest was plain, but so was his concern over the events to come.

"How certain are you? Do your visions ever fail to come true?" he asked.

Ellie had not yet corrected him. It was easier to let him think she had visions than to tell him that she was from the future. Neither of them being good options, somehow, having visions seemed the lesser of two evils. It was slightly more believable, even to her own mind, than the concept of time travel which still seemed like magic to her. Though, she still worried that he would rat her out to Thomas at some point, and they would lock her up.

"So far, they've all come true," she said.

"Do you have visions of the people around you?"

Shaking her head, she told him she only saw larger things, global events for the most part. He accepted her response and asked her what other global events she saw, wanting to know how far into the future she could see.

Ellie laughed and told him, "Almost three hundred years."

Shocked by her answer, he was immediately filled with questions. They chatted for some time about the course the country would take before he stopped and thought about a different question that had been plaguing both him and Thomas.

"From where do you come, Miss Ellie?" he asked.

After spending hours discussing future events openly, Ellie suddenly became quiet. She looked away from Robert and quietly said, "Please don't ask me that. I will tell you anything else I can, but not that."

Robert raised her chin to meet his warm brown eyes. "Were you driven out for having visions?"

Ellie fought back the tears. "I really don't have any answers and that is the absolute truth. I come from somewhere far away and have no idea how I got here or how to get back. That's all I can say."

Searching her face, Robert read the truth of her words. He released her chin then and patted her hand. "Very well, Ellie."

They were quiet for a moment as Robert absorbed everything they had discussed and the implications of her ability. Her gift had possibly saved his life. Who was he to punish her for that?

"It's a gift from God," he decided.

Ellie did not believe in God but kept her opinion to herself. There was no reason to not allow him to think what he wanted.

"I should tell Thomas." It had been on her mind for a long time. She hated hiding things from him and desperately wanted to tell him who she was and where she came from.

Robert paused for a moment before answering carefully. "Not only is it a difficult thing to believe for a man of reason, but foretelling the future is illegal. Granted the law is meant to protect others from charlatans operating under the pretense of having foreknowledge of the future in order to commit fraud, but you should have a care with whom you share this information. Thomas is a man of science, believing what he can see and prove. He may not understand this. Worse, he may have you arrested if he believes you to be such a charlatan."

Recalling her conversation with Thomas about witchcraft and believing in things that were unheard of there, she remembered that he had thought the ideas incredulous. Understanding swept across Ellie. She was open-minded, but much the same, not believing anything on faith or another person's word alone. If it could not be proven, she had a tendency to not believe it. This was probably one of the reasons she was struggling to understand what had happened to her. Everything she had ever known about the world suggested that what she had experienced both with the time travel and the healing abilities should be impossible. They may as well be magic. Yet they were happening, even if she could not prove where she came from. She had to accept them as a possibility, even if she did not understand them, but Thomas did not.

Chapter 27

October 1757

Many of the excess troops had been dismissed immediately after the massacre and were sent home on August 17. By mid-September, the provincial troops were moved to the island. The fort began to feel smaller, and life was starting to feel almost normal again, though what classified as normal for Ellie was anything but. By late October, they discovered that enemy scouts were still prowling the woods near the fort when two men were found shot dead near the brick kilns south of the creek on two separate nights. It was a reminder to not wander off from the encampment.

The trio had resumed meeting as often as they could, taking respite from the turmoil of their duties in their nightly tai chi exercises. When not doing tai chi, Ellie watched as Robert and Thomas practiced swordplay. They had grown up learning it together, honing their skills while at school across the ocean. It was uncommon in the colonies, but quite popular in France and still regularly practiced in England.

Though they had learned on rapiers, they now carried the sabers of officers and practiced as often as they could.

Their nearly nightly visits had become an escape for them all, but also a way to stay connected. After finishing a round of tai chi, Thomas went over to where he had left his coat and pulled something from the pocket. He smiled shyly while handing Ellie a book.

She was surprised by the gift. "You brought me a present? It's not even my birthday! Not until the end of the month anyway."

"Your birthday? Why would that matter?"

"Because you brought me a present."

At the confused looks before her, she added, "You know... because birthdays are when people generally give gifts. The celebration of someone's birth every year. Well, birthdays and Christmas."

"Only the birthdays of kings or governors, or other persons of great importance are celebrated."

"You're kidding."

Robert and Thomas exchanged confused looks. Thomas shrugged and Robert turned to Ellie, asking for clarification, "*Kidding?*"

"Joking? Jesting? Teasing?"

"I see," Thomas replied. "No. I am not *kidding*. Are you accustomed to celebrating your birthday, Miss Ellie?"

"Maybe not every year, exactly, but yes. At the very least, everyone I know reaches out to me and wishes me a happy birthday."

"Are you endeavoring to tell us something, Ell? Are you a member of the royal family," Robert teased.

"Royalty? Hardly," Ellie scoffed. Turning her nose up in the air, she inflected her voice with the haughtiest tone she could muster. "I, sir, am a goddess; materialized from thin air, taking on human form to walk the earth with you mere mortals."

"That's the most plausible explanation you've given me thus far," Thomas deadpanned. "It does accord with your arrival as you most assuredly did appear out of thin air." He studied her for a moment while she rolled her eyes in amusement and added, "*Mea dea.*"

When Ellie cocked her head inquisitively at him, he responded, "I forget you do not know Latin. I thought with your medical knowledge…"

He trailed off while Ellie shook her head, prompting him to explain his words. "It means 'My Goddess.'"

Laughing and shaking her head, she asked, "You really don't do anything on birthdays here for people close to you?"

"Most do not even have knowledge of the date of their birth. It would be difficult to mark the occasion with presents."

"Do you both know your dates of birth?"

"August 8, 1730," replied Robert.

"April 18, 1730," added Thomas. "Do you know yours?"

"October 26."

"You know not the year?" Thomas asked.

"I do. I'd just rather not say." She could not very well say *1976.*

"You do not wish us to know how old you are? Is this because you are so much older than we?" Thomas asked with a twinkle in his eye. Ellie knew he was teasing, but Robert did not understand the joke. Thomas enlightened him. "She's rather an old woman."

Ellie played along. With a teasing smile, she said, "That's exactly why."

Momentarily done with her teasing, she turned her attention to the gift in her hand. "Thank you for the book."

She opened it up to see that it was a book of poems by Thomas Gray.

"I know you enjoyed that one from my collection, and wished you to have it," Thomas said.

"I get to keep it? Thank you. I love it. But, you know you have to inscribe it, right?"

"Do I?" he asked.

"Of course. You can't gift someone a book without an inscription. It's bad luck." Trying to convince him to add an inscription, Ellie had made up the last part. Having always loved getting books as gifts, it made it so much more personal when they were inscribed.

"Bring it to me tomorrow and I shall inscribe it for you."

Robert was not finished with the teasing. He asked Ellie mischievously, "Do tell, how old shall you be at the end of the month?"

Turning up her nose, she said playfully, "A lady never tells."

Thomas chimed in with, "She must be near five and eighty now, is that not right?"

Her eyes widened and she swatted him on the arm. "I may have been slightly mistaken in my calculations," he said. "Five and seventy, was it?"

After more goading by the two of them, she finally said, "I am old. I'll be forty-six."

An incredulous Robert blurted out, "That's not possible."

Ellie told him the same thing she had told Thomas all those months ago, "I'm older than I look."

"Yes, but six and forty? I believe it not for a minute."

Thomas agreed with Robert's assessment as Ellie smiled at them, rolling her eyes.

With the joviality winding down, none was particularly eager to leave for the night. Robert commented that the weather was beginning to turn. "We shall be going to winter quarters soon."

They had noticed that snow was not far off. Thomas agreed, "Campaign season is near over. I wonder what next year shall hold."

Robert immediately looked at Ellie, who shook her head almost imperceptibly. He turned back to Thomas. "Will you return home this year?"

"With no smallpox to contend with, I believe I shall."

The mood had immediately changed, and Ellie tried to find something with which to busy herself, pretending she was no longer listening to the conversation as she gathered her things. She wished they had been talking about this in the hospital where it would be easier to feign busyness. Or better yet, when she was not there at all. Ellie still had not considered what she would do. Only having been allowed to stay at the fort over the winter last year because of the smallpox outbreak, she was not sure she would be allowed to do so that year. Ellie was kicking herself for becoming complacent and relying on the army to provide her with living accommodations, food, and pay, meager as they were. Having gotten so used to it, she had not even tried to venture outside of the fort and figure out something else. Now she may be out on her ear in time for a New York winter. Robert turned to her then and asked what her plans were.

"I haven't really thought about it," she said nonchalantly.

Beginning to make her excuses about getting to bed early, Ellie tried to rush off. Before she could get far, Thomas slapped Robert on the side of the head, quietly reminding him, "She's nowhere to go."

"Of course she does," Robert said loudly. "She may join me in Williamsburg. I've plenty of room."

Ellie immediately stopped in her tracks while Thomas looked appalled at the thought, as Robert had intended. Before she could respond, Thomas jumped in with, "She most certainly will not. If she is to stay with anyone in Williamsburg, it shall be me."

Already being embarrassed at the reminder of her position, having Thomas dictate what she was 'allowed' to do made her incensed. An indignant Ellie spun on Thomas with her hands on her hips.

"You can keep your macho bullshit to yourself. I'm perfectly capable of making my own damn decisions about what I do and don't do."

While both men were momentarily stunned, Robert recovered first and guffawed at her audacity.

When Thomas realized his mistake, he placed his hands on Ellie's waist, displacing her own hands which moved to his forearms as he pulled her into him.

"Please forgive me, darling. I certainly did not mean to imply otherwise." Running a finger down the side of her face, he continued, "It would bring me great pleasure if you came home with me. I mean no impropriety and you shall be unmolested."

"Well, that's unfortunate," she muttered.

Ellie knew he did not mean the term in a sexual way, but she could not help herself. Both men looked at her with confused expressions once again.

"You wish for harm to befall you?" Robert asked.

"No, sorry. Bad joke. Forget it," she said.

Of all the differences in language that she had encountered, the frequent usage of *unmolested* in a generic reference to safety always threw her off. She was used to the word having entirely different connotations. While her dark sense of humor had led to her making a poor joke about wanting to be molested, even the suggestion of sexual relations with Thomas while he held her like he was now had her mind spinning. Ellie shook herself from the lewd thoughts going through her mind and focused on the conversation. Her annoyance at his possessiveness immediately dissipated with his apology as her heart filled with the idea of spending time alone with Thomas, away from the fort and all the other soldiers. She began to nod her head to say yes but then something occurred to her.

"You'll be there spending Christmas with your family."

Thomas nodded, "Yes."

Shaking her head now, Ellie started to push him away, disentangling herself from his arms. "Thomas, I don't want to intrude on your family Christmas. They haven't even seen you in, how long?"

"Years," he said. "But you shan't be intruding at all." Thomas took her hand, stopping her from leaving. "Spend Christmas with me, Miss Ellie."

She was hesitant. As much as she wanted to spend Christmas with him, she did not want to meet his family. They had not actually been 'courting' as they said there, but Ellie was pretty certain meeting the family of someone with whom you had a romantic involvement of any sort was a big deal in any time period. She did not want him or them to get the wrong idea.

"Would you prefer to remain here in the snow and spend it in a tent with five other women?" he asked.

Robert jumped in to assist. "Christmas is fabulous in Williamsburg. These New Englanders know not how to do Christmas. But Virginians? We know how to do Christmas. Balls every night, feasts, games, the fox hunt, horse races; it shall be a grand time."

Ellie had to admit, it did sound fun. "Fine. I'll go. But don't you go getting any ideas, mister. This doesn't mean anything. I'm only coming because you guys are my friends and I want to spend the holidays with you, not because I particularly want to meet your family."

Narrowing her eyes, she pointed her finger at him while she spoke to emphasize her point. Thomas and Robert laughed at her theatrics, but Robert asked, "What did you call us?"

Ellie paused. What had she said this time? "What? Guys?"

"Yes. What does that mean? Is it another word for friend?"

She shrugged. Every time she thought she was making progress with the speech, there was always something new that came up.

"It's a generic term to refer to a person or group of people," she explained.

"But you will go?" Thomas asked again, trying to make certain she had, in fact, said yes.

When she confirmed that she would go, Thomas hugged her excitedly, lifting Ellie off her feet in the process. He kissed her on the cheek, then set her back down before adding, "The hospital in Philadelphia offers lectures every winter. With the outbreak, I was unable to attend last year, but I shall be in attendance this year. Would you care to accompany me to that after Christmas as well?"

"Are you kidding? You should have led with that. I'd love to."

Thomas asked, "It's a long journey and I'm afraid we'll be on horseback for a significant portion of it. Will you be able to make the journey?"

"Absolutely! I love road trips," Ellie said excitedly, having always loved the open road. Whether in a car or on her motorcycle, there was a freedom to it. She loved driving cross-country by herself, though she did not often have the time or money to do so. Most of her trips involved going as far as Las Vegas to visit Kristy or to other surrounding states.

Both men looked at each other, then back at her with confusion. At the questioning looks, Ellie shook her head and said, "Never mind."

"No one loves to travel," Robert said. "It takes too long to get anywhere. It's filthy. Accommodations are poor at best. And it is oft quite dangerous."

"Oh, come on, Robbie. Where's your sense of adventure?"

November 1757

It was not long before the army was broken up and either released or sent to winter quarters as the campaign season ended for the year. It snowed two inches on October 30, as if to emphasize the point. The inhabitants of the fort spent the next few days packing up and preparing to leave. Ellie put all of her meager belongings into a sack for the journey and they departed from the fort on the cold morning of November 10.

They stopped periodically to rest themselves and the horses, but they made good time, reaching Stillwater by the end of the first day. There was very little there with the town consisting of a rather small settlement. They found the home of a family whom they hoped would allow them to stay overnight. With few hotels or motels in the period, travelers would often knock on the doors of random homes and the people inside would typically allow them in. Ellie found the concept rather bizarre, but also quaint, though it felt like a rather unsafe thing to do.

As they arrived at a home and dismounted, Ellie stood on wobbly legs. Without thinking, she said, "Damn. It's been ages since I've spent that much time in the saddle. I hope I can walk tomorrow."

Thomas stopped unpacking their belongings and turned to her. "I believed you to have never ridden a horse before?"

Thinking about her motorcycle, she was momentarily confused by his question. What did she say? "I hadn't. Not until you taught me how to ride."

"Then how could you have been 'in the saddle?'"

Realization of what she had said suddenly sank in. "Oh. No. Not that kind of saddle."

Both Robert and Thomas were now staring at her, waiting for an explanation. How could she explain her motorcycle?

A thought popped into her head that maybe she would not have to. She tried a different tactic, thinking carefully about her words as she spoke. "We have… contraptions… called bicycles. They're a metal frame on two wheels with pedals that you can turn with your feet to make it go." At this, Ellie did a pedaling motion with her hands. "The seats are called saddles and I used to ride all the time."

At their doubtful expressions, Ellie added, "They're a lot of fun and good exercise, too. Very good for your health."

"Like tai chi?" Thomas asked.

"Exactly," Ellie smiled.

Thomas let it drop, but it was another reminder that he knew nothing of her past. She was still hiding things from him. Was she lying as well? The contraption she described sounded like nothing he had ever heard of before. Ellie had certainly not seemed to know her way around horses when he taught her, but perhaps she had been pretending. Was she that good an actress? That was unlikely. It was always obvious to him when she was speaking falsehoods. Was she simply confused? Sometimes the things she said were so fanciful, they could not possibly be true. Did she merely live in her own imagination, confusing her thoughts for reality? Robert had said he could trust her, and he was working on it but still was not certain. He desperately wanted to, but until she was completely honest with him, he did not know how he could.

***

"So, the Regulars are primarily from England and the provincials are from the colonies?"

They talked along the journey, using it to help pass the time. Ellie had picked up a lot about life in that time, but there was still so much she was missing. She used this opportunity to clarify some of the questions still floating around in her mind.

"Yes," Thomas answered. "Though many of the Regular units contain men from the colonies. The militia also derive of men from the colonies."

"But the militia only enlist as needed, then go home as soon as the campaign ends?"

"Correct. They are usually farmers who need to return to their crops." With Thomas curled behind her on his horse, his words came softly in her ear, sending chills down her spine that had nothing to do with the cold.

"Okay. And the provincial regiments reflect where they're from? So, the Connecticut Regiment is made up of men from Connecticut and the Massachusetts Regiment is all men from Massachusetts?"

Thomas and Robert both nodded.

"So, how is it that if you're both from Virginia, you ended up in a Regular Regiment stationed in New York?" She had been wondering about this one for quite some time. Initially, she had not thought twice about it, knowing how the military operated in her own time, sending troops all over the world as needed, but that was not how things operated in this time period.

"We would have joined a Virginia Regiment, but we both schooled with the major of our regiment in Edinburgh," Robert offered. "When the hostilities began again, he was tasked with enlisting men for his regiment, which was stationed in New York. He had two captain's commissions open for purchase. Since no one in Virginia had two open, we agreed to buy into the Regular Regiment so we could stay together."

"Your officer commissions were purchased?" She had learned that some of the commissions were purchased after hearing of several that had been for sale at the fort, but did not understand how it worked, thinking it was an exception, rather than the norm.

"They're all purchased," Thomas explained, "with rare exceptions. But those are typically reserved for promotions which rarely occur outside of war."

Ellie absorbed the explanations, then turned to Robert as she asked, "You both schooled in Edinburgh?"

A cold breeze swept over them, and Ellie huddled closer. Thomas used the opportunity to wrap his arms more tightly around her, squeezing the great cloak closer together. It felt right holding her in his arms like this, though he had to focus his thoughts the entire journey. Every time she moved, his body came to life.

"I studied law while Thomas studied medicine," Robert explained. "However, unlike Thomas, I returned home when I completed my education.

Ellie turned in the seat, trying to look at Thomas, but they were too close together. Thomas closed his eyes at the effect it had on him and concentrated on her unspoken question.

"After I finished, I pursued additional training in London. There's a charity hospital there that was built in the twelfth century. Saint Thomas's Hospital provides training for a great many British practitioners of medicine."

"Saint Thomas's?" Ellie asked with a smirk. Thomas did not need to see her face to hear the amusement in her voice.

"Yes." He poked a finger into her side to distract her before she could make a joke about him working in a hospital with that name. She laughed and squirmed in her seat, making his attempt at distraction a success, but simultaneously making things more difficult for him. He shifted in the saddle, but it was a small space and there was nowhere for him to go. Thankfully, he did not have to stand anytime soon. He only hoped her skirts were thick enough to prevent her from feeling the effect she was having on him.

Thomas was struggling to control himself with Ellie so close for so long. He did not understand the reaction he was having. It was as if he was a young boy again, coming into adulthood and unable to control himself. He had not had this much difficulty around a woman since he was quite young. But Ellie

Sorenson had such an effect on him. Never having met anyone like her before, he had found her a curiosity at first, with such strange dress, jewelry, tattoos, and vernacular. It took no time at all for her to intrigue him and begin filling him with new ideas. Constantly challenging him, she made him question his own beliefs about the world while making him feel seen and not judged. She was smart, brave, forward thinking, and never took advantage of others, always making people feel at ease, as though they were all her equals. Despite being highly educated and intelligent, she somehow managed to maintain a certain innocence or naivety that he could not quite understand. Unlike the women he had always met in his social circles, she did not seem to be interested in money or social standing. She was eclectic, unlike anyone he had ever met, both in her knowledge and her behavior. He wanted to know everything about her and understand the way her mind worked. Being the focus of her attention was like emerging into the hot summer sun after a long, cold, dark winter. If only he could break through the barriers she kept built up around herself. Perhaps in time, she would let him in.

The group tried to stop in settlements or towns as much as possible. They only had one tent between them and the one night they found themselves between settlements, the men set up the small canvas tent and insisted Ellie take it.

"And where will the two of you sleep?" she asked.

Without hesitation, they both answered in unison, "Out here."

Their answer sounding as though it had been practiced, Ellie laughed at them and shook her head.

"It's too cold out here. There's plenty of space inside the tent for all of us."

Both men immediately balked at her suggestion, arguing over how improper it would be, that they were gentlemen and would never compromise her, and every other excuse they could come up with. Ellie was not having it.

"Stop it. We're all adults and I trust both of you completely. It'll be warmer inside the tent and with all three of us in there, it'll be that much warmer. Now stop acting like children and get inside the tent."

Properly chastised, the men looked at each other and Robert shrugged. They resigned themselves to following Ellie's orders and crawled inside the small space. None of them slept that night, but they were warm while they laid awake.

They rode into New York City with Thomas periodically letting Ellie take the reins and run the horse. Thomas enjoyed the delight on her face whenever they stopped after these bouts. As they approached the outskirts, they stopped for a rest where Robert pointed out the now visible city.

Without thinking, Ellie exclaimed, "Holy shit! That's New York Fucking City? Jesus Christ. I can walk every street in the city in less than a day."

Her eyes were wide, and her heart was racing. It had not even occurred to Ellie to curb her words, as she was too busy trying to not have a panic attack. Her entire body was on alert as she struggled to breathe. After all this time and everything she had seen, she was still not prepared for this. She realized that she had still been picturing her New York City the entire journey thus far. The morgue in which she worked during covid had been across the East River from the Statue of Liberty and Manhattan and she had gotten used to seeing the statue and all of the skyscrapers every day. Now the skyline she had come to know was gone. The thought made her want to cry. Ellie had never had any particular interest in living in New York City, but she had taken care of it while it was sick and dying. This had given her a sense of guardianship over it. Her only condolence was that this period was before and not after her time there. Rather than being over, all of those things were still to come. It did not stop the heartache from coming.

As her eyes filled with tears and she tried to control her anxiety, Ellie's companions were becoming increasingly alarmed. They were both by her side in an instant, trying to see to her welfare. They had thought she was excited until they saw the horror-stricken look on her face and her eyes brimming with tears.

Thomas pulled her to him, whispering soothing words, but he did not understand what was happening, and knew she would not tell him. In an attempt to give them some privacy, Robert saw to the horses. Ellie regained her composure, burying her emotions deep inside once again, something at which she had become an expert over the years. At the sudden change, Thomas was even more concerned.

When he asked if she was alright, she replied, "Yup. All good," and went to assist Robert with the horses. Thomas was disappointed that she would not talk about what had just happened, but Ellie could not talk about it. As much as he hated it, Thomas was getting used to these seemingly random emotional episodes followed by Ellie closing herself off and behaving as though nothing had happened. He wished more than anything that she would open up to him.

***

Once in the city, they found a public house in which to stay, then went to book passage on a ship to Williamsburg for the next day. Ellie was ecstatic at the idea.

"Am I to understand then, that you've never before traveled by ship?" Robert asked.

"Not like this, no," she replied. She had been on a schooner and ferry boats before, but they were short rides, typically around a harbor. This was something entirely different and the prospect excited her greatly.

Thomas found he enjoyed being with her while she had new experiences. After booking passage, they walked around the city. It was a constant struggle for Ellie to keep her emotions in check, which was highly unusual for her. She had never been a particularly emotional person yet found them to always be just under the surface there. They were always ready to spring forth with no notice. Having no control over them was really starting to piss her off.

When they came upon a clothier, Thomas suggested they go inside. Robert continued on to another shop while Ellie looked around and Thomas spoke to the shopkeeper. It was fascinating to see how stores operated in the era. The shopkeeper came back with a gown in his hands and held it out to a confused Ellie. She eyed the beautiful dress while feeling the smooth fabric. The overskirt and bodice were a purple silk covered in delicately embroidered vines and flowers and there was a coat to match.

After complimenting the shopkeeper on such a fine piece of clothing, she turned away to continue window-shopping. Thomas informed her that the dress was for her if she wanted to try it on. She eyed him sideways, and politely declined, knowing she could not afford such a dress. Ellie had been saving as much of her pay as she could, but it was meager, and she still had to buy various sundries from the sutler while at the fort. What she had managed to save certainly did not need to be thrown away on something so extravagant when she already had clothing, assuming she even had enough to cover the cost, which she doubted. The clothes she had may have been rather plain and worn, but they were suf-ficient to meet her needs. Ellie was not concerned with her appearance.

Thomas continued to insist while Ellie tried to discreetly decline, but the man was not taking no for an answer. She finally told him, "It's too much. I can't afford it and these clothes are just fine."

"I don't expect you to purchase it, darling. I shall cover the expense."

"Absolutely not. You already covered the cost of everything else on this journey and the passage to Williamsburg; you don't need to be buying me a dress on top of it."

"And if it is something I wish to do?"

Ellie stood with her arms crossed over her chest, glaring at him. Finally, she decided to walk out of the shop when he stopped her. Spinning on him, she said, "I told you once before, I don't want your char-ity."

"This is not charity, Miss Ellie. Consider it a gift."

That was not much better as far as she was concerned. She said, "I don't want it," and left him standing in the shop.

When he came out behind her, he asked what was wrong. Before she could say anything else, something flashed through Ellie's mind and she asked, "Are you embarrassed by me?"

Thomas stepped back as though she had physically struck him. "Never. I thought the gown to be of your liking."

"It is. But it's too much," she said.

"I can well afford it."

"Is that supposed to make me feel better? I can't repay you. And I don't want your money, Thomas."

As she began walking away, he grabbed her hand, pulling her back. "Ellie, my dear, I am well-aware you're unaccustomed to letting other people do things for you, nor do I believe you to be after my money." He brushed a hair away from her eye and continued, "However, I wish for you to have it. You shall need ball gowns once we arrive in Williamsburg and I do not expect you to repay me. I want of nothing in return. It would give me the greatest pleasure to spoil you. My darling girl, I'd remove you far away from this war and give you everything were it within my power. Please allow me this small thing."

When Ellie still hesitated, he added, "Moreover, you need a proper coat. This one is not fit for a lady."

Thomas tugged on the lapels of the red army uniform coat that had been given to her the previous winter, pulling her into him. He kissed her nose sweetly and brushed his hands along the shoulders of the coat, waiting for her reply.

A long vacation sounded heavenly; just the two of them, a large bed, and room service. She wanted to accept his offer and let him take her away and spoil her. Since she did not know how to be that person, she said instead, "You're an ass."

Thomas smirked. "Yet, you continue to enjoy my presence."

Rolling her eyes, Ellie turned and walked back into the store with a sigh, taking the gown to try it on, the shopkeeper's assistant right behind her. The assistant helped her disrobe and put on all the many new layers. This was entirely different from what she had gotten used to wearing and was not amenable to a lady being able to dress herself. The new ensemble began with a shift much like the one she already wore. However, after the shift came a knee-length petticoat instead of the full-length ones to which she had become accustomed. Unlike the stays she wore daily which laced in both the front and back, this one only laced in the back. Over the pocket bags went a pannier. This padded roll tapered at each end, resting on her low back in order to lift the skirt and emphasize the waist. Another petticoat went on over the top of the pannier, this one full-length. Given that it was winter, this one was quilted. The neckerchief was silk and a decorative V-shaped panel was pinned to the stays underneath. This stomacher matched the silk gown petticoat which was lined with linen. The gown came next which was similar to the short jacket she normally wore, but this one had a full-length attached skirt that went down to the floor. The bodice edges were pinned along the edges of the stomacher and ribbons beneath the skirt tied together to give it a puff. The bodice sleeves and front edges were lined with lace. The final piece was a delicate silk apron which was about half as wide as the ones she normally wore and she was informed it was purely decorative.

When she came out to show off the gown, Thomas's breath hitched, and his handsome face was split by a large smile.

"You look stunning."

"It is beautiful," Ellie admitted.

"I picked this one special for you. I thought you'd favor it, being that it's purple."

Ellie looked at him with a question in her eyes.

"You seem to favor purple. Followed by blue, I believe?" Thomas suddenly seemed unsure. "Did I guess wrong?"

"No. You're dead on. I just can't believe you could tell."

"I notice much when it comes to you, *mea dea*."

She could feel a blush spread across her cheeks, which was entirely unexpected. When was the last time she blushed under a man's attention prior to meeting Thomas. It was entirely unlike her. Yet he seemed to draw it out of her as though she were a teenager. When she turned back to the privacy screen to put her old clothes back on, he stopped her, telling her she should wear the gown.

"I don't want to get it ruined while we travel."

"It will hold," he assured her. It was not proper travel wear, being more suited for the balls they would be attending, but he was not yet ready to see her back in her old attire. This suited her so much better than the old ratty clothes she wore daily.

"It's also a bit too long," she argued. "It needs to be hemmed before I wear it."

Thomas relented and the shopkeeper marked the length where it needed to be hemmed. While Ellie stood there watching him work, Robert came into the shop after having finished his business. When he saw her, he did a double take and whistled. The smile that broke out on Ellie's face lit up the room.

After the bottom of the dress was pinned in place, Ellie went back behind the privacy screen with the assistant and changed back into her regular clothes while Thomas took care of the bill and made arrangements to come by in the morning to pick up the gown. When she came back out, he handed her a new coat that was much like the ones she wore daily but was quilted with sleeves that extended to her wrists. A round fur muff accompanied it to keep her hands warm. It was significantly warmer than what she had and combined with the cloak she wore, it kept her comfortable.

As soon as they walked outside, Ellie placed a hand on Thomas's chest, stood on her tiptoes, and placed a kiss on his lips. When she broke free, she said, "Thank you."

They left the shop with Ellie strutting down the street, an arm attached to each of her best friends in the world, locked in place with her hands now tucked inside the muff. When they told her it was inappropriate, she told them she did not care. They knew she did not, which was one of the things that drew them both in.

They laughed while walking down the street and Ellie called them the Three Musketeers, quoting, "All for one, and one for all," a reference neither understood. Ellie had not thought that a particularly modern story, but apparently it was modern enough.

The next morning, Thomas went back to the dressmaker and loaded the extra luggage onto his horse, walking back to the public house to join

Robert and Ellie before heading to the docks. When Ellie set eyes on the amount of luggage he had, she teased him.

"Got in some extra shopping while you were out did you? Here I thought you were only going to the dressmaker."

"I did. Surely you did not think I would only purchase one gown? We shall have balls to attend every night."

"You didn't?" Ellie was immediately annoyed at his presumptions and grand gesture when he knew she was already uncomfortable with it. Though she knew he was trying to be thoughtful and do something nice, she was not used to that and did not know how to take it.

"I could not let them go to waste. Normally gowns such as these take weeks to make. The dressmaker informed me while you were looking around yesterday that the woman who had ordered them expired before she could pick them up. He kept them as displays but hoped someone would purchase them. In addition to the one you tried on, there are two more gowns and shoes to match."

He was rather smug about slipping it past her and Ellie wanted to throttle him, but it was already done. She tried to accept the gowns for what they were and thanked him again, even though she hated feeling indebted to anyone.

Chapter 29

December 1757

The journey aboard the ship was everything Ellie had hoped it would be. She loved spending
time on the water. Every moment possible
was spent on the deck watching the waves roll by and
feeling the cold salty sea air and the sun on her skin.
Certain she had not stopped smiling the entire way,
Ellie did not even feel the frigidness in the air, bun-
dled up as she was.

The whole trip had taken close to three weeks,
the majority of it getting across New York. When
they arrived in Williamsburg on the first of December, Ellie was instantly taken back to her childhood,
despite not having thought about her time there in
years. When her dad was stationed near Norfolk,
they visited Colonial Williamsburg often. Her grandparents came to visit one year, and the family had
gone to see all of America's Historic Triangle, exploring Colonial Williamsburg, Jamestown, and
Yorktown. They continued going often after that,
enjoying the Christmas season in particular. It was

one of the only memories she had of her parents ever having been involved with her and her siblings. Though the streets were dirt now and a modern city was not visible beyond the historic buildings, this looked remarkably like the town she visited as a child with the houses and shops all lining a single main street, continuing onto a few secondary streets, and spreading out into farmland from there. The vegetation was thicker than what she was used to, but as they walked down Duke of Gloucester Street, she recognized most of the buildings. The Governor's Palace, capitol building, the magazine, courthouse, and Public Gaol were all as she remembered. There were several other buildings that she recognized as well. Much of it looked the same as it had when she was a child.

"I've been away for some time," Thomas said. "Everything has grown substantially since I was last here."

Robert agreed, "It has. Since they rebuilt the capitol building after it burned down a few years ago, everyone seems to be moving here. I would expect the merchants and artisans, but even the planters are moving here now. We shall all have a need to sell off parcels of our own land if it continues."

"I dare say we would get a fair penny for them," Thomas replied. "Come now, Robert, our families have both been here for four generations. I hardly think it shall cause either of our families any concern. If I know my father, he's already found a way to profit from the growth."

Ellie was not listening to the conversation around her. Being there, seeing these places had the most profound effect on her of all the places they had been to yet. Taking in a deep breath, she tried to push away the melancholy she was feeling, toying with the pendants on both of her necklaces as they walked. Even if she was home, her grandparents would not be there. They had both passed years ago. She plastered a smile on her face, but her companions both knew it was forced when it did not reach her eyes. They both also knew she would not tell them what was on her mind and left her to her secrets.

Once off the main street, they mounted the horses and rode the rest of the way, coming up to a large plantation outside the main part of town, spread over acres and acres of land covered in outbuildings. Ellie was struck by the size of it. Visiting plantations as a child had always been a favorite for her, but this was completely different. It was in full operation and her eyes were drawn to the many shacks further out in the field. Though she had never seen those at the plantations she had visited, she knew them to be the slaves' quarters and she was instantly filled with disgust.

Thomas helped her off the horse and took her arm, walking her up to the house. Turning back, she tried to ask about their belongings, but he said someone would come take care of them. Ellie was suddenly filled with nerves and unease and wondered if this had been a good idea while wanting to turn around and run back to New York.

When they went inside, a beautiful older woman with blonde hair under a linen cap came down the stairs to greet them. A tall man came down the hall at nearly the same time. It was easy to see where Thomas got his looks. His mother was a tall woman, and gave off a stern countenance, giving her an imposing air. His father had brown hair that was beginning to gray and seemed far more friendly. Ellie was introduced to James and Martha Burke, whom she thought were probably not much older than she was herself. That did not help her unease. Her heart was racing so fast, she thought everyone could hear it.

Thomas's parents were welcoming enough, even if they appeared surprised at her presence. They greeted Thomas, then Robert, then her, when Thomas was finally able to introduce her. Some of his seven surviving siblings came to greet them next and she could tell how close they had all been, despite the differences in age which ranged from seven to thirty. Robert was like one of the family as well. It all became quite overwhelming rather quickly. Robert headed home and Ellie was shown to her room and to her surprise, her things were already there waiting for her. Thomas could sense her unease and closed the door, despite how it would appear.

He pulled her into him, wrapping his arms around her, rubbing her back and kissing the top of her head. Ellie rested her head on his chest and took comfort from his strength.

His deep voice rumbled in his chest. "I know my family may be a bit overwhelming, however it has been a long time since they've seen me. They're excited to have me home. I'm overjoyed to have you here with me."

"They're fine. Really. Thank you for bringing me. I'm just missing my own family. Guess I'm feeling a little nostalgic."

The attempt to give him a smile was unsuccessful when she did not feel it. He kissed her gently and suggested some rest might help. Ellie was happy to follow his advice. This was the most luxury she had experienced since her arrival in the past. She had a room entirely to herself with a giant, comfortable-looking bed and a fireplace already warming the room. Wanting nothing more than a shower and some sleep, she settled for sleep since a shower was not an option.

Ellie slept through dinner and did not wake until morning, not realizing how tired she had been. Some of her tiredness could be attributed to the emotions that had been wreaking havoc on her throughout the entire journey. When a beautiful young girl with dark skin came in to tend to her needs, Ellie was not sure how to handle the matter. She tried to send the girl away, saying she could manage, but she did not leave. Instead, she began opening the curtains and tending the fire, which Ellie realized was still going. Someone must have come in during the night to tend to it.

When she realized the girl was not going anywhere, Ellie introduced herself and asked her name. Daphne was slow to say anything other than her name, but Ellie confided in her that she had no idea what she was doing there. Despite saying it as if it was a secret, Ellie suspected everyone could see it plain as day. The truth was that Ellie felt more comfortable with this girl than she had with the rest of the family the afternoon before. It felt like she was playing pretend with them but could be herself with Daphne. The girl buried a laugh and Ellie told her she had a beautiful smile. Daphne slowly began to open up to her.

Dressed in clothes that were not her own, but had been in the wardrobe, Ellie could no longer hide in her room, and she slowly made her way down the grand staircase. Daphne had told her where she could find the drawing room, where everyone would gather until breakfast was served. As Ellie walked through the vast estate, she had the urge to look inside every room. She was immediately reminded of the governor's mansion in Colonial Williamsburg, but without all of the armament adorning the entryway and hallways. There were so many rooms, it would have been easy to get lost if Daphne had not told her where to go.

Thomas found Ellie roaming the hallway, looking at the paintings adorning the walls. She looked stunning as always, but he was glad to see his sisters' clothing fit her well. Not as fancy as the ball gowns he had purchased for her, they were far nicer than what she had obtained at the fort. Coming to stand behind her, he explained how he was related to the person in each painting. Her hand on his arm, he escorted her to the drawing room and introduced her to the remaining family members she had not yet met. Ellie wished with all her being that she could be the confident, capable woman she knew herself to be, but in that moment, she was anything but. To her own horror, she found herself almost hiding behind Thomas as they walked in, not wanting the attention she was receiving. Everything in her was screaming to run fast and run far. She wondered briefly if she could find Robert and hide out with him until they left for Philadelphia. The only problem with that option was that he was also with his family. She was stuck there. It was going to be a very long month and a half.

Thomas escorted Ellie into the dining room with his hand on the small of her back, pulled out her chair for her when she sat, and seated himself beside her. The family sat down for the most formal breakfast Ellie had ever attended. She was expecting formal dinners but had not considered breakfast. The long table was set with China, crystal, and silver with flowers and candles decorating the center. If this was breakfast, Ellie wondered what dinner was going to entail. She knew in a household of this standing, it was going to be much more formal than even this and hoped she would be able to conduct herself in a manner that would not embarrass Thomas. Glad she had skipped the meal last night, she planned to use this opportunity to watch her table companions for clues to the proper etiquette. She would do the same at dinner, but this gave her a chance to practice.

Several enslaved women brought in dishes and Ellie thanked each one as they set anything down in front of her, grateful that she recognized everything that was brought in. She opted to skip the coffee as she had never been a fan but had some of the milk that was offered. Being hand-sliced after cooking, the bacon was slightly different from what she was used to, but everything else was recognizable. To go with the bacon, there were also eggs and toast, but the last dish that was brought out gave Ellie a surprise. Thomas had been watching her and leaned in to whisper something to her, but before he could say anything, she looked at him and asked, "Waffles?"

Thomas looked down at her plate and back up at her. She followed his gaze, then smiled at him. "You have waffles here?" she asked.

Thomas warmed at her delight but was confused by her surprise. Waffles were not uncommon in the colonies nor in Europe. The Dutch had actually brought them to the colonies, making them a familiar dish in New York.

"You seem surprised," he observed.

"I am. I didn't know waffles were a thing here," she said with a smile.

"A thing?" he asked, shaking his head with a smirk. He understood her meaning well enough but often found her choice of words amusing. Every so often, he could not hide that amusement. She recognized it for what it was and smiled with him.

The exchange had eased her nerves ever so slightly while also giving Ellie time to observe others at the table. Their manners were precisely what she had expected. The only difference from her standard was that the waffles were always cut with the knife instead of the side of a fork and utensils were used to eat the bacon.

"I'm glad you're pleased," Thomas said quietly to her before taking a bite of egg.

"I'm always pleased when I actually recognize what's placed in front of me. So much of life here is so foreign, it's nice when I'm presented with something familiar."

Thomas paused before his next bite, looking at her for a moment. In all this time, he had not considered how difficult that must have been for her. While he watched her, he noticed that she took dainty bites of her waffle after cutting it with her knife and fork in the same way his mother and sisters had. Though she was far from improper, Ellie was not typically very formal in her table manners at the fort. He had wondered if he would need to guide her on proper etiquette but had forgotten to do so prior to now. He was glad to see it would not be an issue. Though, it once again had him leaning towards her being a gentlewoman prior to appearing at the fort. Continuously going back and forth between that and her being of low breeding while also having spent time with the Indians, he simply could not make sense of her. Perhaps it was time he gave up trying. When she looked up and saw him watching her, she smiled at him, placing another bite of waffle in her mouth. Thomas smiled back at her and turned back to his own breakfast.

Ellie preened under Thomas's warm gaze. This was not as bad as she had thought. Despite the unfamiliar formalities, she could do this. She would simply take one day, one moment, at a time. Being surrounded by people gave her ample opportunities to decide whose lead to follow, though all she had to do was watch Thomas and take her cues from him, knowing he would not steer her wrong. Ellie was starting to feel some of her confidence slowly come back. She would make it through this visit just fine.

While leaving breakfast, Ellie lowered her voice to ask Thomas, "Why are the boys all wearing dresses?"

Thomas looked at her blankly for a moment, then broke out into laughter. "They're not dresses. Boys don't wear breeches until around age seven or eight when they undergo a breeching ceremony. Until then, all children wear gowns."

"I had no idea." She had always thought that children simply wore miniature versions of the same clothes adults wore. Everything there was still a constant surprise.

Chapter 30

December 1757

It took several days, but Ellie slowly relaxed a little and got to know Thomas's family. As much as relaxing around them was possible. They were very formal, and Ellie had to keep reminding herself that Thomas was Captain Burke and Robert was Captain Jensen. Though she was allowed to call his younger siblings by their given names, everyone else was mister or missus. She constantly reminded herself to sit up straight and watch her speech. Ellie had tried to mimic the speech patterns of the people at the fort, adopting some of the more formalized speech and terminology of the period that she heard daily as much as she could. Trying to only relax her speech when she was in private with Robert or Thomas, it often slipped when she was excited or tired. It was all rather exhausting. Every chance she got to slip away with Thomas or his sisters, she gladly took it. The snow began to fall as Christmas got closer and she was surprised to see the amount that fell. It had never snowed that much when she lived there as a child.

They went into town after a heavy snowfall one morning. As Thomas handed her into the sleigh and sat down beside her, Ellie seemed to have found humor in something. Pulling a blanket over their laps, he looked at her rosy cheeks, pink from the cold, and marveled that she was there with him.

"What is it that has brought the laughter to your eyes, my dear?" he asked, but she was enigmatic as always in her answer.

With a spot of mischief in her eye now, she asked him, "This is all just normal for you, isn't it?"

Ellie knew he had no idea what she was talking about, but it did not matter. She had seen the sleighs at the fort all winter the previous year, and knew it was how they got around. But a horse-drawn sleigh ride through the snow was not simply transportation in her time. It had an entirely different connotation for her. Snuggling into him to help ward off the cold, she enjoyed the experience.

Seeing this side of Thomas was a treat. At the fort, he was much more serious most of the time. Though he let his guard down a little when they spent time together outside of the hospital, he spent most of his time as a confident, take charge, and no-nonsense military man. In Williamsburg, he was somehow slightly softer; more relaxed, sweet, and even playful. She was glad she had the opportunity to see him like this, but more so, she was glad he had the opportunity to relax for a while.

James and Martha Burke had a Christmas party—no, a ball, she corrected herself—which seemed to be attended by half the town and surrounding farms. Wearing one of her beautiful new gowns, she was grateful now that Thomas had purchased them for her. Ellie would have felt vastly out of place there in the tattered clothes she had. In addition to the gowns and many layers, there were new shoes and stockings to go with them. Daphne had helped her dress, informing her the garters were tied above the knee. They only went below the knee when being more active. The stockings were embroidered at the ankle in what Daphne had called a cloque. With Daphne's help, she wore her hair half up and half down, again with no cap, though she learned it was slightly more acceptable to go without a head covering for formal occasions. It was the only time a woman was not chastised for leaving her hair uncovered, though many women still covered theirs. Instead, Daphne laced ribbons through the curls atop her head, making Ellie feel entirely like royalty.

When she came down the stairs, Ellie found Thomas exquisitely dressed, wearing a gray coat and pants with a royal blue vest which matched the dress she wore. She knew he had somehow planned it, likely with the help of Daphne, but she liked matching him. With his light brown hair pulled back into a low pony tail and curled at the temples, and lace at his collar and sleeves, he looked every bit the gentleman he was. It was impossible for Ellie to take her eyes off of him.

He was having the same problem. "You look exquisite, *mea dea.*"

There were so many people, she found herself constantly sneaking out. She was happy to see Robert again, though. He spent most of the night escorting her around while Thomas was otherwise engaged and helped her sneak out on more than one occasion, until his sister scolded him for running off with his friend's lady. Ellie got a great kick out of that one and laughed uproariously at his discomfort.

It felt good to be home. Thomas was enjoying not only this time with his family, but with Ellie as well. He loved being with her away from the fort and all of the other soldiers with whom he had to share her. Here, he did not even have to share her with Robert. Or at least, he had not until tonight. Though he was a little jealous that she had been spending most of her night with Robert instead of him, he had been kept plenty busy with all of his friends and neighbors whom he had not seen in years.

There was one guest in particular he had been trying to avoid, but when his mother brought his sister's friend around, there was no avoiding her. Thomas kissed her hand politely, and talked amiably with her, glad for the first time all night that Robert had been keeping Ellie occupied. The young Miss Talbot had turned seventeen this year and his parents wanted him to marry her. He had been aware of her interest in him as a young girl, but being ten years younger than him, he had never paid her any attention. Now that she was of marrying age, she had begun writing him. Thomas was polite, but as disinterested as he could express. The girl had grown into a beautiful woman, but she was not Ellie. The thought had him searching the room, trying to find her. When he caught Robert's eye, he sent him a look of thanks at entertaining Ellie and keeping her away from him while he spoke with the young girl before him.

Thomas managed to finally get some time in with Ellie at the end of the night. They danced after he quickly showed her the steps, and she laughed every time she mis-stepped. Thomas loved that she did not get upset or embarrassed like most women would have. Regardless of whether or not she was doing what everyone else expected, she enjoyed herself and even made up new steps of her own when she became lost. After their dance, he took her outside where they meandered around the veranda. It was cold, but it had been quite warm inside and the cold air felt good. When Ellie's cheeks began turning pink, he put his coat over her.

"Thank you for being here."

Ellie smiled and thanked him for inviting her. They spent a few more minutes outside, then went back in when the guests began to leave. Ellie hugged Robert and kissed him on the cheek, wishing him a Merry Christmas. He returned the kiss to her cheek before shaking hands with Thomas and departing.

Waiting for Thomas in a doorway nearby, she watched while he said his goodbyes to the last of his friends, his parents still seeing people off. Ellie was exhausted and this was not even her party. The thought of changing into some yoga pants and an oversized sweater with no bra or corset and curling up on the couch with a book and tea filled her mind. The mansion now felt empty without the throngs of people occupying every corner. Thomas found her in the doorway and came over to finally spend some time with her and stopped, looking up above her head. Ellie put her hands behind her back and leaned against the door frame, following his eyes to see what had grabbed his attention.

"Do you know what that is?" he asked her in a low voice.

"It's mistletoe," she replied. Apparently, some traditions went back rather far.

Thomas reached up and pulled one of the last berries from the plant. Mistletoe was poisonous and for a moment, she was afraid that he might try to eat it. At her expression, he said loud enough for only her to hear, "It's the cost of a kiss. Once the berries have all been pulled, there are no more kisses."

She whispered back, "That's really sad. There should always be more kisses."

Thomas took her chin in his hand, gently lifting her face to meet his. His kiss was slow and sweet, and Ellie's stomach dropped out the bottom as if she were on a roller coaster. They were not even entwined, with Ellie's hands still behind her back. Thomas stood inches away with one arm against the door frame beside her and the other at his back. Yet it was somehow still incredibly intimate.

When Thomas broke the kiss, they held each other's gaze for a moment before he put his hand on the small of her back and waited for her to direct him where she wished to go.

The next morning was Christmas morning. It was nothing at all like what Ellie was used to. There had been no Christmas tree, and the only presents were those given to the children or servants. While in town with Thomas's sisters, they informed her that adults did not exchange gifts for Christmas. Gifts were only given to children or other subordinates. It had immediately made her again question the dresses Thomas had purchased for her. At the time, she had wanted to be angry with him but tried to let it slide. She had never been materialistic and typically did not celebrate Christmas. If anything, Ellie was more pagan, celebrating the solstice, and she did not believe in purchasing gifts. The only ones who ever received store-bought gifts from her were her young niblings or those who participated in the white elephant gift exchanges at work that she hated so much. As the kids got older, she stopped buying them things as well. Ellie had always preferred giving hand-made gifts, typically something sweet she baked.

After breakfast, the family went to church and to Ellie's great dismay, she was expected to join them. Thomas knew how she felt about religion, and she had thus far managed to avoid it, but there would be no avoiding it today. To her surprise, there were laws in place in Virginia requiring everyone to attend Anglican public worship, which had even led to arrests of Baptist preachers and mobs breaking up prayer meetings and attacking practitioners. Even had it not been the law, these people had opened their home to her and welcomed her during their holiday celebrations, despite never having met her. When they asked her to go to church, she went. Though she did not like it, she felt obligated to go and it was a small price to pay. It was only one service. After church, there was a feast waiting for them. Ellie was proud of herself for being able to keep up with proper dining etiquette by then.

"How did you find yourself following the army?" Martha Burke asked while they ate. "My son informs us you're not there with any family."

"No. I got lost and stumbled into a skirmish." Ellie paused, trying to find the right words. "I was injured and taken to the hospital at Fort Edward. When I recovered and had nowhere to go, Captain Burke arranged for me to stay on as a nurse."

"That was rather generous of him," his mother said with an edge in her voice. Ellie got the impression the woman was suspicious of her. "And now you're traveling with him?"

"The captain has been both generous and helpful. I've been the matron of the hospital for this last campaign. Major Sparks gave me permission to return next season, but Captain Burke invited me to come along with him to attend the medical lectures in Philadelphia," she added excitedly.

As they spoke, Thomas's uncle rose and went to stand in the corner facing the room. Adding to the conversation, he took the side of Thomas's mother. "'Tis quite irregular for a young unmarried woman such as yourself to travel with a single man."

"Oh, I don't worry about Thomas. He's been a perfect gentleman. And Robert also traveled with us the whole way here. They've both been great."

As Ellie responded to him, she realized he was urinating into a chamber pot while they spoke, only feet away from the dinner table. Her voice faltered and her eyes grew big, but she tried to maintain her composure. Looking around the table, no one seemed to be giving him a second thought.

Martha scowled at the use of the men's given names. Clearly, her son was far too familiar with this woman who found herself living alone amongst soldiers. She wondered just how familiar they were with one another. Did this girl who was clearly of lower sorts think to catch him so he would have to marry her and be responsible for her? A waif like her was hardly a suitable match for her son.

"Mother, Mrs. Sorenson has been treated well and given her privacy throughout the entire journey." Thomas deliberately left off the part of the journey where they had all shared the tent, grateful it had only been one night.

Martha huffed. "What are your intentions when the war ends, Mrs. Sorenson? What shall you do when the army no longer has need of you?"

Thomas's uncle returned to the table as soon as he was finished urinating, but Ellie continued directing her stare anywhere but at him. It was difficult to continue eating after the display, but at least he had only urinated. It could have been worse.

"I'm hoping to have a chance to look at the hospital in Philadelphia while we're there. I'm confident I can find work as a nurse somewhere whenever I leave Fort Edward."

"What of your family?" James asked gently.

"I have no family," Ellie said, directing her attention at her dinner.

"You poor dear," his father replied. "Perhaps you'd be better served remaining here when the men return to the fort. We shall help you find a husband."

Ellie was more aghast at that thought than at watching Thomas's uncle pee in the corner during the middle of dinner.

Before she could say anything, Thomas chimed in. "That shan't be necessary. Mrs. Sorenson is needed at the fort. She is held in high regard by the men there and enjoys what she does."

"Only, one so young as herself shan't be wasting her time working when she could be wed and bearing children," Thomas's uncle argued.

Ellie choked on her meal. "I'm not as young as I look. I've been married and I'm perfectly content to continue working as a nurse for the time being."

"Yes, well you say that now, but the longer you wait, the more difficulty you shall have in finding another husband," his mother argued.

Opening her mouth to say something, Thomas stopped her with his own response. "Let's have no more talk on the matter. Mrs. Sorenson has a mind to continue as a nurse. She shall return with me when I leave here."

Ellie turned to find him looking at her. She nodded her thanks, and he gave her a single nod in return.

"Son, it's highly inappropriate," his mother began again.

"Mrs. Sorenson has already made up her mind, mother. The matter is settled."

As Thomas escorted Ellie around after dinner, he questioned whether he had overstepped himself. He was reluctant to say anything but knew he needed to ask.

"I hope I did not speak out of turn at dinner. If you wish to stay, I shall speak with my parents."

"Not at all. I was worried for a minute that they were going to insist upon it. I'm glad you said something."

The relief Thomas felt was palpable. He could only imagine Ellie staying behind and his parents finding someone for her to wed. The thought was more than he could bear, yet he knew it was only a matter of time before the possibility became a reality. If he continued to wait, he would lose his chance with her, though now that she was traveling under his care and protection, he could not declare his intentions without seeming to be taking advantage of her. He would have to wait to remedy it until they returned to the fort.

Chapter 31

December 1757

The festivities did not end on December 25. They continued for the entire 'Twelve Days of Christmas' and included more balls, games, fox hunts, horse races, and feasts almost every night, just as Robert had described. There was drinking, dancing, and merriment every night. Thomas's sisters made sure she had the proper attire for every occasion, supplementing her scant wardrobe.

When they went to the Governor's Palace for the ball there, Ellie was hesitant to go inside. Once again on Thomas's arm, she pulled back as they approached the door. The line of people behind them stalled and Thomas looked down at her to see what was amiss. Ellie saw the concern on his face and gathered herself up, forcing herself to push on. Inside, the palace looked much the same as it had all those years in the future when she had toured it as a child. There were some slight differences, but it was close enough to still be quite familiar. However, the hundreds of firearms and swords adorning the walls in the entryway and throughout the hallways she had always enjoyed seeing were not there now.

As Ellie looked around in confusion, she could not help but ask, "Where are all of the weapons that usually line the walls?"

Thomas stopped abruptly and turned to look at her. "You've been here before?"

Instantly realizing her mistake, Ellie tried to think quickly. "There are empty posts on the walls. It's obvious something is missing. I just assumed, given the outline of them, that it could only be swords and firearms."

He looked at her skeptically, knowing without a doubt that she was not being truthful with him. The knowledge cut through him like one of the missing swords. Instead of pushing her, he took a deep breath and replied, "They're being employed at the moment. The militia has need of them."

As soon as he said it, Ellie remembered the tour guides always saying they had been taken down to be used during the revolution, but she had not made the connection that they also would have been used during this war. She nodded quietly and they continued into the grand ballroom. It was a sight, filled with people dressed in gowns and suits of the era. Gentlemen doffed their hats, showing their wigs underneath. Thomas had foregone a wig, wearing his natural hair in curls at his temples like he had at the last ball at his parents' plantation. She had initially laughed when she had seen him appearing so formal, as she had again that evening. It had taken her by surprise the first time, but he looked so regal, the laughter tonight was more from nerves than mirth. The situation had felt so surreal and absurd that she questioned what she was even doing there, vastly aware of the fact that she did not belong there.

Robert soon found them, and Ellie took in his appearance, with his hair in curls at the temples as well. Ellie wanted to give him a hug after not having seen him in a few days, but she knew this was not the place for it. Much to Thomas's dismay, she had gotten into the habit of giving him a hug every time she saw him when they spent any time apart. Robert had been uncomfortable with it at first, while Thomas had been annoyed by it, admonishing her for being too familiar and too forward. It was improper for a lady to show such displays, particularly to someone to whom she was not wed. But Ellie did not care about being proper. It was her custom to do so, and she continued it. She had done so with Thomas on occasion, but it was different with him. First, they never spent any time apart. More than that, it meant something more when they embraced. They were both aware of it, so Ellie refrained from being too forward with him in public.

As they made their way around the room, Ellie met a vast number of people, including Robert's parents and sister. After meeting them, another young man approached their trio, and Robert made the introductions.

"Mrs. Ellie Sorenson, may I introduce to you Mr. Patrick Henry?"

Ellie's brow furrowed as she tried to remember her history. She knew the name quite well, that he was one of the founding fathers, but could not remember which one he was or what he had done. For that matter, she was not certain this was the same Patrick Henry. After only a moment, she recalled the reenactor of Patrick Henry at Colonial Williamsburg when she was young.

"Patrick Henry? Really?" Ellie looked around the room. "Am I to meet George Washington next?"

"George Washington?" Robert asked.

"Who?" Thomas asked.

"Is he not the young lieutenant colonel of the militia who lost Fort Necessity to the French, effectively starting this war?" Robert offered.

At the mention of Fort Necessity, Thomas recognized the name. "Why would he be in attendance?"

Damn it. She had done it again. Ellie really needed to keep her mouth shut. "He is Virginian, is he not?" At the confused looks, Ellie shook her head. "Never mind."

She turned her attention back to the man in front of her. "Patrick Henry. Of the House of Burgesses?"

"Would that I had that honor," Patrick replied.

"Is your father or uncle also called Patrick Henry or are you the only one?"

The men exchanged more confused glances before Patrick responded. "No, madam. I'm the only one. Of which I'm aware that is." He added the last with a smirk.

"Mr. Henry is teaching himself law." Robert explained. "We've had much to discuss."

"Of course you are," Ellie said with a smile. "You must be in order to get into the House."

Robert tilted his head and furrowed his own brow at the oddness of Ellie's statements. However, he was used to her saying things like this and wondered if it was related to another one of her visions. In an attempt to redirect the conversation away from anything that would draw unwanted attention to her gift, he supplied, "Mrs. Sorenson is a nurse."

Ellie continued looking at the boy in front of her, studying him. It made sense that he was studying law. If memory served, most of the founding fathers had studied law. That was certainly true for most politicians in her own time. But this young man was only starting his career. He was so young; it was hard to reconcile the fact that he would help shape the foundation of this country.

"Do you not agree, Mrs. Sorenson?" Thomas asked.

Pulled from her thoughts by the mention of her name, she had no idea what they had been discussing. Before she could respond, something else clicked in her memory and she spoke the words aloud before she could stop herself.

"Oh! Give me liberty or give me death."

Several heads turned to stare at her outcry that had come out slightly louder than she had anticipated. The men all looked at each other, unsure what to do with her declaration. Ellie finally turned her attention away from a red-faced Patrick Henry to see Thomas and Robert staring at her, confused.

"Sorry," she said quickly. "I was off somewhere else for a moment. Mr. Henry, it was an absolute pleasure to meet you. Good luck with the law and what will be a memorable career."

Turning to walk away, Ellie left the three men behind her utterly bewildered. She heard Thomas make his apologies then come to escort her. Taking her hand, he placed it on his forearm as he opened the door for her and directed her through the dining room to the gardens outside.

"What was that?" he asked as soon as they were out of earshot of anyone else.

"What?"

Thomas dropped his arm, letting her hand fall away as he spun on her. "Do you know Mr. Henry?"

"No. How would I know him?" Ellie knew she was being obstinate and defensive but could not seem to care. She felt overwhelmed. Every minute since she had arrived in Williamsburg had served to remind her of her situation and how stuck she was. Tonight had been exceptionally trying.

"You certainly sounded as though you knew him. And what was that about liberty and death?" Thomas stood with his arms folded across his chest.

Ellie shook her head as if to clear away a fog. "I don't know, Thomas. It was just something that popped into my head." She sighed, knowing this could easily turn into a fight. That was the last thing she wanted. "Sorry. I'm just feeling a little out of sorts tonight. I think I'm over-peopled. This week has been quite full."

He did not understand what had gotten into her since they arrived or what had just happened. Something had shaken her about being there in Williamsburg, more so since they arrived at the governor's palace. Now Ellie had not been able to take her eyes off the man that she seemed to know but claimed to have only just met. Thomas had thought he had moved past being suspicious of her, but he could not help wondering again what she was hiding. She had clearly been there before, despite having told him she had not. Why would she lie about that? Was her past somehow tied to Williamsburg? It was impossible to imagine her ever having been there before without crossing paths with her, though he had been away several years. If she was hiding from something there, why would she willingly come back there with him now? None of this made any sense. He wanted to trust her, but she was making it increasingly difficult.

Ellie put a hand on his arm in a gesture of contrition. With a sigh, his arms dropped, and his hands went to her waist. He leaned forward, momentarily putting his forehead against hers. "Very well, darling. We shall go home and skip the ball tomorrow night."

Her grateful smile did not fully reach her eyes. "Thank you."

As they walked back through the crowd, they passed Robert who was still talking with Patrick Henry. Thomas gave his excuses, telling Robert they were retiring for the evening.

"What was that you said earlier, Mrs. Sorenson? About liberty?" Patrick asked.

"Oh, it was nothing. Forget I said anything."

"How could I forget something so remarkable? I was simply wondering where you'd heard it or if it was something of your own making? Are your beliefs so strong that you would trade your life for an ideal such as liberty?"

At a loss for words, she decided it best not to engage. "The words are yours, Mr. Patrick Henry. Use them as you will."

Forcing a smile then, she wished him and Robert a good night. Thomas held out an arm for her and she gladly took it as he guided her away from the ball.

After three days of festivities and balls, Ellie did not think she could handle any more. Being an introvert, life at the fort had been difficult enough, but this took things to a whole new level. After the night at the governor's palace, she did not think she *should* handle more. It was becoming increasingly more difficult to not slip up. Ellie was more and more aware of Thomas's suspicions about her. She desperately needed some quiet time. Thomas stayed home with her on the fourth night, making his excuses to his parents. Feeling guilty for keeping him from enjoying the festivities, she urged him to go without her, but of course he would not.

Ellie spent most of the evening in the study, looking through books, finding a couple that she pulled down and began reading. Thomas left her alone until she was ready to come out. When she finally was, she found him in the drawing room with his younger siblings and niblings. He had one older brother who had two small children and a younger sister with one. The brother next in line had died as a child, and his next younger sister was the only one not present for the celebrations. Having recently turned nineteen, she had married a sea merchant that year and was currently in South Carolina. There were a couple of age gaps between the next four siblings who were between sixteen and seven. The adults had all gone off to balls, leaving the younger children behind. Ellie came to stand beside the piano as Thomas played.

"Vivaldi?" she asked when he finished playing.

Pleased she recognized it, he nodded with a smile. "Do you play?"

Shaking her head, she replied, "No. I never learned any instruments."

"Your voice is a beautiful instrument. Would you be so good as to sing for us?"

"Oh, I hate singing in front of others. It's not really my thing. I'd much rather enjoy the talents of others."

Not wanting to push it and make her uncomfortable, Thomas guided her over to the sofa–which everyone referred to as either a settee or a settle–where he began telling a story to the children. When he finished his story, Thomas's youngest brother Christopher volunteered Ellie to tell one next. Ellie immediately declined, saying, "I don't know any."

After declining to sing or play anything, the kids were not letting her off that easily, and she laughed at their enthusiasm while they tried to goad her into telling one. Ellie immediately thought of all the movies she had ever loved and could only think of ones that were comic books or sci-fi with concepts like space ships. There was no way she was telling those. However, she was enjoying this. The fireplace was going and though there was no tree, there were other evergreens decorating the room, putting her in a festive spirit. This was far more her style; a cozy Christmas by the fire, telling stories. When Thomas finally came to her defense and told the kids to ease off, she was grateful. Until he said with a twinkle in his eye, "I fear Mrs. Sorenson has lived a rather boring life and knows no stories."

She laughed incredulously at him, knowing he was teasing her, challenging her to come up with something. "Alright. I think I have one. It was one of my favorites as a child."

Kicking off her shoes and curling her feet underneath her on the settee, Ellie got more comfortable and began telling them the story of *The Princess Bride*. She tried to recite as much of the dialogue as she could remember while doing the different voices to match the characters from the movie.

Thomas was fixated on her throughout her animated telling of the story, never having seen a woman make herself so relaxed in front of others. His mother and sisters would never dare remove their shoes in public or sit with their feet anywhere but on the floor. They would have been appalled, but he found it endearing. His four-year-old niece curled up against her, and everyone was enthralled. By the time she finished, it was getting late. The kids were taken to bed, and Thomas told her, "You never cease to amaze me, Ellie. I never thought to feel such fullness in my heart. You shall make a wonderful mother someday."

Ellie smiled, trying to cover up the awkwardness and pain she felt at his remarks. Johnny had never wanted children and she had been content to wait, thinking he would eventually change his mind. He never did. After turning thirty-five, she had given up on the idea of ever having them. It felt wrong to have them past that age. Now she felt younger and healthier than ever but still had not had a period since arriving in this time and was beginning to think she never would. Her birth control shot had only been good for three months and would have worn off long ago. Her period should have returned, but it had been a year and a half now and she knew she was not capable of getting pregnant. Motherhood was something that would forever be out of reach for her.

While the thought saddened her, it was for the best. Having children now would be a complication Ellie did not need. Her future was still anything but certain. The reminder that Thomas wanted children was like a cold splash of water to the face. He had made comments of the sort before, often speaking of having a family of his own one day, but she had not considered it to be something that had anything to do with her. He was still so young while she was anything but.

Ellie reminded herself she needed to put some distance between them yet could not seem to make herself do so. He was getting too serious for her liking. Then again, it was not like they had even discussed a relationship. He often used terms of endearment and they had kissed a few times, but that was it. He was affectionate, but so was Robert. Thomas bought her the gowns, but only because he knew she would need them there in Williamsburg and could not afford them on her own. He brought her home out of pity because he knew she had nowhere else to go and she would be joining him in Philadelphia after the holiday. This was simply easier logistically. If he was really interested, he would have made his intentions clear. That was what men did in this period. Maybe he was only interested in bedding her. Ellie certainly would not object to that. But with no history, no money, and no family in this time, she was clearly in a lower class bracket than he was. Perhaps none of it even mattered because she was not 'good enough' for his family. That was all fine with Ellie. She had never been interested in social standing and if that was what it took to keep things from becoming too serious, she was more than happy to accept it.

Sufficiently convinced that there was nothing serious between her and Thomas, Ellie decided to call it a night. Thomas escorted her up the stairs to her room, where he kissed her thoroughly, then lingered at her door for a while, twirling a strand of her hair between his fingers and caressing her cheek and neck. By the time he left, Ellie was no longer so convinced.

———————

January 1758

The days passed far too quickly, but Thomas took advantage of them. He spent every spare moment he could in Ellie's company, wandering the estate or escorting her around town. They saw Robert several more times, but he had been away from home a long time as well and his family was keeping him busy. Thomas was pleased that his siblings all liked Ellie, though the same could not be said about his parents. He knew they both looked down on her, even if his father was pleasant enough. Ellie's idiosyncrasies had her standing out regardless of how much she tried to fit in. The number of piercings in her ears alone had his family asking the same questions to which she had never given him answers. His mother was quick to inform him that she was hiding something; a fact Thomas knew all too well. She did not trust Ellie and wanted to see him toss her out into the street like the pauper his mother believed her to be. His father kept Martha under control, and allowed Ellie to remain, but he too encouraged Thomas to distance himself from her. They wanted to see him married and were both in favor of a match with his sister's friend. It was his mother who had encouraged her to write to him while he was away. As much as Thomas did not want this respite to end, he was glad to be leaving the suspicious and overbearing discussions with his parents.

Thomas's family had been welcoming enough, but Ellie was ready to leave the plantation. She got the distinct impression that his mother did not like her, and she was increasingly uncomfortable being surrounded by enslaved persons, regardless of how 'well' they were treated. This had been a source of contention between her and Thomas as they walked the property day after day. He had seen her unease every time they crossed paths with the people who worked the fields and in the house. Ellie was always friendly to them, greeting them in passing. When Thomas informed her she did not have to address them, she was appalled at the idea.

"Why wouldn't I?" she asked.

"They're merely slaves," he responded.

"They're people. People who have been forced into the most horrendous situation imaginable."

"You do not approve of slavery?" Though he knew she did not, they had never discussed her beliefs on the matter and his curiosity was piqued.

"It's abhorrent," Ellie spat with vehemence. "People are not property. They're not cattle. They are every bit as human as you and I. How would you feel if you were stolen away from your home and your family and treated the way these people are? I can't even begin to understand how anyone can justify treating another human being the way people of color have been treated in this country. No one deserves this. It's inhumane and just plain wrong. They're human and deserve to be treated as such."

Not yet finished, her voice betrayed her. She was so angry, she was shaking and could no longer speak.

Thomas could see her viewpoint, but simply responded, "Most people believe them to be inferior. They're inherently lazy, dishonest, and immoral. They need the power of the whip and the law administered by White men in order to be productive."

"That's the most ridiculous thing I've ever heard. Simply based on a person's skin color? I thought you were a man of reason, of science and evidence. Where's the evidence for this?"

"Darling, I did not say it was what I believe. To be honest, I never considered it before. It has always simply been the way of the world."

She would not accept this, and could not help her response of, "For now."

"Miss Ellie, you don't understand our ways. It's not likely to change."

"Don't start getting all condescending. I understand your ways better than you think. I simply don't agree with them. I believe in equality regardless of race, gender, or economic status."

Thomas could no longer hold back the smirk that had been threatening to appear on his face. "It gives me great pleasure to see you become impassioned about your beliefs."

She raised her eyebrow in challenge as if his words proved her point.

He threw his hands up in surrender. "I would not condescend to you, *mea dea*, of that you have my word. I know how you feel in regard to people being treated equally, yet I find that I simply cannot resist riling you up on occasion. You are so beautiful, and I find your beliefs to be rather compelling. They make you even more beautiful were that possible."

That stopped Ellie in her tracks. Her hand dropped from his arm and it took him a second for his brain to catch up that she had stopped. He had to turn back to her after he had initially continued walking.

"So, you were just arguing for the sake of being argumentative?" Ellie folded her arms across her chest.

"It was not my intention to be argumentative, my dear. I was merely informing you of what others believe and explaining why things are unlikely to change."

"I see. So you were mansplaining things again?"

"This is something of which you've accused me before. If you're going to continue to do so, you might at least tell me what it is of which you are accusing me."

Ellie began walking again, leaving him to follow. Looking ahead of her, she kept her head held high as she said, "I'm accusing you of being a sexist, egotistical male who speaks down to women condescendingly in order to make himself feel superior because a woman could not possibly know anything on the matter."

The words were harsh, but Thomas could hear the teasing tone in her voice. She had never even hinted at him behaving the way in which she now accused him. As if to make sure he knew she was teasing, she continued mockingly, "Don't mind me. I'm just a weak little girl, incapable of thinking for myself or doing anything without a big strong man to help me and tell me what to think and do."

"You wish to have a big, strong man tell you what to think and do?" he teased back, knowing that unlike most other women, his Ellie was not interested in such.

He tried to reach for her, but she shot out from his grasp, circling around to avoid him. When he gave chase, she squealed and darted around a tree, giggling all the while. When he went to block her path, she darted back the other way. Her previous anger was gone and the look of delight on her face was far better than that when she was riled up. As much as he loved seeing passionate Ellie who was enflamed by her beliefs, playful Ellie took his breath away. She crouched low as they danced around the tree at a stalemate. Bending down, she scooped up a handful of snow, patting it into a ball, her smile mischievous.

"You'd not dare," he teased.

Throwing the snowball at him, he was momentarily stunned when it hit him directly in the face. She squealed again and used his surprise to run away, laughing as she ran. Running up behind her, he quickly caught up to her. When he got to her, he lifted her up easily, spinning around with her, his cold face buried in her warm neck, causing her to squeal even more. Before he could set her down, his foot caught in the uneven ground and he fell, taking her down with him. They toppled to the ground, her landing on top of him, both of them laughing. When they finally collected themselves, he stood quickly, holding out a hand to help her up. Once standing, they brushed the snow off one another. Kissing her forehead, he turned, placing her hand on his arm while he escorted her back to the house. If he stayed out there with her much longer, he would not be able to control himself.

Chapter 32

January 1758

The journey to Philadelphia was far colder than the journey south had been. The January weather was unforgiving as Thomas and Ellie made their way north by ship. This was the largest city they had been to yet. It was strange to think of any city in America being bigger than New York City, yet it was. They had a few days yet before the lectures started and Ellie enjoyed seeing the sights around the city.

Philadelphia was built on a grid, leading out from the Delaware River with the hospital being about a mile from the river. Nothing surrounded it but farmland. The Quaker presence was obvious with meeting houses on what seemed like nearly every corner. Not knowing when it had been built, Ellie had been surprised to see Independence Hall, though it was not called that yet. In this time, it was the Pennsylvania State House. It was surreal to see it before it would become the birthplace of the nation.

They stayed at a public house with each of them in their own rooms. Ellie found it more than a little discomforting that the doors did not have locks on them, but they had requested their rooms be side-by-side. Having Thomas right next door provided some level of comfort. She knew this was only her twenty-first century upbringing making her paranoid, but she could not shake it. Even after spending the previous year and a half sharing quarters with thousands of people, she simply could not get past this at the public house. It was different at the fort where everyone was known, and they all fell under military law. In Philadelphia, she was surrounded by random strangers with no ties to each other. She could not imagine staying at a hotel in her own time without a lock on the door, no matter how normal it was there. It led to many sleepless nights.

Ellie found the medical lectures to be fascinating. It was interesting to obtain more insight into how people treated disease and illness during this time, though much of it made her angry. She wanted to get up on the lectern and set everyone straight on several issues. It was tempting to tell them all the ways they were wrong and that they were killing more patients with their treatments of bloodletting and mercury administration than the diseases were. Some days, it took everything in her to keep her cool.

Of course, Ellie was only permitted to be there as a guest of Thomas's, under the guise of being his betrothed. Even at that, she was barely admitted. Ellie was irked by the exclusion of women, but happy to play along with the ruse they had developed. Though she had no interest in actually being married, she found she did not mind playing the part with Thomas. Of course, he was ever the gentleman, much to her dismay. He kissed her often, and they embraced as often as possible, but that was all Thomas would allow, never taking it further.

As the days rolled on, it was getting harder and harder for Thomas to maintain a distance from Ellie. With her posing as his betrothed, they had fallen into a new level of familiarity with each other. Saying good night to her became increasingly more difficult as the nights went on. He wanted to take her to his bed with him instead of leaving her on her own. Their kisses lingered, becoming increasingly more passionate, and it was all he could do to walk away from her every night.

Thomas enjoyed doting on her and did what he could to see to her comfort. Ellie made it easy as she never asked for anything and often refused his gestures when she felt they were too much. He rarely let her win those arguments and the more she refused, the grander his gestures became. When he purchased her very own horse, she finally stopped refusing him, albeit reluctantly. It was obvious Ellie was torn by the gesture, immediately being apparent how much she loved it and wanted to accept it, but also how much it pained her to do so. She was fiercely independent, his Ellie. Thomas promised he would stop if she accepted this. Of course, he only meant he would stop with the grandness of the gifts; he would not stop the gifts altogether.

This gift also had a practicality to it. They would need the extra horse to carry all of their luggage back to New York. They had managed thus far, but only because they had taken his family carriage to the ship in Williamsburg and did not have far to go once they arrived in Philadelphia. Once they left, they would need the extra transportation to get all the way back to the fort.

Ellie was becoming increasingly divided on how to handle Thomas, caring about him a great deal and being intensely attracted to him. If his intoxicating kisses continued, she was not certain how much longer she could control herself. At the same time, she worried he was becoming too serious about her. She tried telling herself that he was only playing the part of the doting fiancé and that she was reading too much into it, but the voice in the back of her head said that was not the case. Part of her wanted to rip his clothes off and finally have her way with him while the other part of her wanted to run for the hills and never see him again. Ellie knew she was not what he needed in a woman and could never be with him for the long term but wanted to thoroughly enjoy the time they did have together. Most of the time, she tried not to think about it, so that she did not overthink it.

Early March 1758

On their last night in Philadelphia, Thomas took El-lie to see the opera. It had first arrived in the city only the previous winter and was performed by the stu-dents at the College of Philadelphia. It was the first of its kind in the colonies with acting, music, scenery, and costumes all coming together to produce the *Masque of Alfred.* Thomas had been excited to escort Ellie to the performance and was surprised when she informed him that she had been to the opera before.

He immediately asked which one and where out of instinct, but of course she would not tell him where it had occurred. She did tell him she had seen one called *La Boheme*, but he had never heard of it. Ellie had always enjoyed the ballet and she tried mentioning that, but again, he had never heard of the ones she had seen. Not sure when any of them had been written, she did not say anything further.

When they returned to the public house, Thomas escorted Ellie up to her room with her hand on his arm as he had done every night. At her door, she released his arm, and he took her hand and kissed it, bidding her a good night. Neither of them moved for a moment. Unable to take his eyes from hers, he leaned in to kiss her. Wrapping her arms around his neck, they continued kissing with a need that grew more and more urgent. They had done this every night since they left Williamsburg, but the intensity of their connection grew every night. As her tongue plunged into his mouth, his hands began roaming her body. The passion between them continued to grow until they heard people come up the stairs. They reluctantly broke apart before the men reached the landing. Thomas again took her hand, kissing the back of it, and bid her good night.

"Darling, if I don't take leave of you now, I may never," he said with a gruff voice.

"Would that be so terrible?" she asked, her heart racing.

Thomas growled at her and opened her door wide, gesturing for her to go inside.

Forcing herself into her room, Ellie leaned against the closed door after Thomas left, catching her breath. There was never an opportunity there to be together with so many prying eyes and everyone so heavily concerned with propriety. She shook herself off and began undressing, readying herself for bed. Climbing into bed in only her shift, she knew she would not be able to sleep. Between that kiss and the door not having a lock on it, she knew she would be up all night.

Thomas made her laugh and feel as though she was the most important person in the world. The way he looked at her made her feel as though she might combust in an instant. It had been so long since she felt desired like that, if ever. Her and Johnny had met while she was still in high school and though he was much older than her, he had never been anywhere near as mature as Thomas. They were both part of the *Toys 'R' Us* generation, refusing to grow up. But more than that, it had never felt like this with Johnny or any of her other boyfriends. She knew she needed to tread carefully so she did not lose herself with this man, but was it wrong to enjoy everything he had to offer while she could?

Ellie tried to remember the last time she had been with a man, not having had a physical relationship with her husband in years. Johnny had all but abandoned her physically and emotionally. As far as she was concerned, her sex life had become her own years ago and it had nothing to do with him. He gave up that right when he lost interest in her after the accident. Performance had not been a problem for him; he had simply lost interest. She had done everything she could think of to seduce him and continue marital relations, and had even begged him to seek help, but to no avail. It had destroyed her. Johnny's rejection was a betrayal she could not fathom. It had affected her self-esteem and her confidence. She had been neglected for years. Now, she and Thomas had been dancing around it for months and she did not know how much longer she could hold out. A wicked thought popped into her head as she suddenly realized that if her door had no lock, neither did his.

Gathering up what confidence she had, Ellie rose from bed and donned her dressing gown over her shift before she lost her nerve. She quietly opened her door enough to peek down the hallway. When she saw the emptiness, she tiptoed to the room next to hers and quietly rapped on the door, opening it slowly without waiting for an answer.

Thomas still had the fireplace going and a candle burning and had just crawled into bed. He was immediately alarmed and asked, "Miss Ellie? What's wrong?"

"Nothing's wrong," she replied as she closed the door and crossed the room quickly.

"Then what…" he started to ask, then trailed off as she came to the opposite side of the bed from where he was lying.

The blankets covered Thomas to his waist, and his bare abdomen rippled slightly below his hard chest as he propped himself on an elbow to see her. He watched her with brows drawn in confusion while Ellie took off her dressing gown, pulled the covers back, and climbed into bed next to him.

She also propped herself on her elbow, so she was facing him as she slid her free hand up his chest. His free arm instinctively moved to her hip as she pulled him into her, kissing his supple lips.

When Thomas broke the kiss, his breathing was heavy as he practically moaned her name. She could feel his hardness against her leg, though he was still hesitant to act on his desire.

"Ellie," he said admonishingly, "you should not—"

She interrupted him with a finger to his lips before he could say anything to object or send her back to her room.

"I want you, Thomas. Don't you want me?" As if to help convince him, she removed her finger and kissed him again. "I'm not some blushing virgin worried about her maidenhead," she said between kisses, "and I know you've bedded other women. I'm tired of dancing around this. Do you want me half as much as I want you?"

She pulled his mouth back to hers and started sliding her hand down below the covers. Ellie found he had removed his breeches for bed but still had his drawers on, and she glided her fingers along the waistband toward the buttons in the front.

"Tell me you don't want me, and I'll leave right now."

This seemed to have helped Thomas make up his mind. Despite how much he wanted her, he had been resisting the idea before, but in that moment, carnal lust overtook him, and he was no longer worried about what was proper or what he was supposed to do. He wanted Ellie with every fiber of his being.

"Darling, I've wanted you since the moment I saw you climb atop my patient and fight to return him from the dead," he said. "I can't seem to resist you, *mea dea.*"

With that, Thomas grabbed her hand, pinning it above her head while rolling her onto her back. Excitement and delight filled her stomach and a pulsing throb thrummed between her legs.

Thomas hovered over her, using his other hand to slide her other arm up to meet the first. While loosely holding both of her hands in place with one of his, he slowly reached down to untie the collar of her shift. Ellie freed one of her hands and brought it to rest on his cheek while she kissed him. His hand roamed her body, and he broke away from her lips to explore her body with his mouth. Trailing kisses down her neck onto her breast, he slid her shift down as he went. With one breast exposed, he stopped moving and stared at it with wide eyes. He quickly slid her shift down over the other breast as his eyes roamed back and forth between them. Suddenly self-conscious at his scrutiny, Ellie wondered for the first time if this was a good idea.

Thomas looked up at her in awe and asked, "Are those rings? Through holes bored into your nipples?"

"Yes," she said hesitantly.

"I've never seen such a thing. The navel was a surprise when we first met and I tended your injury, but this? Do they hurt? May I touch them?"

Thomas's hand hovered over one breast, waiting for permission. Ellie laughed in relief that he was not repelled by her piercings. That boded well because her nipples and navel were not the only body parts she had pierced. She decided to let him find the other one on his own. Relaxing again, she satisfied his curiosity.

"It hurt a little to have them done, but they healed long ago. If anything, it makes me a little more sensitive to certain sensations," she said with a mischievous smile.

Intrigued, Thomas set about exploring this claim for himself, taking a nipple in his mouth, licking and suckling while pinching the other. Ellie moaned softly, enjoying his ministrations while stroking his muscular back and twining her fingers in his long hair. His hand moved further down, sliding her shift above her hip. As his hand glided along her soft skin, he made his way toward her inner thighs. When he reached the top, he froze once again. Expecting it this time, she was barely holding back her laughter now. He scrambled beneath the covers to get a closer look.

"I find myself at a loss for words. The grooming is quite French, but the ring is far from anything I've ever before seen."

She had forgotten about the lack of hair between her legs. Having groomed herself since she was a teenager, she never thought it unusual or out of the ordinary, keeping her labia free of hair, leaving only a small patch above on the pubis. The lack of hair now had the added benefit of allowing her to feel cleaner in this world without showers. The grooming was not uncommon in her own time, but in this time period, however, it was far from ordinary.

Laughter bubbled forth from her, and she squirmed as he pretended to poke and prod her as if she were a medical curiosity.

"Well, you surprise me, *mea dea*. Is there anything else of which I need know?"

"Mmm. I don't think so. I think you've found them all now."

Thomas had already seen most of her tattoos and her belly ring when he tended to her wound upon her arrival in the past, so those were not a surprise now. Covering this last ring with his mouth, he played it with his tongue. Ellie moaned at the pleasure rolling through her body, the sound driving Thomas to a new level of excitement he had never known.

"You truly are a goddess."

They took their time exploring each other and relishing in the feel of one another. There was an eagerness to their passion, yet they both wanted to savor the time together. He was every bit as skillful and eager as she had fantasized, and together, they brought each other to new heights.

As Ellie lay on Thomas's chest after being fully sated, she looked up at him. "You didn't know about my piercings? I thought you would've seen them when you first tended to my wound."

"I did not. I am a gentleman, after all. I saw only your injury."

"In my ti–" Ellie caught herself before she could say 'time' and restarted. "Where I'm from, the doctors remove all clothing to check for any other injuries that may be present and make it easier to work on the injuries that are there. I was in different clothes when I woke, so I just assumed you'd already seen me naked."

Thomas was aggrieved at her assumption of unseemly behavior.

"I would never. I look only at what is necessary. Mrs. Gibbons removed your clothes and redressed you. She left your," he hesitated for a moment before finding the right word, "breeches on. I only ever saw your abdomen."

Ellie absently played with her braid while they spoke, her pendants brushing his bare chest. Thomas reached out and lifted one, turning it over in his fingers.

"Why do you wear two necklaces?" he asked. "You never remove either, though you remove your rings and bracelets every morning when you enter the hospital."

She shrugged. "They aren't in danger of transferring germs from one person to another. But they also both mean more to me than my rings and bracelets do. I don't want to lose them."

Thomas cocked his head inquisitively, waiting for her to explain.

Reluctantly, she told him, "The amethyst was given to me by my nieces, and I've had my ankh for a very long time. It's hard to explain, but it sort of just became part of me."

"Your nieces?" Thomas was surprised at her answer. She never spoke of her life before arriving at the fort.

Ellie nodded. "It's not particularly valuable, but it reminds me of them."

Thomas could see the pain it brought her to think of her family. What had happened to them? Had they all been killed by Indians while she was spared and taken captive?

"What has become of them?" he asked gently.

Though he expected her to close down as she always did when he asked about her past, he had hoped she would finally open up after what they had just shared. She had told him this much.

"They're gone," she said with a lump in her throat and tears stinging her eyes. "I don't think I'll ever see them again."

She did not say anything more. Thomas desperately wished she would open up to him and tell him about her past, but he could see how much it hurt her to think about. As much as he wanted to push her for more, he hated to see her hurting. Nor did he not want to start an argument with her after such a wonderful night. Putting his hand on the side of her neck, he gently turned her face toward his, kissing her forehead, then slowly working his way around her face, kissing her eyelids, nose, cheeks, and finally landing on her lips. There was no urgency or sexual undertones to the gesture. It was simply supportive and comforting, and it made Ellie's heart swell.

Thomas held onto Ellie while she fell asleep in his arms. He had been shocked by her crawling into bed with him, but it was everything he had wanted for so long, he could not force himself to turn her away, no matter how ungentlemanly it was. Ellie had been exquisite. Passionate and knowledgeable, yet unlike the women he had visited in the French brothels, she was also intelligent, cultured, and soft. She had given him all of her attention, loving him with everything in her. His heart felt ready to burst. Thomas never wanted to let her go.

Ellie woke in the early morning hours and thought it best to go back to her room before everyone began to stir. She gently kissed a sleeping Thomas and carefully slipped out of bed, putting her shift and dressing gown back on. Quietly creeping back to her room, she crawled into her own bed for a few more hours of sleep.

Chapter 33

Early March 1758

When Thomas met Ellie in the morning for breakfast, he desperately wanted to take her in his arms and kiss her until she was again flush with desire. He wanted to take her back to bed and continue their passions from the previous night.

"Good day, *mea dea*," he said with a smile.

"Yes, it is," she replied. "Did you get any sleep?"

"A little. I fear a little bird flew into my bedchamber and kept me awake late into the night," he replied with a smirk. "I finally achieved sleep, however when I awoke this morning, the bird had flown off."

Thomas said the last with a pout. Ellie could barely conceal her mirth at his description. They ate their breakfast and loaded up the horses, getting on the road as early as they could. It was a sunny day and Ellie was glad to have the little bit of extra warmth it provided. With the start of March, spring was not far off, but it was still rather cold. With any luck, it would be warm by the time they reached Fort Edward in a few weeks.

Having the extra horse made a big difference on the return journey. Not only was it more comfortable having a little extra room, but they were able to carry their belongings more easily. Thomas missed having Ellie pressed against him for the journey, but he still had the memory of the previous night to keep him content.

As they got further down the road, he said, "I did not enjoy the most disagreeable circumstance of not waking up to you this morning. I was quite confounded when I saw you gone."

"Sorry," she replied. "I thought it would probably be best if I wasn't seen leaving your room this morning."

"Of course, I pay deference to your decision," he sighed. "Though, it yet saddened me."

"Perhaps tonight, we could continue the pretense and claim to be husband and wife when we stop," she suggested.

Thomas was instantly excited at the thought. One night was not enough. The weeks it would take to get back to the fort would not be enough. If he spent a lifetime with this woman, it would never be enough. Ellie Sorenson stirred something inside him he had not known existed. She was the most uninhibited woman he had ever met, even when it came to sex. She knew what she wanted and was not afraid to go after it. Though he knew the more frequently they engaged in such behavior, the more likely they would be found out. He did not like risking her reputation like that.

When Thomas furrowed his brow, it made Ellie second-guess herself again. Maybe he did not want her again. Maybe he was only being polite. She hated being this insecure, but it was difficult not to be with him. It surprised her to find that she wanted to please him, to see him happy. Though after the rejection from her own husband, it would not surprise her if Thomas now did not want her in his bed again.

"Ellie, I do not wish to dishonor you," he finally said after a brief silence. "I cherished last night so much more than I may ever express, *mea dea*. And by God, would I love to engage in amorous congress with you again, yet I would not have others think of you as a woman of easy virtue or have you compromise your morals for anyone."

It was Ellie's turn to furrow her brow. She did not know whether to be hurt at him for declining her offer or happy of his claim to want her again but was thinking of her reputation above his own desires. She decided anger was a better outlet. Despite his claim, this was all-too-familiar territory, and she could feel the pending rejection. Ellie needed to put her walls back up before he could trample all over her emotions. Anger helped with that.

"You're in luck, because I would never compromise my morals for anyone," she said aloofly.

"Ellie, I gather you came from a place that is vastly different from here," Thomas began slowly. "However, there are certain behaviors in which a lady simply does not engage if she wishes to maintain her respectability. There are certain moral codes by which we live that determine what makes a woman a lady. I would not have you compromise that and be thought unchaste."

Thomas spoke carefully and slowly as though he were explaining this to a teenage girl who had been caught drinking past curfew in a car full of boys. Ellie was not deterred in the least.

"Morality is a construct of a time and place," she told him. "It doesn't make it right. What may work for one group of people may not work for another. The morality and acceptable practices of the people here now would quite possibly shock the Puritan settlers who arrived here a hundred years ago. Just as the practices of people a hundred, two hundred years in the future would shock the hell out of people here now. Every culture has practices that are frowned upon by others even within the same time period. It doesn't necessarily make them wrong. It simply makes them different. Anyone who thinks another inferior because their morals may be different from their own is closed-minded, judgmental, and a little narcissistic.

"Where I'm from," she continued, "no one would ever think poorly of sex outside of marriage or tattoos and piercings or even revealing clothing."

This was a bit of an exaggeration since many people did, in fact, take issue with all of these things, but they had all become much more mainstream and acceptable. It was certainly not untrue. She continued, "Women work and choose whether or not to have children and even choose to have them outside of wedlock. Being a single mother is commonplace. Yet, the thought of owning another human being or treating someone with disdain simply because of the color of their skin would be completely reprehensible. Don't sit there thinking yourself superior simply because your morals are different from mine. If you want to judge me for enjoying sex, I can play that game, too. There's plenty I could judge you for based on my morality. Slavery. Or someone urinating at the dinner table for example. Neither of those would be even remotely acceptable where I'm from. To be honest, I was a little horrified by them both."

Thomas jerked back in surprise. "Were you? Your position on slavery was abundantly clear, though I'd not have guessed the use of the chamber pot to have bothered you."

"Exactly. Because I know that my reaction was based on my own morals, not those of this time and place. But since I don't judge others according to my morals and what I find to be acceptable or not, I did not react outwardly or say anything. I don't expect others to adhere to my standards. They're for me and me alone."

Thomas was amused by her outrage, though her words made sense to him. Instead of commenting on the morality in question, Thomas focused on the first thing she said and asked, "And from where exactly did you come?"

Ellie rolled her eyes at his blatant change of subject and the continued attempt at getting her to tell him where she was from. When Thomas laughed, she knew the tenseness of the conversation had passed.

"Darling, I judge you not for enjoying sex. On the contrary, I'm quite grateful for it and hope to experience the pleasure you take from it again," Thomas said with a lustful glint in his eye which had Ellie wanting to tear his clothes off right then and there. "However," he continued, "I'd not have others judge you and turn you out for unseemly behavior. You are no longer amongst those with the same morals as you, which means you must adhere to the morals of those around you."

"Never," Ellie asserted. "I'll do what I must to fit in and not draw excessive attention to myself, but that doesn't mean I have to change who I am. *That* would be compromising my morals. And as I said, I won't do that for anyone."

Thomas felt a rush of pride in her unwavering belief in her own standards. Ellie was Ellie. She would not change who she was simply to make her life easier or to be accepted by society. He was filled with both envy and admiration for her spirit.

The ride passed quickly as they talked along the way. They both enjoyed flirting with one another, trying to pass the time. Thomas never stopped being a gentleman and Ellie never stopped teasing him.

They stopped for lunch and Ellie kissed Thomas sweetly, promising more to come if he accepted her offer. She could see the war waging within him. He clearly wanted to give in to his desires but was struggling to go against his upbringing and the standards of the time. Thomas never argued with her beliefs. He took them to heart and even agreed with many of them. But it was extremely difficult to go against a lifetime of ingrained ideals. She appreciated the fact that despite this, he was still open to listening and hearing her out. Sometimes she wondered if he would believe her if she told him the truth about where she came from. As much as she wanted to tell him, she thought his open-mindedness only went so far. Self-preservation kept her mouth shut on the matter.

As the sky began to darken, they knew they needed to stop for the night. They had been riding close together, and Ellie reached over and put her hand on Thomas's arm. He looked over at her questioningly.

"Thomas, I don't want you to think I'm pressuring you or 'enchanting' you or any other such nonsense. If you prefer to retain a physical distance, I understand. I'll respect your wishes, whatever you decide."

Thomas sighed and looked over at her. "I think of little else but you, *mea dea*. There is nothing else for which I would care than to spend every moment with you, exploring you, tasting you, loving you. I seem unable to control myself around you. I simply do not wish your reputation to suffer because of my desire to gratify your passions and my inability to control myself. Nor do I wish to see you get caught under these circumstances."

"Get caught? Like we're teenagers? Who's going to catch us?" she laughed.

Thomas frowned. "That was not my meaning. I referred to my seed catching inside your womb."

"Oh," Ellie said, trying to suppress the laughter that continued to bubble up at his obvious discomfort at having this conversation. Or perhaps it was the idea that had him feeling uneasy. Either way, it was not a possibility. "I appreciate your concern, but there's no need for you to worry over my womb. As for my reputation, that's why I suggested we present ourselves as man and wife. No one would think twice about anything 'unseemly.' And really, do you honestly think people don't see the chemistry between us? Everywhere we go, people seem to think we've already been having an affair for a long time. Presenting ourselves as married would most likely help the situation if anything."

Thomas thought about what she said and decided she was right. "I care not for the pretense, but at least then it shan't matter."

Ellie smiled at the prospect.

Spring was the worst time of the year to travel. Their journey south in November had been incredibly cold, but now it was not only the cold with which they had to contend. On warmer days, the snow melted and the rains came, leaving the unpaved roads in a perpetual state of muddiness. It never dried out and it was not only the surface that remained wet. In some spots, the mud and puddles seemed to be several feet deep, leaving roads impassable. The wagons and horses that had come before them left deep ruts in the road and the horses had to move slowly and carefully in order to navigate the muddy paths. Some days, the rain came down in buckets while other times, it turned to sleet or snow, leaving them unable to travel safely. Ellie relished every day they could not travel. Her and Thomas spent most of the day in bed inside their small tent on those days. He worshipped her and she could not get enough of him.

The journey was one of the best times in Ellie's life. The days were short and the nights long, making their journey that much longer, which they both relished. The journey was filled with great conversation and companionship. She enjoyed spending this time with Thomas more than she ever thought she could. He was always a gentleman and treated her with every respect and courtesy he could muster. He opened doors and pulled out chairs for her; always extended an arm while escorting her, keeping himself between her and whatever street on which they walked; and he always helped her on and off of her horse. Thomas put her on a pedestal, to which she was initially unsure of how to respond, but then she accepted it, trying to ignore it as much as possible. Ellie let him worship her and in turn, she opened herself up to him as much as she was able, though not as much as he would have liked.

They spent every night together in each other's arms. Opting to avoid questions and enjoy their time together more fully, they set up the small tent every night instead of trying to find lodging. It allowed them far more freedom than they otherwise would have had. As promised, Thomas explored every inch of Ellie. While lying between her thighs with his head on her stomach one night, Thomas asked her, "Do your tattoos have meaning?"

"Tattoos are very personal to each person who gets them," she explained. "Mine have meaning to me. Each one represents a different time in my life."

"What time does this one represent?" he asked as he kissed the big one on her abdomen.

Her laughter shook him as he lay over her. "You would ask about that one first." She did not want to hide anything more from him than she already was, but knew she had to be careful explaining this one to keep from chasing him off. "I used to dance," she hesitated before saying, "for men."

Thomas looked up at her questioningly. "For men? Do you mean to say, seductively? Were you unclothed? Much like the women in a brothel?"

"Sort of but not quite like a brothel. The customers were not allowed to touch me. I was on a stage where they could only look. And I did not get completely naked." How did Ellie explain panties when no such thing existed there? "I had on something similar to a loin cloth that covered me here," she said as she gestured around her crotch.

Thomas's eyebrows shot up. "Is that all you wore?"

"Eventually," she confirmed. "I always started out wearing more than that but slowly took everything off while I danced. It was just a show; a tease. Nothing more than that."

"Darling, you certainly are good at teasing. Even with your clothes on," he said while nibbling at her nipple. It was easy for him to accept her words at face value, believing there was no physical contact between her and the men who had watched her; he was simply grateful she was sharing something of herself with him. If anything, it seemed to fit her. She lived by her own rules and did what suited her. It was one of the things that drew him to her.

This made Ellie laugh again. Thomas continued on to the next tattoo, moving across her body and kissing the crease of her opposite hip, where it met the thigh.

"What does this one represent?"

"My raven. There was a pandemic a few years ago, and I was called to work in a very busy morgue, collecting the remains of the dead. The building we worked out of had a nest of ravens in the rafters. It always felt like they watched over us, and they became part of our team, a representation of our time there." Ellie knew she could not tell him the pandemic was from covid or that the morgue was in New York, but he would certainly understand the rest of it.

Not knowing of the pandemic of which she spoke, Thomas assumed she meant an epidemic and decided to let that go as well. He wanted to make a life with Ellie and the only way he could do that was by accepting her as she was even if he did not understand or know everything about her. He used this opportunity to practice that and instead nodded his head in understanding and moved further down her body, grabbing her ankle. He kissed the side of her heel and said, "What of this one?"

"That one represents my career as a medic."

Ellie held out her other foot before he got there and added, "And this one is for my time working with the dead." He brought her other ankle to his mouth and kissed the side of that heel.

Slowly moving back up her body, he kissed her skin along the way. Grabbing her wrist, he held it to his lips.

"And this one?"

"Ah. My dandelion seed." Ellie almost gave her standard reply, that the dandelion was the official flower of the military brat, but she held her tongue and instead said, "That one represents my childhood. We moved a lot, but I always managed to plant roots and blossom wherever we ended up, just like a dandelion seed. It's a reminder to me to always be flexible, let the wind take me where it will, and embrace whatever situation I'm thrown into."

Thomas smiled at that one. "You certainly seem to have embraced this situation and even blossomed. Darling, you are one of the most unique women I've ever had the pleasure to know. What shall you get to represent this time in your life?"

"I'm not sure that's an option. I wouldn't even know where to get one here. I think my Lichtenberg figures will represent my time here."

"Your Lichtenberg figures?" Thomas asked.

Ellie held out her right arm and gestured to the tree-like pattern spread from her shoulder to her elbow. It had turned white and was subtle but still visible.

"Ah, yes. I recall you mentioning that before. Why do you call them Lichtenberg figures?"

"I didn't name them. That's what they're called. I would imagine they're named for the man who discovered them."

"This Lichtenberg discovered the marks on you? I thought you obtained them immediately before we met? I don't recall anyone named Lichtenberg being at Fort Edward."

Ellie laughed at the misunderstanding. "No. Lichtenberg discovered that lightning leaves these types of marks. They're basically burns from the capillaries heating up after being struck by lightning. Though they usually clear up in a few days. I'm not sure why mine didn't, but I like them, so I'm glad they stayed."

Thomas kissed her arm, working his way up to Ellie's shoulder, then her neck, and eventually her mouth. He took his time loving her, savoring their time together and the pleasure she gave him. In all his time in the brothels of France, he never imagined sex could be like this.

Chapter 34

March 1758

When they stopped for lunch between settlements, Ellie took advantage of their seclusion. It was a beautiful, sunny day, with the warmth trying to break through the chill in the air. They tied their horses off to a nearby tree and wandered deeper into the wooded area, finding some privacy from anyone wandering by on the roadway. As things began to heat up between them, Ellie began to work her way down Thomas's body, kissing his chest, then his stomach. When she freed him from his breeches and began lowering herself even further, Thomas stopped her and pulled her up as he always did when she began heading that direction.

"Why do you always stop me from wrapping my lips around you? Do you not like it?"

"What? No. I don't..." Thomas stuttered, uncomfortable discussing such matters. The hurt and confusion was visible in her eyes but he did not want to speak about something so improper. It was bad enough she continuously tried to engage in the act.

As much as he wanted her to, he cared too much about her to allow her to degrade herself in such a manner.

"Darling, you should not have to do that."

"I don't *have* to. I *want* to."

His head jerked back in surprise. "You *want* to?"

"Absolutely. Why wouldn't I?"

Thomas hesitated, choosing his words carefully. "I thought ladies did not enjoy such things."

Ellie grinned cheekily. "Many don't." She shrugged. "I do. I love making you feel good. Seeing and feeling you get excited by me gives me pleasure."

Thomas shook his head, scrubbing a hand over his face, unable to believe they were actually talking about this. "You continue to surprise me, *mea dea*. I would have thought such behavior beneath you. You're far too good to engage in such activities."

A burst of laughter erupted from Ellie. "It's the virgin-whore dichotomy."

"The what?" he asked, uncomfortable with her brazenness yet drawn to it all the same.

"It's the idea that women can only be either saintly virgins or whores. Men want the whore in bed but the saint in every other aspect of life, and they can't reconcile both characteristics in the same woman. She has to be either, or; not both at the same time. If she's promiscuous or overly sexual, then she can't possibly be a good person. On the other hand, if she's a good person, she must be chaste in bed."

At a loss for words, all Thomas was capable of was staring back at her. The way she spoke never failed to astonish him. She was brash and fearless and spoke of things that would make other gentlewomen run away in embarrassment, yet it was never vulgar coming from her. Perhaps she was onto something.

Her explanation of the virgin-whore was a perfect description of her, though he would never dream of thinking of her as a whore. She loved sex and was unapologetic about it, but it did nothing to diminish the goodness in her.

"Thomas, if there's something you like or something you want to try, you should feel comfortable enough with me to ask. I promise there's nothing you could possibly ask of me that I would ever ridicule or judge you for. I may not be interested in the same things, but I might be. You don't know until you ask. I want you to be happy."

Thomas brought her hand to his lips and kissed it gently.

"I am incredibly happy, darling," he said.

This made Ellie's heart leap and a smile spread across her face. She kissed his lips, then started moving further down his jaw toward his neck. Pushing him gently until he was on his back, she straddled him, trailing her mouth slowly down his torso. He moaned as her lips roamed his body, then gasped when she finally took him in her mouth. Seeing how much he was enjoying this, she could also tell he was trying to fight the urge to stop her.

"Do you want me to stop?" she asked while looking up at him.

"No," he moaned. His hands were in her hair, and he watched her every move. "You feel extraordinary."

Ellie continued, taking her time. As his moans got louder, she knew he was close, but he stopped her from continuing. When she looked at him in question, he gently pulled her up. She straddled him, leaning down to kiss him while he slid himself inside her. This brought a smile to Ellie's lips as much as his concession to allow her to take him in her mouth had. Initially, he had rarely strayed much from missionary position, flipping her onto her back if she tried straddling him, even when she could see his desire to allow her to do so. He had slowly begun opening up more, exploring other positions, seeing that it was alright to act on his desires with her, rather than adhering to what he thought was acceptable. Glad to see her words getting through to him, she had enjoyed their time together, but it was so much better without him holding himself back. Ellie wanted all of him, unreserved, and uninhibited. They still had a couple weeks before they would reach the fort and she was happy to finally be getting just that. She could hardly wait to see what else she could introduce him to and learn everything she could about what he actually enjoyed.

April 1758

"This is to be our last night like this. We shall be at the fort tomorrow."

Ellie groaned, "Don't remind me. Let's just enjoy tonight. We can figure everything else out tomorrow."

Neither wanted this time together to end. They had been in a bubble for weeks, spending all of their time in a world made up of just the two of them. Thomas had opened up to Ellie in a way he never thought possible. His sexual experience had been limited to the women in the brothels and he had always thought proper ladies demanded a reverence that put severe restrictions on what was acceptable. He knew now that it depended on the woman, but that his Ellie was open to far more than he ever would have imagined. She was a wonder.

When they stopped at night, they always camped out, enjoying the privacy and freedom it afforded them. Neither was ready to be back at the fort where the war would resume, and they would have to sleep apart and go back to being nothing more than colleagues. The thought was killing them both.

They left Stillwater early in the morning, choosing to take their time on the road as much as possible. When they stopped for lunch, they found a quiet spot in the trees beside the Hudson River and lingered, enjoying the last carefree time they would have together. Thomas was lying on the ground, his head in Ellie's lap while she sat, leaning against a tree, playing absently with his golden hair.

"Were we wed, we'd not have to pretend or sneak about."

Ellie had been staring out over the water and absentmindedly murmured her agreement with his statement, adding, "We wouldn't."

Thomas sat up now and took both of her hands in his. Looking into her eyes, he said, "Marry me, Ellie."

Taken aback, Ellie pulled her hands from his without even trying to be subtle about it. "You can't be serious?"

She laughed at the absurdity of it, believing him to be joking. The look on his face told her Thomas was completely serious. She stood up, needing some physical distance between them, feeling as though she could not breathe.

"Thomas, we can't get married just so we can continue having sex. We'll find a way to be together. If we have to sneak around then we will."

Thomas stood now, too. "I do not wish to sneak around. And continuing to lay with you is not my sole purpose for proposing marriage. I do not wish to use you merely to satisfy my lust. I had planned on making my intentions to court you known upon our return to the fort but it seems we've foregone that step. I've not known anyone like you. I'm intrigued by the way you see everything. Darling, you occupy my every waking thought, my nightly reveries. When you're not near, I scarce think of anything else but the time in which we shall once again come to be together. I love you to distraction, Ellie. I've loved you since Albany. It would fill me with immense pleasure to be your husband."

Thomas's declaration of love took her by surprise, even more so than his proposal. Ellie had convinced herself that he was merely enjoying their time together and was no more serious than she was. She cared for him deeply and considered his offer ever so briefly. Under other circumstances, she may even admit she loved him, too. But she would not permit herself to admit that now. His proposal had made sure of that. She had to remain logical and do what was best for them both.

"Albany?" she echoed, surprised. "I was a moody bitch in Albany."

Thomas chuckled. "I cannot disagree with that. However, you were also intelligent, brave, curious, and somehow innocent."

"Innocent? There's something I've never been accused of."

The corner of his lip lifted in a half smile. "You have an almost childlike wonder about you. I understand it not, yet I find it rather intriguing. And when we were attacked on the journey back to the garrison," he paused, collecting himself. "Darling, I thought I'd lost you. When I saw that savage with his knife to your forehead," he was visibly shaking as he recalled the memory. "I knew in that moment that I was in love with you and I would have done anything to trade places with you."

While Ellie was elated at his feelings for her, it was absurd. He was far too young for her to marry. She finally understood why the size of the age gap between them had bothered her. At nineteen years his senior, she was old enough to be his mother. However, it was not his physical age that bothered her so much as his lack of life experience. Thomas had served as a doctor in war for the last two years and seen plenty for his age, and men there seemed so much more mature than in her own time, not being allowed to remain children very long. The problem was that he had yet to have a family which he badly wanted, and his career was in its infancy. He still had so much ahead of him that was already behind her.

Ellie had always felt older than her years and married young, at age seventeen. For years, she had felt like an old woman. Though, being there in the past had her feeling younger and younger as time went on. The changes she had noticed were not only physical. She somehow felt younger mentally as well and almost felt like she had when she first married. Perhaps it was having to learn how to navigate life in this world. Her arrival was like a rebirth. Having arrived with no property and no money, she initially had no way to take care of herself. Even the clothes on her back had been cut off of her in order to treat her injuries. She had nothing upon her arrival. If that was not enough, even the language and beliefs were barriers. The thinking seemed so primitive compared to her twenty-first century worldview. While everyone spoke English, the vernacular was different enough that it felt as though she had to learn a new language. Add to that the fact that the majority of the soldiers were uneducated and spoke differently from the officers who were primarily upper class and it was like adding a second new language.

Despite feeling and looking young, the fact remained that she was not young. Regardless of anything else, she could not give Thomas what she knew he wanted. Ellie could not have children. Nor could she be the 'lady of the manor' that he would need in the person he married. More than that, she was also still jaded from her current marriage. Was she even still married? She was not sure it counted since Johnny was not alive at this time. That suited her fine. As far as she was concerned, she was entirely single. But marriage was the furthest thing from her mind at that time. As Ellie had told Lucas, she was not a forever kind of girl.

Thomas could see the panic and doubt rising within Ellie. He was still waiting for an answer, but she had gone entirely too quiet.

Ellie tried to be gentle in her refusal. "Thomas, I'm not in a place to be married right now."

"No. Obviously not," he said, looking around at the trees and water that surrounded them, opting to take her literally. "We shall do it as soon as we reach the fort. I must receive permission from my commanders before we do, but with your history at the hospital, I don't foresee that being a problem."

Had the situation not been so serious, Ellie would have laughed. "That's not what I meant. I can't marry anyone right now. Not here. Not now. I mean, what's the rush anyway? Why don't we just live together?"

Thomas scoffed. "My parents would never accept that. And what of any babes that come along? Would you have them be bastards?"

"Babies?" was all Ellie managed to choke out. It was getting more and more difficult to breathe.

"Of course. I wish to give you as many babies as we may have. You shall make a wonderful mother. It means living a life attached to the army, but the children shall grow up loved and will have a good life. I've already received my inheritance from my father and can provide a comfortable life for you."

"Jesus, Thomas."

Ellie's head was spinning. She felt physically ill, as if she might vomit any minute. How had this simple affair spun so far out of control, so quickly? Panic began to course through her and she could hardly look at him. How much would she have to tell him to get him to understand? What would he do with the information if she told him?

"I'm not going to just marry the first person who comes along and smiles at me just so I can squeeze out a bunch of brats. Just because you whisper sweet nothings in my ear, I'm supposed to go all gooey and melt and be something I'm not?" Ellie's words were harsher than she had intended but she was panicking.

Thomas threw her own words back at her. "Tell me you don't want me, Ellie. Tell me you don't want me, and I shall leave you be."

"That's not fair."

"Is it not?"

"I never asked you for forever." Ellie's panic was quickly turning to anger.

"I can take care of you," he tried again.

This did not help Ellie's anger. "I don't need someone to take care of me. I've been doing that for thirty years and am perfectly capable of continuing to do so." She was yelling now.

"Do you love me, Ellie?" There was a pleading in his voice; a begging to say that yes, she did love him.

Ellie felt her heart breaking as her anger melted away. Just when she thought she was incapable of ever loving anyone again, Thomas had come along and opened her up to it. Unlike so many men she had known, Thomas had not merely been interested in bedding her. Instead, he had genuinely seemed to enjoy her company and had somehow managed to break through her barriers when she had not been looking. He had broken through her walls and wormed his way into her heart, awakening something in her that she thought had long since been dead. Unfortunately, she was in no position to give in to the newfound emotions she was experiencing. It would have been better had she continued to not feel anything. She was certain she would never recover from the heartbreak this time. The tears rolled down her cheeks as she stepped in close to him.

Putting her palm on his cheek, Ellie kissed his lips sweetly. "I'm sorry, Thomas. You deserve so much more. I can't be what you need in a wife."

Turning away from him then, Ellie started packing up the remains of their picnic. With the conversation over, she loaded the horses while Thomas walked away down to the river, taking a minute to collect himself and dry his tears before taking over the loading. She may have just ripped his heart out, but he was still a gentleman and would not see her doing the work while he merely stood there.

Ellie knew this was the right thing to do. Why did it feel so wrong then?

Chapter 35

April 1758

Ellie's new tent was as far from the hospital as possible. Women and children were always placed at the edge of camp and it was more than a mile to the hospital now. Construction on the King's Hospital, which had begun the previous year, was now finished and Thomas would be working there on the island while Ellie would still be inside the main fort. Having become accustomed to having Thomas in her life every day, it pained her to not see him daily and be near him now, but given the circumstances, it was for the best. She would still be required to assist on the island periodically, much as Thomas and Gideon Anwar would occasionally come back to the main fort, but they would not interact daily.

Captain Jensen arrived back at the fort shortly after they did and noticed the tension immediately. He was surprised to see Thomas and Ellie working in the separate hospitals and even more surprised to learn they were not speaking. When he tried asking them what had happened, neither would talk about it. Ellie had even seemed distant with him when he first saw her again. He was not certain what had happened, but he would have an answer.

When Ellie saw Robert, she was initially excited to see him. But the situation with Thomas complicated everything. He was Thomas's best friend. What would that mean for the relationship between her and Robert? She knew far too many people who lost friends in a breakup and despite Robert being one of her only friends there, she knew she would lose if it came to him having to decide between them. He would likely side with Thomas, not only because they had been childhood friends, but because of the way she had treated Thomas. Ellie had broken his heart and that would be enough for Robert to hate her as much as Thomas now did. So, she took the decision away from him and tried to keep her distance.

When he came into the hospital to see her, she smiled when she saw him but then held back, waiting for the lecture she knew was coming. He had likely already seen Thomas and she imagined he would have told Robert everything. In their world, she was nothing more than a woman of easy virtue who threw herself at Thomas then refused to marry him. Ellie was surprised and grateful when Robert treated her no different than he always had. At least she still had one friend there. Still, she could not help but wonder how long it would last. Maybe Thomas had not told him yet, and it was only a matter of time. Ellie decided it best to continue keeping her distance with Robert as well.

There was one person who was happy to see the rift between Ellie and Thomas. Gideon Anwar gloated at what he saw as Ellie's fall from favor. This seemed to give him leave to treat her with even more contempt and disrespect than he always had. If Thomas had noticed, he would have put a stop to it, but he was in a separate building now and too far into his own despair to notice much other than what was immediately before him. He threw himself into his work and focused on the patients and administrative tasks he was required to do. At least with Gideon Anwar being in the King's Hospital, Ellie did not have to see him as much.

Ellie did much the same as Thomas. Work was her respite from the heartache she felt. When she had time off, she spent it close to her tent. The nightly tai chi sessions had not resumed. Instead, Ellie spent her nights reading the poetry book Thomas had given her months ago. It felt like the only thing she still had left of Thomas, and she cherished it more now than she ever had. Wanting to keep it close, she carried it in her pocket at all times. She often opened the cover, reading only the inscription he had written, without reading any of the poetry.

My Dearest Ellie,

May the words on these pages bring you the joy your friendship has brought to me.

Your Obedient Servant,
Thomas

Ellie could not count how many times since their return she had opened the cover and traced the words with her fingers. Some nights, she would cry while tracing them. It felt as though there was a hole in her heart that would never fill again. She wanted to let go and let him love her; to be everything he was asking her to be, but she knew she could not. Ellie was not that person. Love was not real. It inevitably ended and then there was only resentment. Divorce happened there, but it was rare and not widely accepted. She would be trapped yet again when things soured. Then there was the financial aspect of marriage in this time. Women gave up everything in a divorce including any money or property they owned prior to getting married. Everything became the property of the husband. There was no way in hell she was going to put herself in that position. She did not have any money or property there, but she would be damned if she was going to willingly trap herself yet again or worse, make herself become the property of anyone else, regardless of how she felt about him.

"What happened, Thomas?"

After getting the brush-off from his friend for several nights, Robert followed Thomas out of the hospital and walked with him to his quarters.

"Nothing you need concern yourself with, Robert," he replied in an icy tone.

Robert stopped him with a hand on his arm, turning Thomas to face him. In as stern a voice as he could muster, he tried again. "I shall have an answer if I must receive it from her. I wished to pay deference to our friendship and ask you first."

There was no need to say who she was, as there had been no need to clarify what he referred to when he asked what had happened. Thomas knew exactly who and what his friend was asking about. However, he still was not ready to discuss it or tell his friend that the woman he loved had broken his heart. Thomas turned and continued walking.

"Leave it alone," he warned.

"Jesus, Thomas. I never thought you capable of such disagreeable conduct as to hurt a lady. Perhaps I should have accompanied you to Philadelphia. What did you do?"

"Damn your blood Robert, you said I could trust her." He never should have let her into his bed. What had he been thinking? He knew he could not trust her.

Robert was more confused than ever. Had Ellie told him of her visions and Thomas reacted badly?

"You may. What happened?"

Thomas was becoming angry now. Anger felt better than the pain he felt, yet he did not want to rehash this out with Robert. Closing the gap between them, he got in Robert's face to yell at him but did not know where to begin. Thomas was too ashamed to admit that this woman with nothing had turned down his proposal of marriage after what had been the best weeks of his life. He had given her everything he could think of, but it was not enough. Thomas had thought Ellie would have jumped at his proposal. He could provide for her and give her anything she wanted including a life it did not sound like she had ever experienced. Had he not shown her that in Williamsburg and Philadelphia? Any number of women would be happy to accept his proposal. He did not understand how he had read the situation as wrong as he had. Thomas lost his steam and turned around, walking away.

"Nothing of consequence. Ellie and I wish for different things."

When he could not get an answer from Thomas, Robert decided to get one from Ellie. She had shared other confidences with him, he thought she may be forthcoming about this as well. He found her in their old tai chi spot and decided to try a different tactic with her.

Ellie looked up from her reading when Robert sat down beside her. It was the first time they had spent any time together since being back at the fort. Robert asked her about what she was reading. Holding up the book, she kept her answers brief. After a few minutes of brevity, Robert sighed and took the book from Ellie, setting it down. He took her hands in his, resting their arms between them.

"Miss Ellie, this is unlike you. I know not what happened between you and Thomas, but do not punish me for whatever disagreeable thing he did. I believed us to be friends?"

It was a low blow and he knew it, but that had always been what she had said about them. Regardless of how often they had told her it was inappropriate, she never listened. Ellie had always insisted none of that mattered and that she would not let other people dictate who her friends were or how she behaved.

It had the exact effect he had hoped for, and she finally said to him, "We are friends, Rob. At least I hope we are. I wasn't so sure you'd still want to be anymore."

"Why would I not?"

Ellie sighed, turning to the side in order to discretely pull her hands from his. "I don't want to come between you and Thomas."

"Why would you? Look Ell, I know not what even happened. What did Thomas do?"

Knowing how persistent Robert could be, she was all too aware that he would not give up until he got what he was after. She let out a breath and tried to tell him what happened while not going into details. He may have kept her confidence about her knowledge of the future, but she was afraid anything she said about Thomas would get back to him. And she certainly did not hate him or wish him ill. She only wanted the best for Thomas, which was why she turned him down to begin with.

"Thomas didn't do anything."

"Did you tell him? About your visions?"

"No. He just wants more than I can give him," she shrugged.

Robert immediately jumped to his own conclusions. His back stiffened in alarm as he asked her, "Did he push himself on you, Ellie?"

Where had she heard that before? Why was that the first place people there always went?

"Of course not. Hell, if anything I did." She mumbled the last, but he still heard it.

"You pushed yourself on him?" he asked, doubtful.

"Thomas did nothing wrong. He's perfect, okay?"

"That does not accord with the manner in which you are both behaving now. I've seen you together. I know how you each feel toward one another. Your conduct would not be what it is now had something not happened."

"Nothing happened, Rob, I promise. Like I said, he just wanted more than I could give."

"I am left perplexed. He only wants you, Ell. Thomas would walk to the ends of the earth for you. He would never ask more of you than what you are.

I'm quite certain it was only a misunderstanding. If he's pressuring you for a physical relationship, I'm sure—"

"That's the problem," Ellie cut him off. "It wasn't a misunderstanding. I'm the one who seduced him. He asked me to marry him."

"Ell, that's wonderful," Robert said with a smile.

Before he could get even more excited, Ellie interrupted him again. "I can't marry him, Robert." At his confused expression, she continued, "Been there, done that. It's not something I plan on ever doing again. Thomas needs someone who will stick around, and that's not me. I don't know how long I'll even be here."

"Are you leaving us, Miss Ellie?" There was more sadness in Robert's voice than she would have expected.

She sank as she tried to clear things up the best she was able. Ellie had been referring to the possibility of going home again, but maybe this was a different way out. There were other things she needed to start thinking about.

"I wasn't planning on it, but now I'm not sure. Thomas doesn't want me here and honestly, it's probably best I figured out how to take care of myself in this world."

The look on Robert's face would have broken her if she had not already been. She decided to give him something to hold onto.

"Look, I'm not planning on leaving anytime soon. I don't even have anywhere to go right now. I just mean that I need to start looking at alternatives. Who knows how long it could take to find something? I don't like being dependent on others and I can't be stuck at the end of campaign season with nowhere to go this year."

Robert looked away as he said quietly, "You shall always have somewhere to go, my dear."

Her hand came up to rest on his cheek. "Thank you, Robert. I want you to know I appreciate your friendship more than you'll ever know."

The last thing Robert wanted to hear from her lips was what a great friend he was. Thomas was a fool.

"Give him some time."

Ellie nodded but knew things would never be the same between her and Thomas. At least she still had Robert. That gave her some comfort.

May 1758

It was easy enough to avoid Thomas most of the time now that they were in separate buildings. Ellie knew his schedule well enough and knew when he went to the stables every day, so when she wanted to see her horse, she always tried to plan her visits around that. While visiting one evening, she heard someone come in. People often came and went, so she did not think anything of it, but was surprised when she looked up to see Thomas entering the stall next to hers.

As Thomas noticed her presence, Ellie stopped brushing her horse and turned to put the brush down. "Sorry, I just wanted to see her."

Though she did not think of Bella as hers, Ellie visited nightly, petting and brushing off the beautiful black creature. She was comforted by the routine and the appreciation from the animal as she cared for her.

"There's no need to explain," Thomas said. "It's not my business."

"Of course it is, you bought her."

"Yes, but she's your horse."

That was not what Ellie had been expecting, instead assuming Thomas would not want her to keep Bella and would take her back. She should have known; Thomas was not petty. Still, keeping the horse felt wrong, as if everything she had done was some sort of payment or manipulation in order to get Thomas to buy the horse for her. That was not who she was.

"I can't keep her," she said.

Thomas sighed. He had removed his coat, hanging it on a hook and was beginning to gather tools to care for his own horse. "Miss Ellie, I purchased her for you. I'd not deprive you of her. I wish for you to have her."

"Thomas—" she began.

Before she could say anything, he set down the brush and cut her off. "Ellie, I cannot..."

Closing his eyes, he turned away from her, then grabbed his coat. He started to leave, then stopped. Without looking at her, he said, "I shall continue to cover the expense of keeping Bella while you're here."

As he started forward again to leave, she called after him, "Please talk to me, Thomas." Ellie hated the pleading in her voice, but she missed him and this was eating her up.

Thomas finally turned to look at her. "Have your sentiments changed as to what it is you want?"

Ellie shook her head sadly, her eyes downcast. "No, but you don't understand."

He spun on her then, coming close enough to touch her.

"No. I don't. I understand you not at all. I foolishly believed you held affection for me and wished to be with me. However, I am deceived. To what end, Miss Ellie? I never thought you a spy or a harlot, but now I know not what to think."

"I never lied to you, Thomas. And I certainly am not a harlot." His remarks cut her, but she knew he was hurt and angry and tried to not let them get to her.

"Have you not? From where did you come before arriving here?"

It was the same question, yet again. She considered, for just a moment, telling him the truth. It was easy to imagine his reaction and she did not think it would be any better than his current disposition. Instead, she decided to continue as she had.

"I've told you; I have no explanation for that."

That was the truth. Though Ellie could explain that she had come from the future, she had no idea how it had happened. She really did not have any explanations.

Thomas nodded his head sadly. "Yes, you have told me. That is all you have ever told me. I know nothing of you, yet you wish me to believe in your honesty and trust you? How can I possibly do so?"

Ellie's eyes filled with tears. Her throat closed up and she felt as though she could not speak. Nothing she could do would make him understand. It was pointless to even try. The truth would only make him believe her even less. He would think she was simply making up a story to avoid telling him whatever the truth may be. She shrugged and said, "I guess you can't."

"You say you're not a harlot, Miss Ellie, yet did you not get expensive gowns and a horse out of me?"

"I never asked for those!" she interrupted.

"I took you to meet my family, all the while you had no intention of remaining with me. How long did you plan on keeping up the pretense? How much more did you plan on bilking me for?" he seethed. The accusations were meant to hurt. His Ellie was not like that and he knew it. But he wanted her to hurt as much as he did and could not stop the words from coming out. It was a bad habit of his to lash out with his words, wounding others that way when he was upset rather than with his fists like so many other men.

Ellie was shaking her head. "That's not what I was doing."

"Is it not? I'll not ask for them back. Keep them. It shall be a lesson to myself to not be so free with my affections."

Ellie wanted to rage at him. She wanted to yell and scream and tell him he was wrong. Instead, she reminded herself that she was the one who refused him. He was in pain, and she was the reason for it. There was nothing she could say now that would make his pain go away. It was better to let him take his anger out on her. He would come to see in the long run that he was better off without her.

Thomas turned his back on Ellie once again, trying to rein in his temper. He turned back only long enough to say, "To subject myself to this again, I cannot. I think it best we keep a distance between us."

Ellie choked down the bile rising in her stomach and bit back the tears. This was what she had wanted, was it not? No, this was not what she wanted. She knew their relationship would not last forever; nothing ever did. But she had hoped it would have lasted just a little longer. Ellie wished they could have enjoyed each other without any strings attached and then somehow part as friends and remain in each other's lives on good terms. Why did Thomas have to go and get serious? Why did it have to be all or nothing? Why did he need forever? Why could they not simply continue as they were?

She said as stoically as she could, "I understand. I'll stay out of your way."

Standing tall and shutting off her emotions, Ellie walked past Thomas, leaving the stables before anyone else came in. She had become an expert at burying her emotions over the years, but her control over them would only last so long when she was this raw. She did not want an audience when the dam finally broke.

Chapter 36

June 1758

Ellie began trying to find alternatives to staying with the army. Once she had left being a paramedic behind, she never had a desire to go back to medicine, but there was always a need for it there. Her knowledge gave her an edge over others, making her an asset despite her gender.

Joining the hospital in Albany was a possibility, but that would also be under the purview of the army. It was an option as it would not have been difficult to get a referral from the commanders at the fort, but she wanted a clean break. She did not want to have to rely on the army for anything. Ellie thought of the hospital in Philadelphia and began making inquiries there, thinking if she could at least get a position there and begin working, it would be a way to support herself until she could find something else. Once she was there, it would be easier to find other work or maybe even move south.

Having loved growing up in the south, Ellie considered moving back to either North or South

Carolina. She had enjoyed Virginia as well but could not live there now, not with Thomas's family there. The only problem with moving to the Carolinas was the slavery issue. It still occurred in the north as well, but it was much more prevalent in the south and would continue there after the Revolutionary War. There would be no escaping it. At that point, it did not matter. She still had to get somewhere and have employment once she got there. Philadelphia was her best option, though Albany could be a temporary solution if she did not hear back from Philadelphia. Hopefully, she would hear something before the end of campaign season.

The fort was a hotbed of activity as summer rolled in. In early June, troops began amassing there, only to continue on later in the month. They began departing with the first three thousand troops marching to Lake George on the seventeenth. Along with the troops went 173 teams of oxen with provisions, ninety wagons carrying bateaux, and thirty whale boats hauled out by hand on long carriages. The army would be camping out at the south end of Lake George where the ruins of Fort William Henry remained, then using the bateaux and whale boats to make their way up the lake to attack Fort Carillon once the rest of the army arrived. Regiments and companies continued to arrive at Fort Edward for weeks on their way north. At one time, there were over sixteen thousand troops at Fort Edward. By early July, the largest army ever assembled in North America was at Lake George, with over seventeen thousand men, making it the largest city in the colonies, bigger than both New York City and Philadelphia.

Robert found Ellie at the stream doing laundry, singing softly to herself as he approached. When she saw him, she looked up and smiled. She was so beautiful; he wondered, not for the first time, how Thomas could possibly let her go.

"I'm to go to Lake George," he said.

Robert had not wanted to tell her and thought it best to just come out with it. The smile on her face immediately fell and he could see the concern in her eyes.

Ellie stood from the creek, a soaking wet skirt in her hands. When she realized the water was flowing off the skirt, soaking her, she dropped it in the grass. Her brows furrowed, she said, "I wish I knew more about this war and the outcome."

Smiling at her desire to protect him, Robert put a hand on her shoulder. "Do not fret, Ell. I shall be quite well. I've trained for this. Circumstances last year kept me from peril, but it was always inevitable."

"That doesn't mean I have to like it," she said. "I've heard the talk. You're all going to Fort Carillon? I'm not even sure where that is, exactly. I never heard of it until I got here."

"Fort Carillon is at the north end of Lake George, between there and Lake Champlain."

"I thought the only forts up there were Ticonderoga and Crown Point?"

It was Robert's brows that furrowed in confusion now. "There are no forts in that area by either of those names. Though, 'Ticonderoga' is the Iroquois word to mean where two waters meet, which describes where Fort Carillon is located. If we capture the fort, it shall be renamed. Perhaps that is a sign to indicate we shall be triumphant in this siege."

Ellie grabbed onto the hope. Though she knew the British would win the war, she knew nothing of the individual battles and attacks. She hated not being able to give her friend more information to keep him safe.

When it came time for Robert to leave, Ellie embraced him in a lingering hug. "Be safe," she said quietly in his ear. Still holding each other, she pulled back to look at him and added, "And come back to us."

Robert nodded in acquiescence. "I shall do my best."

It was all he could do and Ellie accepted that this was out of their control, though she did not like it.

Before releasing her, Robert added, "Ell, you be careful as well. There's been an increase in attacks along the road all spring and summer thus far. Promise me you shan't leave or wander outside the fort on your own."

Promising she would be careful, Ellie nodded. Robert was still hesitant. "I take no pleasure from leaving you here under these circumstances. If you've need of anything, go to Thomas. He's hurt right now, but he still holds affection for you, Ell. He will protect you."

Ellie pulled away from Robert at this. Turning away, she looked down at the laundry at her feet. "I'll be okay, Rob. I don't need anyone to protect me."

He put his hand under her chin, turning her head to look at him. "Promise me, Ell."

When she promised, he added, "And promise me you shall be here upon my return."

They both knew there were no guarantees they would ever see each other again. He may not come back from the siege, and she may be in Philadelphia by the time the army returned to the fort. There were too many unknowns. The promises they were making to each other were promises that this would not be the end for them; that no matter what happened, they would see one another again.

Knowing it was something out of her control, Ellie nodded and said, "I promise."

***

July 1758

The army moved on in a column which stretched two miles long. On July 6, a detachment of three hundred and fifty French had accidentally stumbled onto the British Army in the forest and opened fire. General Lord George Howe had been at the front of the charge, advancing with the infantry, when he was shot under the left breast with grapeshot. It killed him instantly. His body was transported by wagon back to Fort Edward, then placed in a scow which traveled down the Hudson River to Albany where he was buried. Beloved by the men, his death was a pall over the army. An order was given for all of the wounded to be sent back to Fort Edward, but the army continued.

By the time they reached Fort Carillon on July 8, the Regulars were cut down so fast that it had been difficult for the remaining troops to get over the dead and wounded. The French had mounted swivel guns at the fort which had been filled with more grape-shot. Once fired, the shells split apart, releasing individual lead balls like shotgun pellets causing as much damage as possible with each burst. It killed almost everyone in the trenches surrounding the French-held fort.

The Highlander Regiment charged for three hours without a break and without retreating. Chaos reigned and soon, there were no instructions being given by commanders. Robert could only focus on what was in front of him and staying alive. There had been no orders given to retreat, but he could see many of the men leaving. That evening, another attempt was made on the fort which continued until sunset, to no avail. Men continued to retreat after sunset. As it became obvious their effort was futile, Robert and his company left as well, fighting their way out of the area. There were so many dead and wounded in the road, he could hardly walk without stepping on them. The injuries he had sustained in battle made this feat even more difficult. They could do nothing for the dead and wounded but leave them where they lay. He was only glad to not be one of them.

After the battle, the army was mustered at midnight where they received word that the French were now coming down the lake to cut off their retreat and take their bateaux. Scrambling to prevent this, they had worked through the night. With no sleep, they departed the lake at nine the next morning. By the time they reached the south end of Lake George that evening, the men were dejected and melancholy.

Feeling just as dejected and melancholy as the men, Ellie had been running ragged for days. The wounded had started coming in after the first encounter with the French on the sixth and had not stopped. It was easy to pinpoint exactly when the army made its attempt on the fort when the number of wounded suddenly increased throughout the hospital. She kept looking to see if Captain Jensen was among them and was both relieved and disappointed every time a new batch of wounded came through without him in it. Ellie had not wanted Robert to be wounded and was glad when he was not amongst those men, but she wanted to see him safe. The longer he was away, the more concerned she became.

With the fort devoid of soldiers, Thomas avoiding her, and Robert gone, the fort felt emptier than it ever had. There were only six companies remaining at the fort, leaving less than three hundred men. Ellie stayed within the garrison as she had promised Robert.

If she received word that she had been accepted at the hospital in Philadelphia, she would have to make the journey on her own. This thought made her more grateful than ever that Thomas had given her the horse. It would be a treacherous journey for a single woman to travel that great a distance, between towns and cities, on her own. Traveling in convoys as much as she was able would help and she would plan her departure to coincide with a convoy to Albany or New York City if possible. She did not like it, but she would manage. Ellie would not let the possible danger deter her. Until then, she did not take any unnecessary risks and stayed as safe as she could.

With the wounded men having begun to trickle in shortly over two weeks after the army departed, the hospitals at Fort Edward filled quickly and they were all kept quite busy. The wounded were not only their own men, but those of the enemy as well.

Prisoners were sent to Fort Edward and those wounded amongst them were sent to the hospitals.

Men were spread out between the various hospitals at the fort. Many of the officers went to the island while the majority of men Ellie saw were prisoners. She rushed between them, trying to do what she could to treat them or stabilize them for travel to Albany. With the influx of patients, Thomas had even come to assist with the wounded prisoners. She was doing her best to skirt around him and stay out of his way.

"Madam, leave that man. The captain here is in need of your assistance."

Ellie looked up from the Native American who was bleeding out before her to see a man helping another into a chair. The one being seated was not visibly bleeding. Ellie thought perhaps he had internal injuries and rushed over to him after telling the Native who had escorted her patient to keep applying pressure on his wound.

"Where are you injured?" she asked the captain hurriedly.

"My leg," he replied. "I believe it to be broken."

Ellie's patience had run out long ago. She had been on edge since Thomas's proposal and worrying about Robert was not helping her frayed nerves. Nor was having Thomas in her part of the hospital that day. Try as she might, it was impossible to ignore him. The last thing she needed was to be bossed around by a bunch of men with superiority complexes who took her away from patients who were actually in urgent need of assistance.

"You'll hold," she said while going back to her patient.

The man who had called her over was not having it.

"I told you to come see to him. The captain is in a great deal of pain. He's an officer and you shall put him ahead of that savage."

Ellie turned on the man, about to unload on him when she regained what little control she had. Taking a deep breath, she turned to the captain instead.

"Sir, if you had been captured by the French and were bleeding to death, would you like it if they stopped tending to you and let you die in order to fix the broken leg of one of their officers?"

The confused and shamed looks on their faces gave her some level of satisfaction.

"No miss. I'd not. You go and do what you might to save that man's life. I shall be here when you finish."

Going back to the dying man, she continued working to get the bleeding under control. When she finished stitching him up, she went back to the captain as promised and saw to him. The rest of the day was spent running from patient to patient, helping where she could.

When she needed help with any of the prisoners, none of the medical staff at the fort would assist. They were the enemy, and the hospital staff always put their own people first. The concept of triage and working according to the severity of injury was a foreign concept. Ellie grabbed the Native American who had assisted her before and put him to work. He only had minor injuries, which she treated quickly as soon as she had a spare moment.

"What's your name?" she asked him, hoping he spoke English. He was sharp and she could see the intelligence behind his eyes. He did not speak much, but took everything in.

"I am called Dajoji," he answered. "Of the clan of the wolf, of the Onoñdowa'ga:' Nation, of the League of the Haudenosaunee, known to the White man as the Iroquois."

"Thank you for your help, Dajoji."

Surprised, he nodded and continued assisting her. Dajoji checked in on his friend periodically but otherwise stayed by Ellie's side all day. As she slowly made headway amongst the wounded, Ellie came across one with a bullet in his arm. Everyone else was just as busy with other patients, so she prepared to remove the bullet. He was not a prisoner, but because he was a person of color, he had been put aside to treat officers with injuries less severe. Allowing the anger to flow through her, she then released it so she could do what needed to be done. She sterilized the instruments once again after her last patient, setting them up on a table next to the man's bed.

"What's your name?" she asked as she made her preparations.

"Peleg Foster, miss," he said on a groan.

Ellie tried to keep him talking and guided Dajoji over to help her. He had assisted her not only with the other Native American patients, but with any others she needed help. When she was ready to remove the bullet, Dajoji held the man down and Ellie set to digging out the musket ball. Peleg screamed out in pain, but she kept going, hating this part of the job. Having to operate on a patient while he was awake and had no anesthesia whatsoever was always brutal for both her and the patient. She could feel the ball and was almost close enough to pull it out when the man screamed again. This time, Dajoji was caught off balance and his hold on the man slipped. Peleg sat upright and his free arm flailed out, scratching her neck.

"Hold him," Ellie admonished her assistant.

Dajoji regained control of him, pulling him back down to the table and firming up his grasp. Ellie was able to finish the surgery and closed and bandaged the wound. As soon as she was done, the man sheepishly held up his good arm. Ellie looked down at the black cord with the amethyst crystal pendant on it and immediately reached for her neck, feeling its absence.

"I be sorry miss. I din't mean ta," he said with remorse in his eyes.

Knowing it had been an accident, she took the cord with the now broken clasp and put it in her pocket. She set the man's conscience at ease and moved onto the next patient.

Dajoji was quiet but watched Ellie carefully throughout the day and into the next. The hostility and suspicion in his eyes that she saw upon first seeing him were gone by the end of the day, but only when he looked at her. They were still present whenever he looked at anyone else. When she came in a couple mornings later, he was gone. Ellie thought they had moved him out of the hospital in order to make room for others and wondered briefly where they were holding the prisoners who were uninjured. He had been such a help; she was sad to see him gone.

On July 10, Ellie looked up from the patient she was patching up and saw Robert in the doorway. She dropped her bandages and ran to him, pulling him into a hug. The relief washed through her at seeing him standing there and he wrapped one arm around her, holding her close. He kissed the top of her head, and she pulled back, regaining her composure. Ellie was aware that everyone in the hospital was watching them, and this was considered highly inappropriate, but she could not care less.

When she finally stood back, she wanted to see for herself that he was okay. As she looked at him, she saw that his uniform was in a state. Robert was dirty and covered in blood, cradling his left arm. Ellie brought him to a table where she could tend to him. Not only was his arm broken, but he had received a stab wound to the thigh which needed stitches and cleaning.

"Have you been to see Thomas yet?"

"Not as of yet," he answered. "I wanted to stop here first."

At that, Ellie smacked his good arm and scolded him. "You should have stopped to see him and let him know you're okay."

Robert smirked. "He'll hold. I knew you'd be far more concerned than he."

He was probably right, but she did not want Thomas to have any more reason to hate her. She did not want him to think that she was stealing his friend away from him on top of everything else. When she suggested Robert go see him to get his wounds tended, he said he would rather she did it. Ellie shook her head and tended to him while he recounted his experience.

Normally, Captain Jensen would never share his experience of war with a woman. He did not know of any women who were capable of handling the horrors of the experience. None, except Ellie. She always listened and made him feel as though he could tell her anything. Somehow, she would not only understand what he had experienced but also would not judge him for it or for sharing it with her. Robert knew she would never shrink away from the horrors he experienced, and it always felt good to talk with her. He opened up and shared everything.

Chapter 37

July 20, 1758

In the days following the battle, an outbreak of dysentery and diarrhea spread through the camp, followed by cases of smallpox as the wounded and sick continued to be transported to Fort Edward. By July 12, they had counted 1,944 men either killed or wounded in the battle with more succumbing to their wounds over the following days. There were reports that the French were killing prisoners who remained at Fort Carillon after the British had retreated.

Ambushes continued throughout the region and on July 20, there was one close to the fort. On their way to Lake George, General Abercrombie had stopped at Halfway Brook and ordered a picket fort to be built there. Having been the halfway point between Fort Edward and Fort William Henry, it made a good stopping point for troops, but there was nothing there but a brook.

Construction commenced immediately and it took no time for the stockade to be erected with sharpened stakes making up the walls. A regiment from Massachusetts was stationed there when a detachment of six hundred Natives and Canadians were sent from Carillon to annoy and intercept wagons. As a wagon train was making its way through the area, the detachment did what they had been sent to do. When they attacked the wagons, the men at the stockade heard the shots being fired and immediately ran to engage the enemy and aid the victims, causing the French to turn their attention to the soldiers.

Word of the skirmish quickly reached Fort Edward. There were twenty-six soldiers killed, wounded, or missing. As they retrieved the bodies, they were mangled and mutilated, with most of them being scalped. The surgeon at the post could not handle the amount of wounded and Thomas and Gideon were sent to assist.

Thomas was happy to get out of the fort, even under such circumstances. Life at the garrison had become suffocating. Ellie was everywhere. Though they worked in separate buildings most of the time, they still saw each other more frequently than he would have liked. Even when she was not there in front of him, she was not only on his mind but also on those of the other soldiers. He constantly heard reports of her work and her care of the wounded soldiers. She had a way with people and the men had always praised her work. It was the reason she had been allowed to stay after the first year, then come back again this year. Thomas was not sure what he would do at the end of this campaign season. He could not petition whoever would be commanding the fort for her return if he could not be in the same room with her. Yet, he could not simply turn her out, either. She still had nowhere to go. Perhaps he could have her assigned to another fort or the hospital in Albany.

Captain Burke and Gideon Anwar assisted with the wounded at Halfway Brook over the next few days. As Thomas assessed the situation at the post, he determined they needed more medical supplies and considered speaking with Colonel Ebenezer Nichols about having Ellie stay on and assist with wounded at the small post. However, he was uncertain about this option. It would get her away from him, but this post was not as well protected as the fort. It was also the place she had been stabbed and nearly died when she first came to them. Would she be safe there?

Thomas had sent word back to the fort with a list of provisions and Ellie gathered them together, preparing to leave when Robert found her. He urged her not to go with the convoy.

"I'll be fine, Rob. I'm not traveling alone. I can stay there for a while, leaving Thomas and Mr. Anwar to come back here. He said they've taken care of the most serious cases already, and now they mostly just need aftercare and supplies."

Robert was more insistent. "I like it not, Ell. There aren't enough guards and with my wrist broken, I shan't be able to protect you. The red man is vicious and brutal. They won't give pause to attacking you simply because you're a woman."

"I know, but I need to go. They need me and I don't need you to protect me."

When they said goodbye, it was much like it had been when Robert left, but this time, he was the one concerned for her safety. Ellie was looking forward to escaping the fort, even if it was only for a short time. While packing a few things, she came across her necklace that had broken while removing the musket ball from Peleg's arm.

She examined the broken cord, trying to determine how to fix it. Ellie had not seen anything like the clasp she was familiar with since her arrival there, which meant she would likely have to get a new cord altogether. It saddened her, but at least she still had the amethyst. It would have broken her heart to have lost the stone that she held as a reminder of her nieces. She carefully wrapped it in linen and tucked it safely amongst her things, stuffing it inside the pouch that matched one of the gowns Thomas had bought her, hoping no one would go through her things while she was gone. Ellie packed enough for a few days and left the rest there for her return. She would have to look for something with which to fix the clasp as soon as she left the fort. Being able to do so was one more advantage to working for a hospital someplace as big as Philadelphia. She had not been interested in doing much shopping thus far, but found herself looking forward to the possibility now. Exploring the city would be a good distraction to help get her mind off Thomas. Or so she hoped. If only she would hear back from them.

July 28, 1758

The convoy consisted of about sixty carts, forty wagons being pulled by four or more oxen, and fifty guards. They had only made it five miles north of the fort when they heard the war cries of the Native Americans. The musket blasts soon followed.

Ellie spun on her horse, trying to see where they were coming from and where she could go to get away. The convoy broke down into a random scattering of people as everyone tried running. They were surrounded by thick forest and the noise was deafening. The Natives continued their war cries, muskets fired, people and animals screamed as they were cut down. Ellie wanted to help, but there was nothing she could do, unable to tend to the wounded and dying in the middle of the activity and not having any weapons with which to fight back. Her horse wanted to buck her off and run and it was all she could do to keep Bella under control. The lessons she had received from Thomas two summers ago did not cover how to control a horse while it was trying to buck her off.

While Ellie fought to regain control of Bella in order to flee the scene, she saw a woman jump from a wagon and run off while a little girl tried to follow her. The girl ran into the dirt path and a wagoner saw her. He immediately cut the horse's ropes from the wagon and rode back along the road after her. Taking her by the hand, he scooped her up, saving her life as they rode away.

Unable to move forward or back, Ellie felt as though she was frozen, stuck in the middle of the carnage as the people around her were killed. Her horse finally succeeded in throwing her off and she found her way under a wagon, trying to find any sort of shelter from the battle raging around her. She was trying to make her way to the trees but could not get through the enemy. They were everywhere. Ellie was reminded of the battle she had stumbled into when she first arrived there in nearly this same spot so long ago. However. this one was far more intense. The other one had been nearing the end when she stumbled onto it, and most of it had been hidden by the trees, preventing her from seeing the entirety of the carnage. Her interaction in that one was very brief. This was something so much more.

Just as Robert had said, the Natives did not care if their targets were soldiers or not. They attacked women and children as well. When someone fell victim to them, the person was scalped and mutilated, the body stripped and cut up.

A woman fell nearby after being shot in the stomach and Ellie crawled over to try and help her. Wanting to stay hidden but knowing there were too many people in need around her, she could not stay there. It spurred her to action as she tried to help in any small way she could.

Thomas heard the commotion from the stockade as did everyone else. They all immediately went running to assist. He knew Ellie would likely bring his requested provisions herself when he had sent word that they would need continued assistance at the post once he left with Gideon. Despite what had happened between them, the thought of her in the middle of another Indian attack chilled his blood. When the provincials ran out to assist, he was in the middle of them, with Gideon trailing behind him, urging him not to go.

What Thomas saw in front of him nearly gutted him. There were at least four hundred Canadians, Iroquois, and Abenaki surrounding the convoy. He searched in vain for Ellie but did not see her. He tried calling her name but was not heard above the din of the battle. As he searched the road for her, his eyes fell on the provisions scattered across the road. The wagons had been destroyed and the oxen killed along with men, women, and children from the convoy. Chocolate had begun to melt in the roadway, mixing with the blood that was now forming rivulets. Wagons were being set aflame as the enemy continued their assault on the provincials and remaining survivors. Thomas was frantic.

Ellie continued to watch, looking for her chance to flee. While helping the injured when she could, she had tried to stay as close to the wagons as possible, pulling wounded with her. With the wagons being set on fire now, she knew her time was quickly running out. She would have to make a run for it. As she moved to assist another woman, she saw Thomas in the middle of the battle. She called to him, but he could not hear her. Running towards him, she was almost there when she saw an Abenaki on the side of the road pull back his bow, aiming at Thomas. Ellie screamed and jumped in front of him, trying to push him out of the way. A sharp pain surged through her chest as she collapsed at his feet. When Ellie looked down, she saw the shaft of an arrow sticking out of her chest. She looked up at a surprised Thomas who knelt down, immediately assessing her injury.

Knowing better than to pull out an object that had pierced the skin, she also knew she was beyond saving. Ellie's brain disengaged and without thinking, she yanked out the arrow, causing blood to ooze out with it. It had been lodged in deep, past the arrowhead and up the shaft a way. Thomas pulled her into his arms and cried, "No!"

Only moments away from death, Ellie reflected back on how she came to be there and everything that had happened since. She had spent so much time trying to figure out how to get back to her own time, to go 'home,' but in that moment, she only wanted to stay. Not knowing the extent of her injuries the last three times she had a brush with death, she had justified her recoveries as having been because the injuries had not been fatal. This time, she knew how bad it was. She was not certain her magical healing powers would be able to save her again. There was not a doubt in her mind this one was fatal.

To her surprise, her life did not flash in front of her eyes, though it had not done so any of the other times she had nearly died, either. Instead, she remembered sitting at the lake with Lisa and Kristy when Lisa had asked if she was happy. At the time, several images had flashed through her mind but they all fell away now as her thoughts turned to Thomas.

The world fell away around them as Thomas rocked her in his arms. They were in the tree line, partially obscured from the bulk of the attacking detachment. Stroking her face and brushing the hair from her forehead, he realized the wetness on her cheeks was coming from his own tears.

Kissing her face, he whispered, "Darling, forgive me. I'm so sorry. I love you with all my heart, Ellie. Please forgive me, *mea dea*."

Unable to move any longer, there was so much Ellie wished she could say to Thomas, wanting to undo everything that had happened between them. For the entirety of her adult life, no one had ever looked out for her or taken care of her. Everything she had obtained or accomplished had been due to her own hard work. Thomas had arranged for her to stay on at the fort with both lodging and pay when he did not even know her, and he had always watched out for her. He had followed her in Albany and made sure she was safe from those thugs, ran in after her during the attack at Stillwater, and even dragged her in from the possibility of being hit by lightning. He had even tried to pay her out of his own pocket when he knew she had nothing. She knew what a good man he was, and she hated that she had caused him so much pain already but would cause him even more now with her death.

It was too little, too late, but she looked up into his devastated face and whispered, "I love you, Thomas." Every word was an effort, but she needed to say them. She needed to tell him how she felt. "I didn't want to, but I do. I– I love–"

Her breathing was quickly slowing to a stop. All she could do was lay there in his arms as the tears rolled down his cheeks. She could no longer feel anything. It did not take long before her heart stopped altogether.

Ellie laid dead in Thomas's arms as the carnage continued around him. He did not even care about the ensuing slaughter. He wanted to follow her. The sound of Gideon Anwar calling out in French reached his ears.

"No. He's a physician."

Looking up, Thomas saw a French soldier only feet away. There was no time to do anything before the soldier hit him over the head with the butt of his rifle. The blood trickled down his face as everything went blissfully black.

Chapter 38

July 28, 1758

Ellie woke with a gasp to shouting as Thomas was being pulled out from underneath her. She was initially confused. Did she just die? Why did her chest itch? Was she alive now? Struggling to clear the fog from her brain and remember the last few minutes, she realized a Native American was tugging at an unconscious Thomas while pushing her off of him. He was trying to rouse Thomas while pulling him out from under her.

By her counting, this was the fourth time Ellie had possibly died. Unless the lightning had not killed her, too. Lightning was not always fatal so she was not sure she could count that one. Lightning aside, she was also not sure she was in a position to give an accurate account of all of her brushes with death since her trip to New York. She wished she knew how bad her previous injuries had been, though she was starting to suspect they had all been fatal. In addition to the many possible near-death experiences, she knew small wounds healed unusually fast. Cuts and abrasions would heal in minutes. But this? This was far more than a little cut or abrasion. How was this possible? Why was it happening? Was she somehow immortal? Did it have something to do with her travel through time? But the traffic accident had occurred before she traveled through time.

Her confusion was interrupted by the sight of Thomas being hauled away by a Native American. He appeared to be alive but unconscious. Ellie tried standing, stumbling slowly to her knees as she cried out for them not to take him. The Native turned his attention to her.

"Stop. Please don't take him," she pled.

"We need a healer," was all he said in response, as if it justified them killing dozens of people and kidnapping even more.

She did not think Thomas would fare well under captivity by the French or the Native Americans. There had been too many reports of prisoners being tortured or killed and their bodies mutilated. Looking at the carnage around them, she decided they were most likely not unfounded rumors.

"I'm a healer. Please, take me instead."

Though she had no idea what to expect, Ellie knew she did not belong there. Thomas did. She had nothing there, not even Thomas. He had made his feelings clear over the last few months. Despite that, she would do whatever she could to save him. Planning on leaving the fort anyway, it would be better for them all if she went with the Natives.

Just then, Gideon was pulled from behind a tree where he had been hiding. Another Native had him by his collar and was pulling him towards the rest of the war party which was now preparing to leave with their captives. He was trying to bargain with them and convince them not to take him. The Natives spoke amongst themselves for a moment. Gideon finally realized what she had said and seized the opportunity to save himself.

"Listen to her. She's a-speakin' the truth. She also were a healer and shall do well for you, she shall."

Oh, now he would acknowledge her medical abilities? Ellie did not think she could hate him any more than she already had, but she was wrong. She would happily trade her life for Thomas's, but that was her decision to make, not his. Gideon was proving himself to be just as cowardly as she had always suspected him to be.

The warriors continued to confer for another moment. Ellie recognized the one holding Gideon as the Iroquois warrior who had helped her with the injured prisoners only weeks ago after Carillon. Dajoji, was it? Ellie tried to remember his name. She had thought he had been taken away as a prisoner when he had disappeared from the hospital but realized now that he had escaped. He approached her and squatted, pulling her blood-soaked bodice aside, exposing her wound. There was a gash in her skin, but it did not appear to be very deep.

"If he stays, you will come with us and not try to run away?" Dajoji asked.

"I won't run," she agreed with a nod. "I will stay as long as you need me and do what I can to help, but you have to leave now and do no more harm to anyone here." She pointed at Thomas, now lying on the ground. "He lives, stays here, and suffers no further injuries. Mr. Anwar stays to tend to him."

Dajoji nodded and lifted her to her feet, dragging her away from the unconscious Thomas while the other warrior released him to Gideon. His still body being dragged back towards the post by Gideon was the last thing she saw as they walked away. Ellie gave her word that she would not try to escape her captors, and for Thomas's sake, she would keep it. For all she knew, they would come back for him if she ran away from them.

As they fled the carnage, all Ellie could think was that now she would not have to figure out how to get out from under the British Army and stand on her own. It looked like she would not be doing that any time soon. She had looked forward to the independence of living on her own, but now had only captivity to look forward to, wondering what it would be like and how badly she would be treated. If the rumors they had heard at the fort were any indication, she could expect a considerable amount of mistreatment and physical abuse. Her only hope was that the connection she had previously made with Dajoji and her knowledge of medicine would encourage them to have mercy and treat her decently. If she was being honest with herself, Ellie had always craved the unknown and as terrified as she was, part of her could not help wonder what adventure lay ahead.

I've tried to keep the historical aspects of the book as close to being accurate as I could get. While not a historian, I am a researcher and did what I could to ensure historical accuracy. However, many aspects have been imagined for the sake of the story. *Old Fort Edward before 1800: An Account of the Historic Ground Now Occupied by the Village of Fort Edward, New York* by William H. Hill was an invaluable resource for what life was like during this era and for many of the people and events that surrounded life at the fort during the French and Indian War. Additional resources that were extremely helpful were *Empires in the Mountains: French and Indian War Campaigns and Forts in the Lake Champlain, Lake George, and Hudson River Corridor* by Russell Bellico, *Hodges' Scout: A Lost Patrol of the French and Indian War* by Len Travers, and various journals from people who served in the war in some capacity.

The war waged in North America from 1756 to 1763 is often referred to as both the French and Indian War and The Seven Years' War. There's considerable debate as to which name should be used with most Americans referring to it as the former and most Canadians using the latter. As most Americans are more familiar with the French and Indian War moniker, I opted to use that. Though the fighting continued for more than seven years, the dates from when war was officially declared until the peace treaty was signed consisted of seven years. However, there had been nearly continuous military action in the colonies for close to a hundred years prior to this war and continued after the peace treaty was signed.

Nearly all of the military actions in this story were based on facts. The raids on Halfway Brook in which Ellie found herself were both actual events. Raids on convoys occurred there on June 17, 1756, and July 28, 1758, with another having occurred shortly after the picket fort was built there on July 20, 1758. The attack on a work party one mile from the fort on July 23, 1757, also occurred, bringing men from all over the fort to respond, including Rangers from the island. Likewise, the attack on Fort William Henry around Saint Patrick's Day 1757 and the siege and subsequent massacre on that fort are both based on real accounts of the events, as was the siege on Fort Carillon, which was eventually captured and renamed Fort Ticonderoga.

The only attack that was not based on a specific event was the raid in Stillwater on the return trip from Albany on Sunday July 11, 1756. While these trips to move patients to the hospital were regularly undergone, this trip was entirely made up for the story. Native American scouts roamed the areas near the English forts looking for anyone wandering away and often attacked whenever opportunity presented itself. Larger war parties were also prevalent in the area and would attack work parties or other groups on the road.

A permanent corps of Rangers was established at Fort Edward and Fort William Henry during April 1756 to counter the attacks from French and Indian scouts. Robert Rogers was appointed commander of this group. He appointed his brother Richard as his first lieutenant and John Stark as his second lieutenant. Rogers is thought to be the father of the US Army Rangers. It was his techniques and guidelines for wilderness fighting that were used for the foundation of the Rangers and also contributed to the colonists winning the Revolutionary War.

The smallpox outbreak in the winter of 1756 was widespread throughout the army and the region. It killed countless people, both military and civilian alike. Robert Rogers contracted the illness and was bedridden from March 5 to April 15, 1757. Surgeon Thomas Williams was a real doctor who was at Fort Edward during the outbreak, attributing the cause of it to be bad air, but also due to the people being sinful. He argued that if people repented and reformed, the disease would abate.

Along with Surgeon Williams and Robert Rogers, the commanders of the forts and the generals mentioned were all real people. Command of Fort Edward passed hands often and during Ellie's time there, it would have been commanded first by Colonel Whiting, then Major Sparks, and finally Colonel Ebenezer Nichols. Generals Loudon, Abercrombie, William Johnson, Lyman, and Webb; General Lord George Howe, General Marquis de Montcalm, and Lieutenant Colonel George Munro; Major Prevost; and Israel Putnam were all involved in the war and any mention of each was based on historical record. Any reference to the character of real persons was based entirely on my interpretation of the research I conducted and the needs of the story. The reports of General Lord George Howe's death in the siege of Fort Carillon on July 6, 1758, were based on fact. By all accounts, he was quite admired and respected, leaving his death to weigh heavily on the entire army.

The military punishments described were also based on real accounts. It was not uncommon to have been beaten with the cat of nine tails for most offenses while desertion was typically punished by death, though on occasion could also be punished with the cat of nine tails in lieu of death. The strict discipline within the army was not only for the soldiers but applied to all of the camp followers as well. Women and children could just as easily find themselves being whipped if they were found to have committed a crime.

Triage was a foreign concept during this time period. Rather than treating people according to the severity of their injuries, people were treated according to rank and position in society. Higher ranking officers would have been treated first, while servants then enslaved persons would have been the last ones to have received treatment. Women and enslaved persons were not considered people but were property. This would have put servants slightly above enslaved persons, though only just.

As most officers purchased their commissions, higher ranking officers tended to be wealthier as those commissions fetched a higher price. It was not unheard of for families to purchase a commission of major or even colonel for a child of seven years old. Titled nobility often entered service as a general with no prior military experience. On the other end of the spectrum, the militia was mostly made up from farmers or lower-class individuals with little to no education.

The subject of witchcraft often came up when I began working on this story. There is a misconception that people in every time period before the modern era adhered to strong beliefs in witchcraft and women were always being punished for such whenever they displayed any unusual knowledge or behavior. While this is true for many periods throughout history, by this point, it had begun waning.

After the tragedy of the Salem Witch Trials, public opinion began to change regarding the accusation and treatment of those being charged as witches. This also coincided with the start of The Enlightenment or the Age of Reason in which superstition gave way to scientific reasoning. The Witchcraft Act of 1735 declared it illegal to accuse a person of having magical powers or of being guilty of practicing witchcraft. Prior to the Act, witchcraft was considered a real practice whereas by the time the Act passed, it was recognized as a way to deceive people in an attempt to defraud them. While it did not stop highly superstitious people from believing a person may be a witch, it prevented people from being formally prosecuted as such based on the accusations of others. Instead, the act focused on prosecuting those who pretended to conjure spirits, foretell the future, and cast spells rather than those who may have actually practiced.

ACKNOWLEDGMENTS

Thanks to David Sorum who allowed me to bounce ideas around and helped me work through the concepts on which I got stuck. I appreciate the time you've spent on the artwork for this.

To Marki Henricksen and Mason McNamara, I appreciate both of you reviewing the medical scenarios for me and helping me make them better and bring them to life. Thank you for your time and your feedback.

A huge thanks to Lisa Lambert and Billy Romero who gave me continuous feedback throughout working on this story and discussed ideas with me at length, letting me ramble on and on endlessly.

A special thanks to all those who helped encourage me and gave me input to improve the story. It would not be what it is without the contributions of each of you.

To my readers, I appreciate you taking the time to read my works. I hope you enjoy them as much as I have.

Also by Veronique Holloway

Ichabod's Curse Endures: The Headless Horseman
Rides Again

Time and Other Lies
Volume 1: Pulled Through Time
Volume 2: Time of the White Raven
Volume 3: Time Alone
Volume 4: A Time of Madness
Volume 5: A Time of War
Volume 6: Forward in Time
Volume 7: Learning Time
Volume 8: At Home in Time

For additional information, maps, and
insights, visit VHBooks.net